The frontispiece from the 1820 edition
of 'The Bride of the Isles'.

Dracula's Brethren

*Edited by Richard Dalby
and Brian J. Frost*

With an Introduction and Bibliography by

BRIAN J. FROST

HARPER

HARPER

An imprint of HarperCollins*Publishers*
1 London Bridge Street
London SE1 9GF
www.harpercollins.co.uk

Published by HarperCollins*Publishers* 2017

1

Selection, Introduction, and Notes © Richard Dalby
and Brian J. Frost 2017

A catalogue record for this book
is available from the British Library

ISBN 978-0-00-821648-1

Typeset by Palimpsest Book Production Ltd, Falkirk, Stirlingshire

Printed and bound in Great Britain by Clays Ltd, St Ives plc

FSC™ is a non-profit international organisation established to promote
the responsible management of the world's forests. Products carrying the
FSC label are independently certified to assure consumers that they come
from forests that are managed to meet the social, economic and
ecological needs of present and future generations,

and other controlled sources.

Find out more about HarperCollins and the environment at

CONTENTS

INTRODUCTION

ARRANGED chronologically, the nineteen stories in this anthology are culled from books and magazines published between 1820 and 1910, a period noted for producing some of the finest vampire tales ever written. The first vampire story to make a significant impact on European literature was 'The Vampyre,' by John William Polidori, which set a precedent by depicting the vampire as an aristocrat. Erroneously attributed to Lord Byron when it was first published in the April 1819 issue of *The New Monthly Magazine*, this story subsequently inspired a surge of popular interest in vampires and established the vampire's image as a fatal lover.

In 1820 the French author Cyprien Bérard penned a novel-length sequel to Polidori's story, titling it *Lord Ruthwen ou les Vampires*. This, in turn, formed the basis for James R. Planché's play *The Vampire; or, The Bride of the Isles*, which had its first performance on the London stage in August 1820. Not long afterwards an anonymously-written short story adapted from the play, bearing the title 'The Bride of the Isles: A Tale Founded on the Popular Legend of the Vampire,' was put on sale by an enterprising Dublin publisher. Better than most vampire tales written in the early 1800s, its inclusion in the present volume marks its first appearance in an anthology exclusively devoted to vampire fiction.

The earliest known vampire story by an American writer, Robert C. Sands' 'The Black Vampyre: A Legend of Saint Domingo' (1819), broke new ground by featuring a mulatto vampire. A more significant innovation, the introduction of the female vampire into prose fiction, is the main claim to fame of Ernst Raupach's 'Wake Not the Dead,' which was, for many years, falsely attributed to Johann Ludwig Tieck. A cautionary tale about the folly of bringing the dead back to life, it was originally published in Leipzig in 1822, and received its first English translation a year later when it was included in *Popular Tales and Romances of the Northern Nations*. Less well-known is the quaintly titled story 'Pepopukin in Corsica,' in which a disagreeable suitor is sent packing by inspiring in him a dread of vampires. Originally published in 1827, in *The Stanley Tales, Vol. 1*, where it was credited to 'A. Y.', it was recently claimed that the author these initials belonged to was Arthur Young. Another story from the 1820s, this time by a French writer, is 'The Unholy Compact Abjured' (1825), by Charles Pigault-Lebrun, in which a soldier seeking shelter for the night encounters demonic vampires in a spooky chateau.

Russian literature's first major contribution to the vampire canon was Nikolai Gogol's 'Viy,' which comes from his 1835 collection *Mirgorod*. Described by Edmund Wilson as 'one of the most terrific things of its kind ever written,' it is about a young philosopher's frightening encounter with a witch-vampire and monstrous winged creatures under the control of the King of the Gnomes. The most famous vampire story from the 1830s is undoubtedly 'La Morte Amoureuse' (1836), by the French author Théophile Gautier. Anthologised many times under different titles (e.g. 'Clarimonde,' 'The Dreamland Bride,' and 'The Beautiful Dead'), it tells of a young priest's illicit relationship with a dead courtesan, whose beguiling revenant draws him into a fantastical dreamworld and nightly sucks small quantities of his blood to sustain her life-in-death existence.

Meanwhile, in America, Edgar Allan Poe was turning out a string of morbid horror tales, several of which dealt with unusual forms of vampirism. In 'Ligeia' (1838), for instance, he introduced the idea of mental vampirism, linking it with the allied theme of metempsychosis. The ill-fated title character, a beautiful, highly intelligent woman, gradually wastes away as a result of her husband's obsessive desire to know her completely; but, in a final twist, retribution for this subconscious act of vampirism seems likely when the dead woman's spirit possesses the body of her marital successor, suggesting that the roles of vampire and victim will shortly be reversed. A variation on the same theme occurs in another of Poe's stories, 'The Oval Portrait' (1845), in which an artist totally absorbed in capturing an absolute likeness of his lovely young bride is unaware of the devitalising effect it is having on her frail constitution, and fails to notice that with each sitting the woman's life force is ebbing away. Psychic vampirism of an even more bizarre kind is the underlying theme of Poe's masterpiece, 'The Fall of the House of Usher' (1839). In this story the psychic vampire is the ancestral home of the Usher family, and its victims are the current occupants, Roderick Usher and his sister Madeline. By some hideous process, the ancient mansion – a sentient stone organism impregnated with the evil emanations of past generations of Ushers – is having a devitalising effect on the doomed couple, bringing the horror of madness into their lives. These three stories, along with two others utilising the vampire theme, 'Morella' (1835) and 'Berenice' (1835), were collected together in *Dead Brides: Vampire Tales* (1999).

A story by one of Poe's contemporaries, James Kirke Paulding's 'The Vroucolacas,' has, in the past, attracted the curiosity of vampire aficionados due to its extreme rarity, but since it has become accessible on an internet website any hopes that it might turn out to be a forgotten gem have sadly been dashed. Originally published in the June 1846 issue of *Graham's Magazine*, it is about a frustrated suitor pretending to be a vampire in order to win the hand of his sweetheart. Vampiric possession is the theme of Erckmann-Chatrian's 'The Burgomaster in Bottle,' which first appeared in the French journal *Le Démocrate du Rhin* in 1849. Since then, this story has strangely been overlooked by compilers of vampire anthologies, a situation finally rectified by its inclusion within these pages. The most frequently anthologised vampire tale from the 1840s is 'The Mysterious Stranger,' the bloodsucking villain of which, Azzo von Klatka, is thought to have been the model for Count Dracula. Formerly uncredited, it has recently been established that the author of this story was a little-known German writer named Karl von Wachsmann, and it first appeared in print in 1844, which is much earlier than was previously supposed. Hereditary vampirism is the theme of Aleksey K. Tolstoy's 'Upyr,' which was first published in 1841 under the pseudonym 'Krasnorogsky.' Also worth a brief mention is the vampire episode from Alexandre Dumas's *The*

Thousand and One Phantoms (1848), which usually bears the title 'The Pale Lady' when it is published separately.

Novels with a vampire as the central character were something of a rarity in the first half of the nineteenth century, and the only one remembered today is *Varney the Vampyre; or, The Feast of Blood*, which was originally published in weekly instalments between 1845 and 1847, coming out in book form immediately afterwards. The vampiric hero-villain of this long, rambling narrative is Sir Francis Varney, a tall, gaunt figure with cadaverous features, who is made even more frightening to look at by his glassy eyes, taloned hands, and fang-like teeth. He is also incredibly strong, can move about rapidly, and is a master of disguise. Even on those occasions where he is seemingly killed, he is subsequently revived by the Moon's rays, allowing him to resume his nefarious activities. Finally, after an interminable series of escapades, Varney becomes tired of his life of horror, and ends it all by throwing himself into the crater of Mount Vesuvius. Currently available in a number of paperback editions, in which the novel's authorship is attributed to either James Malcolm Rymer or Thomas P. Prest, this crudely-written 'penny dreadful' is really only noteworthy for the influence it had on later writers, who reworked the variations on the vampire theme which it had introduced.

In comparison with the previous decade, the 1850s were lean years for vampire fiction. The only work of any significance was Charles Wilkins Webber's *Spiritual Vampirism* (1853), which had the distinction of being the first novel to have psychic vampirism as its theme. The following decade was more fruitful, producing some notable short stories featuring female vampires. Of these, none are more highly regarded than Ivan Turgenev's 'Phantoms' (1864), the hero of which is repeatedly visited at night by a phantasmal female figure, who he suspects is secretly sucking his blood. The first vampire story by an Australian author, 'The White Maniac: A Doctor's Tale' (1867), by Mary Fortune, centres on events that take place inside a strange house where everything in it is coloured white. A doctor's desire to solve the mystery leads to the shocking discovery that this has been done by the owner of the property to placate his ward, a beautiful young noblewoman, who suffers from a rare type of anthropophagy, making her prone to homicidal rages whenever she sees something coloured scarlet. One of the earliest appearances of the 'vamp' – the name usually given to a heartless, man-eating seductress – was in 'A Vampire,' an episode in G. J. Whyte-Melville's *Bones and I; or, The Skeleton at Home* (1868). Calling herself Madame de St Croix, this insatiable sexual vampire has remained youthful and desirable over many years and has acquired a string of lovers, all of whom have died in mysterious circumstances. On more traditional lines is William Gilbert's 'The Last Lords of Gardonal' (1867), in which a nobleman is attacked by his beautiful bride on their wedding night, unaware that she has been brought back to life by a wizard's magical powers, and can only survive in her present state by sucking her husband's blood.

Vampirism of a much more unusual kind occurs in Louisa May Alcott's 'Lost in a Pyramid; or, The Mummy's Curse' (1869). In this chilling tale an ancient curse is activated when a seed found in a mummy's wrappings is planted, and the white flower it bears slowly absorbs the vitality of a young woman after she pins it to her dress. One of the least effective stories from the 1860s is 'The Vampire; or, Pedro Pacheco and the Bruxa' (1863), by William H. G. Kingston. Although the main narrative is preceded by a fascinating account of the activities of vicious Portuguese vampires called Bruxas, their non-appearance in the story itself is something of a letdown.

The only vampire-themed novels from the 1860s remembered today are *Le Chevalier Ténèbre* (1860) and *La Vampire* (1865), both of which were written by Paul Féval. In the earlier novel, two notorious male siblings, one a ghoul, the other a vampire, periodically emerge from their 400-year-old graves and go on the rampage. The later novel features the equally formidable Countess Addhema – a pale, fleshless old woman with a bald pate – who is temporarily transformed into a ravishing beauty every time she applies to her bare skull a living head of hair torn from one of her beautiful young female victims. Féval added to his tally of vampire novels in the following decade, penning *La Ville Vampire* in 1874. A parody of early nineteenth century Gothic novels, its unlikely heroine is the real-life author Ann Radcliffe, who mounts an expedition to find the legendary vampire-infested city of Selene, hoping to rescue a friend who has been taken there following her abduction by the evil vampire lord Otto Goetzi.

The first story to feature a lesbian vampire was Joseph Sheridan Le Fanu's 'Carmilla' (1871). In this frequently anthologised classic a young woman named Laura is visited nightly in her bedchamber by the new house guest, the alluring Carmilla, and is drawn into an increasingly intimate relationship with her. Thereafter, Laura's health declines, raising fears that she is the victim of a vampire. It eventually transpires that Carmilla is the revenant of Countess Mircalla Karnstein, who has been dead for more than one hundred and fifty years.

In the 1880s – looked on today as the beginning of supernatural fiction's golden era – there was a noticeable broadening of the vampire story's scope. For example, bigotry, and the tragic circumstances that may arise from it, provides the basis for Eliza Lynn Linton's 'The Fate of Madame Cabanel' (1880), in which a young Englishwoman living among superstitious French peasants is brutally murdered after being mistaken for a vampire. In contrast, Phil Robinson's 'The Man-Eating Tree' (1881) is about an arboreal vampire poetically described as 'a great limb with a thousand clammy hands.' In another offbeat story, Karl Heinrich Ulrichs' 'Manor' (1884), a drowned sailor's corpse becomes reanimated and issues from its grave at night to suck the blood of a youth who had been in a homosexual relationship with the dead man. A unique story from 1886 which is still capable of sending shivers up and down readers' spines is Guy de Maupassant's 'The Horla,' the narrator of which fears he has become the plaything of an invisible vampire. Psychic vampirism is the theme of Frank R. Stockton's 'A Borrowed Month' (1886), in which a young man suffering from a debilitating illness discovers that, by the force of his will, he can draw energy and vitality from his friends. Psychic vampirism of a more sinister kind is practised in Conan Doyle's 'John Barrington Cowles' (1884); this time the perpetrator is a beautiful, sadistic woman who luxuriates in her ability to destroy her lovers.

Sabine Baring-Gould's 'Margery of Quether' (1884) is, without doubt, one of the oddest vampire stories in English literature. Satirising the politics of its day – with many references to the controversial reforms to the land laws – it was popular for a while, but soon sank into a lengthy period of obscurity. However, since its inclusion in *Vintage Vampire Stories* (2011) this story's cynical humour can now be savoured once again. A more conventional story, Aleksey K. Tolstoy's 'The Family of the Vourdalak,' draws its inspiration from Serbian folklore. Originally written in 1839, but not published until 1884, it tells of a French diplomat's frightening encounter with vampires, which happens when he stops for the night at a village, and discovers it is deserted apart from a single family, all of whom have been transformed into vampires after the head of the household was bitten by one.

Two other significant stories from the 1880s are 'Ken's Mystery' (1883), by Julian Hawthorne, and 'A Mystery of the Campagna' (1887), by 'Von Degen' (pseudonym of Anne Crawford). In the former, the hero becomes romantically entangled with a legendary vampiress after travelling with her into the past through the agency of a magic ring; and, in the latter, a composer holidaying in Italy becomes the victim of a centuries-old vampiress whose sarcophagus is concealed in an underground burial chamber.

As might be expected from one of the most fertile periods in the history of supernatural fiction, the final decade of the nineteenth century yielded a rich harvest of vampire stories, several of which are among the finest ever written. Particularly outstanding is Arthur Conan Doyle's 'The Parasite,' which is a compelling tale about a psychic vampire. Originally published in *Harper's Weekly*, 10 November–1 December 1894, it revolves around the machinations of a frail, middle-aged spinster who is able to control the thoughts and actions of other people by her amazing mental powers. In particular, she conceives a passion for a university professor, whom she hypnotises in an attempt to make him reciprocate her love, eventually resorting to vampiric possession when this ploy fails.

One of the few stories from the 1890s to feature a psychic vampire of the male gender is 'Old Aeson' (1890), by Arthur Quiller-Couch, which tells how a man who gives shelter in his home to a decrepit stranger soon lives to regret his charity when his guest usurps his position in the household by stealing his youth and most of his substance. Two other stories from the 1890s with psychic vampirism as their main motif are 'A Modern Vampire' (1894), by W. L. Alden, in which an author has his energy drained by a pretty young woman he has befriended; and 'A Beautiful Vampire' (1896), by Arabella Kenealy, whose central character, a menopausal woman, steals beauty and sexual energy from those around her in order to remain attractive to members of the opposite sex.

New medical procedures being introduced around this time may have inspired 'Good Lady Ducayne' (1896), by Mary E. Braddon. In this lacklustre yarn a latter-day Elizabeth Bathory has survived well beyond the normal lifespan by getting her private physician to inject her with blood he has drained from his employer's young female companions, all of whom fade away and die. A far superior story by this author is 'Herself' (1894), which was included in *Vintage Vampire Stories* after years of undeserved neglect. Set in Italy, it chronicles the gradual decline in health of a bubbly young woman after she becomes morbidly enraptured by an antique mirror, which steals some of her vitality every time she gazes into its depths.

A female vampire of royal blood, who comes to life and sucks the blood of an Englishman after her ancient resting-place is disturbed, is featured in 'The Tomb Among the Pines' (1894), an uncredited story which was initially published in the British periodical *Household Words*. One of the most exotic vampiresses from the 1890s is the evil enchantress in 'The Crimson Weaver' (1895), by R. Murray Gilchrist. Incredibly old yet stunningly beautiful, she lures a knight into her magical domain and kills him horribly after enslaving him with a kiss. Similarly, in Arthur Quiller-Couch's 'The Legend of Sir Dinar' (1891) an Arthurian knight seeking the Holy Grail is held in thrall by a beautiful vampiress who steals his youth. There can be no doubt, however, that the deadliest female vampire from this period is Annette, the central character in Dick Donovan's 1899 story 'The Woman with the "Oily Eyes".' An irredeemably evil monster in womanly form, she attracts upright men against their will and brings about their destruction, using her mesmeric eyes to subjugate them. Another story from 1899, Vincent O'Sullivan's 'Will,' is notable for its effective use of the 'biter bit' scenario. Similar in style to Poe's macabre tales, it tells how a man with an irrational hatred for his wife relentlessly draws out and absorbs her life force by gazing at her intently for hours on end, until eventually she dies. The tables are turned, however, when the dead woman constantly haunts her husband, sapping his will to live.

One of the most unconventional vampire stories from the late Victorian era is 'A Kiss of Judas' by 'X. L.' (pseudonym of Julian

Osgood Field). First published in 1893, it is based on the curious legend of the Children of Judas, the substance of which is that the lineal descendants of the arch-traitor are prowling about the world intent on doing harm to anyone who offends them. Luring their victims into their clutches by any means necessary, they kill them with one bite or kiss, which is so deadly it drains the blood from their bodies, leaving a wound on the flesh like three X's, signifying the thirty pieces of silver paid to Christ's betrayer. Another offbeat story is Count Eric Stenbock's 'The True Story of a Vampire,' which comes from his 1894 collection *Studies of Death*. Count Vardalek, whose activities this story chronicles, is a male version of Le Fanu's Carmilla, but whereas she was homoerotically attracted to another woman, Vardalek has similar feelings about a young boy.

'The Priest and His Cook' and 'The Story of Jella and the Macic' are two folkloric tales that have recently been extracted from *The Pobratim*, an 1895 novel by Professor P. Jones. The former appeared for the first time in *Vintage Vampire Stories*, and the latter makes its debut in the present volume. Two better-known stories from the 1890s that have turned up in vampire anthologies on more than one occasion are 'Let Loose' (1890), by Mary Cholmondeley, and 'The Death of Halpin Frayser' (1891), by Ambrose Bierce. Both are difficult to classify, but a case for including them in the vampire canon can be made if one views them as stories about the dead returning to wreak vengeance on the living, using methods akin to vampirism. There are, however, no such doubts about the eligibility of H. B. Marriott Watson's 'The Stone Chamber' (1898) to be categorised as a vampire story. Set in rural England, it tells how guests staying at Marvyn Abbey awake in the morning feeling exhausted and have red marks on their necks, a tell-tale sign that they have been preyed upon by a vampire.

Stories about vampires of the non-human kind were also popular during the final decade of the nineteenth century. For instance, in H. G. Wells' 'The Flowering of the Strange Orchid' (1894), a collector of exotic plants is attacked by a bloodsucking orchid growing in his hothouse; while in Fred M. White's 'The Purple Terror' (1899) a group of explorers are menaced by vampire-vines in the Cuban jungle. Even more loathsome is the vampire-like monstrosity in Erckmann-Chatrian's 'The Crab Spider' (1893), in which animals and people who enter a cave at a German health resort are attacked and have their bodies drained of blood by a giant arachnid. In another fascinating story, Sidney Bertram's 'With the Vampires' (1899), explorers journeying up the Amazon encounter cave-dwelling vampire bats. The same geographical location is also the setting for Phil Robinson's 'The Last of the Vampires' (1893), in which a German trader comes across a huge vampire-pterodactyl, to which human sacrifices are made.

A psychic detective whose cases sometimes involved vampire-like phenomena is Flaxman Low, who appeared in a series of allegedly real ghost stories in *Pearson's Magazine* between 1898 and 1899 under the byline of E. & H. Heron, a pseudonym used by the mother-and-son writing team Kate and Hesketh Prichard. In 'The Story of Baelbrow,' for instance, Low investigates mysterious deaths at a reputedly haunted house, and discovers that a previously ineffectual spirit-vampire has become a deadly killer by activating an Egyptian mummy in his client's private museum. In another exploit, 'The Story of the Moor Road,' a malevolent elemental becomes palpable after absorbing an invalid's vitality; and, in 'The Story of the Grey House,' guests staying at a secluded country house are strangled and drained of blood by a demoniacal creeper growing in the shrubbery.

The 1890s was also a productive decade for vampire novels, but apart from a select few most are forgotten today. Towering above them all is Bram Stoker's *Dracula*, which, since its launch in 1897, has gone on to sell millions of copies around the world and is undoubtedly the most influential vampire novel ever written. Surviving changes in fashion and numerous indignities at the hands of clumsy editors, it has, over time, earned itself a unique place in the vampire canon, and has deservedly achieved the status of a classic of English literature. The enduring appeal of this novel is primarily due to its sensational plot and Stoker's spellbinding narrative power, but it is also noteworthy for two other reasons. Firstly, it has systemised the rules of literary and cinematic vampirology for all time, and secondly we have in Count Dracula the definitive incarnation of the human bloodsucker.

The only novel from the 1890s to rival Stoker's *magnum opus* in popularity is H. G. Wells' *The War of the Worlds* (1898), which was the first novel to feature alien vampires. For the benefit of those who haven't read Wells' classic, or are only familiar with the plot through watching adulterated film versions, the vampires are the invading Martians, who, we learn, turned to vampirism after their digestive tracts atrophied almost completely, making them solely reliant on blood for sustenance. Initially they preyed on their fellow Martians, but when supplies of the life-giving fluid became exhausted they were forced to look beyond their own planet for survival, and found just what they needed on neighbouring Earth.

J. Maclaren Cobban's *Master of His Fate* (1890), which was strongly influenced by Robert Louis Stevenson's *The Strange Case of Dr Jekyll and Mr Hyde*, concerns the tragic fate of a scientist who has discovered a formula that enables him to renew his youth by absorbing energy from other people merely by touching them. However, as the necessity to absorb larger amounts of energy arises, he is forced to commit suicide to prevent the deaths of his 'donors,' who include the woman he loves. Another novel probably inspired by Stevenson's split-personality classic is Oscar Wilde's *The Picture of Dorian Gray* (1891). While not usually thought of as a vampire, Gray can quite legitimately be likened to one in view of his destructive, self-indulgent lifestyle, an essential part of which is the consumption of other people's life-energy in order to gain eternal youth. Vampirism of a similar nature is practised in H. J. Chaytor's *The Light of the Eye* (1897) and L. T. Meade's *The Desire of Men: An Impossibility* (1899). In the former, a man's eyes have the power to suck out people's vitality, while Meade's thriller revolves around weird experiments in a strange house, where the aged regain their lost youth at the expense of the young. Other novels from the 1890s with vampirism as the main or subsidiary theme are: *The Soul of Countess Adrian* (1891), by Mrs Campbell Praed; *The Strange Story of Dr Senex* (1891), by E. E. Baldwin; *Sardia: A Story of Love* (1891), by Cora Linn Daniels; *The Fair Abigail* (1894), by Paul Heyse; *The Lost Stradivarius* (1895), by J. Meade Falkner; *Lilith* (1895), by George MacDonald; *The Blood of the Vampire* (1897), by Florence Marryat; *In Quest of Life* (1898), by Thaddeus W. Williams; and *The Enchanter* (1899), by U. L. Silberrad.

The only vampire novels from the first decade of the twentieth century of any significance are *In the Dwellings of the Wilderness* (1904), by C. Bryson Taylor; *The Woman in Black* (1906), by M. Y. Halidom;

and *The House of the Vampire* (1907), by George Sylvester Viereck. In the first of these, a party of American archaeologists is attacked vampirically by the revivified mummy of an Egyptian princess; while the novel by the pseudonymous M. Y. Halidom features a glamorous seductress who has retained her beauty and youthful appearance for centuries by sucking the blood of her lovers. In contrast, the vampire in Viereck's novel – an arrogant, self-centred writer – acts like a psychic sponge, stealing the most creative thoughts of his protégés and passing them off as his own.

A short story from the turn of the century which has remained popular over the years is F. G. Loring's 'The Tomb of Sarah.' First published in the December 1900 issue of *Pall Mall Magazine*, it centres on the nocturnal activities of an undead witch who has been accidentally released from the confinement of her tomb during renovations to a church. For a while her nightly forays in search of blood cause great concern among the local community, but she is eventually caught and permanently laid to rest by the time-honoured ritual of driving a stake through her heart. A much more sensational story from this period, Richard Marsh's 'The Mask' (*Marvels and Mysteries*, 1900), is about a homicidal madwoman adept in the art of mask-making who transforms herself into a raving beauty and tries to suck the blood of the story's hero. Female vampires are also featured in two stories in Hume Nisbet's collection *Stories Weird and Wonderful* (1900). In 'The Vampire Maid' a weary traveller finds lodgings at an isolated cottage on the Westmorland moors, only to be preyed on during the night by the landlady's vampire daughter; and in 'The Old Portrait' a woman depicted in a painting comes to life and tries to suck out the vitality of the picture's owner with a long, lingering kiss. Offering more substantial fare, Phil Robinson's 'Medusa,' a well-crafted story from *Tales by Three Brothers* (1902), is about a seductive femme fatale who feeds on the life force of her male admirers. A more subtle threat is posed in Mary E. Wilkins Freeman's 'Luella Miller' (1902), the title character of which unconsciously absorbs the vitality of her nearest and dearest, causing them to languish while she blooms. On more traditional lines is F. Marion Crawford's vampire classic 'For the Blood is the Life' (1905), in which a gypsy girl returns from the dead to vampirize the man who had spurned her love. In another first-rate story, R. Murray Gilchrist's

'The Lover's Ordeal' (1905), a young woman challenges her fiancé to pass through an ordeal before she will consent to marry him. This involves spending the night at a haunted house; but, unbeknown to the couple, a beautiful vampiress is lurking in one of the rooms, waiting patiently for her next victim to come along. An inconsequential piece, by comparison, is 'The Vampire,' by Hugh McCrae, which was originally published under the pseudonym 'W. W. Lamble' when it appeared in the November 1901 edition of *The Bulletin*.

One of the Edwardian era's finest vampire stories is 'Count Magnus,' by M. R. James, which has been anthologised many times since its debut in *Ghost Stories of an Antiquary* (1904). Among this author's spookiest tales, it chronicles the events leading up to the gruesome death of an English scholar, who becomes a doomed man after delving too deeply into suppressed legends about a notorious seventeenth-century Swedish nobleman. A minor story, 'The Vampire' (1902), by Basil Tozer, has seemingly sunk into oblivion, a fate that may well have befallen Frank Norris's 'Grettir at Thorhallstead' (1903) had it not been rescued from obscurity by fantasy historian Sam Moskowitz, who reprinted it in his 1971 anthology *Horrors Unknown*. Not entirely original, Norris's story is a retelling of an episode in *Grettir's Saga*, in which the legendary Icelandic hero has a fateful encounter with a vampire. Coincidentally, the same episode also provided the inspiration for Sabine Baring-Gould's 'Glámr,' which was included in his *A Book of Ghosts* (1904). Another vampire story from this collection is 'A Dead Finger,' in which the hapless protagonist is preyed on by the disembodied spirit of a dead man, which is gradually stealing his vitality in an attempt to create a new body for itself. On similar lines to this story are Luigi Capuana's 'A Vampire' (1907), which describes how the disembodied spirit of a woman's deceased husband attempts to suck the blood of her infant child; and Lionel Sparrow's 'The Vengeance of the Dead' (1910), in which a thoroughly evil man has, since his demise, existed in a state of life-in-death by stealing vitality from the living and transferring it to his corpse. More ambitiously, the unscrupulous scientist in C. Langton Clarke's 'The Elixir of Life' (1903) has isolated the vitic force and found a way to transfer it from others to himself, thereby attaining a kind of immortality. More conventional in their treatment of the vampire theme are 'The Vampire Nemesis' (1905), by 'Dolly,' and 'The Singular Death of Morton' (1910), by Algernon Blackwood. In the former story a suicide is reincarnated as a giant vampire bat; and, in the latter, two men holidaying in France encounter a sinister woman, who lures one of them to a cemetery and sucks all the blood from his body.

Some of the best stories from the Edwardian era feature vampires in unusual guises. In Morley Roberts' 'The Blood Fetish' (1909), for example, a severed hand lives on as an independent entity by absorbing the blood of both animal and human victims. In another morbid tale, Horacio Quiroga's 'The Feather Pillow' (1907), a young woman has all the blood gradually sucked out of her by a monstrous insect secreted inside the pillow on her bed; and in F. H. Power's 'The Electric Vampire' (1910) a mad scientist creates a giant, electrically-charged insect which feeds on blood. Even more bizarre is Louise J. Strong's 'An Unscientific Story' (1903), in which a professor who has succeeded in breeding the 'life-germ' in his laboratory soon realises the folly of his experiments when his creation grows at a fantastic rate and within a short time forms itself into a humanoid creature which exhibits a craving for blood.

The first anthology to gather together a sizeable number of stories from this golden age of vampire fiction was Richard Dalby's *Dracula's Brood* (1987), which contained twenty-three rare stories written by friends and contemporaries of Bram Stoker. Then, after years of searching through dusty old books and defunct magazines, Richard and fellow vampire enthusiast Robert Eighteen-Bisang compiled an even rarer collection of stories for their 2011 anthology *Vintage Vampire Stories*. Now, after more diligent searching, Richard and I have put together this stunning new collection of stories, nearly all of which have been unavailable for many years, and include several forgotten gems whose resurrection from an undeserved obscurity should finally bring them the recognition they deserve.

BRIAN J. FROST

THE BRIDE OF THE ISLES

A Tale Founded on the Popular Legend of the Vampire

Anonymous

When this story, which is based on James Robinson Planché's play *The Vampire; or, The Bride of the Isles*, received its first publication in 1820, the publisher, J. Charles of Dublin, took the liberty of falsely attributing it to Lord Byron, and the real author is unknown. Nevertheless, it is an excellent example of the bluebook or 'Shilling Shocker,' which were the terms usually used to describe short Gothic tales published in booklet form during the early 19th century. Retailing between sixpence and a shilling, they were about four by seven inches in size, and their closely printed pages were stitched into a cover made of flimsy blue paper. These luridly illustrated publications were especially popular with members of the lower classes, many of whom craved the thrill of reading stories revolving around shocking, mysterious and horrid incidents, but couldn't afford to buy expensive Gothic novels, which were often published in three volumes. A copy of the rare 1820 first edition, complete with its coloured frontispiece, fetched £2000 at auction three years ago.

'THOUGH the cheek be pale, and glared the eye, such is the wondrous art the hapless victim blind adores, and drops into their grasp like birds when gazed on by a basilisk.'

THERE IS A popular superstition *still extant* in the southern isles of Scotland, but not with the force as it was a century since, that the souls of persons, whose actions in the mortal state were so wickedly atrocious as to deny all possibility of happiness in that of the next; were doomed to everlasting perdition, but had the power given them by infernal spirits to be for a while the scourge of the living.

This was done by allowing the wicked spirit to enter the body of another person at the moment their own soul had winged its flight from earth; the corpse was thus reanimated – the same look, the same voice, the same expression of countenance, with physical powers to eat and drink, and partake of human enjoyments, but with the most wicked propensities, and in this state they were called vampires. This second existence as it may not improperly be termed, is held on a tenure of the most horrid and diabolical nature. Every *All-Hallow E'en*, he must wed a lovely virgin, and slay her, which done, he is to catch her warm blood and drink it, and from this draught he is renovated for *another* year, and free to take *another* shape, and pursue his Satanic course; but if he failed in procuring a wife at the appointed time, or had not opportunity to make the sacrifice before the moon set, the vampire *was no more* – he did not turn into a skeleton, but literally vanished into air and nothingness.

One of these demoniac sprites, Oscar Montcalm, of infamous notoriety in the Scotch annals of crime and murder (who was decapitated by the hands of the common executioner), was a most successful vampire, and many were the poor unfortunate maidens who had been sacrificed to support his supernatural career, roving from place to place, and every year changing his shape as opportunity presented itself, but always chosing to enter the corpse of some man of rank and power, as by that means his voracious appetite for luxury was gratified.

Oscar Montcalm had seen, and distantly adored in his mortal state, the superior beauty of the Lady Margaret, daughter of the Baron of the Isles, the good Lord Ronald; but, such was his situation, he had not dared to address her; however, he did not forget her in his vampire state, but marked her out for one of his victims, in revenge for the scorn with which he had been treated by her father.

Lady Margaret, though lovely and well proportioned, entered her twentieth year unmarried, nor had she ever been addressed by a suitor whom she could regard with the least partiality, and with much anxiety she sought to know whether she should ever enter into wedlock, and what sort of person her future lord would be. With credulity pardonable to the times in which she lived, and the narrow education then given to females, even of rank, she consulted Sage, Seer and Witch, as to this important event; but it is not to be wondered at that she met with many contradictions, everyone telling a different tale. At length urged on by the irresistible desire to pry into futurity, she repaired with her two maidens, Effie and Constance, to the Cave of Fingal, where, cutting off a lock of her hair, and joining it to a ring from her finger, she cast it into the well, according to the directions she had received from Merna, the Hag of the mountains, who had instructed the fair one as to this expedition.

No sooner was the ring flung into the well than a dreadful storm arose; the torches, which the attendant maidens had borne, were extinguished, and the immense cave was in utter darkness: loud and dreadful was the thunder, accompanied by a horrid confusion of sounds, which beggars description.

Margaret and her companions sunk on their knees; but they were too stupefied with horror to pray, or to endeavour to retrace their way out of this den of horrors. Of a sudden, the cave was brilliantly illuminated, but with no visible means of light, for there were neither torch, lamp, or candle. Solemn music was heard, slow and awfully grand, and in a few minutes two figures appeared, one heavy, morose in countenance, and clad in dark robes, who announced herself as Una, the spirit of the storm, and touching a sable curtain, discovered to the view of Margaret the figure of a noble young warrior, Ruthven, Earl of Marsden, who had accompanied her father to the wars. Again the storm resounded, the curtain closed, and the cave resumed its darkness; but this was only transient – the brilliant light returned – Una was gone, and the light figure, dressed in transparent robes, sprinkled over with spangles remained. With her wand she pulled aside the curtain, and a young man of interesting appearance was visible, but his person was a stranger to the fair one. Ariel, the spirit of the Air, then waved her hand to the entrance of the cave, as a signal for them to depart, and bowing low, they withdrew, amid strains of heart-thrilling harmony, rejoiced to find themselves once more in an open space, and they happily returned in safety to the baron's castle. The Lady Margaret was well pleased with what she

had seen, as promising her two husbands, though she was somewhat
puzzled by calling to mind a couplet that Ariel had repeated three
or four times, while the curtain remained undrawn.

> 'But once fair maid, will you be wed,
> You'll know no second bridal bed.'

What could this mean? Surely she would never stoop to illicit
desires or intrigue? She thought she knew her own heart too well.

The vampire had seen into the designs of Margaret to visit the
Cave of Fingal, and he sought out Ariel and Una, to whom, by
virtue of his supernatural rights, he had easy access. The spirit of
the air would not befriend him, but the spirit of the storm assisted
him to pry into futurity; and to suit his views, she presented the
figure of Ruthven, Earl of Marsden. In the meantime, Marsden had
the good fortune to save Lord Ronald's life in the battle, and the
wars being ended, or at least suspended for a time, he invited the
gallant youth home with him to his castle, to pass a few months
amid the social rites of hospitality and the pleasure of the chase.

The Lady Margaret received her father with dutiful affection, and
gratitude to providence for his safe return, and she beheld young
Marsden with secret delight; but when informed that he had
preserved the baron from overpowering enemies, her gratitude knew
no bounds, and she looked so beautiful and engaging, while
returning her thankful effusions for the service he had rendered
her father, that the earl could not resist the impulse, and from that
hour became deeply enamoured of the lovely fair one.

Marsden's rank and birth were unexceptionable but his fortune
was very inadequate to support a title, which made him (added to
the love of military glory) enter into the profession of arms, of which
he was an ornament.

Margaret was the only child, and her father abounding in wealth
and honours; it might therefore be presumed that an ambition might
lead him to form very exalted views for the aggrandisement of his
heiress; and so he had, but perceiving how high his preserver stood
in the good graces of his darling child, and that the passion was
becoming mutual, he resolved not to give any interruption to their
happiness, but if Marsden could win Margaret to let him have her,

as a rich reward for the service he had performed amid the clang of arms.

Parties were daily formed by the baron for the chase, hawking, or fishing, while the evening was given to the festive dance, or the minstrels tuned their harps in the great hall, and sang the deeds of Scottish chiefs, long since departed, amongst whom the heroic Wallace was not forgot.

The love of Ruthven and Lady Margaret were now generally known throughout the islands and congratulations poured in from every quarter.

A day was fixed for the nuptials, and magnificent preparations were made at the castle for the celebration of the ceremony, when the sudden and severe illness of the baron caused a delay. He wished them not to defer their marriage on his account; but the young people, in this instance would not obey him, declaring their joys would be incomplete without his revered presence.

The baron blessed them for this instance of love and filial duty, but he still felt a strong desire to have the marriage concluded.

The baron was scarce recovered, when he and Ruthven were summoned to the field of battle, a war having broken out in Flanders, and the marriage was deferred till their return; and taking a most affectionate leave of the Lady Margaret, the father and lover left the castle, and the fair one in the charge of old Alexander, the faithful steward, with many commands and cautions respecting the edifice and the lady, whom they both regarded as a gem of inestimable value, with whom they were loath to part, but imperious duty and the calls of honour allowed no alternative.

Robert, the old steward's son, attended the baron abroad; and Marsden took his own servant the faithful Gilbert. They were successful in several skirmishes with the enemy, but in the final engagement Ruthven lost his life, dying in the arms of the Lord of the Isles, who mourned over him as for a beloved son, and he ordered Robert and Gilbert, who were on the spot, to convey the body to a place beyond the carnage, that when the battle was over he might see it (if he himself survived) and have the valued remains interred in a manner that became an earl and a soldier, dying in defending his country's cause.

The battle ended, for the glory and success of Great Britain, and the good Baron of the Isles was unhurt, so was Robert, but Gilbert was amongst the slain.

Lord Ronald, fatigued with the sharp action of the day, in which he had borne his part with a vigour surprising to his time of life, for his head was now silvered over with the honourable badge of age, repaired to his tent to take some refreshment and an hour's rest on his couch, to invigorate his frame. The couch eased his weary limbs, but his eyes closed not, and all his thoughts were on Ruthven, and the distress the sad news would give to his dear child. He arose, and with trembling fingers penned a letter to her, describing the melancholy event, and exhorting her, for the sake of her father, to support this trial with resignation and patience, and bow to the dispensations of Providence, who orders all things eventually for the best, however severe and distressing they seem at the time. He ended his letter by observing that he should return to the castle of the Isles without delay, being anxious to fold her in his arms, and that he should bring the corpse of the brave Marsden to his native land.

The letter being sent off expressly by one of his retainers, the baron ordered some soldiers to attend with a bier, and taking Robert for their guide they went to fetch the body of Ruthven, and in the meantime he had a small tent erected for its reception, surmounted by a sable flag.

But this posthumous attention of the good baron was all in vain, for after a long absence, Robert and the soldiers returned, with the unwelcome news that the body of the gallant Scot was not to be found, but the spot where it had been deposited by the servants was still marked with the blood that had flowed from his gaping wounds and it was presumed that the enemy had found the corpse, and had conveyed it away to some obscure hole out of revenge for the slaughter he had dealt among their leaders before his fall. This event added materially to Ronald's regret and sorrow, for the natives of the Isles of Escotia held a traditional superstition, that while the body lay unburied the spirit wandered denied of rest. He offered rewards for the body without success, and was at length obliged, though with much reluctance, to drop the affair.

The baron was obliged to pay his duty in England to his sovereign before he repaired to the Isles. Unexpected events detained him two months at the British court, but he at last effected his departure to his long wished-for home.

A courier made known his approach, and Lady Margaret, attended by the whole household, dressed in their best array, came forth to meet him, headed by the aged minstrel, and they received their lord with joyous shouts and lively strains, about half a mile from the gates of the castle.

Lord Ronald, as the carriage descended a steep hill that led into the valley, had a full view of the party approaching to meet him, and his heart felt elated at the compliment. He could discern his daughter; but how came it she was not in sables? Surely Ruthven, her betrothed lover, deserved that mark of respect to his memory! But he could observe that she was gaily dressed, and her high plume of feathers waving in the light breeze that adulated the air. The baron cast a look on his own deep mourning, and sighed; he was not pleased – but worse and worse. As he gained a nearer view, he perceived that his daughter was handed along, most familiarly by a knight. I had hoped, said he to himself, that Margaret would have rose superior to the inconstancy and caprice attributed to her sex. Can it be possible, that she has so soon forgot the valiant, accomplished Ruthven! Oh, woman! woman! are ye all alike? As the vehicle entered the valley, Ronald quitted it, to receive the welcome of his child and retainers.

Powers of astonishment! Was it, or was it not, illusion? By what miracle did he behold Ruthven, Earl of Marsden, standing before him, and Lady Margaret hanging with chaste expressions of delight on his arm; there was a scar on his forehead, and he was much paler than before the battle, but no other alteration was visible. As for Robert, he stood aghast, his hair bristled up and his joints trembled, and altogether would have served as a good model of horror to a painter or statuary.

Ruthven stretched forth his hand – 'You seem astonished, my good lord,' said he, 'to find me here before you, or, indeed to find me here at all. I was discovered by some peasants returning from their daily labour, nearly covered with fern and leaves ['Yes,' said Robert, 'that was Gilbert's work and mine.'] by means of a little dog, who had scented out my body from its purposed concealment. They were very poor, and my clothes and decorations were a strong temptation, to which they yielded, they agreed to strip me, sell the clothes, and divide the spoil. While they were thus occupied, they perceived signs of life, and their humanity prevailed over every other consideration, I was conveyed to one of their cottages, and well attended. The man had a wonderful skill in herbs and simples, therefore my cure was rapid, but previous to my leaving them, I well rewarded everyone who had been instrumental in my preservation and freely forgave the intended plunder they had confessed to me, as it was the means directed by fate to prolong my existence, and restore me to my angelic Margaret.

'When I recovered, I found the British forces had quitted Flanders, but I could not learn which direction my friend the baron (you my dear lord) had taken; so I hastened to Scotland with all the speed my situation would admit of, and we were retarded at sea by adverse winds. I found my dear betrothed, and her fair damsels, in deep mourning for my supposed loss; but I soon changed her tears for smiles, and her sables for gayer vestments: but at first her surprise, like yours, Lord Ronald, was too great to admit of utterance, but in time we became composed and grateful, and we agreed not to inform you of my existence, but astonish you on your arrival.'

The baron greeted his young friend most warmly and testified his hope that no more ill-omened events would disappoint the nuptials of the brave earl and Margaret, whom he tenderly clasped to his bosom, and kissing each cheek, remarked that she was the living image of his dear departed wife. He then turned to the old harper, and bidding him strike up a lively strain, proceeded to the castle, where all was joy and festivity; again resounded the song, and again the damsels, with their swains showed off their best reels *à la Caledonia*.

In the old steward's room a plenteous board was spread, for the upper servants and retainers of the hospitable Lord of the Isles, who ordered flowing bowls and well replenished horns to the health of Ruthven and Margaret.

Some of the party were remarking on the wonderful preservation of Marsden's earl by the Flemish peasants, instead of plundering and leaving him to perish, as many would have done to an almost expiring enemy.

'*Almost expiring!*' said Robert, whose cheeks had not yet recovered their usual hue since the meeting in the valley with Ruthven.

'*Almost expiring!*' he repeated; 'I am certain the body of the earl was dead – aye, as dead as my great grandsire – when I and Gilbert carried him from the field of battle; and when we left him under the fern he was as cold as ice, and the blood from his wounds coagulated – No, no, he never came to life again; this Ruthven you have here must be a vampire.'

'*A vampire! a vampire!*' resounded from all the company, with loud shouts of laughter at poor Robert's simplicity. 'Perhaps you are a *vampire*,' said his sweetheart, Effie, joining in the mirth, 'so I shall take care how I trust myself in your power.'

Robert did not reply, and all the rest of the night he had to stand the bantering jests of his companions.

But Robert was right; Marsden's earl died on the field of battle, and the moment the servants quitted the corpse, the vampire, wicked Montcalm, whose relics lay mouldering beneath a stone in Fingal's cave, watching the moment, took possession, and reanimated the body; the wounds instantly healed, but the face wore a pallid hue, the invariable case with the vampires, their blood not flowing in that free circulation which belongs to real mortals.

The story told by the vampire was a fabrication, respecting the peasants, to impose on Lord Ronald and the Lady Margaret as to the appearance of the supposed Ruthven, and he well succeeded.

On previously consulting the Spirit of the Storm, the vampire had discovered that Margaret would be courted by Ruthven, Earl of Marsden; he also discovered, in his peep into futurity, that the young hero would be slain in battle, and this seemed to him a glorious opportunity to obtain possession of the lovely Margaret, and make her his victim, renovate his vampireship, and go on in the most diabolical career, hurling destruction on the human race, and drawing them into crime after crime, till they sank into the gulf of eternal infamy.

It now wanted a month to All-Hallow E'en and it so chanced, that in that year the next coming moon would set on that very eve from its full orbit. The vampire repaired to the cave of Fingal, and by magic means, which he well knew how to put in execution, he raised up some infernal spirits, whom he asked for orders. They told him they would consult their ruler Beelzebub, and he was to come on the third eve from thence for an answer.

This, then, was the decree – he must wed a virgin, destroy her, and drink her blood, before the setting of the moon on All-Hallow E'en, or terminate into mere nonentity; and if the maid was unchaste, the charm was dissolved. If he succeeded he was to quit the form of Earl Marsden and get egress into some other corpse to give it animation.

The supposed death of Ruthven had caused Margaret to imbibe the idea that the two figures she had seen in Fingal's cave, and Ariel's couplet prophetic but of one marriage, now made out by his fall, he being only a betrothed lover, and the stranger knight she regarded as her future spouse; but the return of the Earl again puzzled her, and she knew not what to think, but at length resolved on another visit to the mystic cavern. Possibly ashamed of confessing this weakness to her maidens, or, what is more probable, conscious that from the terrors they had experienced in attending her there, she could not persuade them to go a second time, she went alone, and soon after midnight, when all the castle was hushed in sound repose, save the vampire, who beheld from the lofty casement, the temporary flight of the enterprising Margaret. How did he thirst for her blood – how willingly would he have immolated the lovely maid that moment, and paid the infernal tribute, but for one clause that interposed and saved her from his fangs. This was the necessity of his being first legally married, in all due form, to the intended victim. He regarded her with a diabolical and malicious scowl, while, by as bright a starlight night as ever illumined the heavens, he saw her tripping through the park's wide avenues of stately firs. He wondered where she was going, and felt apprehensive that some event was in agitation that might deprive him of his bride. The vampire had just concluded to follow her, when a heaviness he could neither resist or shake off, overpowered him and sealed his eyes in a deep sleep.

Margaret, in much perturbation and a beating heart, gained the way to the cave; but the interior was so dark that she was obliged to grope on her hands and knees to the magic well, and cast in the accustomed charm. The thunder rolled, and the storm commenced, but with not one quarter of the violence as on her preceding visit. The music followed in an harmonious strain, and the spirits of the storm and air soon stood before her. The beauty, the innocence, of the noble maid, her virtues and her benevolence, had interested these mystical beings in her behalf – yes, even the stern and oft obdurate

Una felt for Margaret, and wished to save her. They could not alter the decree of fate, nor had they power over the vampires; the only thing that remained was to warn the enquirer, if possible, of her danger. For this purpose, they unfolded the curtain, and presented to her view, the real Ruthven on the field of battle, bleeding and a corpse. She heard his last sigh, saw his last convulsive motion – *a grisly fleshless skeleton stood by his side, and at that moment entered his corpse, which sprung up reanimated*! Margaret knew well the traditional tales of the vampires, and shuddered as she beheld one before her; for what could be more plain? No further vision was shown her – she was warned from the cave, and the fair one returned to the castle, dejected and spiritless. What did this mean? Ruthven, her adored Ruthven, could be no vampire – impossible – so accomplished, so clever, superior in most things to others of his rank. She passed the intervening hours in a very restless state, till they met at their morning repast in the small saloon. The vampire handed her to a chair; she remembered the scene in the cave, and shrank back with a feeling of disgust; but this was not lasting; the labours of the spirit of the storm and the air had not their intended effect; like advice given to young maidens that accords not with the inclination, it sank before the fascination of the object beloved, and she regarded what had been shown her as wayward spite in Una and Ariel; so ready are we to twist circumstances to act in conformity with our own inclination.

The dews of night, the chilling breeze, the damp of the magic cave of Fingal, joined to the fatigue and agitation of the noble maiden, caused a fever which confined her to her chamber several days, and again delayed the marriage. The vampire grew impatient, and before the Lady Margaret was scarce convalescent, he began to press for the nuptial ceremony, with what the good baron thought indecorous haste, though he made all possible allowance for repeated disappointments and youthful passions.

Robert, much better read than the warrior, his master, in the traditional tales of his country, and its popular superstitions, had not yet got the better of his shock at the reappearance of Ruthven in his native valley, when he felt convinced that Marsden's earl died of his wounds on the field of battle at Flanders. 'Aye, by the holy rood, he did,' would the youth often mutter to himself. 'May I never live to be married to my gentle Effie, and it wants but three days and three nights to that happy morn, if I did not see Ruthven's eye-strings crack, and his heart's veins burst assunder: this is a vampire, and this is the moon when those foul fiends pay their tribute, and now he is all impatience to wed my young mistress, forsooth – Yes, yes, 'tis plain enough: but what is the use of saying anything about it, my father and all the servants laugh at me; even my intended turns into ridicule, anything I advance on the subject, and calls me Robert, the vampire hunter: but I will not be deterred from doing my duty like an honest servant, let them jeer as they will. I am resolved to tell the baron all that I know, that is, all I think of his guest, and then he may please himself, and come what will, my conscience will be clear.'

Robert had courage to face a cannon, and never turned his back on the bravest foe, but he felt daunted at the disclosure he meant to make to Lord Ronald; the subject was awkward, and the vampire (if vampire he was) might take a summary revenge on him for his interference. Yet his resolution was not shaken, and seeking the cellar-man he procured a glass of cordial and a horn of ale to revive his spirits, and then, finding himself what he called his own man again, he sought the baron, whom he happened to find alone and taking his evening walk in the grounds, while Margaret and her lover were sitting at their music.

Robert told his tale with much hesitation and faltering, but the baron heard him with more patience than he expected, and made him recount every particular of his suspicions. ''Tis strange! 'tis marvellous strange!' replied the good Lord Ronald; 'for I have seen many persons from Flanders, and yet they never heard of the Earl of Marsden being saved by the peasants: one would have thought such news would have spread like wildfire.'

'Neither does he go to mass or prayer,' observed Robert, 'as a Christian warrior ought to do; nor does he take salt on his trencher.[1] And All-Hallow E'en is fast approaching,' continued Robert: 'this is the fatal moon, and my young mistress—'

'Shall never be his,' exclaimed the baron, ''till the moon sets, and the night, so tragic and pregnant of evil to many a spotless maid, is gone by; then if Ruthven is Marsden's true earl, he may

---

1 This remark of Robert's was another popular superstition of the Isles.

have my Margaret. She shall then be his, and I will turn all my fish ponds into bowls for whisky punch, and the great fountain in the forecourt shall flow with ale till not a Scot around can stand upon his legs, or he is no well-wisher to me or mine; but if he is an infernal vampire, his reign will be over. Faith, by St Andrew, I know not what to think, but I have had fearful dreams, portentous of evil to my ancient house.'

The baron dismissed Robert with a present, and many encomiums on his fidelity and zeal for him and the Lady Margaret. 'My father,' said the honest fellow, 'has lived with you from youth to age: I was born within these walls, and my deceased mother suckled your amiable heiress; treachery in me would be double guilt: no, I would die to serve the house of Ronald!'

When the baron entered his daughter's apartment, a group met his eyes, very ill calculated to give him pleasure in his present frame of mind full of supernatural ideas, and teeming with dread suspicions; Margaret had changed her robes of plaid silk for virgin white, her neck chain, bracelets and other ornaments of filigree silver, most exquisitely wrought. Ruthven was also dressed with elegance. The fair one's attendants were also in their best. The steward and the physician of the household were present, and the chaplain stood with the sacred book in his hand.

'We were waiting for you, my dear Lord Baron,' said the vampire, Ruthven; 'I have persuaded my lovely betrothed to be mine this very evening. We have been so very unfortunate, that I dread further delay, and think every hour teeming with evil till she is mine irrevocably.'

'You have no rival,' answered the baron, much alarmed and piqued: 'you are secure in Margaret's love and my consent. My friends and tenants will ill brook such privacy; they have been accustomed to see the daughters of the Lord of the Isles wedded in public pomp and magnificence, and to share in the festive and abundant hospitalities. No, by the shades of my ancestors, I will have no such doings.'

Ruthven pleaded hard, but the baron heeded not his arguments or eloquence, for the more he seemed bent on espousing Margaret then, the old lord thought more on Robert's report and his own suspicions. Margaret, infatuated by the spell that cast an illusion over her senses, seemed to forget her proper dignity and the delicate decorum of her sex, and joined in the solicitations of her lover. 'My dear father,' said the beauteous maiden, 'Ruthven and myself are in unison with each other's sentiments; we seek not in pomp and glare for happiness; we place our prospects of future bliss in elegant retirement and domestic pleasures. Allow us to be now united, I entreat you, and you can afterwards treat your neighbours, retainers, and servants, as plenteously as you like, but I shrink from the idea of a public marriage.'

Ruthven took the hand of his betrothed, which she presented to him with the most endearing smiles, while her eyes modestly bent down and her cheeks covered with roseate blushes, and never did Lady Margaret look so irresistibly captivating as at that moment.

The baron, while she was speaking, trembled with emotion – Not for a single hour, said he, mentally, would I defer their happiness on account of bridal pomp, if I thought all was right; but I will not risk the sacrificing of so much loveliness, and that my only child, the image of my lost Cassandra, to a vampire; but he did not like to disclose the suspicions he had imbibed, for if they were founded in error, how grossly ridiculous would he appear, and he resolved to delay the nuptials, and stay the test of the moon. He therefore said, 'It is my pleasure to give a full month to splendid preparation, 'tis but a short delay, and let me have the satisfaction to have the nuptials as I would wish them to be, in honour of Marsden's earl and Ronald's daughter.'

The baron observed the lover give a start at the words 'a full month', and his eyes shot forth a most malicious glance. He still held Margaret's hand. 'Nonsense! my good friend,' said he, 'this is not fair, from one warrior to another – Chaplain, begin the ceremony.'

The enraged baron flung off his guard, snatched the book from the hands of the priest, and bade Margaret retire with her maidens to another room, accusing Ruthven of being a vampire.

This was strongly resented by the accused, and, indeed, every one took his part, and laughed at the suggestion. This raised the baron's passion so high that he was declared by the physician to be insane, and they coercively conveyed him to his chamber, and barred him in, where he was on the point of becoming frantic indeed, from the thoughts of his injunctions, for he was more convinced than ever of Ruthven being a supernatural imposter, or he would never have acted so uncourteous to a knight in his own castle.

Robert having heard from his father, the old steward, of the interruption of the marriage through the baron's mania, in thinking the Earl of Marsden a vampire, and his lord's confinement in the western turret, observed that he supposed the nuptials then were all off. His parent answered no, that the young people were not forced to obey such whims; that Lady Margaret was retired for an hour to regain her composure, and the chaplain would then perform the ceremony. 'And who is to be the bride's father?' said Robert. – 'I am to have that honour,' replied the steward. – 'And much good may it do you,' said the son: 'but if I was you, I'd cater better for the noble Lady Margaret than to give her to an evil spirit.' – 'Go to, for an ungracious bird,' exclaimed Alexander; 'you are as mad as your master; poor Effie will have but a crazy husband at the best of it.' – 'Better a crazy one, than a bloodthirsty vampire, father,' observed Robert, who quitted the room, vexed at the loud peal of laughter, which was now set up against him.

Robert went out into the park, but returned privately into the castle by a bypath and a private door, of which he had a key, having procured it some time before he went to the wars, for he was then a rakish youth, and loved to steal out to the village dance or festival, after he was supposed to retire to rest for the night; but now he was contracted to the languishing blue-eyed Effie he was reformed, and voluntarily relinquished all such stolen delights. The key was now regarded by him as a treasure. 'It helped me,' said he to himself, 'to sow my wild oats; it shall now aid me to perform a more laudable purpose. Little did I think to see the good Baron of the Isles a captive in his own castle; and for what, but that he is in too much possession of his senses to sacrifice his lovely virgin daughter to a vampire, for such, by the holy rood, is this fine Earl of Marsden. Why his face is the image of death itself, and his eyes glare; yet my Lady Margaret forsooth! thinks him very handsome, now she is under the influence of the wicked spell; the real Ruthven looked not so when he came to woo the noble fair one; but he says 'tis through his wounds in battle: I think by St Cuthbert, he has had time enough to get his complexion again, and he eats and drinks voraciously, it makes me sick to see him as I stand in waiting, and no salt – faugh!'

This long soliloquy, brought the faithful youth to the door of the baron's prison; he drew the bolts and entered; his lord was pacing the chamber with unmeasured strides, and beating his forehead, while heavy sighs burst from his aged bosom. He started and stood still on Robert's entrance.

'Friend or foe?' said he. – 'Friend,' replied Robert, 'and when I prove otherwise to my most noble master and commander, may I be seized by the foul fiend and made food for vulture.'

'I am not mad,' said the good old veteran, 'but I think I may say, I am distracted with grief.'

'You are no more mad than I, my lord; I do not join in that absurd tale; but hasten and arm yourself. The marriage is to take place almost immediately – let us hasten and prevent it, ere it is too late.'

Lord Ronald was doubly shocked – his suspicions of the vampire were increased by this obstinate persisting in the nuptials against his command, and the want of tenderness and filial love testified by his daughter. How changed was Margaret! Did she choose for her bridal hours those of confinement to her sire – had she not supposed him insane, it is not to be thought she would have suffered him to be thus treated; this then was her season for connubial joys – the sudden insanity of her only surviving parent, he who had so ardently strove not only to fulfil his own duties, but to supply the place as far as possible of the late Lady Cassandra, his amiable wife, and he felt there was no sting so keen as a child's ingratitude. The barbed arrow seemed to touch his very vitals, and for the first time in his life the brave Ronald shed tears.

'Take courage, my lord,' said Robert, 'if they dare still to oppose your authority, this trusty falchion, this well-tried steel, shall prove if Ruthven is common flesh and blood or no.'

'Moderation! moderation! Robert,' replied the baron, as he led the way to Lady Margaret's apartment, where he did not arrive one minute too soon – the ceremony was on the point of commencing, and 'tis possible a few of the first words had been pronounced by the priest.

The baron's entrance caused a universal consternation – the maidens shrieked, and the vampire began to bluster, but Lord Ronald took prompt measures. He solemnly protested that he was in the full use and exercise of his senses, and charged his daughter, on the penalty of incurring his curse, not to enter into wedlock with Marsden's earl till he sanctioned it. She did not choose to disobey on such an awful threat, but casting a look of anguish and tenderness on her lover, she burst into tears, and leaning on the arms of her sympathising maidens, withdrew to her chamber, where throwing herself on a couch, gave way to a full tide of sorrow. 'Cruel father!' she exclaimed. 'Ridiculous superstition! I feel I never shall be the bride of my truly adored and adoring Ruthven, so many fatal interruptions seem as if the fates forbid our union – spirits of the storm and air, are ye not too in league against me?'

The vampire now besought the baron's forgiveness and friendship, attributing his recent behaviour to excess of love, that did not brook delay; he also interceded for the chaplain, whom Lord Ronald was about to dismiss for his presumption, and peace was again restored in the Castle of the Isles.

Wine was called for, and a repast was spread and the vampire so artfully strove against the suspicions of the baron, that the prejudices of the latter were nearly done away; and Robert blamed for his credulous folly; yet the false earl could not obtain from the old nobleman a promise to allow him to wed before the setting of the moon, for Ronald still adhered to that test, nor would abridge aught of a term that now waxed very short.

The vampire concealed his chagrin and feigned content; he thought it best to keep a firm footing in the castle, as some chance might still operate in his favour, founding his hopes on the spell he had obtained over Lady Margaret, and the strong affection with which she beheld him, and he scarcely admitted a doubt of success, if he could get the baron and Robert out of the way; for no one else in the castle had the least doubt of his being the real Earl of Marsden.

The baron, however, watched with great vigilance, and Robert never stirred from a station he had taken that commanded a view of the door of Lady Margaret's chamber. Time seemed to ride on swift pinions with the vampire – his fears were stronger than his hopes – he had never been so foiled before in his attempts, and he thought it best to provide against the coming danger, and leave the mistress alone for her maid the blue eyed Effie; whom he would lure from her allegiance to Robert, persuade her to wed himself, and then sacrifice her to pay his annual demoniac tribute. This would serve two purposes, renew his vampireship, and be a deadly revenge on the interfering Robert, on whom he longed to wreak his diabolical rage.

It seemed rather a difficult achievement to gain the affections of a young and certainly most virtuous maiden (who was to be married in a few hours to the object of her first choice) from that object, but the vampire's case grew desperate, and he resolved to try if the charm would operate.

While Robert was watching the lady, the vampire resolved to seize on the more ignoble prize, and he assailed Effie with every alluring temptation. He told the poor girl that he was tired of pursuing the match with Lady Margaret, and abhorred the thought of allying himself to such a piece of dotage as the credulous baron, who was grown superannuated, and only fit to sit amongst the old wives a-spinning, and tell legendary tales of hobgoblins, and water sprites. He said Effie's beauty and innocence had charmed him – that she wanted nothing but dress and rank to be level with her mistress, and that would be hers by marrying Marsden's earl.

'But I am ignorant, and can neither play music, sing, dance, or do the honours of a table, like Lady Margaret.' This reply pleased the vampire; it seemed one of a very yielding nature, if she had no scruples but what arose from a fear of her own demerits.

'All these can soon be taught,' said the deceiver. 'I must seek some lady of fallen fortune, but elegant accomplishment, to polish your native gracefulness; she shall be your companion in my absence, and your tutoress, and I will join in the delightful task; therefore that can be no objection.' Effie raised several other difficulties, but all were successfully combated, and the vampire earl promised to make the foresaken Robert amends for the loss of his bride by a noble sum and a pretty damsel from off his own estate.

Effie yielded; and though by this act she justly incurred censure and reproach, yet we must do her the justice to remember that the vampire had a tongue to charm his victims, and eyes that are described like the fascination of a basilisk; and to have a powerful earl sighing for her love, might have tempted a higher maid than the simple Effie, the mere child of nature.

Having gained her consent, he hastened to secure his prize; he persuaded her that they must instantly flee, lest the lynx-eyed Robert should grow jealous, and interrupt their promised happiness; he therefore told her to meet him in an hour, at the end of the long avenue in the castle park, and he would be prepared with a horse to convey her to the next convent (about five miles distant) where the priest could join their hands.

That he intended to wed Effie was too true; in that promise lurked no deceit, but the ceremony over, he meant to take her into an adjacent wood, offer up his sacrifice by immolating her with his own hands, and drinking her heart's blood; then seek out some noble form just departed – enter it – and woo Lady Margaret in a new character, and finally triumph over the baron, for he hated all who opposed him in his designs.

Poor unsuspecting Effie, thy head ran on nothing but the glare of thy expected coronet, and thou felt no pity for thy so lately loved Robert, or thy kind and generous mistress, though both were to be betrayed by this clandestine step.

She was true to her appointment and crossed the park with light steps – the vampire was in waiting – he assisted her to mount the horse, and then sprung up behind her. – The steed bounded off like lightning. In an instant Robert rushed from a copse and cried out for the fugitives to stop, but instead of obeying him the vampire spurred his horse to quicken him on. The baron had taken Robert's post to watch the Lady Margaret while the latter made an excursion for air; his gun was loaded, and vengeance nerved the young soldier's arm with so sure an aim that the corporeal part of the vampire fell mortally wounded to the ground, dragging Effie after it loudly shrieking, and all her new-raised love extinguished – for the illusion had vanished, and the image of Robert again filled her virgin heart. Most happily for her future peace the secret of her consenting to the supposed earl's passion was known to her alone – there had been no witness of that degrading incident so fatal to her integrity; and Robert believing she was carried off against her will, all ended well – she was espoused to her faithful suitor at the appointed time, and made an excellent wife; for her dereliction had made her watchful over herself – she often thought of the precipice on which she had stood and trembled. Her beauty long after her marriage gained her admirers, but they were soon dismissed with spirit, and taught to keep at a proper distance, for Effie was now proof against seduction.

But to return to the vampire. He lay bleeding on the ground, while Robert conveyed Effie to the castle, cautioning her to secrecy as she valued his life, for he knew not what might be the result of this act, if it was indeed Marsden's earl he had slain. He sought the baron who was much vexed at the recital, though he acknowledged that Robert had much provocation, and Ruthven's elopement with Effie was an insult on the Lady Margaret not to be borne. The Lord of the Isles and his faithful follower repaired to the spot where the latter had left the treacherous earl.

'I wonder,' said Robert, as they proceeded thither, and calling to mind the scene in Flanders, 'whether we shall find his lordship there, or whether Beelzebub has given him a second life.' The vampire, however, was there, bleeding copiously, but in full possession of his senses. He declared life to be ebbing fast, and that he forgave Robert his death wound; also, he ascribed his carrying off Effie as a mere frolic to alarm her and that he had intended to convey her back in safety to the castle. 'I do not like such jests,' said the indignant Robert, 'and you have paid for an act you had better have left alone.'

The false earl then proceeded to state, on the oath of a dying man, that he was no vampire. This gave a sad pang both to the baron and Robert, and the former testified his regret at the conduct such suspicions had given rise to. He then demanded of Ruthven if he had any commission to charge him with, and it should be punctually executed.

'Swear it,' exclaimed the vampire, eagerly.

The baron drew forth his sword and swore on it.

'Give me that topaz ring from off your finger,' said the vampire; 'let me die with it on, in token of your renewed amity, and allow it to be buried with me.' To this the Lord Ronald most readily consented.

'Next,' said the vampire, drawing it forth from his bosom, where it hung extended by a hair chain, 'take this ring of twisted gold, and cast it into a well that stands on the north side of Fingal's cave – 'tis a charm given by the mighty Stuffa. I shall thus have a vow performed that will give peace to my soul, and save it from wandering after it has quitted its mortal clay-built tenement. In a few minutes I shall be no more – draw my body aside into the copse, and tomorrow at your return you can seek it, and give me burial; but for the present conceal my death from all you meet: name it not until the ring is in the cave.'

In a few minutes the vampire seemed to die with a heavy groan, and the afflicted baron and his attendant proceeded to obey the last injunctions thus received, both conscience-stricken at having thus treated Marsden's earl, and feeling assured, from the manner of his death, that he was a mortal man. They returned to the castle to prepare for their journey to the cave; but mentioned not the decease of Ruthven; and even Effie was imposed on to believe that the wounds, though they had bled much, were but trifling. This gave much comfort to the damsel, as it cleared her Robert of a deed of blood.

The baron and Robert set out as soon as it dawned for the cave of Fingal, to perform what they thought an imperious duty, for as such they considered a posthumous request made under such distressing circumstances.

Little did the credulous pair suspect that they were now made the agents of the wicked vampire, for this is the true story of the magic ring.

The outer part of the vampire was not subject to disease, and it was invincible to the sword. If they could contrive to have Stuffa's ring flung into the well of the cave of Fingal within twenty-four hours after the death wound it was restored to its vile career for the appointed time, and for that season the malignant spirit hovered round the body.

The good Lord of the Isles and Robert arrived safe there, and with little difficulty found the well, for report had spread its situation far and wide owing to its magic qualities. Lord Ronald cast in the ring – instantaneously a hissing, as if of snakes, followed, but soon all was silent as the grave.

They left the cavern and found themselves in the midst of a pelting storm, and their horses, which they had left tied to a tree, were unloosened and they sought in vain for them. As they continued their search a sweet musical voice was heard by the wanderers.

> ''Tis Ariel bids you haste away,
> 'Tis Ariel warns you not to stay;
> Hie and stop a horrid scene,
> 'Tis the fatal *Hallow E'en*,
> Haste and save the destin'd fair
> From the treacherous vampire's snare!'

'Robert,' said the Baron, 'did you hear ought or do my ears deceive me?' – again was the verse repeated with this additional stanza—

> 'Lose not time but quickly see
> Whose the triumph is to be,
> Margaret must be no more,
> Or the vampire's reign is o'er'

'Tis plain enough, my lord; Ariel, who is always reckoned a benign spirit, warns us. – We are deceived. – Oh this cursed vampire! I see it now, he made us tools for his own purpose.'

'Nonsense, my good fellow,' said the baron, 'it must be some new plot against my peace – a real vampire, for we left Marsden's Earl quite dead.'

'Oh, he was dead enough in Flanders,' observed Robert, 'but he seems to have as many lives as the Witch of Endor's tabby cat. My mind forbodes horrid things. – No harm, however, in getting home quick.'

But they were involved in the intricacies of the forest, and it required both patience and perseverance to find the right track; at length they succeeded, and walked on with rapid strides, for the evening wore away. At this juncture some horsemen overtook them. – It was quite dusk and objects scarce discernible.

'Hoy, holla, my good foresters! can you put us in the way for Baron Ronald's castle; the Lord of the Isles we mean,' said the foremost of the cavaliers.

'What want you there?' replied the baron (himself), 'let us know ere we guide you, for we are going thither.'

'I am Hildebrand, Lord Gowen's sister's son, sent by my mother to pay my respects and duty to him as becomes a nephew and a godson, nor has he seen me since my infancy.'

'Welcome! Welcome!' exclaimed the baron, 'son of my beloved Ellen, I am thy uncle, but by some strange accidents, here on foot with one single follower.'

''Tis lucky,' replied the youth, springing from his steed and embracing the baron, 'that we have some led horses in our train.' Lord Ronald and Robert were glad to hear of this seasonable supply, and mounting the noble beasts, set off at full speed.

Hildebrand, as they rode along, was made acquainted with recent events by his worthy uncle – he was struck with terror, and felt much interested for the Lady Margaret; for young Gowen had imbibed from the countess (his mother) a strong belief of the exist-ence of vampires, and he intimated, though respectfully, to his venerable uncle, that he had done wrong by throwing the ring into the well, as by that means it was most probable the wicked sprite had acquired reanimation.

Again the storm arose and served to retard their progress, for the steeds affrighted at the vivid and incessant lightning, could with difficulty be got forward. At length they arrived at the copse, and Robert with two of Earl Gowen's serving men dismounted to seek for the body, but it was not there. 'Just as I thought to find it,' said the former. 'Beshrew me it is an industrious sprite; but the moon will soon set,' and as the benign Ariel sang—

> 'Let's haste and save the destin'd fair
> From the treacherous vampire's snare.'

They spurred their horses, and the storm having made a temporary stop they were soon across the park. Music was sounding – they could distinguish the harper's strain – the great hall was lighted up most brilliantly – a sumptuous altar had been erected at one end – and for the third time, the marriage ceremony was about to begin, when the baron, Lord Gowen and Robert rushed in and secured the intended bride, who fainted immediately, for in the person of her noble cousin she beheld the form shown her by Una and Ariel in the cave of Fingal, and the vampire's charm vanished away like snow before the meridian sun.

The vampire seemed armed with supernatural strength – he resisted all their efforts to subdue him – and their swords made no impression – he struggled hard to bear away the Lady Margaret from the midst of her protectors, and the amazing efforts of the vampire spread horror and alarm, for that he was an evil sprite no one now doubted. He had returned to the castle that evening, and said he came with the baron's consent (who had undertaken a sudden journey) to wed the Lady Margaret, and had brought her father's ring as a token. All was now bustle, preparation and joy,

till the unexpected entrance of the Lord of the Isles and his companions, and had it not been for the providence of Gowen seeking the
castle that night, the fiend would have triumphed, for they could
not have got home on foot in time enough to save her.

But the fiend was not to be overpowered – he jumped on the
temporary altar, sword in hand (after having wounded and bit with
his teeth several of the domestics), insisting he would yet have his
bride. In an instant the scene changed – the moon set – the thunder
rolled over the castle, and the bolt fell on the vampire – he rolled
lifeless upon the floor, and after a terrific yell, melted into thin air,
incorporeal and invisible to every eye. Thus ended the wicked sprite.

Some months after this event Margaret was happily united to
Earl Gowen, with whom she led a happy life till they both sunk
into the grave, venerable with age, making good the prediction of
the spirits of the cave of Fingal—

'Ne'er but once was she to wed,
Or have a second bridal bed.'

THE UNHOLY COMPACT ABJURED

Charles Pigault-Lebrun

Charles Pigault-Lebrun (1753–1835) was a Calais-born French novelist and playwright whose real name was Charles-Antoine-Guillaume Pigault de l'Epinoy. His most celebrated novels are *L'Enfant du Carnaval* (1792) and *Angelique et Jeanneton de la Place Maubert* (1799). Not so well-known is his short story 'The Unholy Compact Abjured,' which, according to Peter Haining, received its first English translation in 1825 for its appearance in a British weekly magazine titled *The French Novelist*.

───────────

In the churchyard of the town of Salins, department of Jura, may still be seen the remains of a tomb, on which is sculptured in figures as rude as the age in which they were carved, a representation of a soldier, firmly clasped in the arms of a maiden; near them stands the devil in a menacing attitude. Though the inhabitants of the town are all ready to swear to the truth of the story, they are not agreed as to the time when it happened; so that we can only say, that some centuries have rolled away, since a young soldier named St Amand, a native of Salins, was returning after a long absence to the bosom of his family. He walked with quick and cheerful steps, carrying with ease, in a small knapsack, the whole of his worldly goods. Never since he quitted the paternal roof, had he felt so happy; for he hoped ere night, to see his pretty cousin, Ninette, whom he loved with all his heart, and whom he intended to make his wife.

He walked on, gaily carolling, till he saw a crossroad before him, and uncertain of his way, he called to an old woman, with her back towards him, to direct him. She was silent: and, as he approached, he repeated the call, and she raised her head to answer it. The stout heart of the young soldier quailed, as he cast his eyes upon a countenance, such as never before had met his gaze. He had, indeed, reason to tremble; for he had just disturbed in the middle of an incantation, one of the most powerful witches in the country. She regarded him with a demoniac smile, and said in a tone which froze his blood, 'Turn where thou wilt, thy road is sure, – it leads to death!'

For some moments, he stood as if rooted to the spot; but, soon, fear of the sorceress, who remained gazing upon him, gave him strength to flee. He ran forward, nor stopped till he had completely lost sight of the fearful being, whose dreadful prediction had struck him with such horror. Suddenly a frightful storm arose; the thunder growled, and the lightning flashed round the weary traveller, who, drenched with rain, and overcome with fatigue, had hardly strength to proceed. How great was his joy, when he saw at a distance, a magnificent chateau, the gate of which stood open. He exerted all his remaining strength to reach it, and precipitately entered a large hall. There he stopped, expecting every moment to see some domestics, but no one appeared. He remained some time, watching the progress of the storm: at length it began to abate, and he determined to pursue his way; but as he approached the door, it closed with a loud noise, and all his efforts to open it were in vain.

Struck with astonishment and dismay, the young soldier now believed that the prediction of the witch was about to be accomplished, and that he was doomed to fall a sacrifice to magic art. Exhausted by his vain efforts to open the ponderous door, he sank for a moment in helpless despondency, on the marble pavement; put his trust in providence, and soon revived. He said his prayers, and rising, waited with firmness the issue of this extraordinary adventure. When he became composed enough to look round him, he examined the hall in which he was: a pair of folding doors at the further end, flattered him with the hope of escape that way; but they too, were fastened. The hall was of immense size, entirely unfurnished; the walls, pavement and ceiling, were of black marble; there were no windows, but a small sky-light faintly admitted the light of day, into this abode of gloom, where reigned a silence like that of the tomb. Hour after hour passed; this mournful silence remained still undisturbed; and St Amand, overcome with fatigue and watching, at length sunk into a deep, though perturbed slumber.

His sleep was soon disturbed by a frightful dream: he heard all at once, the sound of a knell, mingled with the cries of bats, and owls, and a hollow voice, murmured in his ear, '*Woe to those who trouble the repose of the dead!*' He started on his feet, but what a sight met his eyes! The hall was partially illuminated by flashes of sulphurous fire; on the pavement was laid the body of a man newly slain, and covered with innumerable wounds, from which a band of unearthly forms, whose fearful occupation proclaimed their hellish origin, were draining the yet warm blood.

St Amand uttered a shriek of terror, and was in an instant surrounded by the fiends: already were their fangs, from which the remains of their horrid feast still dripped, extended to grasp him, when he hastily made the sign of the cross, and sank senseless upon the ground. When he regained his senses, the infernal band had vanished, and he saw bending over him, an old man, magnificently but strangely dressed: his silken garments flowed loosely around him, and were embroidered with figures of different animals, and mystic devices. His countenance was majestic, and his venerable white beard descended below his girdle: but his features had a wild and gloomy expression: his eyes, above all, had in their glance, that which might appal the stoutest heart. St Amand shrunk from this mysterious being, with awe, mingled with abhorrence, and a cold shudder ran through his veins, as the old man bent upon him his piercing eyes.

'Rash youth,' cried he in a severe tone, 'how is it that thou hast dared to enter this place, where never mortal foot save mine has trod?'

'I came not willingly,' replied St Amand, trembling; 'an evil destiny, and not vain curiosity brought me hither.'

'Thou wouldst not the less have expiated thy presumption with thy life, but for my aid,' returned the old man, austerely. 'I have saved thee from the vampires who guard it, and it depends upon me, whether thou shalt not still become their prey.'

'Oh! save me, then, I pray thee!'

'And why should I save thee?' demanded the venerable magician. 'What price art thou willing to give me for thy life?'

'Alas! I have nothing worthy of thy acceptance,' sighed St Amand.

'But thou may'st have; and it is only through thee that I can obtain what I most desire.'

'How?'

'The blood of a dove, for me, would be a treasure, but I may not kill one; she must be slain for me, by one whose life I have saved. Should I liberate thee, a dove will fly to thy bosom; swear that thou wilt instantly sacrifice her for me, and thou shalt be free.'

'I swear it!'

Hardly had St Amand uttered the words, when he found himself in the chamber of Ninette, who, with a cry of joy, rushed into his arms. He pressed her with transport to his breast; but scarcely had he embraced her, when he saw the magician standing by his side.

'Wretch!' cried he, 'is it thus thou keepest thine oath? Pierce her heart – she is the dove that thou must instantly sacrifice, if thou wilt not become a feast for the vampires!'

'Sacrifice her? Never! Never!'

'Then, thou art my prey!' and the fiend assuming his own form, sprang towards his victim; but he stopped suddenly – he dared not seize him: for the maiden held him firmly clasped in her arms, and the little cross of gold, which night and day she wore upon her bosom, had been blest by the venerable priest, whose gift it was. Thus, nought unholy dared approach the maiden, and the baffled fiend fled with a tremendous yell, as the crowing of the cock announced the approach of dawn.

The cries of the maiden soon brought the neighbours to her chamber, and among them was the pastor, to whom St Amand related his adventure. 'Oh, my son!' said the good priest, 'what have you done? See you not, that you have entered into a contract with the powers of darkness? Unable to wreak their vengeance on you, when you had guarded yourself with the blessed sign of our redemption, the fiend has had recourse to craft to draw you into his power. You have promised a sacrifice, to the enemy of God and man, but you have done it in ignorance. Abjure then, solemnly, the cursed contract, and dread no longer the vengeance of the fiend.'

The young soldier made the required abjuration, during which, the most dreadful noises were heard: it was the last effort of the demon's vengeance; for, from that time, he was never seen, nor heard of. St Amand married Ninette, who had given him such a courageous proof of her love; and the cross transmitted from her, to her descendants, was always considered by them as the most precious part of their inheritance. In process of time, the family became wealthy, and a great grandson of St Amand erected the monument we have described, to commemorate the miraculous escape of his ancestor.

VIY

Nikolai Gogol

NikolaiVasilievich Gogol (1809–1852) was a Russian dramatist, novelist, and short story writer of Ukrainian ethnicity. While in his early twenties, Gogol's first volume of stories, *Evenings on a Farm Near Dikanka* (1831), met with immediate success; and a second volume, *Mirgorod* (1835), was equally well received. By far the strangest story in the latter is 'Viy,' the title of which is the name given to the King of the Gnomes. It should be pointed out, however, that this grotesque entity is not an authentic figure from Ukrainian folklore, as Gogol had claimed in an introductory note to the story, but is probably based on an old folk tradition surrounding St Cassian, the Unmerciful, who was said to have had eyebrows that descended to his knees, whereas, in Gogol's story, the King of the Gnomes is depicted as having eyelids that reach to the ground.

As soon as the rather musical seminary bell which hung at the gate of the Bratsky Monastery rang out every morning in Kiev, school-boys and students hurried thither in crowds from all parts of the town. Students of grammar, rhetoric, philosophy and theology trudged to their classrooms with exercise books under their arms. The grammarians were quite small boys: they shoved each other as they went along and quarrelled in a shrill alto; they almost all wore muddy or tattered clothes, and their pockets were full of all manner of rubbish, such as knucklebones, whistles made of feathers, or a half-eaten pie, sometimes even little sparrows, one of whom

suddenly chirruping at an exceptionally quiet moment in the classroom would cost its owner some sound whacks on both hands and
sometimes a thrashing. The rhetoricians walked with more dignity;
their clothes were often quite free from holes; on the other hand,
their countenances almost all bore some decoration, after the style
of a figure of rhetoric; either one eye had sunk right under the
forehead, or there was a monstrous swelling in place of a lip, or
some other disfigurement. They talked and swore among themselves
in tenor voices. The philosophers conversed an octave lower in the
scale; they had nothing in their pockets but strong, cheap tobacco.
They laid in no stores of any sort, but ate on the spot anything they
came across; they smelt of pipes and vodka to such a distance that
a passing workman would sometimes stop a long way off and sniff
the air like a setter dog.

As a rule the market was just beginning to stir at that hour, and
the women with bread-rings, rolls, melon seeds, and poppy cakes
would tug at the skirts of those whose coats were of fine cloth or
some cotton material.

'This way, young gentlemen, this way!' they kept saying from all
sides: 'here are bread rings, poppy cakes, twists, good white rolls;
they are really good! Made with honey! I baked them myself.'

Another woman lifting up a sort of long twist made of dough would
cry: 'Here's a breadstick! Buy my breadstick, young gentlemen!'

'Don't buy anything off her; see what a horrid woman she is,
her nose is nasty and her hands are dirty . . .'

But the women were afraid to worry the philosophers and the
theologians, for the latter were fond of taking things to taste and
always a good handful.

On reaching the seminary, the crowd dispersed to their various
classes, which were held in low-pitched but fairly large rooms, with
little windows, wide doorways, and dirty benches. The classroom
was at once filled with all sorts of buzzing sounds: the 'auditors'
heard their pupils repeat their lessons; the shrill alto of a grammarian
rang out, and the windowpane responded with almost the same
note; in a corner a rhetorician, whose mouth and thick lips should
have belonged at least to a student of philosophy, was droning
something in a bass voice, and all that could be heard at a distance
was 'Boo, boo, boo . . .' The 'auditors,' as they heard the lesson,

kept glancing with one eye under the bench, where a roll or a
cheese-cake or some pumpkin seeds were peeping out of a scholar's
pocket.

When this learned crowd managed to arrive a little too early, or
when they knew that the professors would be later than usual, then
by general consent they got up a fight, and everyone had to take
part in it, even the monitors whose duty it was to maintain discipline
and look after the morals of all the students. Two theologians usually
settled the arrangements for the battle: whether each class was to
defend itself individually, or whether all were to be divided into
two parties, the bursars and the seminarists. In any case the grammarians first began the attack, and, as soon as the rhetoricians
entered the fray, they ran away and stood at points of vantage to
watch the contest. Then the devotees of philosophy, with long black
moustaches, joined in, and finally those of theology, very thick in
the neck and attired in shocking trousers, took part. It commonly
ended in theology beating all the rest, and the philosophers, rubbing
their ribs, would be forced into the classroom and sat down on the
benches to rest. The professor, who had himself at one time taken
part in such battles, could, on entering the class, see in a minute
from the flushed faces of his audience that the battle had been a
good one and, while he was caning a rhetorician on the fingers, in
another classroom another professor would be smacking philosophers' hands with a wooden bat. The theologians were dealt with
in quite a different way: they received, to use the expression of a
professor of theology, 'a peck of peas apiece,' in other words, a
liberal drubbing with short leather thongs.

On holidays and ceremonial occasions the bursars and the seminarists went from house to house as mummers. Sometimes they
acted a play, and then the most distinguished figure was always
some theologian, almost as tall as the belfry of Kiev, who took the
part of Herodias or Potiphar's wife. They received in payment a
piece of linen, or a sack of millet or half a boiled goose, or something
of the sort. All this crowd of students – the seminarists as well as
the bursars, with whom they maintain an hereditary feud – were
exceedingly badly off for means of subsistence, and at the same time
had extraordinary appetites, so that to reckon how many dumplings
each of them tucked away at supper would be utterly impossible,

and therefore the voluntary offerings of prosperous citizens could not be sufficient for them. Then the 'senate' of the philosophers and theologians despatched the grammarians and rhetoricians, under the supervision of a philosopher (who sometimes took part in the raid himself), with sacks on their shoulders to plunder the kitchen gardens – and pumpkin porridge was made in the bursars' quarters. The members of the 'senate' ate such masses of melons that next day their 'auditors' heard two lessons from them instead of one, one coming from their lips, another muttering in their stomachs. Both the bursars and the seminarists wore long garments resembling frock coats, 'prolonged to the utmost limit,' a technical expression signifying below their heels.

The most important event for the seminarists was the coming of the vacation: it began in June, when they usually dispersed to their homes. Then the whole high-road was dotted with philosophers, grammarians and theologians. Those who had nowhere to go went to stay with some comrade. The philosophers and theologians took a situation, that is, undertook the tuition of the children in some prosperous family, and received in payment a pair of new boots or sometimes even a coat. The whole crowd trailed along together like a gipsy encampment, boiled their porridge, and slept in the fields. Everyone hauled along a sack in which he had a shirt and a pair of leg-wrappers. The theologians were particularly careful and precise: to avoid wearing out their boots, they took them off, hung them on sticks and carried them on their shoulders, particularly if it was muddy; then, tucking their trousers up above their knees, they splashed fearlessly through the puddles. When they saw a village they turned off the high-road and, going up to any house which seemed a little better looking than the rest, stood in a row before the windows and began singing a chant at the top of their voices. The master of the house, some old Cossack villager, would listen to them for a long time, his head propped on his hands, then he would sob bitterly and say, turning to his wife: 'Wife! What the scholars are singing must be very deep; bring them fat bacon and anything else that we have.' And a whole bowl of dumplings was emptied into the sack, a good-sized piece of bacon, several flat loaves, and sometimes a trussed hen would go into it too. Fortified with such stores, the grammarians, rhetoricians, philosophers and theologians went on their way again. Their numbers lessened, however, the further they went. Almost all wandered off towards their homes, and only those were left whose parental abodes were further away.

Once, at the time of such a migration, three students turned off the high-road in order to replenish their store of provisions at the first homestead they could find, for their sacks had long been empty. They were the theologian, Halyava; the philosopher, Homa Brut; and the rhetorician, Tibery Gorobets.

The theologian was a well-grown broad-shouldered fellow; he had an extremely odd habit – anything that lay within his reach he invariably stole. In other circumstances, he was of an excessively gloomy temper, and when he was drunk he used to hide in the rank grass, and the seminarists had a lot of trouble to find him there.

The philosopher, Homa Brut, was of a cheerful temper, he was very fond of lying on his back, smoking a pipe; when he was drinking he always engaged musicians and danced the trepak. He often had a taste of the 'peck of peas,' but took it with perfect philosophical indifference, saying that there is no escaping what has to be. The rhetorician, Tibery Gorobets, had not yet the right to wear a moustache, to drink vodka, and to smoke a pipe. He only wore a curl round his ear, and so his character was as yet hardly formed; but, judging from the big bumps on the forehead, with which he often appeared in class, it might be presumed that he would make a good fighter. The theologian, Halyava, and the philosopher, Homa, often pulled him by the forelock as a sign of their favour, and employed him as their messenger.

It was evening when they turned off the high-road; the sun had only just set and the warmth of the day still lingered in the air. The theologian and the philosopher walked along in silence smoking their pipes; the rhetorician, Tibery Gorobets, kept knocking off the heads of the wayside thistles with his stick. The road ran between scattered groups of oak and nut trees standing here and there in the meadows. Sloping uplands and little hills, green and round as cupolas, were interspersed here and there about the plain. The cornfields of ripening wheat, which came into view in two places, showed that some village must soon be seen. It was more than an hour, however, since they had passed the cornfields, yet they had come upon no dwelling. The sky was now completely wrapped in darkness, and only in the west there was a pale streak left of the glow of sunset.

'What the devil does it mean?' said the philosopher, Homa Brut. 'It looked as though there must be a village in a minute.'

The theologian did not speak, he gazed at the surrounding country, then put his pipe back in his mouth, and they continued on their way.

'Upon my soul!' the philosopher said, stopping again, 'not a devil's fist to be seen.'

'Maybe some village will turn up further on,' said the theologian, not removing his pipe.

But meantime night had come on, and a rather dark night. Small storm clouds increased the gloom, and by every token they could expect neither stars nor moon. The students noticed that they had lost their way and for a long time had been walking off the road.

The philosopher, after feeling about with his feet in all directions, said at last, abruptly: 'I say, where's the road?'

The theologian did not speak for a while, then after pondering, he brought out: 'Yes, it is a dark night.'

The rhetorician walked off to one side and tried on his hands and knees to feel for the road, but his hands came upon nothing but foxes' holes. On all sides of them there was the steppe, which, it seemed, no one had ever crossed.

The travellers made another effort to press on a little, but there was the same wilderness in all directions. The philosopher tried shouting, but his voice seemed completely lost on the steppe, and met with no reply. All they heard was, a little afterwards, a faint moaning like the howl of a wolf.

'I say, what's to be done?' said the philosopher.

'Why, halt and sleep in the open!' said the theologian, and he felt in his pocket for flint and tinder to light his pipe again. But the philosopher could not agree to this: it was always his habit at night to put away a quarter loaf of bread and four pounds of fat bacon, and he was conscious on this occasion of an insufferable sense of loneliness in his stomach. Besides, in spite of his cheerful temper, the philosopher was rather afraid of wolves.

'No, Halyava, we can't,' he said. 'What, stretch out and lie down like a dog, without a bite or a sup of anything? Let's make another try for it; maybe we shall stumble on some dwelling-place and get at least a drink of vodka for supper.'

At the word 'vodka' the theologian spat to one side and brought out: 'Well, of course, it's no use staying in the open.'

The students walked on, and to their intense delight caught the sound of barking in the distance. Listening which way it came from, they walked on more boldly and a little later saw a light.

'A village! It really is a village!' said the philosopher.

He was not mistaken in his supposition; in a little while they actually saw a little homestead consisting of only two cottages looking into the same farmyard. There was a light in the windows; a dozen plum trees stood up by the fence. Looking through the cracks in the paling-gate the students saw a yard filled with carriers' waggons. Stars peeped out here and there in the sky at the moment.

'Look, mates, don't let's be put off! We must get a night's lodging somehow!'

The three learned gentlemen banged on the gates with one accord and shouted, 'Open!'

The door of one of the cottages creaked, and a minute later they saw before them an old woman in sheepskin.

'Who is there?' she cried, with a hollow cough.

'Give us a night's lodging, granny; we have lost our way; a night in the open is as bad as a hungry belly.'

'What manner of folks may you be?'

'Oh, harmless folks: Halyava, a theologian; Brut, a philosopher; and Gorobets, a rhetorician.'

'I can't,' grumbled the old woman. 'The yard is crowded with folk and every corner in the cottage is full. Where am I to put you? And such great hulking fellows, too! Why, it would knock my cottage to pieces if I put such fellows in it. I know these philosophers and theologians; if one began taking in these drunken fellows, there'd soon be no home left. Be off, be off! There's no place for you here!'

'Have pity on us, granny! How can you let Christian souls perish for no rhyme or reason? Put us where you please; and if we do aught amiss or anything else, may our arms be withered, and God only knows what befall us – so there!'

The old woman seemed somewhat softened.

'Very well,' she said, as though reconsidering, 'I'll let you in, but

I'll put you all in different places; for my mind won't be at rest if you are all together.'

'That's as you please; we'll make no objection,' answered the students.

The gate creaked and they went into the yard.

'Well, granny,' said the philosopher, following the old woman, 'how would it be, as they say . . . upon my soul I feel as though somebody were driving a cart in my stomach: not a morsel has passed my lips all day.'

'What next will he want!' said the old woman. 'No, I've nothing to give you, and the oven's not been heated today.'

'But we'd pay for it all,' the philosopher went on, 'tomorrow morning, in hard cash. Yes!' he added in an undertone, 'the devil a bit you'll get!'

'Go in, go in! and you must be satisfied with what you're given. Fine young gentlemen the devil has brought us!'

Homa the philosopher was thrown into utter dejection by these words, but his nose was suddenly aware of the odour of dried fish; he glanced towards the trousers of the theologian who was walking at his side, and saw a huge fishtail sticking out of his pocket. The theologian had already succeeded in filching a whole carp from a waggon. And as he had done this from no interested motive but simply from habit, and, quite forgetting his carp, was already looking about for anything else he could carry off, having no mind to miss even a broken wheel, the philosopher slipped his hand into his friend's pocket, as though it were his own, and pulled out the carp.

The old woman put the students in their several places: the rhetorician she kept in the cottage, the theologian she locked in an empty closet, the philosopher she assigned a sheep's pen, also empty.

The latter, on finding himself alone, instantly devoured the carp, examined the hurdle-walls of the pen, kicked an inquisitive pig that woke up and thrust its snout in from the next pen, and turned over on his right side to fall into a sound sleep. All at once the low door opened, and the old woman bending down stepped into the pen.

'What is it, granny, what do you want?' said the philosopher.

But the old woman came towards him with outstretched arms.

'Aha, ha!' thought the philosopher. 'No, my dear, you are too old!'

He turned a little away, but the old woman unceremoniously approached him again.

'Listen, granny!' said the philosopher. 'It's a fast time now; and I am a man who wouldn't sin in a fast for a thousand golden pieces.'

But the old woman opened her arms and tried to catch him without saying a word.

The philosopher was frightened, especially when he noticed a strange glitter in her eyes. 'Granny, what is it? Go – go away – God bless you!' he cried.

The old woman said not a word, but tried to clutch him in her arms.

He leapt on to his feet, intending to escape; but the old woman stood in the doorway, fixed her glittering eyes on him and again began approaching him.

The philosopher tried to push her back with his hands, but to his surprise found that his arms would not rise, his legs would not move, and he perceived with horror that even his voice would not obey him; words hovered on his lips without a sound. He heard nothing but the beating of his heart. He saw the old woman approach him. She folded his arms, bent his head down, leapt with the swiftness of a cat upon his back, and struck him with a broom on the side; and he, prancing like a horse, carried her on his shoulders. All this happened so quickly that the philosopher scarcely knew what he was doing. He clutched his knees in both hands, trying to stop his legs from moving, but to his extreme amazement they were lifted against his will and executed capers more swiftly than a Circassian racer. Only when they had left the farm, and the wide plain lay stretched before them with a forest black as coal on one side, he said to himself: 'Aha! she's a witch!'

The waning crescent of the moon was shining in the sky. The timid radiance of midnight lay mistily over the earth, light as a transparent veil. The forests, the meadows, the sky, the dales, all seemed as though slumbering with open eyes; not a breeze fluttered anywhere; there was a damp warmth in the freshness of the night; the shadows of the trees and bushes fell on the sloping plain in pointed wedge shapes like comets. Such was the night when Homa Brut, the philosopher, set off galloping with a mysterious rider on his back. He was aware of an exhausting, unpleasant, and at the

same time, voluptuous sensation assailing his heart. He bent his
head and saw that the grass which had been almost under his feet
seemed growing at a depth far away, and that above it there lay
water, transparent as a mountain stream, and the grass seemed to
be at the bottom of a clear sea, limpid to its very depths; anyway,
he saw clearly in it his own reflection with the old woman sitting
on his back. He saw shining there a sun instead of the moon; he
heard the bluebells ringing as they bent their little heads; he saw a
water-nymph float out from behind the reeds, there was the gleam
of her leg and back, rounded and supple, all brightness and shimmering. She turned towards him and now her face came nearer,
with eyes clear, sparkling, keen, with singing that pierced to the
heart; now it was on the surface, and shaking with sparkling laughter
it moved away; and now she turned on her back, and her cloud-like
breasts, dead-white like unglazed china, gleamed in the sun at the
edges of their white, soft and supple roundness. Little bubbles of
water like beads bedewed them. She was all quivering and laughing
in the water . . .

Did he see this or did he not? Was he awake or dreaming? But
what was that? The wind or music? It is ringing and ringing and
eddying and coming closer and piercing to his heart with an insufferable thrill . . .

'What does it mean?' the philosopher wondered, looking down
as he flew along, full speed. The sweat was streaming from him.
He was aware of a fiendishly voluptuous feeling, he felt a stabbing,
exhaustingly terrible delight. It often seemed to him as though his
heart had melted away, and with terror he clutched at it. Worn out,
desperate, he began trying to recall all the prayers he knew. He
went through all the exorcisms against evil spirits, and all at once
felt somewhat refreshed; he felt that his step was growing slower,
the witch's hold upon his back seemed feebler, thick grass touched
him, and now he saw nothing extraordinary in it. The clear, crescent
moon was shining in the sky.

'Good!' the philosopher Homa thought to himself, and he began
repeating the exorcisms almost aloud. At last, quick as lightning, he
sprang from under the old woman and in his turn leapt on her back.
The old woman, with a tiny tripping step, ran so fast that her rider
could scarcely breathe. The earth flashed by under him; everything

was clear in the moonlight, though the moon was not full; the ground was smooth, but everything flashed by so rapidly that it was confused and indistinct. He snatched up a piece of wood that lay on the road and began whacking the old woman with all his might. She uttered wild howls; at first they were angry and menacing, then they grew fainter, sweeter, clearer, then rang out gently like delicate silver bells that stabbed him to the heart; and the thought flashed through his mind: was it really an old woman?

'Oh, I can do no more!' she murmured, and sank exhausted on the ground.

He stood up and looked into her face (there was the glow of sunrise, and the golden domes of the Kiev churches were gleaming in the distance): before him lay a lovely creature with luxuriant tresses all in disorder and eyelashes as long as arrows. Senseless she tossed her bare white arms and moaned, looking upwards with eyes full of tears.

Homa trembled like a leaf on a tree; he was overcome by pity and a strange emotion and timidity, feelings he could not himself explain. He set off running, full speed. His heart throbbed uneasily as he went, and he could not account for the strange new feeling that had taken possession of it. He did not want to go back to the farm; he hastened to Kiev, pondering all the way on this incomprehensible adventure.

There was scarcely a student left in the town. All had dispersed about the countryside, either to situations, or simply without them; because in the villages of Little Russia they could get dumplings, cheese, sour cream, and puddings as big as a hat without paying a kopeck for them. The big rambling house in which the students were lodged was absolutely empty, and although the philosopher rummaged in every corner, and even felt in all the holes and cracks in the roof, he could not find a bit of bacon or even a stale roll such as were commonly hidden there by the students.

The philosopher, however, soon found means to improve his lot: he walked whistling three times through the market, finally winked at a young widow in a yellow bonnet who was selling ribbons, shot and wheels – and was that very day regaled with wheat dumplings, a chicken . . . in short, there is no telling what was on the table laid for him in a little mud house in the middle of a cherry orchard.

That same evening the philosopher was seen in a tavern: he was lying on the bench, smoking a pipe as his habit was, and in the sight of all he flung the Jew who kept the house a gold coin. A mug stood before him. He looked at all that came in and went out with eyes full of cool satisfaction, and thought no more of his extraordinary adventure.

Meanwhile rumours were circulating everywhere that the daughter of one of the richest Cossack *sotniks*,[2] who lived nearly forty miles from Kiev, had returned one day from a walk, terribly injured, hardly able to crawl home to her father's house, was lying at the point of death, and had expressed a wish that one of the Kiev seminarists, Homa Brut, should read the prayers over her and the psalms for three days after her death. The philosopher heard of this from the rector himself, who summoned him to his room and informed him that he was to set off on the journey without any delay, that the noble *sotnik* had sent servants and a carriage to fetch him.

The philosopher shuddered from an unaccountable feeling which he could not have explained to himself. A dark presentiment told him that something evil was awaiting him. Without knowing why, he bluntly declared that he would not go.

'Listen, Domine Homa!' said the rector. (On some occasions he expressed himself very courteously with those under his authority.) 'Who the devil is asking you whether you want to go or not? All I have to tell you is that if you go on jibbing and making difficulties, I'll order you such a whacking with a young birch tree, on your back and the rest of you, that there will be no need for you to go to the bath after.'

The philosopher, scratching behind his ear, went out without uttering a word, proposing at the first suitable opportunity to put his trust in his heels. Plunged in thought he went down the steep staircase that led into a yard shut in by poplars, and stood still for a minute, hearing quite distinctly the voice of the rector giving orders to his butler and some one else – probably one of the servants sent to fetch him by the *sotnik*.

2 An officer in command of a company of Cossacks, consisting originally of a hundred, but in later times of a larger number. – (*Translator's Note.*)

'Thank his honour for the grain and the eggs,' the rector was saying: 'and tell him that as soon as the books about which he writes are ready I will send them at once, I have already given them to a scribe to be copied, and don't forget, my good man, to mention to his honour that I know there are excellent fish at his place, especially sturgeon, and he might on occasion send some; here in the market it's bad and dear. And you, Yavtuh, give, the young fellows a cup of vodka each, and bind the philosopher or he'll be off directly.'

'There, the devil's son!' the philosopher thought to himself. 'He scented it out, the wily long-legs!' He went down and saw a covered chaise, which he almost took at first for a baker's oven on wheels. It was, indeed, as deep as the oven in which bricks are baked. It was only the ordinary Cracow carriage in which Jews travel fifty together with their wares to all the towns where they smell out a fair. Six healthy and stalwart Cossacks, no longer young, were waiting for him. Their tunics of fine cloth, with tassels, showed that they belonged to a rather important and wealthy master; some small scars proved that they had at some time been in battle, not ingloriously.

'What's to be done? What is to be must be!' the philosopher thought to himself and, turning to the Cossacks, he said aloud: 'Good day to you, comrades!'

'Good health to you, master philosopher,' some of the Cossacks replied.

'So I am to get in with you? It's a goodly chaise!' he went on, as he clambered in, 'we need only hire some musicians and we might dance here.'

'Yes, it's a carriage of ample proportions,' said one of the Cossacks, seating himself on the box beside the coachman, who had tied a rag over his head to replace the cap which he had managed to leave behind at a pot-house. The other five and the philosopher crawled into the recesses of the chaise and settled themselves on sacks filled with various purchases they had made in the town. 'It would be interesting to know,' said the philosopher, 'if this chaise were loaded up with goods of some sort, salt for instance, or iron wedges, how many horses would be needed then?'

'Yes,' the Cossack, sitting on the box, said after a pause, 'it would need a sufficient number of horses.'

After this satisfactory reply the Cossack thought himself entitled to hold his tongue for the remainder of the journey.

The philosopher was extremely desirous of learning more in detail, who this *sotnik* was, what he was like, what had been heard about his daughter who in such a strange way returned home and was found on the point of death, and whose story was now connected with his own, what was being done in the house, and how things were there. He addressed the Cossacks with inquiries, but no doubt they too were philosophers, for by way of a reply they remained silent, smoking their pipes and lying on their backs. Only one of them turned to the driver on the box with a brief order. 'Mind, Overko, you old booby, when you are near the tavern on the Tchuhraylovo road, don't forget to stop and wake me and the other chaps, if any should chance to drop asleep.'

After this he fell asleep rather audibly. These instructions were, however, quite unnecessary for, as soon as the gigantic chaise drew near the pot-house, all the Cossacks with one voice shouted: 'Stop!' Moreover, Overko's horses were already trained to stop of themselves at every pot-house.

In spite of the hot July day, they all got out of the chaise and went into the low-pitched dirty room, where the Jew who kept the house hastened to receive his old friends with every sign of delight. The Jew brought from under the skirt of his coat some ham sausages, and, putting them on the table, turned his back at once on this food forbidden by the Talmud. All the Cossacks sat down round the table; earthenware mugs were set for each of the guests. Homa had to take part in the general festivity, and, as Little Russians infallibly begin kissing each other or weeping when they are drunk, soon the whole room resounded with smacks. 'I say, Spirid, a kiss.' 'Come here, Dorosh, I want to embrace you!'

One Cossack with grey moustaches, a little older than the rest, propped his cheek on his hand and began sobbing bitterly at the thought that he had no father nor mother and was all alone in the world. Another one, much given to moralising, persisted in consoling him, saying: 'Don't cry; upon my soul, don't cry! What is there in it . . .? The Lord knows best, you know.'

The one whose name was Dorosh became extremely inquisitive, and, turning to the philosopher Homa, kept asking him: 'I should like to know what they teach you in the college. Is it the same as what the deacon reads in church, or something different?'

'Don't ask!' the sermonising Cossack said emphatically: 'let it be as it is, God knows what is wanted, God knows everything.'

'No, I want to know,' said Dorosh, 'what is written there in those books? Maybe it is quite different from what the deacon reads.'

'Oh, my goodness, my goodness!' said the sermonising worthy, 'and why say such a thing; it's as the Lord wills. There is no changing what the Lord has willed!'

'I want to know all that's written. I'll go to college, upon my word, I will. Do you suppose I can't learn? I'll learn it all, all!'

'Oh my goodness . . .!' said the sermonising Cossack, and he dropped his head on the table, because he was utterly incapable of supporting it any longer on his shoulders. The other Cossacks were discussing their masters and the question why the moon shone in the sky. The philosopher, seeing the state of their minds, resolved to seize his opportunity and make his escape. To begin with he turned to the grey-headed Cossack who was grieving for his father and mother.

'Why are you blubbering, uncle?' he said, 'I am an orphan myself! Let me go in freedom, lads! What do you want with me?'

'Let him go!' several responded, 'why, he is an orphan, let him go where he likes.'

'Oh, my goodness, my goodness!' the moralising Cossack articulated, lifting his head. 'Let him go!'

'Let him go where he likes!'

And the Cossacks meant to lead him out into the open air themselves, but the one who had displayed his curiosity stopped them, saying: 'Don't touch him. I want to talk to him about college: I am going to college myself . . .'

It is doubtful, however, whether the escape could have taken place, for when the philosopher tried to get up from the table his legs seemed to have become wooden, and he began to perceive such a number of doors in the room that he could hardly discover the real one.

It was evening before the Cossacks bethought themselves that they had further to go. Clambering into the chaise, they trailed along the road, urging on the horses and singing a song of which nobody could have made out the words or the sense. After trundling on for the greater part of the night, continually straying off the road, though they knew every inch of the way, they drove at last down a steep hill into a valley, and the philosopher noticed a paling or hurdle that ran alongside, low trees and roofs peeping out behind it. This was a big village belonging to the *sotnik*. By now it was long past midnight; the sky was dark, but there were little stars twinkling here and there. No light was to be seen in a single cottage. To the accompaniment of the barking of dogs, they drove into the court-yard. Thatched barns and little houses came into sight on both sides; one of the latter, which stood exactly in the middle opposite the gates, was larger than the others, and was apparently the *sotnik's* residence. The chaise drew up before a little shed that did duty for a barn, and our travellers went off to bed. The philosopher, however, wanted to inspect the outside of the *sotnik's* house; but, though he stared his hardest, nothing could be seen distinctly; the house looked to him like a bear; the chimney turned into the rector. The philosopher gave it up and went to sleep.

When he woke up, the whole house was in commotion: the *sotnik's* daughter had died in the night. Servants were running hurriedly to and fro; some old women were crying; an inquisitive crowd was looking through the fence at the house, as though something might be seen there. The philosopher began examining at his leisure the objects he could not make out in the night. The *sotnik's* house was a little, low-pitched building, such as was usual in Little Russia in old days; its roof was of thatch; a small, high, pointed gable with a little window that looked like an eye turned upwards, was painted in blue and yellow flowers and red crescents; it was supported on oak posts, rounded above and hexagonal below, with carving at the top. Under the gable was a little porch with seats on each side. There were verandahs round the house resting on similar posts, some of them carved in spirals. A tall pyramidal pear tree, with trembling leaves, made a patch of green in front of the house. Two rows of barns for storing grain stood in the middle of the yard, forming a sort of wide street leading to the house. Beyond the barns, close to the gate, stood facing each other two three-cornered store-houses, also thatched. Each triangular wall was painted in various designs and had a little door in it. On one of them was depicted a

Cossack sitting on a barrel, holding a mug above his head with the inscription: 'I'll drink it all!' On the other, there was a bottle, flagons, and at the sides, by way of ornament, a horse upside down, a pipe, a tambourine, and the inscription: 'Wine is the Cossack's comfort!' A drum and brass trumpets could be seen through the huge window in the loft of one of the barns. At the gates stood two cannons. Everything showed that the master of the house was fond of merry-making, and that the yard often resounded with the shouts of revellers. There were two windmills outside the gate. Behind the house stretched gardens, and through the treetops the dark caps of chimneys were all that could be seen of cottages smothered in green bushes. The whole village lay on the broad sloping side of a hill. The steep side, at the very foot of which lay the courtyard, made a screen from the north. Looked at from below, it seemed even steeper, and here and there on its tall top uneven stalks of rough grass stood up black against the clear sky; its bare aspect was somehow depressing; its clay soil was hollowed out by the fall and trickle of rain. Two cottages stood at some distance from each other on its steep slope; one of them was overshadowed by the branches of a spreading apple tree, banked up with soil and supported by short stakes near the root. The apples, knocked down by the wind, were falling right into the master's courtyard. The road, coiling about the hill from the very top, ran down beside the courtyard to the village. When the philosopher scanned its terrific steepness and recalled their journey down it the previous night, he came to the conclusion that either the *sotnik* had very clever horses or that the Cossacks had very strong heads to have managed, even when drunk, to escape flying head over heels with the immense chaise and baggage. The philosopher was standing on the very highest point in the yard. When he turned and looked in the opposite direction he saw quite a different view. The village sloped away into a plain. Meadows stretched as far as the eye could see; their brilliant verdure was deeper in the distance, and whole rows of villages looked like dark patches in it, though they must have been more than fifteen miles away. On the right of the meadowlands was a line of hills, and a hardly perceptible streak of flashing light and darkness showed where the Dnieper ran.

'Ah, a splendid spot!' said the philosopher, 'this would be the place to live, fishing in the Dnieper and the ponds, bird-catching with nets, or shooting king-snipe and little bustard. Though I do believe there would be a few great bustards too in those meadows! One could dry lots of fruit, too, and sell it in the town, or, better still, make vodka of it, for there's no drink to compare with fruit-vodka. But it would be just as well to consider how to slip away from here.'

He noticed outside the fence a little path completely overgrown with weeds; he was mechanically setting his foot on it with the idea of simply going first out for a walk, and then stealthily passing between the cottages and dashing out into the open country, when he suddenly felt a rather strong hand on his shoulder.

Behind him stood the old Cossack who had on the previous evening so bitterly bewailed the death of his father and mother and his own solitary state.

'It's no good your thinking of making off, Mr Philosopher!' he said: 'this isn't the sort of establishment you can run away from; and the roads are bad, too, for anyone on foot; you had better come to the master: he's been expecting you this long time in the parlour.'

'Let us go! To be sure . . . I'm delighted,' said the philosopher, and he followed the Cossack.

The *sotnik*, an elderly man with grey moustaches and an expression of gloomy sadness, was sitting at a table in the parlour, his head propped on his hands. He was about fifty; but the deep despondency on his face and its wan pallor showed that his soul had been crushed and shattered at one blow, and all his old gaiety and noisy merrymaking had gone for ever. When Homa went in with the old Cossack, he removed one hand from his face and gave a slight nod in response to their low bows.

Homa and the Cossack stood respectfully at the door.

'Who are you, where do you come from, and what is your calling, good man?' said the *sotnik*, in a voice neither friendly nor ill-humoured.

'A bursar, student in philosophy, Homa Brut . . .'

'Who was your father?'

'I don't know, honoured sir.'

'Your mother?'

'I don't know my mother either. It is reasonable to suppose, of course, that I had a mother; but who she was and where she came from, and when she lived – upon my soul, good sir, I don't know.'

The old man paused and seemed to sink into a reverie for a minute.

'How did you come to know my daughter?'

'I didn't know her, honoured sir, upon my word, I didn't. I have never had anything to do with young ladies, never in my life. Bless them, saving your presence!'

'Why did she fix on you and no other to read the psalms over her?'

The philosopher shrugged his shoulders. 'God knows how to make that out. It's a well-known thing, the gentry are for ever taking fancies that the most learned man couldn't explain, and the proverb says: "The devil himself must dance at the master's bidding."'

'Are you telling the truth, philosopher?'

'May I be struck down by thunder on the spot if I'm not.'

'If she had but lived one brief moment longer,' the *sotnik* said to himself mournfully, 'I should have learned all about it. "Let no one else read over me, but send, father, at once to the Kiev Seminary and fetch the bursar, Homa Brut; let him pray three nights for my sinful soul. He knows . . .!" But what he knows, I did not hear: she, poor darling, could say no more before she died. You, good man, are no doubt well known for your holy life and pious works, and she, maybe, heard tell of you.'

'Who? I?' said the philosopher, stepping back in amazement. 'I – holy life!' he articulated, looking straight in the *sotnik*'s face. 'God be with you, sir! What are you talking about! Why – though it's not a seemly thing to speak of – I paid the baker's wife a visit on Maundy Thursday.'

'Well . . . I suppose there must be some reason for fixing on you. You must begin your duties this very day.'

'As to that, I would tell your honour . . . Of course, any man versed in holy scripture may, as far as in him lies . . . but a deacon or a sacristan would be better fitted for it. They are men of understanding, and know how it is all done; while I . . . Besides I haven't the right voice for it, and I myself am good for nothing. I'm not the figure for it.'

'Well, say what you like, I shall carry out all my darling's wishes, I will spare nothing. And if for three nights from today you duly recite the prayers over her, I will reward you, if not . . . I don't advise the devil himself to anger me.'

The last words were uttered by the *sotnik* so vigorously that the philosopher fully grasped their significance.

'Follow me!' said the *sotnik*.

They went out into the hall. The *sotnik* opened the door into another room, opposite the first. The philosopher paused a minute in the hall to blow his nose and crossed the threshold with unaccountable apprehension.

The whole floor was covered with red cotton stuff. On a high table in the corner under the holy images lay the body of the dead girl on a coverlet of dark blue velvet adorned with gold fringe and tassels. Tall wax candles, entwined with sprigs of guelder rose, stood at her feet and head, shedding a dim light that was lost in the brightness of daylight. The dead girl's face was hidden from him by the inconsolable father, who sat down facing her with his back to the door. The philosopher was impressed by the words he heard:

'I am grieving, my dearly beloved daughter, not that in the flower of your age you have left the earth, to my sorrow and mourning, without living your allotted span; I grieve, my darling, that I know not him, my bitter foe, who was the cause of your death. And if I knew the man who could but dream of hurting you, or even saying anything unkind of you, I swear to God he should not see his children again, if he be old as I, nor his father and mother, if he be of that time of life, and his body should be cast out to be devoured by the birds and beasts of the steppe! But my grief it is, my wild marigold, my birdie, light of my eyes, that I must live out my days without comfort, wiping with the skirt of my coat the trickling tears that flow from my old eyes, while my enemy will be making merry and secretly mocking at the feeble old man . . .'

He came to a standstill, due to an outburst of sorrow, which found vent in a flood of tears.

The philosopher was touched by such inconsolable sadness; he coughed, uttering a hollow sound in the effort to clear his throat. The *sotnik* turned round and pointed him to a place at the dead girl's head, before a small lectern with books on it.

'I shall get through three nights somehow,' thought the philosopher: 'and the old man will stuff both my pockets with gold pieces for it.'

He drew near, and clearing his throat once more, began reading, paying no attention to anything else and not venturing to glance at the face of the dead girl. A profound stillness reigned in the apartment. He noticed that the *sotnik* had withdrawn. Slowly, he turned his head to look at the dead, and . . .

A shudder ran through his veins: before him lay a beauty whose like had surely never been on earth before. Never, it seemed, could features have been formed in such striking yet harmonious beauty. She lay as though living: the lovely forehead, fair as snow, as silver, looked deep in thought; the even brows – dark as night in the midst of sunshine – rose proudly above the closed eyes; the eyelashes, that fell like arrows on the cheeks, glowed with the warmth of secret desires; the lips were rubies, ready to break into the laugh of bliss, the flood of joy . . . But in them, in those very features, he saw something terrible and poignant. He felt a sickening ache stirring in his heart, as though, in the midst of a whirl of gaiety and dancing crowds, someone had begun singing a funeral dirge. The rubies of her lips looked like blood surging up from her heart. All at once he was aware of something dreadfully familiar in her face. 'The witch!' he cried in a voice not his own, as, turning pale, he looked away and fell to repeating his prayers. It was the witch that he had killed!

When the sun was setting, they carried the corpse to the church. The philosopher supported the coffin swathed in black on his shoulder, and felt something cold as ice on it. The *sotnik* walked in front, with his hand on the right side of the dead girl's narrow resting home. The wooden church, blackened by age and overgrown with green lichen, stood disconsolately, with its three cone-shaped domes, at the very end of the village. It was evident that no service had been performed in it for a long time. Candles had been lighted before almost every image. The coffin was set down in the centre opposite the altar. The old *sotnik* kissed the dead girl once more, bowed down to the ground, and went out together with the coffin bearers, giving orders that the philosopher should have a good supper and then be taken to the church. On reaching the kitchen all the men who had carried the coffin began putting their hands on the stove, as the custom is with Little Russians, after seeing a dead body.

The hunger, of which the philosopher began at that moment to be conscious, made him for some minutes entirely oblivious of the dead girl. Soon all the servants began gradually assembling in the kitchen, which in the *sotnik*'s house was something like a club, where all the inhabitants of the yard gathered together, including even the dogs, who wagging their tails, came to the door for bones and slops. Wherever anybody might be sent, and with whatever duty he might be charged, he always went first to the kitchen to rest for at least a minute on the bench and smoke a pipe. All the unmarried men in their smart Cossack tunics lay there almost all day long, on the bench, under the bench, or on the stove – anywhere, in fact, where a comfortable place could be found to lie on. Then everybody invariably left behind in the kitchen either his cap or a whip to keep stray dogs off or some such thing. But the biggest crowd always gathered at supper-time, when the drover who had taken the horses to the paddock, and the herdsman who had brought the cows in to be milked, and all the others who were not to be seen during the day, came in. At supper, even the most taciturn tongues were moved to loquacity. It was then that all the news was talked over: who had got himself new breeches, and what was hidden in the bowels of the earth, and who had seen a wolf. There were witty talkers among them; indeed, there is no lack of them anywhere among the Little Russians.

The philosopher sat down with the rest in a big circle in the open air before the kitchen door. Soon a peasant woman in a red bonnet popped out, holding in both hands a steaming bowl of dumplings, which she set down in their midst. Each pulled out a wooden spoon from his pocket, or, for lack of a spoon, a wooden stick. As soon as their jaws began moving more slowly, and the wolfish hunger of the whole party was somewhat assuaged, many of them began talking. The conversation naturally turned on the dead maiden.

'Is it true,' said a young shepherd who had put so many buttons and copper discs on the leather strap on which his pipe hung that he looked like a small haberdasher's shop, 'is it true that the young lady, saving your presence, was on friendly terms with the Evil One?'

'Who? The young mistress?' said Dorosh, a man our philosopher already knew, 'why, she was a regular witch! I'll take my oath she was a witch!'

'Hush, hush, Dorosh,' said another man, who had shown a great disposition to soothe the others on the journey, 'that's no business of ours, God bless it! It's no good talking about it.'

But Dorosh was not at all inclined to hold his tongue; he had just been to the cellar on some job with the butler, and, having applied his lips to two or three barrels, he had come out extremely merry and talked away without ceasing.

'What do you want? Me to be quiet?' he said, 'why, I've been ridden by her myself! Upon my soul, I have!'

'Tell us, uncle,' said the young shepherd with the buttons, 'are there signs by which you can tell a witch?'

'No, you can't,' answered Dorosh, 'there's no way of telling: you might read through all the psalm-books and you couldn't tell.'

'Yes, you can, Dorosh, you can; don't say that,' the former comforter objected; 'it's with good purpose God has given every creature its peculiar habit; folks that have studied say that a witch has a little tail.'

'When a woman's old, she's a witch,' the grey-headed Cossack said coolly.

'Oh! you're a nice set!' retorted the peasant woman, who was at that instant pouring a fresh lot of dumplings into the empty pot; 'regular fat hogs!'

The old Cossack, whose name was Yavtuh and nickname Kovtun, gave a smile of satisfaction seeing that his words had cut the old woman to the quick; while the herdsman gave vent to a guffaw, like the bellowing of two bulls as they stand facing each other.

The beginning of the conversation had aroused the philosopher's curiosity and made him intensely anxious to learn more details about the *sotnik's* daughter, and so, wishing to bring the talk back to that subject, he turned to his neighbour with the words: 'I should like to ask why all the folk sitting at supper here look upon the young mistress as a witch? Did she do a mischief to anybody or bring anybody to harm?'

'There were all sorts of doings,' answered one of the company, a man with a flat face strikingly resembling a spade. 'Everybody remembers the dog-boy Mikita and the . . .'

'What about the dog-boy Mikita?' said the philosopher.

'Stop! I'll tell about the dog-boy Mikita,' said Dorosh.

'I'll tell about him,' said the drover, 'for he was a great crony of mine.'

'I'll tell about Mikita,' said Spirid.

'Let him, let Spirid tell it!' shouted the company.

Spirid began: 'You didn't know Mikita, Mr Philosopher Homa. Ah, he was a man! He knew every dog as well as he knew his own father. The dog-boy we've got now, Mikola, who's sitting next but one from me, isn't worth the sole of his shoe. Though he knows his job, too, but beside the other he's trash, slops.'

'You tell the story well, very well!' said Dorosh, nodding his head approvingly.

Spirid went on: 'He'd see a hare quicker than you'd wipe the snuff from your nose. He'd whistle: "Here, Breaker! here Swift-foot!" and he in full gallop on his horse; and there was no saying which would outrace the other, he the dog, or the dog him. He'd toss off a mug of vodka without winking. He was a fine dog-boy! Only a little time back he began to be always staring at the young mistress. Whether he had fallen in love with her, or whether she had simply bewitched him, anyway the man was done for, he went fairly silly; the devil only knows what he turned into . . . pfoo! No decent word for it . . .'

'That's good,' said Dorosh.

'As soon as the young mistress looks at him, he drops the bridle out of his hand, calls Breaker Bushy-brow, is all of a fluster and doesn't know what he's doing. One day the young mistress comes into the stable where he is rubbing down a horse.

'"I say, Mikita," says she, "let me put my foot on you." And he, silly fellow, is pleased at that. "Not your foot only," says he, "you may sit on me altogether." The young mistress lifted her foot, and, as soon as he saw her bare, plump, white leg, he went fairly crazy, so he said. He bent his back, silly fellow, and, clasping her bare legs in his hands, ran galloping like a horse all over the countryside. And he couldn't say where he was driven, but he came back more dead than alive, and from that time he withered up like a chip of wood; and one day when they went into the stable, instead of him they found a heap of ashes lying there and an empty pail; he had burnt up entirely, burnt up of himself. And he was a dog-boy such as you couldn't find another all the world over.'

When Spirid had finished his story, reflections upon the rare qualities of the deceased dog-boy followed from all sides.

'And haven't you heard tell of Sheptun's wife?' said Dorosh, addressing Homa.

'No.'

'Well, well! You are not taught with too much sense, it seems, in the seminary. Listen, then. There's a Cossack called Sheptun in our village – a good Cossack! He is given to stealing at times, and telling lies when there's no occasion, but . . . he's a good Cossack. His cottage is not so far from here. Just about the very hour that we sat down this evening to table, Sheptun and his wife finished their supper and lay down to sleep, and, as it was fine weather, his wife lay down in the yard, and Sheptun in the cottage on the bench; or no . . . it was the wife lay indoors on the bench and Sheptun in the yard . . .'

'Not on the bench, she was lying on the floor,' put in a peasant woman who stood in the doorway with her cheek propped in her hand.

Dorosh looked at her, then looked down, then looked at her again, and after a brief pause, said: 'When I strip off your petticoat before everybody, you won't be pleased.'

This warning had its effect; the old woman held her tongue and did not interrupt the story again.

Dorosh went on: 'And in the cradle hanging in the middle of the cottage lay a baby a year old – whether of the male or female sex I can't say. Sheptun's wife was lying there when she heard a dog scratching at the door and howling fit to make you run out of the cottage. She was scared, for women are such foolish creatures that, if towards evening you put your tongue out at one from behind a door, her heart's in her mouth. However, she thought: "Well, I'll go and give that damned dog a whack on its nose, and maybe it will stop howling," and taking the oven-fork she went to open the door. She had hardly opened it when a dog dashed in between her legs and straight to the baby's cradle. She saw that it was no longer a dog, but the young mistress, and, if it had been the young lady in her own shape as she knew her, it would not have been so bad. But the peculiar thing is that she was all blue and her eyes glowing like coals. She snatched up the child, bit its throat, and began sucking its blood. Sheptun's wife could only scream: "Oh, horror!" and rushed towards the door. But she sees the door's locked in the passage; she flies up to the loft and there she sits all of a shake, silly woman; and then she sees the young mistress coming up to her in the loft; she pounced on her, and began biting the silly woman. When Sheptun pulled his wife down from the loft in the morning she was bitten all over and had turned black and blue; and next day the silly woman died. So you see what uncanny and wicked doings happen in the world! Though it is of the gentry's breed, a witch is a witch.'

After telling the story, Dorosh looked about him complacently and thrust his finger into his pipe, preparing to fill it with tobacco. The subject of the witch seemed inexhaustible. Each in turn hastened to tell some tale of her. One had seen the witch in the form of a haystack come right up to the door of his cottage; another had had his cap or his pipe stolen by her; many of the girls in the village had had their hair cut off by her; others had lost several quarts of blood sucked by her.

At last the company pulled themselves together and saw that they had been chattering too long, for it was quite dark in the yard. They all began wandering off to their several sleeping places, which were either in the kitchen, or the barns, or the middle of the court-yard.

'Well, Mr Homa! now it's time for us to go to the deceased lady,' said the grey-headed Cossack, addressing the philosopher; and together with Spirid and Dorosh they set off to the church, lashing with their whips at the dogs, of which there were a great number in the road, and which gnawed their sticks angrily.

Though the philosopher had managed to fortify himself with a good mugful of vodka, he felt a fearfulness creeping stealthily over him as they approached the lighted church. The stories and strange tales he had heard helped to work upon his imagination. The darkness under the fence and trees grew less thick as they came into the more open place. At last they went into the church enclosure and found a little yard, beyond which there was not a tree to be seen, nothing but open country and meadows swallowed up in the darkness of night. The three Cossacks and Homa mounted the steep steps to the porch and went into the church. Here they left the philosopher with the best wishes that he might carry out his duties satisfactorily, and locked the door after them, as their master had bidden them.

The philosopher was left alone. First he yawned, then he

stretched, then he blew into both hands, and at last he looked about him. In the middle of the church stood the black coffin; candles were gleaming under the dark images; the light from them only lit up the ikon-stand and shed a faint glimmer in the middle of the church; the distant corners were wrapped in darkness. The tall, old-fashioned ikon stand showed traces of great antiquity; its carved fretwork, once gilt, only glistened here and there with splashes of gold; the gilt had peeled off in one place, and was completely tarnished in another; the faces of the saints, blackened by age, had a gloomy look. The philosopher looked round him again. 'Well,' he said, 'what is there to be afraid of here? No living man can come in here, and to guard me from the dead and ghosts from the other world I have prayers that I have but to read aloud to keep them from laying a finger on me. It's all right!' he repeated with a wave of his hand, 'let's read.' Going up to the lectern he saw some bundles of candles. 'That's good,' thought the philosopher; 'I must light up the whole church so that it may be as bright as by daylight. Oh, it is a pity that one must not smoke a pipe in the temple of God!'

And he proceeded to stick up wax candles at all the cornices, lecterns and images, not stinting them at all, and soon the whole church was flooded with light. Only overhead the darkness seemed somehow more profound, and the gloomy ikons looked even more sullenly out of their antique carved frames, which glistened here and there with specks of gilt. He went up to the coffin, looked timidly at the face of the dead – and could not help closing his eyelids with a faint shudder: such terrible, brilliant beauty!

He turned and tried to move away; but with the strange curiosity, the self-contradictory feeling, which dogs a man especially in times of terror, he could not, as he withdrew, resist taking another look. And then, after the same shudder, he looked again. The striking beauty of the dead maiden certainly seemed terrible. Possibly, indeed, she would not have overwhelmed him with such panic fear if she had been a little less lovely. But there was in her features nothing faded, tarnished, dead; her face was living, and it seemed to the philosopher that she was looking at him with closed eyes. He even fancied that a tear was oozing from under her right eyelid, and, when it rested on her cheek, he saw distinctly that it was a drop of blood.

He walked hastily away to the lectern, opened the book, and to give himself more confidence began reading in a very loud voice. His voice smote upon the wooden church walls, which had so long been deaf and silent; it rang out, forlorn, unechoed, in a deep bass in the absolutely dead stillness, and seemed somehow uncanny even to the reader himself. 'What is there to be afraid of?' he was saying meanwhile to himself. 'She won't rise up out of her coffin, for she will fear the word of God. Let her lie there! And a fine Cossack I am, if I should be scared. Well, I've drunk a drop too much – that's why it seems dreadful. I'll have a pinch of snuff. Ah, the good snuff! Fine snuff, good snuff!' However, as he turned over the pages, he kept taking sidelong glances at the coffin, and an involuntary feeling seemed whispering to him: 'Look, look, she is going to get up! See, she'll sit up, she'll look out from the coffin!'

But the silence was deathlike; the coffin stood motionless; the candles shed a perfect flood of light. A church lighted up at night with a dead body in it and no living soul near is full of terror!

Raising his voice, he began singing in various keys, trying to drown the fears that still lurked in him, but every minute he turned his eyes to the coffin, as though asking, in spite of himself: 'What if she does sit up, if she gets up?'

But the coffin did not stir. If there had but been some sound! some living creature! There was not so much as a cricket churring in the corner! There was nothing but the faint splutter of a far-away candle, the light tap of a drop of wax falling on the floor.

'What if she were to get up . . .?'

She was raising her head . . .

He looked at her wildly and rubbed his eyes. She was, indeed, not lying down now, but sitting up in the coffin. He looked away, and again turned his eyes with horror on the coffin. She stood up . . . she was walking about the church with her eyes shut, moving her arms to and fro as though trying to catch someone.

She was coming straight towards him. In terror he drew a circle round him; with an effort he began reading the prayers and pronouncing the exorcisms which had been taught him by a monk who had all his life seen witches and evil spirits.

She stood almost on the very line; but it was clear that she had not the power to cross it, and she turned livid all over like one who has been dead for several days. Homa had not the courage to look at her; she was terrifying. She ground her teeth and opened her dead eyes; but, seeing nothing, turned with fury – that was apparent in her quivering face – in another direction, and, flinging her arms, clutched in them each column and corner, trying to catch Homa. At last she stood still, holding up a menacing finger, and lay down again in her coffin.

The philosopher could not recover his self-possession, but kept gazing at the narrow dwelling place of the witch. At last the coffin suddenly sprang up from its place and with a hissing sound began flying all over the church, zigzagging through the air in all directions.

The philosopher saw it almost over his head, but at the same time he saw that it could not cross the circle he had drawn, and he redoubled his exorcisms. The coffin dropped down in the middle of the church and stayed there without moving. The corpse got up out of it, livid and greenish. But at that instant the crow of the cock was heard in the distance; the corpse sank back in the coffin and closed the lid.

The philosopher's heart was throbbing and the sweat was streaming down him; but, emboldened by the cock's crowing, he read on more rapidly the pages he ought to have read through before. At the first streak of dawn the sacristan came to relieve him, together with old Yavtuh, who was at that time performing the duties of a beadle.

On reaching his distant sleeping-place, the philosopher could not for a long time get to sleep; but weariness gained the upper hand at last and he slept on till dinner-time. When he woke up, all the events of the night seemed to him to have happened in a dream. To keep up his strength he was given at dinner a mug of vodka.

Over dinner he soon grew lively, made a remark or two, and devoured a rather large sucking pig almost unaided; but some feeling he could not have explained made him unable to bring himself to speak of his adventures in the church, and to the inquiries of the inquisitive he replied: 'Yes, all sorts of strange things happened.' The philosopher was one of those people who, if they are well fed, are moved to extraordinary benevolence. Lying down with his pipe in his teeth he watched them all with a honied look in his eyes and kept spitting to one side.

After dinner the philosopher was in excellent spirits. He went round the whole village and made friends with almost everybody; he was kicked out of two cottages, indeed; one good-looking young woman caught him a good smack on the back with a spade when he took it into his head to try her shift and skirt, and inquire what stuff they were made of. But as evening approached the philosopher grew more pensive. An hour before supper almost all the servants gathered together to play *kragli* – a sort of skittles in which long sticks are used instead of balls, and the winner has the right to ride on the loser's back. This game became very entertaining for the spectators; often the drover, a man as broad as a pancake, was mounted on the swineherd, a feeble little man, who was nothing but wrinkles. Another time it was the drover who had to bow his back, and Dorosh, leaping on it, always said: 'What a fine bull!' The more dignified of the company sat in the kitchen doorway. They looked on very gravely, smoking their pipes, even when the young people roared with laughter at some witty remark from the drover or Spirid. Homa tried in vain to give himself up to this game; some gloomy thought stuck in his head like a nail. At supper, in spite of his efforts to be merry, terror grew within him as the darkness spread over the sky.

'Come, it's time to set off, Mr Seminarist!' said his friend, the grey-headed Cossack, getting up from the table, together with Dorosh; 'let us go to our task.'

Homa was taken to the church again in the same way; again he was left there alone and the door was locked upon him. As soon as he was alone, fear began to take possession of him again. Again he saw the dark ikons, the gleaming frames, and the familiar black coffin standing in menacing stillness and immobility in the middle of the church.

'Well,' he said to himself, 'now there's nothing marvellous to me in this marvel. It was only alarming the first time. Yes, it was only rather alarming the first time, and even then it wasn't so alarming; now it's not alarming at all.'

He made haste to take his stand at the lectern, drew a circle around him, pronounced some exorcisms, and began reading aloud, resolving not to raise his eyes from the book and not to pay attention to anything. He had been reading for about an hour and was beginning to cough and feel rather tired; he took his horn out of his pocket and, before putting the snuff to his nose, stole a timid look at the coffin. His heart turned cold; the corpse was already standing before him on the very edge of the circle, and her dead, greenish eyes were fixed upon him. The philosopher shuddered, and a cold chill ran through his veins. Dropping his eyes to the book, he began reading the prayers and exorcisms more loudly, and heard the corpse again grinding her teeth and waving her arms trying to catch him. But, with a sidelong glance out of one eye, he saw that the corpse was feeling for him where he was not standing, and that she evidently could not see him. He heard a hollow mutter, and she began pronouncing terrible words with her dead lips; they gurgled hoarsely like the bubbling of boiling pitch. He could not have said what they meant; but there was something fearful in them. The philosopher understood with horror that she was making an incantation.

A wind blew through the church at her words, and there was a sound as of multitudes of flying wings. He heard the beating of wings on the panes of the church windows and on the iron window-frames, the dull scratching of claws upon the iron, and an immense troop thundering on the doors and trying to break in. His heart was throbbing violently all this time; closing his eyes, he kept reading prayers and exorcisms. At last there was a sudden shrill sound in the distance; it was a distant cock crowing. The philosopher, utterly spent, stopped and took breath.

When they came in to fetch him, they found him more dead than alive; he was leaning with his back against the wall while, with his eyes almost starting out of his head, he stared at the Cossacks as they came in. They could scarcely get him along and had to support him all the way back. On reaching the courtyard, he pulled himself together and bade them give him a mug of vodka. When he had drunk it, he stroked down the hair on his head and said: 'There are lots of foul things of all sorts in the world! And the panics they give one, there . . .' With that the philosopher waved his hand in despair.

The company sitting round him bowed their heads, hearing such sayings. Even a small boy, whom everybody in the servants' quarters felt himself entitled to depute in his place when it was a question of cleaning the stables or fetching water, even this poor youngster stared open-mouthed at the philosopher.

At that moment the old cook's assistant, a peasant woman, not yet past middle age, a terrible coquette, who always found something to pin to her cap – a bit of ribbon, a pink, or even a scrap of coloured paper, if she had nothing better – passed by, in a tightly girt apron, which displayed her round, sturdy figure.

'Good day, Homa!' she said, seeing the philosopher. 'Aie, aie, aie! what's the matter with you?' she shrieked, clasping her hands.

'Why, what is it, silly woman?'

'Oh, my goodness! Why, you've gone quite grey!'

'Aha! why, she's right!' Spirid pronounced, looking attentively at the philosopher. 'Why, you have really gone as grey as our old Yavtuh.'

The philosopher, hearing this, ran headlong to the kitchen, where he had noticed on the wall a fly-blown triangular bit of looking-glass before which were stuck forget-me-nots, periwinkles and even wreaths of marigolds, testifying to its importance for the toilet of the finery-loving coquette. With horror he saw the truth of their words: half of his hair had in fact turned white.

Homa Brut hung his head and abandoned himself to reflection. 'I will go to the master,' he said at last. 'I'll tell him all about it and explain that I cannot go on reading. Let him send me back to Kiev straight away.'

With these thoughts in his mind he bent his steps towards the porch of the house.

The *sotnik* was sitting almost motionless in his parlour. The same hopeless grief which the philosopher had seen in his face before was still apparent. Only his cheeks were more sunken. It was evident that he had taken very little food, or perhaps had not eaten at all. The extraordinary pallor of his face gave it a look of stony immobility.

'Good day!' he pronounced on seeing Homa, who stood, cap in hand, at the door. 'Well, how goes it with you? All satisfactory?'

'It's satisfactory, all right; such devilish doings, that one can but pick up one's cap and take to one's heels.'

'How's that?'

'Why, your daughter, your honour . . . Looking at it reasonably, she is, to be sure, of noble birth, nobody is going to gainsay it; only, saving your presence, God rest her soul . . .'

'What of my daughter?'

'She had dealings with Satan. She gives one such horrors that there's no reading scripture at all.'

'Read away! read away! She did well to send for you; she took much care, poor darling, about her soul and tried to drive away all evil thoughts with prayers.'

'That's as you like to say, your honour; upon my soul, I cannot go on with it!'

'Read away!' the *sotnik* persisted in the same persuasive voice, 'you have only one night left; you will do a Christian deed and I will reward you.'

'But whatever rewards . . . Do as you please, your honour, but I will not read!' Homa declared resolutely.

'Listen, philosopher!' said the *sotnik*, and his voice grew firm and menacing. 'I don't like these pranks. You can behave like that in your seminary; but with me it is different. When I flog, it's not the same as your rector's flogging. Do you know what good leather whips are like?'

'I should think I do!' said the philosopher, dropping his voice; 'everybody knows what leather whips are like: in a large dose, it's quite unendurable.'

'Yes, but you don't know yet how my lads can lay them on!' said the *sotnik*, menacingly, rising to his feet, and his face assumed an imperious and ferocious expression that betrayed the unbridled violence of his character, only subdued for the time by sorrow.

'Here they first give a sound flogging, then sprinkle with vodka, and begin over again. Go along, go along, finish your task! If you don't – you'll never get up again. If you do – a thousand gold pieces!'

'Oho, ho! he's a stiff one!' thought the philosopher as he went out: 'he's not to be trifled with. Wait a bit, friend; I'll cut and run, so that you and your hounds will never catch me.'

And Homa made up his mind to run away. He only waited for the hour after dinner when all the servants were accustomed to lie about in the hay in the barns and to give vent to such snores and wheezing that the backyard sounded like a factory.

The time came at last. Even Yavtuh closed his eyes as he lay stretched out in the sun. With fear and trembling, the philosopher stealthily made his way into the pleasure garden, from which he fancied he could more easily escape into the open country without being observed. As is usual with such gardens, it was dreadfully neglected and overgrown, and so made an extremely suitable setting for any secret enterprise. Except for one little path, trodden by the servants on their tasks, it was entirely hidden in a dense thicket of cherry-trees, elders and burdock, which thrust up their tall stems covered with clinging pinkish burs. A network of wild hop was flung over this medley of trees and bushes of varied hues, forming a roof over them, clinging to the fence and falling, mingled with wild bell-flowers, from it in coiling snakes. Beyond the fence, which formed the boundary of the garden, there came a perfect forest of rank grass and weeds, which looked as though no one cared to peep enviously into it, and as though any scythe would be broken to bits trying to mow down the stout stubbly stalks.

When the philosopher tried to get over the fence, his teeth chattered and his heart beat so violently that he was frightened at it. The skirts of his long coat seemed to stick to the ground as though someone had nailed them down. As he climbed over, he fancied he heard a voice shout in his ears with a deafening hiss: 'Where are you off to?' The philosopher dived into the long grass and fell to running, frequently stumbling over old roots and trampling upon moles. He saw that when he came out of the rank weeds he would have to cross a field, and that beyond it lay a dark thicket of blackthorn, in which he thought he would be safe. He expected after making his way through it to find the road leading straight to Kiev. He ran across the field at once and found himself in the thicket.

He crawled through the prickly bushes, paying a toll of rags from his coat on every thorn, and came out into a little hollow. A willow with spreading branches bent down almost to the earth. A little brook sparkled pure as silver. The first thing the philosopher did was to lie down and drink, for he was insufferably thirsty. 'Good water!' he said, wiping his lips; 'I might rest here!'

'No, we had better go straight ahead; they'll be coming to look for you!'

These words rang out above his ears. He looked round – before him was standing Yavtuh. 'Curse Yavtuh!' the philosopher thought in his wrath; 'I could take you and fling you . . . And I could batter in your ugly face and all of you with an oak post.'

'You needn't have gone such a long way round,' Yavtuh went on, 'you'd have done better to keep to the road I have come by, straight by the stable. And it's a pity about your coat. It's good cloth. What did you pay a yard for it? But we've walked far enough; it's time to go home.'

The philosopher trudged after Yavtuh, scratching himself. 'Now the cursed witch will give it to me!' he thought. 'Though, after all, what am I thinking about? What am I afraid of? Am I not a Cossack? Why, I've been through two nights, God will succour me the third also. The cursed witch committed a fine lot of sins, it seems, since the Evil One makes such a fight for her.'

Such were the reflections that absorbed him as he walked into the courtyard. Keeping up his spirits with these thoughts, he asked Dorosh, who through the patronage of the butler sometimes had access to the cellars, to pull out a keg of vodka; and the two friends, sitting in the barn, put away not much less than half a pailful, so that the philosopher, getting on his feet, shouted: 'Musicians! I must have musicians!' and without waiting for the latter fell to dancing a jig in a clear space in the middle of the yard. He danced till it was time for the afternoon snack, and the servants who stood round him in a circle, as is the custom on such occasions, at last spat on the ground and walked away, saying: 'Good gracious, what a time the fellow keeps it up!' At last the philosopher lay down to sleep on the spot, and a good sousing of cold water was needed to wake him up for supper. At supper he talked of what it meant to be a Cossack, and how he should not be afraid of anything in the world.

'Time is up,' said Yavtuh, 'let us go.'

'A splinter through your tongue, you damned hog!' thought the philosopher, and getting to his feet he said: 'Come along.'

On the way the philosopher kept glancing from side to side and made faint attempts at conversation with his companions. But Yavtuh said nothing; and even Dorosh was disinclined to talk. It was a hellish night. A whole pack of wolves was howling in the distance, and even the barking of the dogs had a dreadful sound.

'I fancy something else is howling; that's not a wolf,' said Dorosh. Yavtuh was silent. The philosopher could find nothing to say.

They drew near the church and stepped under the decaying wooden domes that showed how little the owner of the place thought about God and his own soul. Yavtuh and Dorosh withdrew as before, and the philosopher was left alone.

Everything was the same, everything wore the same sinister familiar aspect. He stood still for a minute. The horrible witch's coffin was still standing motionless in the middle of the church.

'I won't be afraid; by God, I will not!' he said, and, drawing a circle around himself as before, he began recalling all his spells and exorcisms. There was an awful stillness; the candles spluttered and flooded the whole church with light. The philosopher turned one page, then turned another and noticed that he was not reading what was written in the book. With horror he crossed himself and began chanting. This gave him a little more courage; the reading made progress, and the pages turned rapidly one after the other.

All of a sudden . . . in the midst of the stillness . . . the iron lid of the coffin burst with a crash and the corpse rose up. It was more terrible than the first time. Its teeth clacked horribly against each other, its lips twitched convulsively, and incantations came from them in wild shrieks. A whirlwind swept through the church, the ikons fell to the ground, broken glass came flying down from the windows. The doors were burst from their hinges and a countless multitude of monstrous beings trooped into the church of God. A terrible noise of wings and scratching claws filled the church. All flew and raced about looking for the philosopher.

All trace of drink had disappeared, and Homa's head was quite clear now. He kept crossing himself and repeating prayers at random. And all the while he heard the unclean horde whirring round him, almost touching him with their loathsome tails and the tips of their wings. He had not the courage to look at them; he only saw a huge monster, the whole width of the wall, standing in the shade of its matted locks as of a forest; through the tangle of hair two eyes glared horribly with eyebrows slightly lifted. Above it something was hanging in the air like an immense bubble with a thousand claws and scorpion-stings stretching from the centre; black earth hung in clods on them. They were all looking at him, seeking him, but could not see him, surrounded by his mysterious circle. 'Bring Viy! Fetch Viy!' he heard the corpse cry.

And suddenly a stillness fell upon the church; the wolves' howling was heard in the distance, and soon there was the thud of heavy footsteps resounding through the church. With a sidelong glance he saw they were bringing a squat, thickset, bandy-legged figure. He was covered all over with black earth. His arms and legs grew out like strong sinewy roots. He trod heavily, stumbling at every step. His long eyelids hung down to the very ground. Homa saw with horror that his face was of iron. He was supported under the arms and led straight to the spot where Homa was standing.

'Lift up my eyelids. I do not see!' said Viy in a voice that seemed to come from underground – and all the company flew to raise his eyelids.

'Do not look!' an inner voice whispered to the philosopher. He could not restrain himself, and he looked.

'There he is!' shouted Viy, and thrust an iron finger at him. And all pounced upon the philosopher together. He fell expiring to the ground, and his soul fled from his body in terror.

There was the sound of a cock crowing. It was the second cock-crow; the first had been missed by the gnomes. In panic they rushed pell-mell to the doors and windows to fly out in utmost haste; but they could not; and so they remained there, stuck in the doors and windows.

When the priest went in, he stopped short at the sight of this defamation of God's holy place, and dared not serve the requiem on such a spot. And so the church was left for ever, with monsters stuck in the doors and windows, was overgrown with forest trees, roots, rough grass and wild thorns, and no one can now find the way to it.

When the rumours of this reached Kiev, and the theologian, Halyava, heard at last of the fate of the philosopher Homa, he spent a whole hour plunged in thought. Great changes had befallen him during that time. Fortune had smiled on him; on the conclusion of his course of study, he was made bell ringer of the very highest belfry, and he was almost always to be seen with a damaged nose, as the wooden staircase to the belfry had been extremely carelessly made.

'Have you heard what has happened to Homa?' Tibery Gorobets, who by now was a philosopher and had a newly-grown moustache, asked, coming up to him.

'Such was the lot God sent him,' said Halyava the bell ringer.

'Let us go to the pot-house and drink to his memory!'

The young philosopher, who was beginning to enjoy his privileges with the ardour of an enthusiast, so that his full trousers and his coat and even his cap reeked of spirits and coarse tobacco, instantly signified his readiness.

'He was a fine fellow, Homa!' said the bell ringer, as the lame innkeeper set the third mug before him. 'He was a fine man! And he came to grief for nothing.'

'I know why he came to grief: it was because he was afraid; if he had not been afraid, the witch could not have done anything to him. You have only to cross yourself and spit just on her tail, and nothing will happen. I know all about it. Why, all the old women who sit in our market in Kiev are all witches.'

To this the bell ringer bowed his head in token of agreement. But, observing that his tongue was incapable of uttering a single word, he cautiously got up from the table, and, lurching to right and to left, went to hide in a remote spot in the rough grass; from the force of habit, however, he did not forget to carry off the sole of an old boot that was lying about on the bench.

THE BURGOMASTER IN BOTTLE

Erckmann-Chatrian

One of the most successful plays staged and constantly revived by Henry Irving and Bram Stoker at the Royal Lyceum Theatre was *The Bells*. First produced in 1871, the role of Mathias, a respectable Alsatian mayor who murders a Jew for his money and is subsequently haunted by the sound of the bells on his victim's sleigh, catapulted Irving to stardom, and remained one of his favourite parts for over thirty years. The London production was adapted from the French play *Le Juif Polonais* (*The Polish Jew*) by the immensely popular writing duo, Émile Erckmann (1822-1899) and Alexandre Chatrian (1826-1890), who, under the byline Erckmann-Chatrian, penned many historical novels and short stories, the earliest collection of which was titled *Histoires et Contes Fantastiques* (1849).

When Erckmann-Chatrian's play *The Polish Jew* was published in book form in London by Ward, Lock in 1873, together with ten of their earlier fantastic tales, it included a long-forgotten vampire story set in the region where the renowned French vineyards are located. Titled 'The Burgomaster in Bottle,' it originally appeared, as 'Le Bourgmestre en Bouteille,' in the June 1849 edition of *Le Démocrate du Rhin*, and was later reprinted, alongside *Le Juif Polonais*, in *Contes Populaires* (1866), prior to the bulk of their strange and unusual tales being translated into bestselling English editions during the 1870s, following the success of *The Bells*.

I HAVE always professed the highest esteem, and even a sort of vener-
ation, for the Rhine's noble wine; it sparkles like champagne, it
warms one like Burgundy, it soothes the throat like Bordeaux, it
fires the imagination like the juice of the Spanish grape, it makes us
tender and kind like lacryma-christi; and last, but not least, it helps
us to dream – it unfolds the extensive fields of fancy before our eyes.

In 1846, towards the end of autumn, I had made up my mind
to perform a pilgrimage to Johannisberg. Mounted on a wretched
hack, I had arranged two tin flasks along his hollow ribs, and I made
the journey by short stages.

What a fine sight a vintage is! One of my flasks was always
empty, the other always full; when I quitted one vineyard, there
was the prospect of another before me. But it quite troubled me
that I had not any one capable of appreciating it to share this enjoy-
ment with me.

Night was closing in one evening; the sun had just disappeared,
but one or two stray rays were still lingering among the large vine-
leaves. I heard the trot of a horse behind me. I turned a little to the
left to allow him to pass me, and to my great surprise I recognised
my friend Hippel, who as soon as he saw me uttered a shout of delight.

You are well acquainted with Hippel, his fleshy nose, his mouth
especially adapted to the sense of taste, and his rotund stomach. He
looked like old Silenus in the pursuit of Bacchus. We shook hands
heartily.

The aim of Hippel's journey was the same as mine; in his quality
of first-rate connoisseur he wanted to confirm his opinion as to the
peculiarities of certain growths about which he still entertained some
doubts.

So we continued our route together. Hippel was extremely gay;
he traced out our route among the Rhingau vineyards. We halted
occasionally to devote our attention to our flasks, and to listen to
the silence which reigned around us.

The night was far advanced when we reached a little inn perched
on the side of a hill. We dismounted. Hippel peeped through a small
window nearly level with the ground. A lamp was burning on a
table, and by it sat an old woman fast asleep.

'Hallo!' cried my comrade; 'open the door, mother.'

The old woman started, got up and came to the window, and

pressed her shrunken face against the panes, You would have taken it for one of those old Flemish portraits in which ochre and bistre predominate.

As soon as the old sybil could distinguish us she made a grimace intended for a smile, and opened the door for us.

'Come in, gentlemen – come in,' cried she with a tremulous voice; 'I will go and wake my son; sit down – sit down.'

'A feed of corn for our horses and a good supper for ourselves,' cried Hippel.

'Directly, directly,' said the old woman assiduously.

She hobbled out of the room, and we could hear her creeping up stairs as steep as a Jacob's ladder.

We remained for a few minutes in a low smoky room. Hippel hurried to the kitchen, and returned to tell me that he had ascertained there were certain sides of bacon by the chimney.

'We shall have some supper,' said he, patting his stomach; 'yes, we shall get some supper.'

The flooring creaked over our heads, and almost immediately a powerful fellow with nothing but his trousers on, his chest bare, and his hair in disorder, opened the door, took a step or two forward, and then disappeared without saying a word to us.

The old woman lighted the fire, and the butter began to frizzle in the frying-pan.

Supper was brought in; a ham put on the table flanked by two bottles, one of red wine, the other of white.

'Which do you prefer?' asked the hostess.

'We must try them both first,' replied Hippel, holding his glass to the old woman, who filled it with red.

She then filled mine. We tasted it; it was a strong rough wine. I cannot describe the peculiar flavour it possessed – a mixture of vervain and cypress leaves! I drank a few drops, and my soul became profoundly sad. But Hippel, on the contrary, smacked his lips with an air of satisfaction.

'Good! very good! Where do you get it from, mother?' said he.

'From the hillside close by,' replied the old woman, with a curious smile.

'A very good hillside,' returned Hippel, pouring himself out another glass.

It seemed to me like drinking blood.

'What are you making such faces for, Ludwig?' said he. 'Is there anything the matter with you?'

'No,' I answered, 'but I don't like such red wine as this.'

'There is no accounting for tastes,' observed Hippel, finishing the bottle and knocking on the table.

'Another bottle of the same,' cried he, 'and mind, no mixing, lovely hostess – I am a judge! Morbleu! this wine puts life into me, it is so generous.'

Hippel threw himself back in his chair; his face seemed to undergo a complete transformation. I emptied the bottle of white wine at a draught, and then my heart felt gay again. My friend's preference for red wine seemed to me ridiculous but excusable.

We continued drinking, I white and he red wine, till one o'clock in the morning.

One in the morning! It is the hour when Fancy best loves to exercise her influence. The caprices of imagination take that opportunity of displaying their transparent dresses embroidered in crystal and blue, like the wings of the beetle and the dragonfly.

One o'clock! That is the moment when the music of the spheres tickles the sleeper's ears, and breathes the harmony of the invisible world into his soul. Then the mouse trots about, and the owl flaps her wings, and passes noiselessly over our heads.

'One o'clock,' said I to my companion; 'we must go to bed if we are to set off early tomorrow morning.'

Hippel rose and staggered about.

The old woman showed us into a double-bedded room, and wished us goodnight.

We undressed ourselves; I remained up the last to put the candle out. I was hardly in bed before Hippel was fast asleep; his respiration was like the blowing of a storm. I could not close my eyes, as thousands of strange faces hovered round me. The gnomes, imps, and witches of Walpurgis night executed their cabalistic dances on the ceiling all night. Strange effect of white wine!

I got up, lighted my lamp, and, impelled by curiosity, I went up to Hippel's bed. His face was red, his mouth half-open, I could see the blood pulsating in his temples, and his lips moved as if he wanted to speak. I stood for some time motionless by his side; I tried to see into the depths of his soul, but sleep is an impenetrable mystery; like death, it keeps its secrets.

Sometimes Hippel's face wore an expression of terror, then of sadness, then again of melancholy; occasionally his features contracted; he looked as if he was going to cry.

His jolly face, which was made for laughter, wore a strange expression when under the influence of pain.

What might be passing in those depths? I saw a wave now and then mount to the surface, but whence came those frequent shocks? All at once the sleeper rose, his eyelids opened, and I could see nothing but the whites of his eyes; every muscle in his face was trembling, his mouth seemed to try to utter a scream. Then he fell back, and I heard a sob.

'Hippel! Hippel!' cried I, and I emptied a jug of water on his head. This awoke him.

'Ah!' cried he, 'God be thanked, it was but a dream. My dear Ludwig, I thank you for awakening me.'

'So much the better, and now tell me what you were dreaming about.'

'Yes, tomorrow; let me sleep now. I am so sleepy.'

'Hippel, you are ungrateful; you will have forgotten it all by tomorrow.'

'Morbleu,' replied he, 'I am so sleepy, I must go to sleep; leave me now.'

I would not let him off.

'Hippel, you will have the same dream over again, and this time I shall leave you to your fate.'

These words had the desired effect.

'The same dream over again!' cried he, jumping out of bed. 'Give me my clothes! Saddle my horse! I am off! This is a cursed place. You are right, Ludwig, this is the devil's own dwelling place. Let us be off!'

He hurried on his clothes. When he was dressed I stopped him.

'Hippel,' said I, 'why should we hurry away? It is only three o'clock. Let us stay quietly here.'

I opened the window, and the fresh night air penetrated the room, and dissipated all his fears. So he leaned on the window-sill, and told me what follows:—

'We were talking yesterday about the most famous of the Rhingau vineyards. Although I have never been through this part of the country, my mind was no doubt full of impressions regarding it, and the heavy wine we drank gave a sombre tinge to my ideas. What is most extraordinary, in my dream I fancied I was the burgomaster of Welcke' (a neighbouring village), 'and I was so identified with this personage, that I can describe him to you as minutely as if I was describing myself. This burgomaster was a man of middle height, and almost as fat as I am. He wore a coat with wide skirts and brass buttons; all down his legs he had another row of small nail-headed buttons. On his bald head was a three-cornered cocked hat – in short, he was a stupidly grave man, drinking nothing but water, thinking of nothing but money, and his only endeavour was to increase his property.

'As I had taken the outward appearance of the burgomaster, so had I his disposition also. I, Hippel, should have despised myself could I have recognised myself, what a beast of a burgomaster I was. How far better it is to lead a happy life, without caring for the future, than to heap crowns upon crowns and only distil bile! Well, here I am, a burgomaster.

'When I leave my bed in the morning the first thing which makes me uneasy is to know if the men are already at work among my vines. I eat a crust of bread for breakfast. A crust of bread! what a sordid miser! I who have a cutlet and a bottle of wine every morning! Well, never mind, I take – that is, the burgomaster takes his crust of bread and puts it in his pocket. He tells his old housekeeper to sweep the room and have dinner ready by eleven. Boiled beef and potatoes I think it was – a poor dinner. Well, out he goes.

'I could describe the road he took, the vines on the hillside, to you exactly,' continued Hippel; 'I see them before me now.

'How is it possible that a man in a dream could conceive such an idea of a landscape? I could see fields, gardens, meadows, and vineyards. I knew this belongs to Pierre, that to Jacques, that to Henri; and then I stopped before one of these bits of ground and said to myself – "Bless me, Jacob's clover is very fine." And farther on, "Bless me, again, that acre of vines would suit me wonderfully." But all the time I felt a sort of giddiness, an indescribable pain in the head. I hurried on, as it was early morning. The sun soon rose, and the heat became oppressive. I was then following a narrow path which crossed through the vines towards the top of the hill. This path led past the ruins of an old castle, and beyond it I could see my four acres of vineyard. I made haste to get there; as I was quite blown when I reached the ruins, I stopped to recover breath, and the blood seemed to ring in my ears, while my heart beat in my breast like a hammer on an anvil. The sun seemed on fire. I tried to go on again, but all at once I felt as if I had received a blow from a club; I rolled under a part of a wall, and I comprehended I had a fit of apoplexy. Then the horror of despair took possession of me. "I am a dead man," said I to myself; "the money I have amassed with so much trouble, the trees I have so carefully cultivated, the house I have built, all, all are lost – all gone into the hands of my heirs. Now those wretches to whom in my lifetime I refused a kreutzer will become rich at my expense. Traitors! how you will rejoice over my misfortune! You will take the keys from my pockets, you will share my property among yourselves, you will squander my gold; and I – I must be present at this spoliation! What a hideous punishment!"

'I felt my spirit quit the corpse, but remain standing by it.

'This spiritual burgomaster noticed that its body had its face blue, and yellow hands.

'It was very hot, and some large flies came and settled on the face of the corpse. One went up his nose. The body stirred not! The whole face was soon covered with them, and the spirit was in despair because it was impotent to drive them away.

'There it stood. There, for minutes which seemed hours. Hell was beginning for it already. So an hour went by. The heat increased gradually. Not a breath in the air, nor a cloud in the sky.

'A goat came out from among the ruins, nibbling the weeds which were growing up through the rubbish. As it passed my poor body it sprang aside, and then came back, opened its eyes with suspicion, smelt about, and then followed its capricious course over the fallen cornice of a turret. A young goatherd came to drive her back again; but when he saw the body he screamed out, and then set off running towards the village with all his might.

'Another hour passed, slow as eternity. At last a whispering, then steps were heard behind the ruins, and my spirit saw the magistrate coming slowly, slowly along, followed by his clerk and several other persons I knew every one of them. They uttered an exclamation when they saw me—

'"It is our burgomaster!"

'The medical man approached the body, and drove away the flies, which flew swarming away. He looked at it, then raised one of the already stiffened arms, and said with the greatest indifference—

'"Our burgomaster has succumbed to a fit of apoplexy; he has probably been here all the morning. You had better carry him away and bury him as soon as possible, for this heat accelerates decomposition."

'"Upon my word," said the clerk, "between ourselves, he is no great loss to the parish. He was a miser and an ass, and he knew nothing whatever."

'"Yes," added the magistrate, "and yet he found fault with everything."

'"Not very surprising either," said another; "fools always think themselves clever."

'"You must send for several porters," observed the doctor; "they have a heavy burden to carry; this man always had more belly than brains."

'"I shall go and draw up the certificate of death. At what time shall we say it took place?" asked the clerk.

'"Say about four o'clock this morning."

'"The skinflint!" said a peasant, "he was going to watch his workmen to have an excuse for stopping a few sous off their wages on Saturday."

'Then folding his arms and looking at the dead body—

'"Well, burgomaster," said he, "what does it profit you that you squeezed the poor so hard? Death has cut you down all the same."

'"What has he got in his pocket?" asked one.

'They took out of it my crust of bread.

'"Here is his breakfast!"

'They all began to laugh.

'Chattering as they were the groups prepared to quit the ruins; my poor spirit heard them a few moments, and then by degrees the noise ceased. I remained in solitude and silence.

'The flies came back by millions.

'I cannot say how much time elapsed,' continued Hippel, 'for in my dream the minutes seemed endless.

'However, at last some porters came; they cursed the burgomaster and carried his carcass away; the poor man's spirit followed them plunged in grief. I went back the same way I came, but this time I saw my body carried before me on a litter. When we reached my house I found many people waiting for me, I recognised male and female cousins to the fourth generation! The bier was set down – they all had a look at me.

'"It is he, sure enough," said one.

'"And dead enough too," rejoined another.

'My housekeeper made her appearance; she clasped her hands together, and exclaimed—

'"Such a fat, healthy man! who could have foreseen such an end? It only shows how little we are."

'And this was my general oration.

'I was carried upstairs and laid on a mattress. When one of my cousins took my keys out of my pocket I felt I should like to scream with rage. But, alas! spirits are voiceless; well, my dear Ludwig, I saw them open my bureau, count my money, make an estimate of my property, seal up my papers; I saw my housekeeper quietly taking possession of my best linen, and although death had freed me from all mundane wants, I could not help regretting the sous of which I was robbed.

'I was undressed, and then a shirt was put on me; I was nailed up in a deal box, and I was, of course, present at my own funeral.

'When they lowered me into the grave, despair seized upon my spirit; all was lost! Just then, Ludwig, you awoke me, but I still fancy I can hear the earth rattling on my coffin.'

Hippel ceased, and I could see his whole body shiver.

We remained a long time silent, without exchanging a word; a cock crowing warned us that night was nearly over, the stars were growing pale at the approach of day; other cocks' shrill cry could be heard abroad challenging from the different farms. A watchdog came out of his kennel to make his morning rounds, then a lark, half awake only, warbled a note or two.

'Hippel,' said I to my comrade, 'it is time to be off if we wish to take advantage of the cool morning.'

'Very true,' said he, 'but before we go I must have a mouthful of something.'

We went downstairs; the landlord was dressing himself; when he had put his blouse on he set before us the relics of our last night's supper; he filled one of my flasks with white wine, the other with red, saddled our hacks, and wished us a good journey.

We had not ridden more than half a league when my friend Hippel, who was always thirsty, took a draught of the red wine.

'P-r-r-r!' cried he as if he was going to faint, 'my dream – my last night's dream!'

He pushed his horse into a trot to escape this vision, which was visibly imprinted in striking characters on his face; I followed him slowly, as my poor Rosinante required some consideration.

The sun rose, a pale pink tinge invaded the gloomy blue of the sky, then the stars lost themselves as the light became brighter. As the first rays of the sun showed themselves Hippel stopped his horse and waited for me.

'I cannot tell you,' said he, 'what gloomy ideas have taken possession of me. This red wine must have some strange properties; it pleases my palate, but it certainly attacks my brain.'

'Hippel,' replied I, 'it is not to be disputed that certain liquors contain the principles of fancy and even of phantasmagoria. I have seen men from gay become sad, and the reverse; men of sense become silly, and the silly become witty, and all arising from a glass or two of wine in the stomach. It is a profound mystery; what man, then, is senseless enough to deny the bottle's magic power? Is it not the sceptre of a superior incomprehensible force before which we must be content to bow the head, for we all some time or other submit to its influence, divine or infernal, as the case may be?'

Hippel recognised the force of my arguments and remained silently lost in reverie. We were making our way along a narrow path which winds along the banks of the Queich. We could hear the birds chirping, and the partridge calling as it hid itself under the broad vine leaves. The landscape was superb, the river murmured as it flowed past little ravines in the banks. Right and left, hillside after hillside came into view, all loaded with abundant fruit. Our route formed an angle with the declivity. All at once my friend Hippel stopped motionless, his mouth wide open, his hands extended

in an attitude of stupefied astonishment, then as quick as lightning
he turned to fly, when I seized his horse's bridle.

'Hippel, what's the matter? Is Satan in ambuscade on the road,
or has Balaam's angel drawn his sword against you?'

'Let me go!' said he, struggling; 'my dream – my dream!'

'Be quiet and calm yourself, Hippel; no doubt there are some
injurious qualities contained in red wine; swallow some of this; it
is a generous juice of the grape which dissipates the gloomy imag-
inings of a man's brain.'

He drank it eagerly, and this beneficent liquor reestablished his
faculties in equilibrium.

He poured the red wine out on the road; it had become as black
as ink, and formed great bubbles as it soaked in the ground, and I
seemed to hear confused voices groaning and sighing, but so faint
that they seemed to escape from some distant country, and which
the ear of flesh could hardly hear, but only the fibres of the heart
could feel. It was as Abel's last sigh when his brother felled him to
the ground and the earth drank up his blood.

Hippel was too much excited to pay attention to this phenomenon, but I was profoundly struck by it. At the same time I noticed
a black bird, about as large as my fist, rise from the bushes near,
and fly away with a cry of fear.

'I feel,' said Hippel, 'that the opposing principles are struggling
within me, one white and the other black, the principles of good
and evil; come on.'

We continued our journey.

'Ludwig,' my comrade soon began, 'such extraordinary things
happen in this world that our understandings ought to humiliate
themselves in fear and trembling. You know I have never been here
before. Well, yesterday I dreamt, and today I see with open eyes
the dream of last night rise again before me; look at that landscape
– it is the same I beheld when asleep. Here are the ruins of the old
château where I was struck down in a fit of apoplexy; this is the
path I went along, and there are my four acres of vines. There is
not a tree, not a streamlet, not a bush which I cannot recognise as
if I had seen them hundreds of times before. When we turn the
angle of the road we shall see the village of Welcke at the end of
the valley; the second house on the right is the burgomaster's; it

has five windows on the first floor and four below, and the door. On the left of my house – I mean the burgomaster's – you see a barn and a stable. It is there my cattle are kept. Behind the house is the yard; under a large shed is a two-horse wine-press. So, my dear Ludwig, such as I am you see me resuscitated. The poor burgomaster is looking at you out of my eyes; he speaks to you by my voice, and did I not recollect that before being a burgomaster and a rich sordid proprietor I have been Hippel the bon vivant, I should hesitate to say who I am, for all I see recalls another existence, other habits and other ideas.'

Everything was in accordance with what Hippel had described. We saw the village at some distance down in a fertile valley between hillsides covered with vines, houses scattered along the banks of the river; the second on the right was the burgomaster's.

And Hippel had a vague recollection of every one we met; some seemed so well known to him that he was on the point of addressing them by name; but the words died away on his lips, and he could not disengage his ideas. Besides, when he noticed the look of indifferent curiosity with which those we met regarded us, Hippel felt he was entirely unknown, and that his face, at all events, sufficed to mask the spirit of the defunct burgomaster.

We dismounted at an inn which my friend assured me was the best in the village; he had known it long by reputation.

A second surprise. The mistress of the inn was a fat gossip, a widow of many years' standing, and whom the defunct burgomaster had once proposed to make his second wife.

Hippel felt inclined to clasp her in his arms; all his old sympathies awoke in him at once. However, he succeeded in moderating his transports; the real Hippel combated in him the burgomaster's matrimonial inclinations. So he contented himself with asking her as civilly as possible for a good breakfast and the best wine she had.

While we were at table, a very natural curiosity prompted Hippel to inquire what had passed in the village since his death.

'Madame,' said he with a flattering smile, 'you were doubtless well acquainted with the late burgomaster of Welcke?'

'Do you mean the one that died in a fit of apoplexy about three years ago?' said she.

'The same,' replied my comrade, looking inquisitively at her.

'Ah, yes, indeed, I knew him!' cried the hostess; 'that old curmudgeon wanted to marry me. If I had known he would have died so soon I would have accepted him. He proposed we should mutually settle all our property on the survivor.'

My dear Hippel was rather disconcerted at this reply; the burgomaster's amour propre in him was horribly ruffled. He nevertheless continued his questions.

'So you were not the least bit in love with him, madame?' he asked.

'How was it possible to love a man as ugly, dirty, repulsive, and avaricious as he was?'

Hippel got up and walked up to the looking-glass to survey himself. After contemplating his fat and rosy cheeks he smiled contentedly, and sat down before a chicken, which he proceeded to carve.

'After all,' he said, 'the burgomaster may have been ugly and dirty; that proves nothing against me.'

'Are you any relation of his?' asked the hostess in surprise.

'I! I never even saw him. I only made the remark some are ugly, some good-looking; and if one happens to have one's nose in the middle of one's face, like your burgomaster, it does not prove any likeness to him.'

'Oh no,' said the gossip, 'you have no family resemblance to him whatever.'

'Moreover,' my comrade added, 'I am not by any means a miser, which proves I cannot be your burgomaster. Let us have two more bottles of your best wine.'

The hostess disappeared, and I profited by this opportunity to warn Hippel not to enter upon topics which might betray his incognito.

'What do you take me for, Ludwig?' cried he in a rage. 'You know I am no more the burgomaster than you are, and the proof of it is my papers are perfectly regular.'

He pulled out his passport. The landlady came in.

'Madame,' said he, 'did your burgomaster in any way resemble this description?'

He read out—

'Forehead, medium height; nose, large; lips, thick; eyes, grey; figure, full; hair, brown.'

'Very nearly,' said the dame, 'except that the burgomaster was bald.'

Hippel ran his hand through his hair, and exclaimed—

'The burgomaster was bald, and no one dare to say I am bald.'

The hostess thought he was mad, but as he rose and paid the bill she made no further remark.

When we reached the door Hippel turned to me and said abruptly – 'Let us be off!'

'One moment, my friend,' I replied; 'you must first take me to the cemetery where the burgomaster lies.'

'No!' he exclaimed – 'no! never! do you want to see me in Satan's clutches? I stand upon my own tombstone! It is against every law in nature. Ludwig, you cannot mean it?'

'Be calm, Hippel!' I replied. 'At this moment you are under the influence of invisible powers; they have enveloped you in meshes so light and transparent that one cannot see them. You must make an effort to burst them; you must release the burgomaster's spirit, and that can only be accomplished upon his tomb. Would you steal this poor spirit? It would be a flagrant robbery, and I know your scrupulous delicacy too well to suppose you capable of such infamy.'

These unanswerable arguments settled the matter.

'Well, then, yes,' said he, 'I must summon up courage to trample on those remains, a heavy part of which I bear about me. God grant I may not be accused of such a theft! Follow me, Ludwig; I will lead you to the grave.'

He walked on with rapid steps, carrying his hat in his hand, his hair in disorder, waving his arms about, and taking long strides, like some unhappy wretch about to commit a last act of desperation, and exciting himself not to fail in his attempt.

We first passed along several lanes, then crossed the bridge of a mill, the wheel of which was gyrating in a sheet of foam; then we followed a path which crossed a field, and at last we arrived at a high wall behind the village, covered with moss and clematis; it was the cemetery.

In one corner was the ossuary, in the other a cottage surrounded by a small garden.

Hippel rushed into the room; there he found the gravedigger; all along the walls were crowns of immortelles. The gravedigger was carving a cross, and he was so occupied with his work that he got up quite alarmed when Hippel appeared. My comrade fixed his eyes upon him so sternly that he must have been frightened, for during some seconds he remained quite confounded.

'My good man,' I began, 'will you show us the burgomaster's grave?'

'No need of that,' cried Hippel; 'I know it.'

Without waiting for us he opened the door which led into the cemetery, and set off running like a madman, springing over the graves and exclaiming—

'There it is; there! here we are!'

He must evidently have been possessed by an evil spirit, for in his course he threw down a cross crowned with roses – a cross on the grave of a little child!

The gravedigger and I followed him slowly.

The cemetery was large; weeds, thick and dark-green in colour, grew three feet above the soil. Cypresses dragged their long foliage along the ground; but what struck me most at first was a trellis set up against the wall, and covered with a magnificent vine so loaded with fruit that the bunches of grapes were growing one over the other.

As we went along I remarked to the gravedigger—

'You have a vine there which ought to bring you in something.'

'Oh, sir,' he began in a whining tone, 'that vine does not produce me much. No one will buy my grapes; what comes from the dead returns to the dead.'

I looked the man steadily in the face. He had a false air about him, and a diabolical grin contracted his lips and his cheeks. I did not believe what he said.

We now stood before the burgomaster's grave. Opposite there was the stem of an enormous vine, looking very like a boa-constrictor. Its roots, no doubt, penetrated to the coffins, and disputed their prey with the worms. Moreover, its grapes were of a red violet colour, while the others were white, very slightly tinged with pink. Hippel leaned against the vine, and seemed calmer.

'You do not eat these grapes yourself,' said I to the gravedigger, 'but you sell them.'

He grew pale, and shook his head in dissent.

'You sell them at Welcke, and I can tell you the name of the inn where the wine made from them is drunk – it is the Fleur de Lis.'

The gravedigger trembled in every limb.

Hippel seized the wretch by the throat, and had it not been for me he would have torn him to pieces.

'Scoundrel!' he exclaimed, 'you have been the cause of my drinking the quintessence of the burgomaster, and I have lost my own personal identity.'

But all on a sudden a bright idea struck him. He turned towards the wall in the attitude of the celebrated Brabançon Männe-Kempis.

'God be praised!' said he, as he returned to me, 'I have restored the burgomaster's spirit to the earth. I feel enormously relieved.'

An hour later we were on our road again, and my friend Hippel had quite recovered his natural gaiety.

LOST IN A PYRAMID; OR, THE MUMMY'S CURSE

Louisa May Alcott

One of the most popular authors of her day, Louisa May Alcott (1832–1888) was born in Germantown, Pennsylvania, but spent most of her early life in Boston and in Concord, where she became acquainted with prominent literary figures, including Ralph Waldo Emerson and Henry David Thoreau. According to *The Louisa May Alcott Encyclopedia* (2001), 'Lost in a Pyramid' – which ingeniously amalgamates the mummy and vampire themes – was written in late 1868 or the first week of 1869, and was the last of a string of sensational thrillers Alcott wrote prior to the publication of her classic children's novel *Little Women*. 'Lost in a Pyramid' first appeared in Frank Leslie's magazine *The New World*, on the 16th of January 1869, earning Miss Alcott a fee of $25. Becoming lost over the years, it was rediscovered in 1998 by British Egyptologist Dominic Montserrat, who found it buried deep in the periodicals collection of the Library of Congress in Washington, D.C.

I

'AND what are these, Paul?' asked Evelyn, opening a tarnished gold box and examining its contents curiously.

'Seeds of some unknown Egyptian plant,' replied Forsyth, with a sudden shadow on his dark face, as he looked down at the three scarlet grains lying in the white hand lifted to him.

'Where did you get them?' asked the girl.

'That is a weird story, which will only haunt you if I tell it,' said Forsyth, with an absent expression that strongly excited the girl's curiosity.

'Please tell it, I like weird tales, and they never trouble me. Ah, do tell it; your stories are always so interesting,' she cried, looking up with such a pretty blending of entreaty and command in her charming face, that refusal was impossible.

'You'll be sorry for it, and so shall I, perhaps; I warn you before-hand, that harm is foretold to the possessor of those mysterious seeds,' said Forsyth, smiling, even while he knit his black brows, and regarded the blooming creature before him with a fond yet foreboding glance.

'Tell on, I'm not afraid of these pretty atoms,' she answered, with an imperious nod.

'To hear is to obey. Let me read the facts, and then I will begin,' returned Forsyth, pacing to and fro with the far-off look of one who turns the pages of the past.

Evelyn watched him a moment, and then returned to her work, or play, rather, for the task seemed well suited to the vivacious little creature, half-child, half-woman.

'While in Egypt,' commenced Forsyth, slowly, 'I went one day with my guide and Professor Niles, to explore the Cheops. Niles had a mania for antiquities of all sorts, and forgot time, danger and fatigue in the ardour of his pursuit. We rummaged up and down the narrow passages, half choked with dust and close air; reading inscriptions on the walls, stumbling over shattered mummy-cases, or coming face to face with some shrivelled specimen perched like a hobgoblin on the little shelves where the dead used to be stowed away for ages. I was desperately tired after a few hours of it, and begged the professor to return. But he was bent on exploring certain places, and would not desist. We had but one guide, so I was forced to stay; but Jumal, my man, seeing how weary I was, proposed to us to rest in one of the larger passages, while he went to procure another guide for Niles. We consented, and assuring us that we were perfectly safe, if we did not quit the spot, Jumal left us, promising to return speedily. The professor sat down to take notes of his researches, and stretching myself on the soft sand, I fell asleep.

'I was roused by that indescribable thrill which instinctively warns us of danger, and springing up, I found myself alone. One torch burned faintly where Jumal had struck it, but Niles and the other light were gone. A dreadful sense of loneliness oppressed me for a moment; then I collected myself and looked well about me. A bit of paper was pinned to my hat, which lay near me, and on it, in the professor's writing were these words:

'"I've gone back a little to refresh my memory on certain points. Don't follow me till Jumal comes. I can find my way back to you, for I have a clue. Sleep well, and dream gloriously of the Pharaohs. N.N."

'I laughed at first over the old enthusiast, then felt anxious then restless, and finally resolved to follow him, for I discovered a strong cord fastened to a fallen stone, and knew that this was the clue he spoke of. Leaving a line for Jumal, I took my torch and retraced my steps, following the cord along the winding ways. I often shouted, but received no reply, and pressed on, hoping at each turn to see the old man poring over some musty relic of antiquity. Suddenly the cord ended, and lowering my torch, I saw that the footsteps had gone on.

'"Rash fellow, he'll lose himself, to a certainty," I thought, really alarmed now.

'As I paused, a faint call reached me, and I answered it, waited, shouted again, and a still fainter echo replied.

'Niles was evidently going on, misled by the reverberations of the low passages. No time was to be lost, and, forgetting myself, I stuck my torch in the deep sand to guide me back to the clue, and ran down the straight path before me, whooping like a madman as I went. I did not mean to lose sight of the light, but in my eagerness to find Niles I turned from the main passage, and, guided by his voice, hastened on. His torch soon gladdened my eyes, and the clutch of his trembling hands told me what agony he had suffered.

'"Let us get out of this horrible place at once," he said, wiping the great drops off his forehead.

'"Come, we're not far from the clue. I can soon reach it, and then we are safe"; but as I spoke, a chill passed over me, for a perfect labyrinth of narrow paths lay before us.

'Trying to guide myself by such landmarks as I had observed in my hasty passage, I followed the tracks in the sand till I fancied we must be near my light. No glimmer appeared, however, and kneeling down to examine the footprints nearer, I discovered, to my dismay, that I had been following the wrong ones, for among those marked by a deep bootheel, were prints of bare feet; we had had no guide there, and Jumal wore sandals.

'Rising, I confronted Niles, with the one despairing word, "Lost!" as I pointed from the treacherous sand to the fast-waning light.

'I thought the old man would be overwhelmed but, to my surprise, he grew quite calm and steady, thought a moment, and then went on, saying, quietly:

'"Other men have passed here before us; let us follow their steps, for, if I do not greatly err, they lead toward great passages, where one's way is easily found."

'On we went, bravely, till a misstep threw the professor violently to the ground with a broken leg, and nearly extinguished the torch. It was a horrible predicament, and I gave up all hope as I sat beside the poor fellow, who lay exhausted with fatigue, remorse and pain, for I would not leave him.

'"Paul," he said suddenly, "if you will not go on, there is one more effort we can make. I remember hearing that a party lost as we are, saved themselves by building a fire. The smoke penetrated further than sound or light, and the guide's quick wit understood the unusual mist; he followed it, and rescued the party. Make a fire and trust to Jumal."

'"A fire without wood?" I began; but he pointed to a shelf behind me, which had escaped me in the gloom; and on it I saw a slender mummy-case. I understood him, for these dry cases, which lie about in hundreds, are freely used as firewood. Reaching up, I pulled it down, believing it to be empty, but as it fell, it burst open, and out rolled a mummy. Accustomed as I was to such sights, it startled me a little, for danger had unstrung my nerves. Laying the little brown chrysalis aside, I smashed the case, lit the pile with my torch, and soon a light cloud of smoke drifted down the three passages which diverged from the cell-like place where we had paused.

'While busied with the fire, Niles, forgetful of pain and peril, had dragged the mummy nearer, and was examining it with the interest of a man whose ruling passion was strong even in death.

'"Come and help me unroll this. I have always longed to be the first to see and secure the curious treasures put away among the folds of these uncanny winding-sheets. This is a woman, and we may find something rare and precious here," he said, beginning to unfold the outer coverings, from which a strange aromatic odour came.

'Reluctantly I obeyed, for to me there was something sacred in the bones of this unknown woman. But to beguile the time and amuse the poor fellow, I lent a hand, wondering as I worked, if this dark, ugly thing had ever been a lovely, soft-eyed Egyptian girl.

'From the fibrous folds of the wrappings dropped precious gums and spices, which half intoxicated us with their potent breath, antique coins, and a curious jewel or two, which Niles eagerly examined.

'All the bandages but one were cut off at last, and a small head laid bare, round which still hung great plaits of what had once been luxuriant hair. The shrivelled hands were folded on the breast, and clasped in them lay that gold box.'

'Ah!' cried Evelyn, dropping it from her rosy palm with a shudder.

'Nay; don't reject the poor little mummy's treasure. I never have quite forgiven myself for stealing it, or for burning her,' said Forsyth, painting rapidly, as if the recollection of that experience lent energy to his hand.

'Burning her! Oh, Paul, what do you mean?' asked the girl, sitting up with a face full of excitement.

'I'll tell you. While busied with Madame la Momie, our fire had burned low, for the dry case went like tinder. A faint, far-off sound made our hearts leap, and Niles cried out: "Pile on the wood; Jumal is tracking us; don't let the smoke fail now or we are lost!"

'"There is no more wood; the case was very small, and is all gone," I answered, tearing off such of my garments as would burn readily, and piling them upon the embers.

'Niles did the same, but the light fabrics were quickly consumed, and made no smoke.

'"Burn that!" commanded the professor, pointing to the mummy.

'I hesitated a moment. Again came the faint echo of a horn. Life was dear to me. A few dry bones might save us, and I obeyed him in silence.

'A dull blaze sprung up, and a heavy smoke rose from the burning mummy, rolling in volumes through the low passages, and threatening to suffocate us with its fragrant mist. My brain grew dizzy, the light danced before my eyes, strange phantoms seemed to people the air, and, in the act of asking Niles why he gasped and looked so pale, I lost consciousness.'

Evelyn drew a long breath, and put away the scented toys from her lap as if their odour oppressed her.

Forsyth's swarthy face was all aglow with the excitement of his story, and his black eyes glittered as he added, with a quick laugh:

'That's all; Jumal found and got us out, and we both forswore pyramids for the rest of our days.'

'But the box: how came you to keep it?' asked Evelyn, eyeing it askance as it lay gleaming in a streak of sunshine.

'Oh, I brought it away as a souvenir, and Niles kept the other trinkets.'

'But you said harm was foretold to the possessor of those scarlet seeds,' persisted the girl, whose fancy was excited by the tale, and who fancied all was not told.

'Among his spoils, Niles found a bit of parchment, which he deciphered, and this inscription said that the mummy we had so ungallantly burned was that of a famous sorceress who bequeathed her curse to whoever should disturb her rest. Of course I don't believe that curse has anything to do with it, but it's a fact that Niles never prospered from that day. He says it's because he has never recovered from the fall and fright and I dare say it is so; but I sometimes wonder if I am to share the curse, for I've a vein of superstition in me, and that poor little mummy haunts my dreams still.'

A long silence followed these words. Paul painted mechanically and Evelyn lay regarding him with a thoughtful face. But gloomy fancies were as foreign to her nature as shadows are to noonday, and presently she laughed a cheery laugh, saying as she took up the box again:

'Why don't you plant them, and see what wondrous flower they will bear?'

'I doubt if they would bear anything after lying in a mummy's hand for centuries,' replied Forsyth, gravely.

'Let me plant them and try. You know wheat has sprouted and grown that was taken from a mummy's coffin; why should not these pretty seeds? I should so like to watch them grow; may I, Paul?'

'No, I'd rather leave that experiment untried. I have a queer feeling about the matter, and don't want to meddle myself or let anyone I love meddle with these seeds. They may be some horrible poison, or possess some evil power, for the sorceress evidently valued them, since she clutched them fast even in her tomb.'

'Now, you are foolishly superstitious, and I laugh at you. Be generous; give me one seed, just to learn if it will grow. See I'll pay for it,' and Evelyn, who now stood beside him, dropped a kiss on his forehead as she made her request, with the most engaging air.

But Forsyth would not yield. He smiled and returned the embrace with lover-like warmth, then flung the seeds into the fire, and gave her back the golden box, saying, tenderly:

'My darling, I'll fill it with diamonds or bonbons, if you please, but I will not let you play with that witch's spells. You've enough of your own, so forget the "pretty seeds" and see what a Light of the Harem I've made of you.'

Evelyn frowned, and smiled, and presently the lovers were out in the spring sunshine revelling in their own happy hopes, untroubled by one foreboding fear.

II

'I have a little surprise for you, love,' said Forsyth, as he greeted his cousin three months later on the morning of his wedding day.

'And I have one for you,' she answered, smiling faintly.

'How pale you are, and how thin you grow! All this bridal bustle is too much for you, Evelyn,' he said, with fond anxiety, as he watched the strange pallor of her face, and pressed the wasted little hand in his.

'I am so tired,' she said, and leaned her head wearily on her lover's breast. 'Neither sleep, food, nor air gives me strength, and a curious mist seems to cloud my mind at times. Mamma says it is the heat, but I shiver even in the sun, while at night I burn with fever. Paul, dear, I'm glad you are going to take me away to lead a quiet, happy life with you; but I'm afraid it will be a very short one.'

'My fanciful little wife! You are tired and nervous with all this worry, but a few weeks of rest in the country will give us back our blooming Eve again. Have you no curiosity to learn my surprise?' he asked, to change her thoughts.

The vacant look stealing over the girl's face gave place to one of interest, but as she listened it seemed to require an effort to fix her mind on her lover's words.

'You remember the day we rummaged in the old cabinet?'

'Yes,' and a smile touched her lips for a moment.

'And how you wanted to plant those queer red seeds I stole from the mummy?'

'I remember,' and her eyes kindled with sudden fire.

'Well, I tossed them into the fire, as I thought, and gave you the box. But when I went back to cover up my picture, and found one of those seeds on the rug, a sudden fancy to gratify your whim led me to send it to Niles and ask him to plant and report on its progress. Today I hear from him for the first time, and he reports that the seed has grown marvellously, has budded, and that he intends to take the first flower, if it blooms in time, to a meeting of famous scientific men, after which he will send me its true name and the plant itself. From his description, it must be very curious, and I'm impatient to see it.'

'You need not wait; I can show you the flower in its bloom,' and Evelyn beckoned with the *méchante* smile so long a stranger to her lips.

Much amazed, Forsyth followed her to her own little boudoir, and there, standing in the sunshine, was the unknown plant. Almost rank in their luxuriance were the vivid green leaves on the slender purple stems, and rising from the midst, one ghostly-white flower, shaped like the head of a hooded snake, with scarlet stamens like forked tongues, and on the petals glittered spots like dew.

'A strange, uncanny flower! Has it any odour?' asked Forsyth, bending to examine it, and forgetting, in his interest, to ask how it came there.

'None, and that disappoints me, I am so fond of perfumes,' answered the girl, caressing the green leaves which trembled at her touch, while the purple stems deepened their tint.

'Now tell me about it,' said Forsyth, after standing silent for several minutes.

'I had been before you, and secured one of the seeds, for two fell on the rug. I planted it under a glass in the richest soil I could find, watered it faithfully, and was amazed at the rapidity with which it grew when once it appeared above the earth. I told no-one, for I meant to surprise you with it; but this bud has been so long in blooming, I have had to wait. It is a good omen that it blossoms today, and as it is nearly white, I mean to wear it, for I've learned to love it, having been my pet for so long.'

'I would not wear it, for, in spite of its innocent colour, it is an evil-looking plant, with its adder's tongue and unnatural dew. Wait till Niles tells us what it is, then pet it if it is harmless. Perhaps my sorceress cherished it for some symbolic beauty – those old Egyptians were full of fancies. It was very sly of you to turn the tables on me in this way. But I forgive you, since in a few hours, I shall chain this mysterious hand forever. How cold it is! Come out into the garden and get some warmth and colour for tonight, my love.'

But when night came, no-one could reproach the girl with her pallor, for she glowed like a pomegranate flower, her eyes were full of fire, her lips scarlet, and all her old vivacity seemed to have returned. A more brilliant bride never blushed under a misty veil, and when her lover saw her, he was absolutely startled by the almost unearthly beauty which transformed the pale, languid creature of the morning into this radiant woman.

They were married, and if love, many blessings, and all good gifts lavishly showered upon them could make them happy, then this young pair were truly blest. But even in the rapture of the moment that made her his, Forsyth observed how icy cold was the little hand he held, how feverish the deep colour on the soft cheek he kissed, and what a strange fire burned in the tender eyes that looked so wistfully at him.

Blithe and beautiful as a spirit, the smiling bride played her part in all the festivities of that long evening, and when at last light, life and colour began to fade, the loving eyes that watched her thought it but the natural weariness of the hour. As the last guest departed, Forsyth was met by a servant, who gave him a letter marked 'Haste.' Tearing it open, he read these lines, from a friend of the professor's:

'DEAR SIR – Poor Niles died suddenly two days ago, while at the Scientific Club, and his last words were: "Tell Paul Forsyth to beware of the Mummy's Curse, for this fatal flower has killed me." The circumstances of his death were so peculiar, that I add them as a sequel to this message. For several months, as he told us, he had been watching an unknown plant, and that evening he brought us the flower to examine. Other matters of interest absorbed us till a late hour, and the plant was forgotten. The professor wore it in his buttonhole – a strange white, serpent-headed blossom, with pale glittering spots, which slowly changed to a glittering scarlet, till the leaves looked as if sprinkled with blood. It was observed that instead of the pallor and feebleness which had recently come over him, that the professor was unusually animated, and seemed in an almost unnatural state of high spirits. Near the close of the meeting, in the midst of a lively discussion, he suddenly dropped, as if smitten with apoplexy. He was conveyed home insensible, and after one lucid interval, in which he gave me the message I have recorded above, he died in great agony, raving of mummies, pyramids, serpents, and some fatal curse which had fallen upon him.

'After his death, livid scarlet spots, like those on the flower, appeared upon his skin, and he shrivelled like a withered leaf. At my desire, the mysterious plant was examined, and pronounced by the best authority one of the most deadly poisons known to the Egyptian sorceresses. The plant slowly absorbs the vitality of whoever cultivates it, and the blossom, worn for two or three hours, produces either madness or death.'

Down dropped the paper from Forsyth's hand; he read no further, but hurried back into the room where he had left his young wife. As if worn out with fatigue, she had thrown herself upon a couch, and lay there motionless, her face half-hidden by the light folds of the veil, which had blown over it.

'Evelyn, my dearest! Wake up and answer me. Did you wear that strange flower today?' whispered Forsyth, putting the misty screen away.

There was no need for her to answer, for there, gleaming spectrally on her bosom, was the evil blossom, its white petals spotted now with flecks of scarlet, vivid as drops of newly spilt blood.

But the unhappy bridegroom scarcely saw it, for the face above it appalled him by its utter vacancy. Drawn and pallid, as if with some wasting malady, the young face, so lovely an hour ago, lay before him aged and blighted by the baleful influence of the plant which had drunk up her life. No recognition in the eyes, no word upon the lips, no motion of the hand – only the faint breath, the fluttering pulse, and wide-opened eyes, betrayed that she was alive.

Alas for the young wife! The superstitious fear at which she had smiled had proved true: the curse that had bided its time for ages was fulfilled at last, and her own hand wrecked her happiness for ever. Death in life was her doom, and for years Forsyth secluded himself to tend with pathetic devotion the pale ghost, who never, by word or look, could thank him for the love that outlived even such a fate as this.

PROFESSOR BRANKEL'S SECRET

Fergus Hume

Fergus Hume (1859–1932) was born in England but spent his formative years in New Zealand. In his youth he attended high school in Dunedin, and later studied law at the University of Otago. It was, however, a career as a writer that he had his heart set upon, eventually achieving success in this field when his novel *The Mystery of a Hansom Cab* (1886) became a worldwide sensation, selling half a million copies in the two years after its publication. Virtually unknown by comparison is the following story, which originally appeared in Dunedin's *Saturday Advertiser* (November–December 1882). Four years later it was published in a cheap paperback edition specially intended for sale at railway bookstalls. Subtitled 'A Psychological Study,' this eerie thriller involves mesmerism, medieval chemistry, and an attempted virgin sacrifice.

I

(Extracts From The Diary of Professor Brankel).

'Of a truth, sir, this oyster may contain a most precious jewel.'

HEIDELBERG, *August 26th*, 1876. – Last night, having to prepare my lecture on chemistry for my students, I left my house and went to the library of the University in order to verify some remarks relative to the chemical discoveries of the fourteenth century. I had no difficulty in finding the books I wanted, all of them being well-known. I had finished, and was about to roll up my notes, when on glancing over them I saw that I had omitted to verify a remark as to Giraldus von Breen.

Giraldus von Breen was a famous but somewhat obscure alchemist of the middle ages, whose life was wholly spent in searching after the philosopher's stone. As the point I wished to elucidate was rather important, I went back to find the 'Giraldus.' I hunted for a long time, but was unable to discover anything of the book I wanted. In despair I consulted the librarian, and he told me that he had seen a copy of the 'Giraldus' in two volumes about a year ago, but had lost sight of it since. He also added that it was but little known, and that until myself no one had inquired for it, with the exception of a young Englishman, who had left Heidelberg about eight or nine months back. Under these circumstances nothing could be done, as the book was evidently not in the library; so, in despair, I took myself home in no very amiable frame of mind at my failure.

August 27th. – I lectured today to my students, and during my discourse I mentioned how unfortunate I had been with regard to the 'Giraldus.' At the end of my lecture Herr Buechler, one of my students, desired to speak with me, and said he thought he could tell me where to find the 'Giraldus.' I asked him where, and he said he had lodged in the same house with a young Englishman called Black, who had left Heidelberg about eight months ago. Of course, I immediately guessed that this was the young Englishman mentioned by the librarian. Herr Buechler also said that the young Englishman was a great admirer of the works of Giraldus von Breen, and constantly studied them. He thought it likely that Herr Black had taken them from the library to read at his lodgings, and, as he had left a number of books behind him, the two volumes might be amongst them. I immediately accompanied Herr Buechler to the late lodgings of the young Englishman, and found there a great number of old books, principally works on chemistry. Both Herr Buechler and myself hunted for a long time without success, but at last the 'Giraldus' was found hidden under a pile of old manuscripts. Thanking Herr Buechler for his trouble, I took the 'Giraldus' home with me, and spent the night in taking notes from it for my next day's lecture on the chemistry of the fourteenth century. It was in the old blackletter type, and bound in faded yellow leather, stamped with the arms of Giraldus. It was a matter of great regret to me that I had only the first volume; doubtless the Englishman had the second, as Herr Buechler and myself had searched too thoroughly among the books to leave any doubt as to it being among them.

August 28*th*. – Coming home tonight, I was smoking in my study after dinner when I caught sight of the 'Giraldus' lying on the table where I had thrown it the previous night. I took it up and began to turn over the leaves idly, when a piece of paper fell out on the floor. I took no notice, as it was evidently only a bookmark, but went on reading and turning over the leaves. I became so absorbed in the book that three o'clock struck before I found that I had finished the volume and had let my pipe go out. I arose, yawned, and proposed to myself to retire, when I thought that I would have one more pipe. I looked about for a piece of paper to light it, when I caught sight of the slip that had dropped out of the 'Giraldus.' It was lying under the table, and, bending forward, I picked it up. Twisting it into shape, I held it over the flame of the lamp. In doing so I caught sight of some writing on it, and, being of a curious turn of mind, I withdrew it and spread it out to make an examination. I found that it was not paper as I had thought, but a piece of parchment yellow with age. It was so very dirty that on close examination all I could make out was the figure *V* and the words *erecipsa* and *is*. I could not guess the meaning of this. I knew that the first was the Roman numeral for five, and that *is* was an English word, but I could not understand the meaning of *erecipsa*. I examined the paper more particularly in order to find out anything likely to elucidate the mystery, and saw that there were other words which I could not decipher, as the paper was so dirty and my light so dim. As this was the case, I thought it best to defer all further examination until next day.

August 29*th*. – As soon as I could get away from my duties, I hurried home, eager to discover the meaning of the mysterious words on the parchment. I washed it gently in warm water in order to remove the dirt, and then, with the aid of a strong magnifying glass, I made out the words. They were in black-letter type, and I translate them word for word into modern writing. The following is a copy of the writing translated from the blackletter type:

IV. X. II. seremun sudlariG, V silev erics arutuf is . . . amenev saecsim euqsatib alli taedua atiretearp erecipsa? . . . is sumina mutnat utitser alos etsev simina ni te silev ereuxe ilos metsev VVRLXXLR.

It was evidently a cryptogram – that is, the words had been purposely thrown into confusion to conceal some secret. I was determined to find it out. Giraldus von Breen, although an obscure chemist, might by some strange chance have discovered a great secret of nature which had escaped his more famed contemporaries. The task which I now set myself to do was to unravel the cryptogram and find out the secret it contained. The question which immediately presented itself was how to begin. There did not seem to be any starting-point, so I laid down the parchment in order to consider some method. By a singular coincidence I had a few months before been reading Jules Verne's scientific romance, 'A Journey to the Centre of the Earth,' and I remembered the clever elucidation of the cryptogram therein. I went to my bookcase, and took down the romance of Monsieur Verne in order to read the part I refer to. Having done so, I again took up my own puzzle, and endeavoured to find out its meaning.

In the first place the figures *VVRLXXLR* at the end were underlined, which evidently showed that they were of great importance. They were rather disconnected from the rest of the writing. I noticed there were two figures of each kind, two fives and two tens. The thought then came into my head to add them up. The total was thirty. I then counted the words of the cryptogram (including also the Roman numerals), and I found they also came to the number of thirty. I was certain now that the figures were a key to the writing, and puzzled over it for four or five hours in order to find out the meaning. At last I gave it up in despair, and went to bed, where I had a nightmare, and thought that I was a cryptogram somebody was trying to elucidate.

August 30*th*. – All day long I have puzzled over that cryptogram, trying to find out the connection between the figures and the writing. When I went home I shut myself up in my study, and proceeded to steadily work out the mystery. Again the figures *VVRLXXLR* met my eyes; and this time I noticed the letters. What might *RL* and *LR* mean? One was the reverse of the other. In puzzling over this, I noticed a Hebrew Talmud lying on my desk, which I had borrowed in order to verify a quotation. While looking at it, the thought came into my head of the strange peculiarity of the Hebrew language, being read backwards, and from right to left. As this struck me, I looked at the figures, and immediately thought of applying it.

VVRL evidently meant, read *V* and *V* from right to left; *XXLR* read *X* and *X* from left to right. The number of words was thirty; and the total of the underlined figures the same. The cryptogram was, without doubt, divided into two sections of five words each, and two sections of ten words each, which made a total of thirty. If I counted five words from the first, and read from right to left, I would get at the meaning. Then the question came, should I count two fives in sequence, and then two tens? I thought not. If there were two fives and two tens, it would be more likely that the maker of the cryptogram only put them thus: *VV*, *RL*, *XX*, *LR*, to mislead, and that the proper way to arrange the words would be to divide them into sections of five, ten, five, ten, and read them as instructed.

Pursuing this method, I read the first five letters from right to left, the next ten from left to right, and did the same with the other two sections. This was the result:—

sudlariG seremun II. X. IV.

V silev erics arutuf is . . . . . . euqsatib saecsim amenev alli taedua

mutnat sumina is . . . . . erecipsa atiretearp

utitsev alos etsev simina ni te silev ereuxe ilos metsev.

Arranging this in its order it came out:—

sudlariG seremun II. X. IV. V. silev erics arutuf is

. . . . *euqsatib saecsim amenev alli taedua mutnat sumina is . . . . .? erecipsa atiretearp utitsev alos etsev simina ni te silev ereuxe ilos metsev.*

Thus far the document had assumed a more feasible aspect, and I had great hopes of unravelling it. On looking at my last effort, however, I found myself as far back as ever, for the words made no sense. In fact, they were not words at all, but a mere jumble of letters. I laid it down at last, and betook myself to my pipe in order to ponder over some method for the solution of the problem. I caught up the romance of Jules Verne, and it opened at the twenty-eighth page. I read carelessly until I came to the last sentence of the page: 'Aha! clever Satenussenum,' he cried, 'you had first written out your sentence the wrong way.'

I immediately dashed down both book and pipe, and with a shout proceeded to apply the idea to my cryptogram with this result:-

Vestum soli exuere velis et in animis veste sola vestitu prae-terita aspicere? Si animus tantum audeat illa venema misceas bitasque. Si futura scire velis V. IV. X. II. numeres Giraldus.

At last I had solved the problem. It was written in Latin, and oh, what vile Latin; but still I easily made it out, and write it down here in good German.

Wouldst thou cast thy vestments of clay, walking unclad, save in thy soul garment, and view past ages? If thy spirit dareth as much, mingle then these drugs, and drink. If thou wouldst know the future add V. IV. X. II., Giraldus.

When I read these marvellous words my brain reeled and, staggering to the table, I filled up a glass with brandy, and drank it off. To think that I had rediscovered this wonderful secret and by the merest chance. What infinite power it would give me: by mingling these drugs. But what drugs? The cryptogram did not mention any. I got out my magnifying glass, and examined the paper carefully. At last I succeeded in making out a number of small red letters, which looked like Greek. My own magnifying glass was not powerful enough; so I sent to my brother-professor, Herr Palamam, to borrow his. When it came, I again applied myself to the red letters, and at last succeeded in making out the names. They are rare and valuable drugs, but I shall not inscribe them even in thee, my diary, for fear they should meet any prying eye. I shall share my mighty power with no one; I shall walk through the realms of the past alone.

II

Extracts From the Diary of Professor Brankel (Continued).

'If it is
Within the circle of this orbëd universe,
I'll have this secret out before the sun.'

OCTOBER 16*th*. – After great trouble I have at last succeeded in obtaining the rare and costly drugs mentioned; I have mingled them in their due proportions as required, and the result is a colourless liquid like water, which has no taste and a faint perfume as of Eastern spices. Tonight I shall try the strength of this drink for the

first time, and, if it fulfils its mission, then who so powerful as I!
Oh, what glories I anticipate! My soul will leave this heavy clinging
garb of clay; it will shake off 'this mortal coil,' as the English
Shakespeare says, and roam light as air through the infinite splendour of the past. The centuries themselves will roll back before me
like the flood of Jordan before the redeemed Israelites. At my bidding
will Time, the insatiable, withdraw the many-tinted curtains of the
past, and usher me into the presence of bygone days. I shall sweep
on wings of light through the countless aeons of the past – yea,
even unto the portals of creation.

October 17*th*. – I have passed the night under the influence of
the elixir, and the result has more than surpassed my thoughts and
desires. Oh, how can I paint the sublime majesty of the scenes
through which I have passed? Tongue of man cannot describe them,
nor pen portray them. They, like the seven thunders in the
Apocalypse, have uttered their voices, and must now be sealed up
– only the spiritual eye of man can behold them, and it would be
vain to give even a faint reflection of their splendours. Weary does
the day seem to me, and eagerly do I wait for the cool, calm night,
in which I can again throw off this cumbersome dress of flesh and
assume my spiritual robes. What monarch is so powerful as I? To
the world I am the professor of chemistry at Heidelberg – to myself
I am a demigod, for to me alone are shown the visions of the past,
and to me alone it is permitted to commune with the mighty dead.

October 18*th*. – Once more have I walked through dead ages. My
feet have pressed the dusty and silent floors of the palace of Time,
and I have wandered spirit-clad through the deserted splendours of
his mansion. But yet there remains the future. How can I lift the
immutable veil which hangs before the altar of Time, and enter the
holy of holies? How can I see with clear eyes the splendid goal
reserved for humanity, the triumphant consummation of the design
of the world? What mean those last mysterious words of the cryptogram? *If thou wouldst know the future, add V IV X II, Giraldus?*
I have searched through the book in vain, and I can find nothing
to give me the slightest clue to their solution. What is the drug
which will admit me behind the veil of Time, and compel him to
reveal his deepest secrets? The secret is evidently contained in the
numerals; but how to discover the meaning? I have puzzled over

this problem for hours, but as yet I am no nearer the end than before.

October 19*th*. – Eureka: I have found it. At last I see the meaning of the mysterious sentence. After a sleepless night I have at last hit on what appears to be the solution of the enigma. After lengthy scrutiny I have come to the conclusion that it means the fifth word of the fourth line of the tenth page of the second volume of Giraldus. But how to get that second volume? I went to the lodgings lately occupied by the young Englishman, and turned over all his books, but was unable to find any trace of the missing volume. I questioned Herr Buechler, and he informed me that the young Englishman had been a student at the University for about two years. (I remembered him, when this was told me, as a thin, cadaverous youth, who attended my chemistry class.) He had left Heidelberg on suddenly being summoned, as he said, to the deathbed of his father. He might have taken the second volume of Giraldus with him, for he was always reading it. I asked Herr Buechler the reason. He replied that Herr Black was trying to find out about the philosopher's stone, and that Giraldus gave an account of it in his second volume. I remembered then that in the first volume Giraldus says he will touch on that branch of chemistry in the second. After this I had not the least doubt in my mind as to the fate of the second volume of the Giraldus. Only one thing remained to me – to leave for England at once, in order to get it. For such a trivial cause as the loss of a book, was I to rest contented, and not avail myself of the splendid promise held out to me? A thousand times no; I shall start as soon as possible for England . . . .

October 29*th*. – I have gathered all the information concerning the young Englishman procurable, and that is very little. The information was furnished me by Herr Buechler, who told me that about two months after the departure of Herr Black from Heidelberg, he had received a letter from him, written from the Anchor Hotel, London. This is all the basis I have to go upon; I have to find out the Anchor Hotel, and depend upon the result of my visit there for my next step. It is understood among my friends that I am going for a little trip to England – I have a letter of introduction to Professor Home, of Oxford, and one to Sir Gilbert Harkness, of Ashton Hall, Hampshire. The latter has an immense library, and a passion for collecting rare and curious books. I look to him to assist me in discovering the 'Giraldus.' But he shall never know what I want with it – no man shall possess my secret; I shall reign alone over the realms of the past.

November 10*th*. – I write this portion of my diary in the Anchor Hotel, London; and I have found out some more particulars concerning the young Englishman. The Anchor Hotel is an obscure inn in a little dark street, and is only frequented by the poorer class. I asked the landlord if he remembered a person named Black staying at his hotel six months ago, and described his personal appearance. The landlord is a big, fat, stupid Saxon, and does not remember, but his wife, a sharp and active woman, does. She said that such a person did reside there for a month. He had paid in advance, but seemed very poor. He was always reading and muttering to himself. He left the hotel one day with his luggage, saying he was going to Black's bookstall, and since then nothing had been heard of him. Thanking the landlord's wife, I set off in search of Black's bookstall. Perhaps Black is his father; he is evidently some relation, or perhaps the bookstall is his own.

November 11*th*. – I have hunted all day without success. Black's bookstall is not very well known, but towards the end of the day I met a policeman who told me that he thought there was a bookstall of that name, in Van Street. I am going tomorrow to see.

November 12*th*. – I have found Black's bookstall, but not the 'Giraldus.' I went to Van Street, and found it there as described by the policeman. It was wedged up between two tall houses, and had a crushed appearance. I entered, and asked to see some book which I named. The owner of the bookstall was a little old man with white hair, dressed in a rusty black suit, who took snuff. I led the conversation up to a certain point, and then asked him if he had a son. He said yes, but that his son was dead. He said that he had sent him to Germany to study about three years ago, but that he had returned to die only three months back. I told him who I was, and the old man seemed pleased. He had been very proud of his son. I asked him if his son had brought home with him from Germany the second volume of the works of Giraldus von Breen. The old man thought for a long time, and replied that he had done so. I asked him where the book now was. He said he had sold it to a literary gentleman about a month ago. I requested the name of the purchaser. The bookstall keeper could not tell me, but he said the gentleman had the largest library of old books in England, and had said he was writing a history of chemistry. It must be Sir Gilbert Harkness. He has a very large library, and I know that he is writing a history of chemistry, for I was told so in Germany. He must have required the 'Giraldus' for reference. I thanked the old man, and left the bookstall. There is no doubt in my mind now but that the book I seek is in the library of Sir Gilbert Harkness. I start for his place tomorrow.

III

In the Library.

> 'Behold this pair, and note their divers looks,
> A man of letters and a man of books;
> With various knowledge each is stuffed and crammed. Oh!
> Yes, they are indeed *arcades ambo.*'

SIR Gilbert Harkness was a bookworm.

All his life he had fed and fattened on books, until they had become part of himself. When they (the books) found themselves in the citadel of his heart, they turned and devoured all the other passions until the heart of their victim was emptied of all save themselves. Sir Gilbert found himself at the age of fifty with a brain weary of its cumbersome load of knowledge, and eyes dim with long study to acquire that same load. Left an orphan at the age of twenty, master of his own actions and a magnificent fortune, he had spent all his time and much of his money in filling the shelves of his library. He spared no cost in procuring any rare and valuable book, and on his frequent visits to London he would be found turning over the dusty treasures of the old bookstalls with eager hands. The nature of the man could be seen at once by the way in which he smoothed and caressed his treasures. How tenderly did he brush the dust off the back of some antique volume; how gloatingly did his eyes dwell on its yellow pages, as they displayed their store of blackletter type. He honoured Fust and Caxton above all men, and looked up to them with as much reverence as the world does to its great heroes. He would descant for hours on the extraordinary excellence of the printing of John de Spira, and would show with pride a quaint old folio of Caxton which he had picked up in some dingy bookstall. But his bookish propensities had devoured dragon-like the rest of his passions, and beyond his library he was a childish and simple man. He never went out save on some bookish expedition, but passed his days in his great library, cataloguing his treasures and writing his history of chemistry. To give an exhaustive and critical work on this subject, he had collected at enormous expense a great number of famous books by German chemists. He was a tall, thin man, with a stoop, doubtless caused by his sedentary habits; and clad in his long velvet dressing gown, with his thin white hair scattered from under a velvet skull cap, he looked like a magician of medievalism. He was standing by the quaint diamond-paned window of his library, examining a book which he had just received from London, and his eyes, dim and blear with work, were bent on the yellow page in a severe scrutiny of the text. All around him were books from floor to ceiling, in all kinds of binding, of shapes and sizes. They had overflowed the shelves, and were piled in little heaps here and there upon the floor. They were scattered on all the chairs, they were heaped upon his writing-table, they were lying on the ledge of the window, they peered out of all the pockets of his dressing-gown – wherever the eye turned it saw nothing but books, books, books.

Good heavens! What an amount of learning of industry was collected between those four walls. East, west, north, south, ancient, mediæval, and modern; representatives of all time and all countries were there. Oh, shades of Fust, Gutenberg, and Caxton, if, indeed, spirits be permitted to revisit the 'glimpses of the moon,' come hither and feast your spiritual eyes on your progeny. In these myriad bindings, many-coloured as the coat of Joseph, is the spirit of past ages preserved. Here you will find the supreme singer of the world, Shakespeare himself, fast bound betwixt these boards, and as securely prisoned as ever the genie was under the seal of Solomon in the Arabian tale. Open yon grim brown folio, and lo! Homer will step forth, followed by all the fresh untrodden generations of the world. Ulysses, with his sea-weary eyes, eagerly straining for the low rocky coast of Ithaca. Helen, with her imperial beauty, standing on the towers of Illium. Achilles, with his angry face set fierce against the walls of windy Troy, over the dead body of his friend. All, all are there, and will appear to thee in their fresh eternal beauty if thou sayest but the word. Truly, the deftest necromancer of the middle ages held not half the airy spirits and fantastic fancies under the spell of his wand as thou dost, oh, Gilbert Harkness.

Outside, the short November twilight is closing in, and Sir Gilbert finds that the fat black letters are all running into one blurred line under his eager eyes. A knock at the door of his library disturbs him, and it is with a spirit of relief that he pitches the volume on the table and calls, 'Come in.' A servant enters with a card, which Sir Gilbert takes to the window, and reads in the failing, grey light: 'Otto Brankel.'

'Show the gentleman in,' he says, and then looks at the card again. 'Brankel? Brankel?' he murmurs, in a dreamy tone; 'where have I heard that name? Nuremburg? Leipzig?'

'No! Heidelberg,' interrupts a voice, and looking up he sees a tall, slender man wrapped in a fur greatcoat, regarding him with a smile.

'Heidelberg,' repeated Sir Gilbert. 'Ah, yes; are you not the Professor of Chemistry there?'

'I have that honour,' replied the visitor, sinking with a complacent sigh into the chair indicated by the baronet. 'I must apologise for this untimely visit, but I have a letter of introduction to you from Professor Schlaadt, and I was so impatient that I thought I would lose no time, but present it at once.'

The baronet took the letter, and glancing rapidly over it, shook the Professor warmly by the hand.

'I am delighted to make your acquaintance, Professor,' he said, eagerly. 'I have heard a great deal about your learning and research.'

'A mere nothing,' said the Professor, with a deprecating glance and a wave of his hand; 'mere scraps of knowledge, picked out of the infinite ocean of learning. You have a wonderful collection of books here. I heard about your library in Germany'; and he cast a keen glance round into all the dark corners of the room.

'Ah, you do not see all,' said Sir Gilbert, with a grateful smile, as the servant brought in a lamp and placed it on the writing-table; 'this dim light does not show it to advantage.'

'The fame of it has penetrated to Heidelberg,' said the Professor, with another glance round.

'Perhaps that is because I have so many of your German works on chemistry,' returned Sir Gilbert. 'You know that I am writing a History of Chemistry.'

'Have you any alchemists of the fourteenth century – any of their works I mean?' asked Brankel, with a faint glow of interest.

'Oh, yes,' answered the baronet, pointing towards a dark corner of the library, where the Professor's gaze eagerly followed him. 'You will find there Rostham von Helme, Gradious, Giraldus.'

The Professor's hands were resting lightly on the arms of the chair, but at the last word he gripped them hard. However, he merely observed coldly:

'"Giraldus" is rather a rare book, is it not?'

'Yes,' replied the baronet, slowly. 'I got it by a curious chance. I—'

'Oh, Governor! Governor!' cried a clear ringing voice, and a young lady in a riding habit, all splashed with mud, stepped lightly through the window into the room. 'Such a splendid run. Fiddle-de-dee carried me splendidly, I was in at the death,' displaying a fox's brush, 'so was Jack. I was the only lady; we came home in about half an hour – both nags quite worn out, which I am sure I don't wonder at. Jack has behaved like a trump all day, so as a reward I have brought him to dinner – come in, Jack.'

A young gentleman in a hunting costume, likewise splashed with mud, in reply to this invitation also came in through the window. He was advancing with a smile towards Sir Gilbert when the young lady suddenly caught sight of the Professor, who had risen at her entry and was standing somewhat in the shade.

'Visitor, dad?' she said, carelessly, shifting the folds of her riding-habit, which was lying on her arm. 'Introduce me, dear.'

'My daughter – Philippa – Professor Brankel,' said Sir Gilbert, in a vexed tone. 'I do wish, Philippa, you would come in at the door like a Christian and not by the window like a—'

'Pagan; eh, dad?' said Philippa, with a laugh.

She was looking at the Professor, and his eyes seemed to have a magnetic attraction for her. The German had stepped out of the shade, and the light of the lamp was striking full on his face, which the girl regarded curiously. It was a remarkable face – a white complexion with jet black hair, brushed back from a high forehead;

dark, bushy eyebrows, with a Mephistophelian curve over light and brilliant eyes, a thin hooked nose, and a nervous cruel mouth unclothed by moustache or beard. Such was the appearance of the famous German Professor of Chemistry. Philippa appeared fascinated by this weird countenance staring at her with flashing eyes. And yet she was not a girl given to superstition – rather the opposite – having a bold audacious nature which did not know fear. But there was something in the steady burning gaze of the German that mastered her at once.

She was a tall slender girl, very beautiful, with masses of dark hair coiled under a coquettish hat set daintily on her well-shaped head. Her eyes flashed with a mixture of fun and mischief, while her rather large mouth displayed a row of very white teeth when she smiled. She looked charming in her dark blue riding-habit and white gloves, with a linen collar at her throat caught by a dainty brooch. She was an extremely self-possessed and self-willed young woman. Her mother died when she was quite a baby, and being neglected by her father, who was too busy with his library to attend to her, the education she received was of a loose and somewhat desultory kind. Sometimes she would learn, and astonish everybody with the rapidity of her progress. At other times she would refuse to open a single book, and alternately teased and delighted her friends by her fantastic moods. She was a splendid rider, and most of her childhood's days were spent in scampering about the country with her Shetland pony and Jack.

Jack, otherwise Lord Dulchester, was the eldest son of the Earl of Chesham, whose estate was next to that of Sir Gilbert Harkness. Jack and Philippa were always together, and the wild young lady followed Jack into whatever scrapes he chose to lead her. She copied Jack's manners and speech, and consequently became proficient in slang. But the longest lane has a turning, and at length Sir Gilbert awoke to the fact that something must be done with his erratic offspring. He wrote to his married sister in London, and she promptly suggested a French boarding-school. So one morning Miss Philippa was violently seized and sent into exile; at the same time her companion in mischief, went to Eton. When Miss Harkness returned from her Gallic exile, she found Jack unaltered, and he found her as jolly as ever (so he put it). Their positions, however, were changed, and instead of Philippa following Jack, Jack followed Philippa. He admired her as being the only girl who could ride straight across country, and discuss horses in a proper way. Besides he had known her such a long time that he had had plenty of opportunity of seeing any faults in her, and he had seen none. Having come to the conclusion that she was 'the jolliest girl he had ever met,' he rode over one morning and promptly asked her to marry him. Philippa as promptly refused, politely telling him not to be an idiot. But Lord Dulchester persisted, and ultimately, Miss Harkness – who was really in love – accepted him, and they were engaged. All the county ladies talked of her as 'that misguided girl,' and lamented that Sir Gilbert had not married again in order to give one of the female sex an opportunity to initiate Philippa into the intricacies of good breeding. They were horrified at her fast ways and strong expressions, which even her French education could not eradicate. It was rumoured that she had actually smoked a whole cigarette, and Philippa had laughingly acknowledged the fact to a lady who questioned her about it. When she secured in Lord Dulchester the matrimonial prize of the county, you may be sure the ladies loved her none the more. They accepted her as an unpleasant fact, and hoped that she would improve in time. The male sex liked Philippa because she was handsome, and said witty things about her neighbours; but it was generally acknowledged that she had a wild eye in her head, and would need breaking in, a task which they did not think Lord Dulchester capable of.

That gentleman was a tawny-haired, clean-limbed son of Anak, who stood six feet, and could ride, shoot, and box better than any man in the county.

He was good-looking; had a title, but no brains; and he adored Philippa.

Miss Harkness withdrew her eyes from the remarkable face before her with an uneasy laugh, and introduced Lord Dulchester.

'You will stay to dinner, I hope, Professor?' said Sir Gilbert.

The Professor bowed, whilst Philippa hurried away to change her dress.

Jack followed soon to make himself a little decent, for the dress in which a man has done a hard day's hunting is certainly not the most presentable for dining.

The Professor, left alone with Sir Gilbert, looked round and thought:

'I wonder where the "Giraldus" can be?'

IV

In the Drawing-Room.

'Do you, believe, sir, in metempsychosis?
Of course you don't, but I can tell you, sir,
He was a serpent ere he was a man.'

THERE is no more charming hour in the whole day than the dinner hour, especially after a hard day's hunting. At least so Lord Dulchester thought. In spite of his splashed dress (which he had made as presentable as he could), he felt a sweet, lazy kind of happiness as he sat down at the dinner-table.

The white cloth, the hothouse flowers, the gleaming and antique silver and delicate china, all assembled under the soft light of rose-coloured lamps, made up a very pleasant picture, and Lord Dulchester felt at peace with all mankind. Beside him sat Philippa, dark and handsome in her dinner dress, vivaciously discussing the day's sport.

At the head of the table sat Sir Gilbert, holding an animated conversation on books with the Professor, who was seated near him.

Dulchester had taken a great dislike to the German and set him down in his own mind as a charlatan, although what reason he had for so doing Heaven only knows.

Perhaps the silvery fluency of the foreigner's conversation, together with the mesmeric glances of his wonderful eyes, helped him to the conclusion.

At any rate, the presence of the Professor was to him the one discordant element of the evening.

'I must apologise for my dress, Sir Gilbert,' he said. 'I wanted to go home and change it, but Phil would not let me.'

'Of course not,' retorted that young lady with a laugh, 'you would not have returned till midnight. And I am sure you need not apologize so much,' she went on, merrily; 'you have done the same thing many times before, and on each occasion you have excused yourself in the same manner. Why don't you practise what you preach?'

'Because you won't let me,' said Jack with a laugh, pouring himself out a glass of wine.

'You had good sport today?' asked the Professor, fixing his piercing eyes on Jack.

'Slashing,' replied that young man enthusiastically, setting down his glass, which was half way to his mouth, in order to give more freedom to his eloquence. 'You should have seen the spin the fox led us. We caught him this side of Masterton's Mill. There was one beautiful hedge and ditch which half the field refused, but Miss Harkness cleared it like a bird, and I followed. I think we were neck and neck, Phil, across the next field,' he added, addressing that young lady who was listening with flashing eyes.

'Rather,' she answered, vivaciously; 'and, by Jove! Jack, what a smash old Squire Damer came.'

'Right into the middle of the ditch.'

'He would insist on giving me the lead, and I did laugh when I saw him flying through the air like a fat goose.'

'Serve him right,' growled Jack, who did not think anyone had a right to give Miss Harkness a lead but himself. 'He's too old for that sort of thing.'

'Oh, yes. You will knock off hunting when you reach his age, eh, Jack?' said Philippa, sarcastically.

'Well, I won't ride so many stone, at any rate,' retorted Jack, evasively, applying himself vigorously to his dinner to prevent the possibility of a reply.

Philippa laughed, and then began talking about some newly-imported mare with miraculous powers of endurance and speed ascribed to her.

Jack responded enthusiastically, and their conversation became so 'horsey' as to be unintelligible, except to a Newmarket trainer, or to one of Whyte-Melville's heroes.

Meanwhile, the two scholars were holding an equally mystical conversation in the higher branches of knowledge on the other side of the table.

At last the Professor, by skilful generalship, led the conversation round to the subject dearest to his heart.

'You were going to tell me where you got the "Giraldus," he said, carelessly playing with his glass.

'Ah, yes,' answered Sir Gilbert, leaning back in his chair. 'It was a most curious chance. I was greatly in want of his works, but had not the least idea where to get them. I went up to London, to see my agent about looking through the Continental libraries for them, when one day I found out an old bookstall, kept by a man named Black.'

'Yes?' interrogatively.

'Well, he had it,' replied Sir Gilbert, nodding his head, 'that is, only the second volume. He said it had been brought from Germany by his son, who had lately died. But it is only the second volume. I wish I knew where the first is.'

'I can satisfy your curiosity,' said the German, bending forward; 'the first volume is in the library at Heidelberg.'

'Indeed.' Sir Gilbert looked amazed. 'How did the two volumes come to be separated?'

'The son of the bookstall keeper whom you mention,' said the Professor, nervously twisting a ring on his finger, 'was a student at the Heidelberg University. Being a great admirer of the works of Giraldus, and leaving Heidelberg hurriedly, he carried with him to England the second volume only. I found the first in his lodgings, by chance.'

'Were you looking for it?' asked Sir Gilbert.

'Yes,' answered Brankel. 'I wanted to illustrate a certain point to my class, which I was unable to do satisfactorily without the aid of Giraldus.'

'I must send this second volume back to Heidelberg,' said the bookworm in a vexed tone, 'as it was taken from there.'

'I don't see it,' replied the Professor, calmly. 'Giraldus is a very obscure alchemist, and if you send the value of the book to the University, I dare say you can have the first volume also. By-the-bye, Sir Gilbert, I think I omitted to tell you that I intend to stay in England for at least six months, and any assistance I can afford you I shall be most happy.'

'Oh, thank you,' answered the baronet, eagerly. 'I shall be delighted to avail myself of it. Where are you staying?'

'At present at an hotel in Launceston,' answered the German;

'but I have taken a house near you, which I am about to fit up. I shall be established in it in about a week, and then you may expect to see me pretty frequently in your library.'

'I shall be glad,' said Sir Gilbert; 'but where is the house you have taken?'

'It is called Wolfden,' replied the Professor.

'Wolfden?' exclaimed Philippa, catching the name. 'Are you going to live there, Professor?'

'Yes, why not?' he asked, rather amused at her sudden entry into the conversation.

'It is such a gloomy place,' she answered, with a little nervous laugh, for those serpent eyes were fixed upon her, 'and has not been inhabited for the last twenty years, except by the ghost of the former proprietor, who hanged himself.'

'Ghost? Bah,' said the Professor with a sneer, which wrinkled up the corners of his thin mouth. 'I'm not afraid of that. This is the nineteenth century.'

'Well, ghosts or no ghosts, I wouldn't live there,' replied Philippa gaily, as she rose, 'it's extremely damp, and bad for the health.' And with a bow she swept out of the door, which the Professor held open, for which civility he was rewarded by a frown from Lord Dulchester, who considered that as his special province.

The two savants began to discuss chemistry over their wine, so Dulchester, after moodily toying with his glass for some minutes, rose and went off to the drawing-room in search of Miss Harkness.

He found that young lady seated by the fire, staring dreamily into the heart of the red coals.

He came forward, and, leaning his elbow on the mantelpiece, looked down on her with a smile.

'Dreaming, Phil?' he asked, softly, as he looked into her face, ringed round with the flare of the fire.

'I was thinking of the Professor, Jack,' she said, abstractedly, leaning back and folding her hands. 'Is he not a strange man?'

'I don't like him,' retorted Jack, bluntly.

'Nor do I,' she answered, 'but he has a remarkable face – like Mephistopheles'. I don't read much poetry, but when I saw his eyes I could not help thinking they were like the witch's in *Christabel* – like a serpent's.'

'Does he stay here long?' asked Dulchester, giving the fire a poke with the toe of his boot, and thereby causing the downfall of a fantastical castle of burning coal.

'About six months,' answered Philippa. 'Hand me that fan, Jack; you have made the fire so hot that it is scorching my face.'

Jack did so, and, kneeling down beside her, looked up into her face with a laugh.

'Let us put away all thought of this Professor, sweetheart,' he said, catching her hand, 'and talk of something interesting.'

It must have been very interesting, for Sir Gilbert and the Professor, coming into the room half an hour afterwards, found them in the same position, with Philippa's hand straying through Jack's chestnut curls.

When discovered thus, Jack sprung to his feet with a growl, and became deeply interested in a picture hanging near him, while Miss Harkness directed her attentions to the Chinese pictorial representations on her fan.

The Professor looked at them with a kind of half-sneer, which made Jack long to knock him down, and then, at Philippa's request, went to the piano, and began to play. Sir Gilbert was sound asleep in his armchair by the fire; Jack sat opposite him with his arm resting on his knee and his chin in his hand, watching Philippa, who was flirting with her fan and staring into the fire. Away in the semi-darkness, sat the Professor at the piano, playing the music of Mendelssohn and Schubert. The situation truly 'had its charm,' as Jack thought; but again the presence of the German seemed an unsympathetic element. Besides, Jack did not care for soft harmonics, and preferred the lusty hunting songs of Whyte-Melville to all the pathos and melody of the masters of music.

Yet there was a kind of dreamy soporific influence about the Professor's playing which, at that time, seemed eminently satisfactory.

Suddenly the Professor stopped playing and began to speak.

'I will play a composition of my own,' he said slowly. 'It is called "A Dream Phantasy."'

He commenced to play again, beginning with a low crescendo of minor arpeggios in the bass, gradually ascending and becoming louder and more agitated, then changed the tempo and dreamily gliding into the swing and rhythm of a cradle-song, as if waves of sleep were closing softly over the head of the dreamer.

Then with an introductory prelude of sharp, clear chords came a grand movement in march-time, with the thunder and tread of many feet, and the silver sound of trumpets drifting into a sorrowful and pathetic melody, which seemed full of the grief and pathos of death.

A shower of silvery tones like the falling of summer rain on the sea, and then a wild, delicious waltz, fantastic and capricious as one of Chopin's ethereal compositions.

Then followed a beautifully smooth modulation with wondrous extended harmonies, and the player glided into a quaint barcarolle, as if a boat were afloat on the breast of a calm summer sea, sailing towards the burning heart of the sunset, and drifting—

'By Jove, you know, Jack, I think the run today was the best of the season.'

Philippa had been thinking for a long time before she delivered this eminently commonplace remark.

The Professor thought that she was listening to his music, whereas, her thoughts were far away with the red-coated field, with the gallant fox flying ahead.

He shut down the piano with a crash, and rose to go.

'You'll come over tomorrow,' said Sir Gilbert, as he shook hands.

'Certainly,' answered the Professor, with a smile. 'Goodnight, Lord Dulchester; you don't come my way?'

'No, I ride home,' answered Dulchester, who had no fancy for a talk with this foreigner.

'I will order the carriage, Professor,' said Sir Gilbert, going to the bell.

'Thanks – no,' returned the German, politely stopping him. 'I prefer to walk. Goodnight once more, and goodnight to you, Miss Philippa. I see you do not care for music.'

And with this parting shaft, the Professor bowed himself out with his cold and sardonic sneer, leaving Philippa angry with herself at having betrayed her thoughts so far, and Lord Dulchester with an unholy desire in his heart to 'punch the foreign beggar's head.'

V

The Effect of the Elixir.

'Dreams are the nightly progeny of sleep,
The ghostly visitants which mock our rest;
And yet methinks they give a sovereignty
Within their airy realms to many a wight,
Who wakes to find himself a ragged knave,
And all the rainbow pageants of the night
Only the idle bubbles of the brain.'

'*Launceston, November* 14*th*. – At last I have found the second volume of "Giraldus." By a strange train of circumstances I have been led step by step towards this successful end. Nothing now remains for me to do but to go over Sir Gilbert's library, take up the "Giraldus," and turn to the page indicated by the cryptogram.

'Then shall I be able to supply the missing drug and add the final ingredient to this marvellous elixir. I have no fear of Sir Gilbert learning why I am so anxious about the "Giraldus." And, truth to tell, he cannot even notice that I am anxious, for I carefully repress all manifestations of interest concerning it, beyond that of an admirer of rare books

'I heard him mention today where it was in his library, with as cool and composed a manner as though I had never heard of the book, while every nerve in my body was tingling with excitement. However, I must now curb my impatience until I can see the volume in the ordinary course. Sir Gilbert is a man wholly devoted to his books, and his desires are bounded by the overflowing shelves of his library. He asked me to stay to dinner, and I was introduced to his daughter and her lover. The lover is one of the aristocracy – a brainless young athlete, with the body of a Milo, and the intellect, as Landor says, "of a lizard." But Miss Philippa Harkness, the daughter, is a very strange young woman. It is a long time since I have studied Lavater, and possibly my skill in physiognomy may have declined, but I have rarely seen a more contradictory face. She has intellect, but does not use it. So far as I can see she has not even the average education of an English lady; all her talk is about field sport and horses, while her conversation is full of words which I am certain are not in the English dictionary – at least, not as far as my acquaintance with it goes. She could be clever if she would, but she will not, for one of the most powerful passions of nature is wanting in her. She is not ambitious, and is quite content to pass the days of her life as her senses dictate, without attempting to rise to eminence.

'Strange that Nature, the bounteous, should be so capricious. To one she gives no talents, and ambition; while to this girl she gives talents without ambition.

'During the evening I made the discovery that Miss Harkness does not like me. She talked gaily and courteously enough, but she avoided my eye, and seemed ill at ease when I addressed her. I suppose it is my manner. A scholastic occupation is certainly not the best for acquiring graces, and I am always rather awkward in the presence of women. I also made the discovery during the evening that she has no soul – at least, not for music. While I was playing my "Dream Phantasy," she suddenly broke in with some remark about her day's sport. Bah! why should I be angry? and yet it wounded my self-esteem. I thought that my playing would hold anyone spellbound, and now I find that it has no effect on this woman. If I took the trouble to hate anybody, I should hate this girl. But I never trouble. Her nature is the opposite to mine, and we seem to have a mutual distrust and dislike of one another. Strange I never felt like this before. I had better master this absurd feeling, as I am to see her almost daily for the next six months. In the meantime all my thoughts are concentrated on the "Giraldus." By this time tomorrow I shall know the secret drug, and then— I must go over tomorrow and look up the "Giraldus" without delay.'

Professor Brankel closed his diary, and prepared for bed. Before he put out the light he went to his desk and took out a small phial filled with a colourless liquid. He swallowed three drops; then, putting the phial away, he went to bed, and was soon wrapped in visions created by the strange power of the elixir.

* * * * * *

Behold I stand under the shadows of a moonless and starless night, divested of that gross garment of clay which is the emblem of mortality. The immortal part of myself is severed from the mortal, and I am an airy spirit, nameless and soulless, for I myself am the soul. Nothing of earth has any part in me; I am formed of the ethereal essence which God breathes into the body of man. I have no feelings, physical or mental, but stand a naked human soul, a citizen of the universe, a partaker of eternity. Time draws back the veil of the past, and I enter into the vast halls of his palace, to wander through the populous courts; to see the splendid kaleidoscope of humanity, and the marvellous colours with which the iridescent dome of life 'stains the white surface of eternity.'

* * * * * *

. . . I stand within the mighty arena of the Colosseum, and above me, tier above tier, I see the blood-loving Roman populace gazing down with wolfish eyes on the blood-stained sands. The bright blue sky gleams through the striped awning which shadows the heads of the people. There is Horace, fresh from his little Sabine farm, laughing with Mæcenas; Virgil, with a placid smile on his face, listening to the witty and epigrammatical conversation of Catullus – the Rochester of his day – who is amusing his fickle Lesbia with remarks on the spectators. And he, the master of the world, rose-crowned, looks down with a serene face at the long train of gladiators. Ave Cæsar . . . . The fight begins . . . a battle of Titans. See how their eyes flash . . . how the sparks fly from their shields at every blow. And Fortune, fickle as a woman, gives her favours now to one again to another . . . See, one has fallen . . . and his triumphant adversary stands over him, looking round for the verdict of the people . . . Habet! And the blood of the conquered sinks into the thirsty sands of the arena – insatiable of blood as the masters of the world . . .

. . . Is it thou, O Athens, the omphalos of Greece . . . set like a jewel in the midst of thy green groves, and filled with the superb intellects of antiquity? . . . Behold the great white streets . . . the vivid, sparkling crowd brimming over with veritable Aristophanic humour . . . the wrangling of the philosophers and their pupils from the porticoes, and the god-like figures of the youths as they haste to the gymnasium. Yes, this is indeed the intellectual capital of the world . . . The great theatre, with the semicircle of eager faces gazing spellbound at the splendid pageantry of the 'Agamemnon' . . . The deep-mouthed roll of the Eschylean line fills the wide-ringed theatre with a sublime thunder, and echoes down the vaulted corridors of Time with ever-increasing volume . . . How magnificent . . . the fiery ring of the speech of Clytemnestra . . . the stately eloquence of the king of men . . . the wild cry of Cassandra, shrinking with prophetic horror from the blood-stained threshold of the palace . . . See . . . Chorus.

(Here the entries in the diary were illegible.)

Hail, Queen, with the snow-white breasts and eyes of fire . . . I pray you, wherefore do you look so eagerly from the mighty walls of wide-streeted Troy? . . . Helen . . . fairest and most imperial of women, thy fatal beauty hath doomed the proud towers of Ilium. Think not that yonder light at which thou gazest as it gleams like a crimson-hearted star . . . think not that it comes from the tent of thy forsaken husband . . .

. . . It lights the funeral couch of Patroclus, and beneath its beam sits the sullen-faced Achilles, gazing with wrathful eyes at the dimly-seen walls of Troy . . . Ai: Ai: . . . The end is near, O Queen . . . Thy fatal beauty hath worked out its evil destiny . . . and already the irrevocable fiat has gone forth from the Fates . . . Ai: Ai: . . . Crafty Ulysses, with the cautious wrinkles round thy deep-set eyes, I pray thee tell me where thou art going . . Ithaca: . . . Push off the galley from the shores of Troy . . . Unloose the ten years' bound sail . . . and let us cross the foaming leagues of perilous seas in search of thine island home . . . Lo: how the great sea freshens and whitens under the caress of the winds, and we feel the salt breath of the wandering fields of foam of large savour in our nostrils . . . But lo: what purple land gleams dimly in the distance? . . . Lotus-eaters . . . (Here the diary is illegible.) See . . . how the nymphs sport in the crystal waters . . . the flash of white bodies; the waving of dishevelled locks . . . Ithaca . . . Turn the galley home to where the ever-weaving Penelope awaits thee . . .

Ah, Ithaca.

* * * * * *

. . . Oh, clash and clamour of music . . . the light tread of slave girls scattering flowers . . . the barbaric gleam of scarlet and gold . . . the

martial bearing of the Roman soldiers . . . and she – the serpent of
the Nile – comes for her Roman lover . . . Ah, Cleopatra. Egypt . . .
he with the passionate face, that stretches out his arms to thee,
would sustain the great diadem of the world on his brow, but for
thee, dark-browed gipsy . . . Hark, how the shrill music sounds . . .
he comes. Anthony.

. . . Ancient Egypt, mysterious and marvellous, wrapped in the
deepest mists of antiquity . . . Long slumbrous ranges of palaces . . .
long trains of painted figures on the walls . . . and symbolical hiero-
glyphics . . . Lift up the dense veil which shrouds thy mysterious . . .
countenance, O Isis . . . Behold how the solemn sphynxes in silent
lines gaze wide-eyed at the mysterious Pyramids . . . O mysterious
Egypt . . . hail . . . Osiris . . . Thoth . . . (Here the writing is illegible.)

. . . Strike the timbrel, for Miriam, the prophetess of the Lord,
sings a pæan of victory, and her great brother towers sublime over
the Redeemed Israelites . . . Golgotha . . . Calvary . . . The Cross
. . . who . . . who hangs upon it so still and lifeless? . . . Behind
. . . reddens the evening sky, and the Cross hangs like a thunder-
cloud over Jerusalem . . . Is it then true . . . this which I deemed
a fable? . . . Didst thou die for humanity, O Christ? . . . Ah, lift not
those pain-charged eyes, O Nazarene: . . . see how the red blood
drips from thy thorn-wreathed diadem . . . Prophet . . . Christianity
. . . I am in space, the centre of the . . . great wheel of the universe
. . . around throng the nebulous masses of worlds . . . and this
heaving mass of fire, is this the earth? . . . I stand before the portals
of creation . . . Open . . . God . . . Fire . . . Chaos . . .

The fresh morning breaks slowly in the East, and the dreamer
awakes to the reality of life.

VI

The Last Ingredient of the Elixir.

'A rarer drug
Than all the perfumed spices of the East.'

PHILIPPA was seated at the window of the breakfast room, dressed in
her riding habit. Engaged that morning to ride with Lord Dulchester,

and longing to be in the saddle, she waited his arrival with some impatience. She was reading the *Field*, her favourite paper; every now and then glancing at the clock, or bending down to caress the huge staghound lying at her feet. At last with a laugh she arose, tossed the paper on the floor, and stepped out on to the terrace followed by her dog.

It was a cold, clear morning, with a brisk wind blowing, which brought the blood into Philippa's cheeks in no time. There were a number of pigeons on the terrace, but at her approach they flew away, and she saw them, whirling specks of white, in the cold, blue sky. Miss Harkness stood staring at them for some time, and then, giving her dog's ears a malicious pull, she began to talk to herself.

'I never did see anyone like that Jack of mine. He is always late; it is about half an hour since the time I told him. Ah, there's that dear old pater hard at work; I shall go in and see him.'

The window of the library was open, and, stepping lightly in, she went to her father. He was bending over his writing-table examining a stray leaf of some book, and looked up with a bewildered expression when her shadow fell on him.

'Well, pater,' she said, gaily, laying her gloved hand on his shoulder, 'hard at work? Why don't you come out for a ride, instead of sitting all day among these musty old books?'

'Bless me, Philippa, how you talk,' answered her father, peevishly. 'How can I spare the time? Besides, Professor Brankel is coming to see the library today.'

Philippa turned round without a word and went on to the terrace, where she stood carelessly flicking at the leaves of a cypress which grew near, and thinking deeply. Her dog lay down at her feet, and put his nose between his paws, keeping one bright eye sharply on his mistress, while the other blinked half-asleep. The thoughts of Miss Harkness were not of a pleasant nature. She had forgotten the German, and her father's reminder had brought to her the unpleasant fact that there was such a person. She was by no means a young lady given to fancies, and yet there was that about this Professor she did not like. Although not of an imaginative tendency, his eyes seemed to fascinate her and again she thought of *Christabel*.

'It's one comfort I shall be away all day,' she muttered to herself, 'and he will be gone by the time I come home, that is, if the pater does not ask—'

'Phil! Phil!' cried a voice almost immediately beneath her, and on looking over she saw her tardy lover, mounted on a splendid horse, and looking handsome and fresh, as a young Briton ought to look on riding five miles on a cold morning, with his ladylove at the end of the fifth mile.

'How late you are, Jack,' she cried, catching up her gloves and flying down the steps. 'I've been waiting quite an hour.'

'Couldn't get away,' replied Dulchester, who had dismounted, and was looking with pride at her eager face. 'The governor wanted to consult me about some things, and it was with great difficulty I could come even now.'

'I am to take that explanation with a grain of salt,' laughed Philippa, whose horse had now been brought round.

'Just as you like – with or without salt,' retorted Jack, flinging the reins of his horse to the groom, and standing ready to assist her to mount.

She laughed lightly, put her foot on his hand, and in another moment was in the saddle. She gathered up her reins, and gave Fiddle-de-dee a sharp stroke with her whip, which caused him to dance about in the most alarming manner.

'Now then, Phil, are you ready?' asked Lord Dulchester, who had mounted his own horse and was steering it beside hers.

'Aye, aye, sir,' and away they went down the avenue, leaving the grooms looking after them with intense admiration.

'They're a rare couple,' said one to the other.

'Aye, the finest this part o' the country,' and with a laugh both went inside.

Meanwhile Miss Harkness and her lover had reached the park gates, and had just passed through them when they saw the Professor coming along the road. Philippa's heart gave a jump as she saw those gleaming eyes once more fixed on hers.

'Good morning, Miss Harkness,' said the Professor; 'I see you are indulging in your favourite pastime. I am calling on Sir Gilbert.'

'You will find him in the library,' said Philippa, bowing coldly, while Dulchester passed him with a curt 'Good morning.'

The Professor stood looking after them with a sneer on his face as they rode away laughing and chatting merrily, and the same envy of their happiness came into his heart as Satan felt when he saw Adam and Eve in the garden.

'Oh, Hell, what do mine eyes with grief behold?'

The feeling, however, soon passed, and with a shrug of his shoulders he resumed his way.

He was immediately ushered into the library on his arrival at the Hall, and found its master anxiously expecting his arrival.

'Ah, Professor,' he said, shaking him heartily by the hand, 'I am so delighted you have come. I want to find out a certain point; but first I must show you all my treasures.'

The Professor assented with delight, for he felt the true joy of a bibliomaniac as he stood in this treasure-house of books. All day long they examined the treasures of the shelves, and ate their lunch as hurriedly as possible, eager to return to the feast of intellect. Sir Gilbert found that he had a truly congenial spirit in the Professor, and expounded his favourite theories and rode his favourite hobbies until the twilight began to close in. All this time the astute Professor had been thinking of the 'Giraldus,' but did not ask where it was, fearing lest too great eagerness on his part might cause suspicion in the jealous breast of the bookworm. He led the conversation round to the request which the baronet had made to him when he came into the room.

'You were saying something about a point you wanted elucidated, when I came in, Sir Gilbert,' he said, looking at him keenly.

'Yes, yes,' replied Sir Gilbert, 'it is in regard to the discovery of the philosopher's stone. Can you tell me any notable work on the subject?'

'I think you will find what you require in "Giraldus,"' said the Professor, whose pulse was beating quickly.

'But he is an obscure chemist,' objected Sir Gilbert.

'You find pearls in oysters,' quoth the German, calmly; 'and the obscure chemist gives the best description of the philosopher's stone I have met with.'

'I thought you had never read the "Giraldus?"' said Sir Gilbert, sharply.

The Professor felt that he was on dangerous ground.

'Not the work itself,' he answered, coolly; 'but other authors which I have studied give extracts, and, putting them together, I have arrived at the conclusion that the work of "Giraldus" is the best on the subject.'

'Well, I had better bring the book, and you can show me the part you refer to,' answered Sir Gilbert, and went off to find it.

The Professor sat down in the baronet's chair by the writing-table, and waited with his heart beating rapidly. At last he had arrived at the consummation of his hope, and in another minute would know the name of the drug which was to be of such value to him. Presently the baronet came back and laid on the table an old yellow book, the counterpart of that stored in the Professor's study at Heidelberg. The Professor took it up and turned over the leaves carelessly, although the touch of every page caused a thrill to go through him.

'You had better get Von Helme too,' he said, looking at the baronet. 'I think he will prove also useful to you.'

Sir Gilbert hurried away well pleased, while the Professor took the 'Giraldus' to the window and turned to the tenth page. Then, counting four lines down, he ran his finger along until it stopped at the fifth word, 'maiden's blood . . .'

When Sir Gilbert came back with the book wanted, he found Brankel standing by the window turning over the leaves of the 'Giraldus.' In handing him Von Helme's work he glanced up to see if it was the one required, but recoiled in a moment with a cry,

'Brankel! What ails you?'

The cold light of the evening was striking fair on the face of the German, and the rest of his body was in the shadow. His face was livid, with great drops of perspiration standing on it, and with the jet-black eyebrows, wild hair, and thin, sneering mouth, he looked the incarnation of the arch-fiend – a modern Mephistopheles. When the baronet spoke he turned to him with a cold smile, and the writhe of pain, passing over his face vanished, and left him with his usual countenance.

'I had a spasm of pain,' he explained, gently going back to the study table; 'it is gone now.'

The baronet looked at him doubtfully, and then suggested that some brandy should be brought.

'Nothing, thank you,' replied the Professor, holding the 'Giraldus' with one hand and waving the other. 'I am subject to these attacks. I am perfectly well now. See, here is the remark of Giraldus on the philosopher's stone.' And they were soon deep in the book.

The Professor refused to stay to dinner on the plea that he had an engagement, and hastened away almost immediately. When he got to his hotel he went to his bedroom, and began to write rapidly, in his diary.

November 15th. – At last I have solved this problem, which has been my aim these many days. I have had the second volume of 'Giraldus' in my hands, and on turning to the page mentioned in the cryptogram I find that the mysterious drug is 'maiden's blood.' To bring out the highest powers of the elixir I must mingle with it the heart blood of a pure maiden. It is a terrible ingredient, and will be difficult to obtain, but I shall not shrink, for I consider it my duty to bring this elixir to its highest state. But where am I to find the maiden from whom to obtain the blood?

Murder is a crime generally punished by the gallows. Bah! why do I bring these things into my thoughts? The killing of a person in the cause of science is no murder. If my own blood were necessary I should not hesitate a moment, but give it freely, in order to consummate this great discovery. Before we can wrest the secrets from the great mother, Nature, we must propitiate her with victims. How many human beings have been slain in a less noble cause than this? Was not the daughter of Agamemnon slain by her own father to satisfy the wrath of Artemis? and shall I shrink from offering up a woman on the altar of science? A thousand times no. The cause of science must be advanced even at the cost of human blood, and I, who am appointed by fate to give this secret of Nature to the world, shall not shrink from my task.

Everything is prepared, the altar, the priest, and the victim, for Miss Harkness will have the honour of contributing her heart's blood to this great discovery. I have made up my mind that she is to die in this cause; and what greater honour can I offer her? Do not the Hindoo maidens immolate themselves cheerfully under the death-dealing wheels of the chariot of their god, and shall an Englishwoman shrink from sacrificing herself in the cause of science? I cannot tell her my wish, for such is the lack of ambition in her soul that she would not comprehend the magnitude of the thing, and doubtless refuse. I must decoy her into my power.

It is a terrible thing to do, no doubt, but in my case must be used the motto of the Jesuits, 'The end justifies the means.' Did I believe in the existence of a Supreme Being I would pray to him to direct me; but as I have no such belief I must kneel to thee, O Science, and entreat thine aid to bring about this sacrifice on thy shrine. The blood of this one maiden will be of more value to the world than that which thousands of human beings have shed on the fields of Marathon and Waterloo.

VII

Wolfden.

'Good gentlemen,
The house is stuffed with ghosts, pray you be wary;
For every footfall wakes a hundred fiends,
Who have the power to do us devilries.'

It was a queer, rambling old place, built of grey stone, almost hidden in dark-green ivy. The stones in some places were so eaten away and cracked by the lapse of years that it seemed to be held together by the clinging parasite. A quaint, picturesque house, it was built in the Elizabethan style of architecture, with narrow, diamond-paned windows, huge stacks of chimneys twisted into all kinds of fantastic shapes; and little red-roofed turrets starting out of the walls at all sorts of odd corners, and clinging to the grey old stones like birds' nests. Under the sloping eaves – where the swallows built every summer – over the great oaken doors, beside the elaborately wrought windows, grotesque faces, carved out of stone into a fixed grin, peered everywhere, like the goblin inhabitants of the deserted mansion. Grass grew between the crevices of the broad stones of the balcony, thistles waved in the deserted courtyard, and everywhere there was a damp, green slime. Some of the shutters, torn off by the force of the wind, were lying half-buried in the grass beneath, while others hung crazily on their broken hinges, and swung noisily with every breeze.

It had formerly been a place of great magnificence, and the lofty ceilings of the state rooms were decorated with beautiful paintings. But the broad oaken stairs, down which had come so many generations, were thick with dust, and the pale moon, looking through the painted windows, saw only dreary rooms filled with floating shadows. But it was not the loneliness of the place that made it such a thing of horror to the simple folk around. There was said to be a curse on it, for the last proprietor had hanged himself, after spending the remains of his fortune in a last banquet. In the great dining-hall a ragged piece of rope, suspended from a hook in the wall, still showed the place where he committed the deed. It was here, after that last terrible orgy was done – after he had exhausted the wine of life, and found that the lees were bitter indeed – that he came and launched himself into another world. His ghost was said to haunt the scene of his former follies, and wail for the past that could not be undone. But the lights which announced his presence were probably only the glimmer of the moon on the glittering windows; and the wail of the wind whistling through the deserted halls, his voice. But the rustics would have been indignant at such a solution, and firmly held to the belief that, whatever modern science might say to the contrary, there were ghosts, and that Wolfden was haunted by one.

On the death of the last squire the estate had gone into Chancery, and the place to rack and ruin. No tenant could be found for it, even in this ghost-despising age, for the place was eerie, and a cloud hung over it. When the German Professor took it he was looked upon as a wonderfully brave man; and, indeed, it was whispered among the village gossips that he must have some acquaintance with the black art itself since he could trust himself so fearlessly among the ghostly inmates of Wolfden. Superstition still has her votaries, even in this enlightened age, among those lonely hills, and the strange-looking foreigner gave rise to many queer surmises.

The Professor did not occupy all the house, but only a small range of rooms on the right side. Those on the left were the state rooms, and these he shut up, leaving them to their dust and loneliness. Immediately above the rooms on the right side was an octagon-shaped apartment, which the Professor turned into a laboratory for the prosecution of his chemical experiments. A light could be

seen in this room far into the small hours, for the Professor preferred
working at night instead of in the daytime. All day he was at the
Hall, in the library with Sir Gilbert, hunting among the books, and
helping the baronet with his History of Chemistry. Sir Gilbert was
the only member at the Hall with whom the German was on friendly
terms. Philippa avoided him, and showed plainly that she did not
relish his company, while Lord Dulchester made no attempt to
conceal his dislike – a dislike which the Professor cordially returned.
The German kept a vigilant watch on Philippa, anxious to seize any
opportunity which might offer itself of getting her into his power,
for he was firmly resolved in his hideous purpose of killing her so
as to add the last ingredient to the elixir. Wherever Philippa went
she found those mesmeric eyes fixed steadily on her, like two evil
planets blighting her with their malignant influence. Under this
continual supervision she began to grow thin and pale. At all times
she felt the burning gaze of those eyes, and would start nervously
at every sound. Nature could not bear the strain, and at last Philippa
saw that unless she removed herself from the influence of the
Professor, she would soon be very ill. To this end she took a sudden
resolution, and unfolded it to Jack in this wise:

'Jack,' said she, one evening, when they were alone in the drawing-room, and the Professor and Sir Gilbert were talking science
over their wine; 'do you believe in the evil eye?'

Lord Dulchester, who was gazing idly into the fire, turned round
in dismay.

'Good heavens, Philippa, what put that idea into your head?'

'I believe the Professor has the evil eye,' went on Philippa, solemnly.
'Whenever I look at him I always find his eyes fixed on me.'

'Just give me leave, and I'll soon settle his eyes,' said Jack, grimly.

'Don't be a fool, Jack,' was Miss Philippa's ungrateful retort; 'he
is a friend of papa's.'

'He doesn't stay here,' replied Dulchester, sulkily.

'I don't see what that has to do with it,' answered Philippa,
candidly; 'he *is* here every day. But, Jack,' she went on, 'I can't
stand this much longer. I am sure I shall be ill—'

'You do look rather pale,' interjected Jack, eyeing her anxiously.

'So I have made up my mind to go up to London and stay with
Aunt Gertrude.'

'Oh!'

Lord Dulchester gave a shiver. He had reason to remember that high-browed, Roman-nosed matron, who had hunted him through several seasons in the most determined manner, to secure him for one of her daughters, who were all equally high-browed and Roman-nosed.

'Don't make faces, Jack,' said Philippa, smiling, for he had confided to her the system of social persecution to which her cousins had subjected him. 'You need not come.'

'Oh, won't I though,' retorted Dulchester, vivaciously. 'I am not afraid; I am an engaged man now.'

'Jack,' said his ladylove, solemnly, with a malicious twinkle in her eye, 'let me implore you not to let my beautiful cousins win your heart from me, for you know your engagement will be no obstacle; and oh, Lord Dulchester, they have brought the art of flirting to a very high state of perfection.'

'Let them try it on,' said Jack, laughing gaily at the idea; 'I am quite willing to risk it, Phil.'

And so it was arranged. Philippa wrote to her aunt and received an effusive answer, stating that she would only be too glad, especially as they were going for the winter to the south of France; did dear Philippa mind? No, dear Philippa didn't; she would have gone to the North Pole if necessary, to escape from those terrible eyes of the Professor. So she began to make arrangements, and fixed an early day for her departure.

* * * * * *

Wolfden, November 22nd. – I have been peculiarly unfortunate with regard to the last ingredient of the elixir. I am no nearer the accomplishment of my desire than before. Miss Harkness persistently avoids me, and I am unable to get her alone. That lover is always with her, and I suspect would have no hesitation in doing me a personal injury. He hates me, I see, for he does not take the least pains to conceal his feelings. This is unfortunate, for it adds to my difficulties in the accomplishment of my design. I have asked Miss Harkness over here, but she persistently refuses to come; and at times I despair of getting her at all. Now, to add to my difficulties in the matter, she has arranged to go to the south of France, where, as she told me, she will probably stay for a long time. It is an impossibility for me to prolong my stay in England beyond the six months, so if she goes away now there is every probability that I shall lose her. There is yet a week before she leaves, so I may think of some plan before then whereby to accomplish my purpose.

The thought often comes across me that if I kill her I shall be liable to the law of England. The law has no sympathy with the sacred cause of science, and would hang me for the murder (as it would call it) as calmly as if I were some common felon who had beaten his wife to death. It cannot be helped. If I wish to perfect this great discovery I see that there is no alternative but to become a victim to the law. But my discovery will live after me, and I shall be looked on as a glorious martyr to the cause of science. I will give this diary – in the event of my being hanged for the sacrifice of this girl on the altar of science – to some learned savant in my own country, to edit, and the world shall see how gradually I was led to the crowning act of my life. I shall be honoured as a martyr; therefore I have no hesitation in committing the deed which is likely to bring me within the arm of the law. 'The blood of the martyrs is the seed of the Church,' and my death shall be the means of giving to man an elixir by which to foresee both past and future. He will be able to see far ahead, and avert from the world those calamities which hitherto have fallen on it owing to the darkness which has veiled the future. What are a few pangs of physical pain in comparison with the splendid future thus open to the world through my agency? My mind is made up – I am ready and willing to fall a martyr in the cause of science against the powers of ignorance, and over my grave shall be inscribed the one word so pregnant with meaning – 'Resurgam!'

* * * * * *

One! strikes slowly with a sound like thunder from the grey old belfry of the church. Midnight – this is the hour during which the earth is thronged with spirits. They pour from the green graveyards, from the charnel house; the murderer descends from his gibbet, and the rich man rises from his vault. The air is filled with ghosts; their incorporeal forms throng in myriads thick as the leaves of Vallombrosa.

Wolfden stands black and dense in front of the calm splendour of the moon; the stars shine on it with their myriad eyes, but they cannot lift the shadow from off it. And he who lies within – is he mingling with the airy spirits of the dead, or dreaming of the accomplishment of his hideous purpose? Is he mad? Is his potent elixir only the outcome of a confused brain? Or is he a glorious genius shaping the form of a great discovery? Is he mad? Was Hamlet?

How still the night; only the murmur of the river as it flows, broad-breasted and fair towards the infinite sea. A few barges lie on the surface of the stream, black, shapeless masses, hanging, as in the centre of a hollow globe, between the star-spread sky and its counterpart in the breast of the river. The distant cry of an owl sounds from the belfry, an answer comes from another at Wolfden, and then the bell again – one! two!

Hark! the wind is rising; the hollow-voiced bell has woke it, and it rushes with wild and querulous voice through the deserted halls. Whew! how it whistles through the great dining-room, and shakes the jagged fragment of rope to and fro as if in glee. The old Squire's spirit is abroad tonight. Whew! how it catches the crazy shutters and shakes them to and fro until one falls with a shriek, and the wind rushes away, rejoicing in its work. Whirr! what a blast down the chimney – the laboratory – what armies of phials, what queer cabalistic apparatus. There are a few ashes in the furnace. How the fierce wind makes them flare and blaze redly like the angry eye of the Cyclops. Away down the old oak stairs, where the moon, looking through the painted windows, casts a red stain on the dust. Whew! into the bedroom of the Professor. Blow the curtains aside, and let yon thin shaft of moonlight strike on his face. How calm, how passionless. Is the spirit indeed in the body, or is his discovery a great truth? How deadly pale, with the black eyebrows, and the black hair wildly tossed about on the pillow. Look how his hand is clenched. A shade sweeps across his face. Is it the spirit returning to the body, or a cloud drifting across the face of the moon? Is he mad? Does that great brow only bind the fantastic humours of a madman's brain? Is he mad? Who can tell? Time alone will work out the solution of that problem. Leave him to his dreams and phantasies. Away! out to sea, where the great ships ride on the white waves. Whew! away! Whirr – whew! Look how the clouds drive across the midnight sky. Oh! this is rare sport; hark! the white surges of the Atlantic cry aloud. Whew! and the wind sweeps away into the black pavilion of clouds which hangs over the boiling gulf of the ocean.

VIII

In the Laboratory.

> 'Whene'er a man
> Is near the pinnacle of his desire,
> "What ho!" cries Death, and lo, he tumbles down.'

JUST outside the gates of Wolfden stood a large hawthorn, whose branches, bare of leaves, were shaking wildly in the keen November blasts. It was raining heavily, and the sky was overcast with heavy clouds, while there was not a speck of blue to give any promise of clearing up.

Under the hawthorn, trying to get some shelter from the driving rain, stood Lord Dulchester and his fiancée. They had come out for a short walk, and had been caught in the full fury of the storm outside the gates of Wolfden. Jack drew Philippa under the hawthorn, but they might as well have been in the open for all the protection that delusive shelter afforded them. They were a quarter of a mile away from the Hall; the storm gave no promise of clearing away, and the nearest place in which they could take shelter was Wolfden, which Philippa resolutely declined to enter.

'I can't go in while that horrible man is there,' she said, in reply to Jack's persistent entreaties.

'I like him as little as you do,' retorted Dulchester, bluntly; 'but I'm not going to have you get your death of cold for anything of that sort. We have no umbrella. Wolfden is the nearest shelter, and the storm won't clear away for some time, so the best thing we can do is to go in.'

Philippa cast a disconsolate look around. It was raining vigorously, and the road was full of little puddles. She had her furs on, but her feet were wet, so at last she consented to try the hospitality of the Professor.

'"Beggars mustn't be choosers,"' she said, miserably. 'Lead on, Macduff.'

Macduff (otherwise Lord Dulchester) pushed open the gate, and, letting Philippa pass through, shut it with a bang. The house looked dreary and gloomy in the rain, but they had little time to inspect it. They hastened up the path, and soon found themselves at the huge oaken door. Jack applied the knocker vigorously, and in a few minutes the door was opened by the Professor himself. He expressed the greatest surprise at seeing them, and inwardly determined that he would accomplish his design at once, since the elements had put his victim into his power.

'You had better come upstairs to my laboratory,' he said, shaking Dulchester by the hand, which civility that gentleman did not at all relish. 'It is the only place where there is a fire.'

'I prefer to wait here,' said Philippa, coldly, looking out at the steady rain.

'Permit me to observe, Miss Harkness,' said the Professor, blandly, 'that I am a bit of a doctor, and you are very likely to catch cold standing here in your wet clothes.'

'You had better go, Phil,' struck in Jack, giving himself a shake like a huge water-dog. 'I'll come too.'

The Professor acquiesced in this arrangement with at least some show of pleasure, and led the way upstairs to his laboratory.

It was an octagon-shaped room, with a triple-arched, diamond-paned window, and a furnace nearly opposite. There were a multitude of instruments, and phials, containing drugs required for chemistry, scattered about, and on a small table were writing materials.

Opposite the door which gave entrance from the body of the house was a smaller and massive-looking door, bound with iron; it was partly open, but nothing could be seen beyond.

The Professor led his unexpected visitors into this workshop of science, and, having apologized for the disorder, put Philippa in a chair in front of the furnace. He removed a portion of the top, so that more heat could get at her, and then asked his visitors if they would take any wine. Both of them declined, so the Professor set his wits to work to get Dulchester out of the way.

Jack was rather taken with the queer apparatus about, and the quick-witted German, seeing this, began explaining various experiments to him. Philippa sat looking dreamily into the fire, and drying her wet boots, while her lover and the Professor moved about. At last Dulchester found himself close to the iron-bound door.

'What have you in here, Professor?' he asked, pushing it slightly open with his hand.

The Professor's eyes flashed. Here was a chance he had not reckoned upon of getting rid of Dulchester.

'Go and see,' he said, with a laugh. Jack, feeling curious, stepped in, upon which the Professor pulled the door to. It was a spring door, and shut with a click. Hearing this Philippa turned round.

'Where is Lord Dulchester?' she asked, rising from her chair in alarm.

'In there,' answered the Professor, with a harsh laugh of triumph, pointing to the door.

'Hallo, Professor, let me out,' called Jack, with a kick at the door.

The Professor paid no attention, but advanced towards Philippa.

'Let him out, Professor,' she said, with a calmness she was far from feeling, for she did not like the look in his eyes. 'I think we will go now; the storm has cleared away.'

The Professor did not answer, but pulling a drawer out of the table, produced from it a long steel knife, the edge of which he felt with a hideous smile. Philippa felt her heart leap, and would have fainted, but that she knew all her courage would be needed in this terrible situation.

'Young lady,' said the Professor, looking at her with a triumphant smile, and speaking slowly, 'some months ago I made a great discovery which requires one thing to perfect it. That is the blood of a pure and innocent maiden. I have chosen you as the person who is to assist at the consummation of this great secret of Nature. You will have had a short life but an eternal fame.'

Philippa's heart turned sick within her as she saw the long blade of the knife, and the wild fire in his eyes.

'It is an honour,' he went on in the same monotonous tone, 'to be an aid to the great cause of science. What is death? Only a pang, and then all is over. Are you prepared?'

The poor girl breathed a prayer to God, and fixed her eyes steadily on the madman.

'You have been my father's guest,' she said in a hard voice, which

sounded unnatural to her own ears. 'Will you stain your hands with
the blood of his daughter?'

'It is an honour,' answered the madman, with a cruel smile,
running his thumb along the edge of the knife. 'Prepare.'

Philippa had retreated to the window as he advanced, and she
looked round for some weapon of defence. On the windowsill by
her side stood a huge bottle filled with some chemical preparation.
At an ordinary time, she could not have lifted it, but at the present
moment the terrible danger gave her strength, and, catching it up,
she turned round on the German.

He was now standing immediately in front of the furnace, and
she could see the fire blazing up behind him.

'Advance another step and I will throw this,' she cried, despairingly.

'It is an honour,' he repeated, still advancing, with a vacant smile.

She closed her eyes in desperation, and flung the bottle at him
with all her strength. It struck the madman on the shoulder, causing
him to stagger against the furnace, and then fell with a crash into
the burning heat of the fire. Immediately there was a terrible explosion, and Philippa saw a wall of flame rise up before her as she
sank insensible on the floor.

* * * * * *

Meanwhile Jack, guessing that there was something wrong,
hammered at the door with unabated vigour, but finding that it
resisted all his efforts, looked round for some way of escape.

He was in a long, narrow room, and at the end a small window
gave an indistinct light. Jack hurried towards this and dashed it
open. He got outside on the ledge which ran round the house, and
found himself about twenty feet from the ground. The ivy which
grew in profusion over the walls offered a natural ladder. So, not
hesitating a moment, he scrambled down. How he reached the
ground he did not know, but as soon as he found himself there he
ran round to the front, in at the door which the Professor had left
open, and up the stairs.

The door of the laboratory was closed. But that was no obstacle,
for the athlete, putting his shoulder to it, burst it open, and on
entering found the room full of smoke. He stumbled over a body

lying on the floor, and on bending down saw it was that of the Professor, lying in a pool of blood.

Hastily he stepped over him, and discovered Philippa lying under the window insensible. He caught her in his arms, and, carrying her downstairs, called loudly for the servants.

On their appearance, he sent them to see after the Professor, while he laid Philippa on a sofa in the sitting-room, and sprinkled her face with water. She opened her eyes with a low moan, and, on seeing Jack's face bending over her, caught his arm with a convulsive sob.

'Oh, Jack,' she gasped, 'what has happened?'

'That's what I should like to know,' said Jack, anxiously, as she sat up.

'The Professor wanted to kill me,' she said, looking at him with a haggard face, 'and I threw some bottle at him. It fell into the fire, there was an explosion, and I knew no more.'

Jack did not say anything, but telling one of the servants to go for the Launceston police took her home.

* * * * * *

Of course the affair caused a nine days' wonder. The back of the Professor's head was blown away, and death must have been instantaneous. The bottle evidently contained some dangerous drug, which exploded on touching the fire. He was buried in England, and news of his death was sent to his relatives in Germany.

Sir Gilbert was horrified at the event, and came to the conclusion, as did everyone else, that the German was mad. Philippa's system sustained a severe shock, and she was ill for a long time.

She is now Lady Dulchester, and her husband is devotedly attached to her.

The diary of the Professor fell into the hands of Sir Gilbert, and it was from it that Lady Dulchester learned the strange series of events which had so nearly cost her her life.

Jack is very proud of his wife's bravery, but she can never recall without a shudder that terrible hour when she discovered the Professor's secret.

* * * * * *

Note by Dr R. Andrews. – I was on a visit to Sir Gilbert Harkness, and in the library found the diary of the late Professor Brankel. I read it, and was deeply interested in the wonderful example which it afforded me of the workings of a diseased brain. Sir Gilbert had a phial of the elixir which the Professor claimed to have discovered, and on analysing it I found that the principal ingredient was opium. Without doubt this was the cause of his visions and hallucinations as described by him in his diary. Whether he did find the cryptogram which led to his discovery I do not know, but the quantity of opium and other drugs which he took must have sent him mad.

From the earlier portions of his diary I am inclined to think that he must have had the germs of insanity in him, which developed under the evil influence of the drink which he called the elixir.

I obtained leave from Sir Gilbert to publish the portions of the diary contained in this story (which I translated from the German), and from what was told me by Lady Dulchester and her husband, I pieced the rest of the story together.

The opium vision in Chapter V. struck me as peculiarly strange. It seems to embrace short and vivid pictures of what the dreamer saw, and must have been written by him immediately after he awoke in the morning. In the diary it was written hurriedly, and was so illegible that I could not make portions of it out.

The workings of this man's mind are peculiarly interesting, and this fact, coupled with the strange series of events linking it to the outer world, led me to publish this story. Of a certainty there is no truer saying than, 'Truth is stranger than fiction.'

JOHN BARRINGTON COWLES

Arthur Conan Doyle

Sir Arthur Ignatius Conan Doyle (1859–1930) was born in Edinburgh, and began writing while studying medicine at the University of Edinburgh. His first published story was 'The Mystery of the Sasassa Valley,' which appeared in *Chambers's Edinburgh Journal* in 1879. Many other works of fiction by this author appeared in print over the next fifty years, but all were eclipsed by his brilliant stories chronicling the adventures of Sherlock Holmes, beginning with *A Study in Scarlet* in 1887. The character's popularity soared to greater heights with the publication of the first series of Sherlock Holmes short stories in *The Strand Magazine*, and within a few years Doyle had become one of Britain's best-paid authors. The following story, 'John Barrington Cowles,' made its first appearance in the April 1884 issue of *Cassell's Saturday Journal*, and received its first book publication in *Dreamland and Ghostland: An Original Collection of Tales and Warnings from the Borderland of Substance and Shadow, Vol. III* (1887). Like many macabre stories from the late 19th century, it reflects Victorian men's anxieties over unleashed female sexuality, as a result of which beautiful, strong-willed women were invariably depicted as seducers and destroyers of men. In this particular instance, the femme fatale is a psychic vampire who uses hypnotism to subjugate her victims.

The Story of a Medical Student.

PART I

It might seem rash of me to say that I ascribe the death of my poor friend, John Barrington Cowles, to any preternatural agency. I am aware that in the present state of public feeling a chain of evidence would require to be strong indeed before the possibility of such a conclusion could be admitted.

I shall therefore merely state the circumstances which led up to this sad event as concisely and as plainly as I can, and leave every reader to draw his own deductions. Perhaps there may be some one who can throw light upon what is dark to me.

I first met Barrington Cowles when I went up to Edinburgh University to take out medical classes there. My landlady in Northumberland Street had a large house, and, being a widow without children, she gained a livelihood by providing accommodation for several students.

Barrington Cowles happened to have taken a bedroom upon the same floor as mine, and when we came to know each other better we shared a small sitting-room, in which we took our meals. In this manner we originated a friendship which was unmarred by the slightest disagreement up to the day of his death.

Cowles' father was the colonel of a Sikh regiment, and had remained in India for many years. He allowed his son a handsome income, but seldom gave any other sign of parental affection – writing irregularly and briefly.

My friend, who had himself been born in India, and whose whole disposition was an ardent tropical one, was much hurt by this neglect. His mother was dead, and he had no other relation in the world to supply the blank.

Thus he came in time to concentrate all his affection upon me, and to confide in me in a manner which is rare among men. Even when a stronger and deeper passion came upon him, it never infringed upon the old tenderness between us.

Cowles was a tall, slim young fellow, with an olive, Velasquez-like face, and dark, tender eyes. I have seldom seen a man who was more likely to excite a woman's interest, or to captivate her imagination.

His expression was, as a rule, dreamy, and even languid; but if in conversation a subject arose which interested him be would be all animation in a moment. On such occasions his colour would heighten, his eyes gleam, and he could speak with an eloquence which would carry his audience with him.

In spite of these natural advantages he led a solitary life, avoiding female society, and reading with great diligence. He was one of the foremost men of his year, taking the senior medal for anatomy, and the Neil Arnott prize for physics.

How well I can remember the first time we met her! Often and often I have recalled the circumstances, and tried to recall what the exact impression was which she produced on my mind at the time.

After we came to know her my judgment was warped, so that I am curious to recollect what my unbiased instincts were. It is hard, however, to eliminate the feelings which reason or prejudice afterwards raised in me.

It was at the opening of the Royal Scottish Academy in the spring of 1879. My poor friend was passionately attached to art in every form, and a pleasing chord in music or a delicate effect upon canvas would give exquisite pleasure to his highly-strung nature. We had gone together to see the pictures, and were standing in the grand central salon, when I noticed an extremely beautiful woman standing at the other side of the room.

In my whole life I have never seen such a classically perfect countenance. It was the real Greek type – the forehead broad, very low, and as white as marble, with a cloudlet of delicate locks wreathing round it, the nose straight and clean cut, the lips inclined to thinness, the chin and lower jaw beautifully rounded off, and yet sufficiently developed to promise unusual strength of character.

But those eyes – those wonderful eyes! If I could but give some faint idea of their varying moods, their steely hardness, their feminine softness, their power of command, their penetrating intensity suddenly melting away into an expression of womanly weakness – but I am speaking now of future impressions!

There was a tall, yellow-haired young man with this lady, whom I at once recognized as a law student with whom I had a slight acquaintance.

Archibald Reeves – for that was his name – was a dashing, handsome young fellow, and had at one time been a ringleader in every university escapade; but of late I had seen little of him, and the report was that he was engaged to be married. His companion was, then, I presumed, his fiancée. I seated myself upon the velvet settee in the centre of the room, and furtively watched the couple from behind my catalogue.

The more I looked at her the more her beauty grew upon me. She was somewhat short in stature, it is true; but her figure was perfection, and she bore herself in such a fashion that it was only by actual comparison that one would have known her to be under the medium height.

As I kept my eyes upon them, Reeves was called away for some reason, and the young lady was left alone. Turning her back to the pictures, she passed the time until the return of her escort in taking a deliberate survey of the company, without paying the least heed to the fact that a dozen pair of eyes, attracted by her elegance and beauty, were bent curiously upon her. With one of her hands holding the red silk cord which surrounded the pictures, she stood languidly moving her eyes from face to face with as little self-consciousness as if she were looking at the canvas creatures behind her. Suddenly, as I watched her, I saw her gaze become fixed and, as it were, intense. I followed the direction of her looks, wondering what could have attracted her so strongly.

John Barrington Cowles was standing before a picture – one, I think, by Noel Paton – I know that the subject was a noble and ethereal one. His profile was turned towards us, and never have I seen him to such advantage. I have said that he was a strikingly handsome man, but at that moment he looked absolutely magnificent. It was evident that he had momentarily forgotten his surroundings, and that his whole soul was in sympathy with the picture before him. His eyes sparkled, and a dusky pink shone through his clear olive cheeks. She continued to watch him fixedly, with a look of interest upon her face, until he came out of his reverie with a start, and turned abruptly round, so that his gaze met hers. She glanced away at once, but his eyes remained fixed upon her for some moments. The picture was forgotten already, and his soul had come down to earth once more.

We caught sight of her once or twice before we left, and each time I noticed my friend look after her. He made no remark, however, until we got out into the open air, and were walking arm-in-arm down Prince's Street.

'Did you notice that beautiful woman, in the dark dress, with the white fur?' he asked.

'Yes, I saw her,' I answered.

'Do you know her?' he asked, eagerly. 'Have you any idea who she is?'

'I don't know her personally,' I replied. 'But I have no doubt I could find out all about her, for I believe she is engaged to young Archie Reeves, and he and I have a lot of mutual friends.'

'Engaged!' ejaculated Cowles.

'Why, my dear boy,' I said, laughing, 'you don't mean to say you are so susceptible that the fact that a girl to whom you never spoke in your life is engaged is enough to upset you?'

'Well, not exactly to upset me,' he answered, forcing a laugh. 'But I don't mind telling you, Armitage, that I never was so taken by any one in my life. It wasn't the mere beauty of the face – though that was perfect enough – but it was the character and the intellect upon it. I hope, if she is engaged, that it is to some man who will be worthy of her.'

'Why,' I remarked, 'you speak quite feelingly. It is a clear case of love at first sight, Jack. However, to put your perturbed spirit at rest, I'll make a point of finding out all about her whenever I meet any fellow who is likely to know.'

Barrington Cowles thanked me, and the conversation drifted off into other channels. For several days neither of us made any allusion to the subject, though my companion was perhaps a little more dreamy and distraught than usual. The incident had almost vanished from my remembrance, when one day young Brodie, who is a second cousin of mine, came up to me on the university steps with the face of a bearer of tidings.

'I say,' he began, 'you know Reeves, don't you?'

'Yes. What of him?'

'His engagement is off.'

'Off!' I cried. 'Why, I only learned the other day that it was on.'

'Oh, yes – it's all off. His brother told me so. Deucedly mean of Reeves, you know, if he has backed out of it, for she was an uncommonly nice girl.'

'I've seen her,' I said; 'but I don't know her name.'

'She is a Miss Northcott, and lives with an old aunt of hers in Abercrombie Place. Nobody knows anything about her people, or where she comes from. Anyhow, she is about the most unlucky girl in the world, poor soul!'

'Why unlucky?'

'Well, you know, this was her second engagement,' said young Brodie, who had a marvellous knack of knowing everything about everybody. 'She was engaged to Prescott – William Prescott, who died. That was a very sad affair. The wedding day was fixed, and the whole thing looked as straight as a die when the smash came.'

'What smash?' I asked, with some dim recollection of the circumstances.

'Why, Prescott's death. He came to Abercrombie Place one night, and stayed very late. No one knows exactly when he left, but about one in the morning a fellow who knew him met him walking rapidly in the direction of the Queen's Park. He bade him goodnight, but Prescott hurried on without heeding him, and that was the last time he was ever seen alive. Three days afterwards his body was found floating in St Margaret's Loch, under St Anthony's Chapel. No one could ever understand it, but of course the coroner brought it in as temporary insanity.'

'It was very strange,' I remarked.

'Yes, and deucedly rough on the poor girl,' said Brodie. 'Now that this other blow has come it will quite crush her. So gentle and ladylike she is, too!'

'You know her personally, then?' I asked.

'Oh, yes, I know her. I have met her several times. I could easily manage that you should be introduced to her.'

'Well,' I answered, 'it's not so much for my own sake as for a friend of mine. However, I don't suppose she will go out much for some little time after this. When she does I will take advantage of your offer.'

We shook hands on this, and I thought no more of the matter for some time.

The next incident which I have to relate as bearing at all upon the question of Miss Northcott is an unpleasant one. Yet I must detail it as accurately as possible, since it may throw some light upon the sequel. One cold night, several months after the conversation with my second cousin which I have quoted above, I was walking down one of the lowest streets in the city on my way back from a case which I had been attending. It was very late, and I was picking my way among the dirty loungers who were clustering round the doors of a great gin-palace, when a man staggered out from among them, and held out his hand to me with a drunken leer. The gaslight fell full upon his face, and, to my intense astonishment, I recognized in the degraded creature before me my former acquaintance, young Archibald Reeves, who had once been famous as one of the most dressy and particular men in the whole college. I was so utterly surprised that for a moment I almost doubted the evidence of my own senses; but there was no mistaking those features, which, though bloated with drink, still retained something of their former comeliness. I was determined to rescue him, for one night at least, from the company into which he had fallen.

'Holloa, Reeves!' I said. 'Come along with me. I'm going in your direction.'

He muttered some incoherent apology for his condition, and took my arm. As I supported him towards his lodgings I could see that he was not only suffering from the effects of a recent debauch, but that a long course of intemperance had affected his nerves and his brain. His hand when I touched it was dry and feverish, and he started from every shadow which fell upon the pavement. He rambled in his speech, too, in a manner which suggested the delirium of disease rather than the talk of a drunkard.

When I got him to his lodgings I partially undressed him and laid him upon his bed. His pulse at this time was very high, and he was evidently extremely feverish. He seemed to have sunk into a doze; and I was about to steal out of the room to warn his landlady of his condition, when he started up and caught me by the sleeve of my coat.

'Don't go!' he cried. 'I feel better when you are here. I am safe from her then.'

'From her!' I said. 'From whom?'

'Her! her!' he answered, peevishly, 'Ah! you don't know her. She is the devil! Beautiful – beautiful; but the devil!'

'You are feverish and excited,' I said. 'Try and get a little sleep. You will wake better.'

'Sleep!' he groaned. 'How am I to sleep when I see her sitting down yonder at the foot of the bed with her great eyes watching and watching hour after hour? I tell you it saps all the strength and manhood out of me. That's what makes me drink. God help me – I'm half drunk now!'

'You are very ill,' I said, putting some vinegar to his temples; 'and you are delirious. You don't know what you say.'

'Yes, I do,' he interrupted sharply, looking up at me. 'I know very well what I say. I brought it upon myself. It is my own choice. But I couldn't – no, by heaven, I couldn't – accept the alternative. I couldn't keep my faith to her. It was more than man could do.'

I sat by the side of the bed, holding one of his burning hands in mine, and wondering over his strange words. He lay still for some time, and then, raising his eyes to me, said, in a most plaintive voice—

'Why did she not give me warning sooner? Why did she wait until I had learned to love her so?'

He repeated this question several times, rolling his feverish head from side to side, and then he dropped into a troubled sleep. I crept out of the room, and, having seen that he would be properly cared for, left the house. His words, however, rang in my ears for days afterwards, and assumed a deeper significance when taken with what was to come.

My friend, Barrington Cowles, had been away for his summer holidays, and I had heard nothing of him for several months. When the winter session came on, however, I received a telegram from him asking me to secure the old rooms in Northumberland Street for him, and telling me the train by which he would arrive. I went down to meet him, and was delighted to find him looking wonderfully hearty and well.

'By the way,' he said suddenly, that night, as we sat in our chairs by the fire, talking over the events of the holidays, 'you have never congratulated me yet!'

'On what, my boy?' I asked.

'What? Do you mean to say you have not heard of my engagement?'

'Engagement! No!' I answered. 'However, I am delighted to hear it, and congratulate you with all my heart.'

'I wonder it didn't come to your ears,' he said. 'It was the queerest thing. You remember that girl whom we both admired so much at the academy?'

'What!' I cried, with a vague feeling of apprehension at my heart. 'You don't mean to say that you are engaged to her?'

'I thought you would be surprised,' he answered. 'When I was staying with an old aunt of mine in Peterhead, in Aberdeenshire, the Northcotts happened to come there on a visit, and as we had mutual friends we soon met. I found out that it was a false alarm about her being engaged, and then – well, you know what it is when you are thrown into the society of such a girl in a place like Peterhead. Not, mind you,' he added, 'that I consider I did a foolish or hasty thing. I have never regretted it for a moment. The more I know Kate the more I admire her and love her. However, you must be introduced to her, and then you will form your own opinion.'

I expressed my pleasure at the prospect, and endeavoured to speak as lightly as I could to Cowles upon the subject, but I felt depressed and anxious at heart. The words of Reeves and the unhappy fate of young Prescott recurred to my recollection, and, though I could assign no tangible reason for it, a vague, dim fear and distrust of the woman took possession of me. It may be that this was foolish prejudice and superstition upon my part, and that I involuntarily contorted her future doings and sayings to fit into some half-formed wild theory of my own. This has been suggested to me by others as an explanation of my narrative. They are welcome to their opinion if they can reconcile it with the facts which I have to tell.

I went round with my friend a few days afterwards to call upon Miss Northcott. I remember that, as we went down Abercrombie Place, our attention was attracted by the shrill yelping of a dog – which noise proved eventually to come from the house to which we were bound. We were shown upstairs, where I was introduced to old Mrs Merton, Miss Northcott's aunt, and to the young lady herself. She looked as beautiful as ever, and I could not wonder at my friend's infatuation. Her face was a little more flushed than usual, and she held in her hand a heavy dog-whip, with which she had been chastising a small Scotch terrier, whose cries we had heard in the street. The poor brute was cringing up against the wall, whining piteously, and evidently completely cowed.

'So, Kate,' said my friend, after we had taken our seats, 'you have been falling out with Carlo again.'

'Only a very little quarrel this time,' she said, smiling charmingly. 'He is a dear, good old fellow, but he needs correction now and then.' Then, turning to me, 'We all do that, Mr Armitage, don't we? What a capital thing if, instead of receiving a collective punishment at the end of our lives, we were to have one at once, as the dogs do, when we did anything wicked. It would make us more careful, wouldn't it?'

I acknowledged that it would.

'Supposing that every time a man misbehaved himself a gigantic hand were to seize him, and he were lashed with a whip until he fainted' – she clenched her white fingers as she spoke, and cut out viciously with the dog-whip – 'it would do more to keep him good than any number of high-minded theories of morality.'

'Why, Kate,' said my friend, 'you are quite savage today.'

'No, Jack,' she laughed. 'I'm only propounding a theory for Mr Armitage's consideration.'

The two began to chat together about some Aberdeenshire reminiscence, and I had time to observe Mrs Merton, who had remained silent during our short conversation. She was a very strange-looking old lady. What attracted attention most in her appearance was the utter want of colour which she exhibited. Her hair was snow-white, and her face extremely pale. Her lips were bloodless, and even her eyes were of such a light tinge of blue that they hardly relieved the general pallor. Her dress was a grey silk, which harmonized with her general appearance. She had a peculiar expression of countenance, which I was unable at the moment to refer to its proper cause.

She was working at some old-fashioned piece of ornamental needlework, and as she moved her arms her dress gave forth a dry, melancholy rustling, like the sound of leaves in the autumn. There was something mournful and depressing in the sight of her. I moved my chair a little nearer, and asked her how she liked Edinburgh, and whether she had been there long.

When I spoke to her she started and looked up at me with a scared look on her face. Then I saw in a moment what the expression was which I had observed there. It was one of fear – intense and overpowering fear. It was so marked that I could have staked my life on the woman before me having at some period of her life been subjected to some terrible experience or dreadful misfortune.

'Oh, yes, I like it,' she said, in a soft, timid voice; 'and we have been here long – that is, not very long. We move about a great deal.' She spoke with hesitation, as if afraid of committing herself.

'You are a native of Scotland, I presume?' I said.

'No – that is, not entirely. We are not natives of any place. We are cosmopolitan, you know.' She glanced round in the direction of Miss Northcott as she spoke, but the two were still chatting together near the window. Then she suddenly bent forward to me, with a look of intense earnestness upon her face, and said—

'Don't talk to me any more, please. She does not like it, and I shall suffer for it afterwards. Please, don't do it.'

I was about to ask her the reason for this strange request, but when she saw I was going to address her, she rose and walked slowly out of the room. As she did so I perceived that the lovers had ceased to talk, and that Miss Northcott was looking at me with her keen, grey eyes.

'You must excuse my aunt, Mr Armitage,' she said; 'she is old, and easily fatigued. Come over and look at my album.'

We spent some time examining the portraits. Miss Northcott's father and mother were apparently ordinary mortals enough, and I could not detect in either of them any traces of the character which showed itself in their daughter's face. There was one old daguerreotype, however, which arrested my attention. It represented a man of about the age of forty, and strikingly handsome. He was clean shaven, and extraordinary power was expressed upon his prominent lower jaw and firm, straight mouth. His eyes were somewhat deeply set in his head, however, and there was a snake-like flattening at the upper part of his forehead, which detracted from his appearance. I almost involuntarily, when I saw the head, pointed to it, and exclaimed—

'There is your prototype in your family, Miss Northcott.'

'Do you think so?' she said. 'I am afraid you are paying me a very bad compliment, Uncle Anthony was always considered the black sheep of the family.'

'Indeed,' I answered; 'my remark was an unfortunate one, then.'

'Oh, don't mind that,' she said; 'I always thought myself that he was worth all of them put together. He was an officer in the forty-first regiment, and he was killed in action during the Persian war – so he died nobly, at any rate.'

'That's the sort of death I should like to die,' said Cowles, his dark eyes flashing, as they would when he was excited; 'I often wish I had taken to my father's profession instead of this vile pill-compounding drudgery.'

'Come, Jack, you are not going to die any sort of death yet,' she said, tenderly taking his hand in hers.

I could not understand the woman. There was such an extraordinary mixture of masculine decision and womanly tenderness about her, with the consciousness of something all her own in the background, that she fairly puzzled me. I hardly knew, therefore, how to answer Cowles when, as we walked down the street together, he asked the comprehensive question—

'Well, what do you think of her?'

'I think she is wonderfully beautiful,' I answered, guardedly.

'That, of course,' he replied, irritably. 'You knew that before you came!'

'I think she is very clever too,' I remarked.

Barrington Cowles walked on for some time, and then he suddenly turned on me with the strange question—

'Do you think she is cruel? Do you think she is the sort of girl who would take a pleasure in inflicting pain?'

'Well, really,' I answered, 'I have hardly had time to form an opinion.'

We then walked on for some time in silence.

'She is an old fool,' at length muttered Cowles. 'She is mad.'

'Who is?' I asked.

'Why, that old woman – that aunt of Kate's – Mrs Merton, or whatever her name is.'

Then I knew that my poor colourless friend had been speaking to Cowles, but he never said anything more as to the nature of her communication.

My companion went to bed early that night, and I sat up a long time by the fire, thinking over all that I had seen and heard. I felt that there was some mystery about the girl – some dark fatality so strange as to defy conjecture. I thought of Prescott's interview with her before their marriage, and the fatal termination of it. I coupled it with poor drunken Reeves' plaintive cry, 'Why did she not tell me sooner?' and with the other words he had spoken. Then my mind ran over Mrs Merton's warning to me, Cowles' reference to her, and even the episode of the whip and the cringing dog.

The whole effect of my recollections was unpleasant to a degree, and yet there was no tangible charge which I could bring against the woman. It would be worse than useless to attempt to warn my friend until I had definitely made up my mind what I was to warn him against. He would treat any charge against her with scorn. What could I do? How could I get at some tangible conclusion as to her character and antecedents? No one in Edinburgh knew them except as recent acquaintances. She was an orphan, and as far as I knew she had never disclosed where her former home had been. Suddenly an idea struck me. Among my father's friends there was a Colonel Joyce, who had served a long time in India upon the staff, and who would be likely to know most of the officers who had been out there since the Mutiny. I sat down at once, and, having trimmed the lamp, proceeded to write a letter to the Colonel. I told him that I was very curious to gain some particulars about a certain Captain Northcott, who had served in the Forty-first Foot, and who had fallen in the Persian war. I described the man as well as I could from my recollection of the daguerreotype, and then, having directed the letter, posted it that very night, after which, feeling that I had done all that could be done, I retired to bed, with a mind too anxious to allow me to sleep.

PART II

I GOT an answer from Leicester, where the Colonel resided, within two days. I have it before me as I write, and copy it verbatim.

'Dear Bob,' it said, 'I remember the man well. I was with him at Calcutta, and afterwards at Hyderabad. He was a curious, solitary sort of mortal; but a gallant soldier enough, for he distinguished himself at Sobraon, and was wounded, if I remember right. He was not popular in his corps – they said he was a pitiless, cold-blooded fellow, with no geniality in him. There was a rumour, too, that he was a devil-worshipper, or something of that sort, and also that he had the evil eye, which, of course, was all nonsense. He had some strange theories, I remember, about the power of the human will and the effects of mind upon matter.

'How are you getting on with your medical studies? Never forget, my boy, that your father's son has every claim upon me, and that if I can serve you in any way I am always at your command.

'Ever affectionately yours,
'EDWARD JOYCE.

'P.S. – By the way, Northcott did not fall in action. He was killed after peace was declared in a crazy attempt to get some of the eternal fire from the sun-worshipper's temple. There was considerable mystery about his death.'

I read this epistle over several times – at first with a feeling of satisfaction, and then with one of disappointment. I had come on some curious information, and yet hardly what I wanted. He was an eccentric man, a devil-worshipper, and rumoured to have the power of the evil eye. I could believe the young lady's eyes, when endowed with that cold, grey shimmer which I had noticed in them once or twice, to be capable of any evil which human eye ever wrought; but still the superstition was an effete one. Was there not more meaning in that sentence which followed – 'He had some strange theories, I remember, about the power of the human will and of the effects of mind upon matter'? I remember having once read a quaint treatise, which I had imagined to be mere charlatanism at the time, of the power of certain human minds, and of effects produced by them at a distance. Was Miss Northcott endowed with some exceptional power of the sort? The idea grew upon me, and very shortly I had evidence which convinced me of the truth of the supposition.

It happened that at the very time when my mind was dwelling upon this subject, I saw a notice in the paper that our town was to be visited by Doctor Messinger, the well-known medium and mesmerist. Messinger was a man whose performance, such as it was, had been again and again pronounced to be genuine by competent judges. He was far above trickery, and had the reputation of being the soundest living authority upon the strange pseudo-sciences of animal magnetism and electrobiology. Determined, therefore, to see what the human will could do, even against all the disadvantages of glaring footlights and a public platform, I took a ticket for the first night of the performance, and went with several student friends.

We had secured one of the side boxes, and did not arrive until after the performance had begun. I had hardly taken my seat before I recognized Barrington Cowles, with his fiancée and old Mrs Merton, sitting in the third or fourth row of the stalls. They caught sight of me at almost the same moment, and we bowed to each other. The first portion of the lecture was somewhat commonplace, the lecturer giving tricks of pure legerdemain, with one or two manifestations of mesmerism, performed upon a subject whom he had brought with him. He gave us an exhibition of clairvoyance too, throwing his subject into a trance, and then demanding particulars as to the movements of absent friends, and the whereabouts of hidden objects, all of which appeared to be answered satisfactorily. I had seen all this before, however. What I wanted to see now was the effect of the lecturer's will when exerted upon some independent member of the audience.

He came round to that as the concluding exhibition in his performance. 'I have shown you,' he said, 'that a mesmerized subject is entirely dominated by the will of the mesmerizer. He loses all power of volition, and his very thoughts are such as are suggested to him by the mastermind. The same end may be attained without any preliminary process. A strong will can, simply by virtue of its strength, take possession of a weaker one, even at a distance, and can regulate the impulses and the actions of the owner of it. If there was one man in the world who had a very much more highly-developed will than any of the rest of the human family, there is no reason why he should not he able to rule over them all, and to reduce his fellow-creatures to the condition of automatons. Happily there is such a dead level of mental power, or rather of mental weakness, among us that such a catastrophe is not likely to occur; but still within our small compass there are variations which produce surprising effects. I shall now single out one of the audience, and endeavour "by the mere power of will" to compel him to come upon the platform, and do and say what I wish. Let me assure you that there is no collusion, and that the subject whom I may select is at perfect liberty to resent to the uttermost any impulse which I may communicate to him.'

With these words the lecturer came to the front of the platform, and glanced over the first few rows of the stalls. No doubt Cowles' dark skin and bright eyes marked him out as a man of a highly nervous temperament, for the mesmerist picked him out in a moment, and fixed his eyes upon him. I saw my friend give a start of surprise, and then settle down in his chair, as if to express his determination not to yield to the influence of the operator. Messinger was not a man whose head denoted any great brainpower, but his gaze was singularly intense and penetrating. Under the influence of it Cowles made one or two spasmodic motions of his hands, as if to grasp the sides of his seat, and then half rose, but only to sink down again, though with an evident effort. I was watching the scene with intense interest, when I happened to catch a glimpse of Miss Northcott's face. She was sitting with her eyes fixed intently upon the mesmerist, and with such an expression of concentrated power upon her features as I have never seen on any other human countenance. Her jaw was firmly set, her lips compressed, and her face as hard as if it were a beautiful sculpture cut out of the whitest marble. Her eyebrows were drawn down, however, and from beneath them her grey eyes seeemed to sparkle and gleam with a cold light.

I looked at Cowles again, expecting every moment to see him rise and obey the mesmerist's wishes, when there came from the platform a short, gasping cry as of a man utterly worn out and prostrated by a prolonged struggle. Messinger was leaning against the table, his hand to his forehead, and the perspiration pouring down his face. 'I won't go on,' he cried, addressing the audience. 'There is a stronger will than mine acting against me. You must excuse me for tonight.' The man was evidently ill, and utterly unable to proceed, so the curtain was lowered, and the audience dispersed, with many comments upon the lecturer's sudden indisposition.

I waited outside the hall until my friend and the ladies came out. Cowles was laughing over his recent experience.

'He didn't succeed with me, Bob,' he cried triumphantly, as he shook my hand. 'I think he caught a Tartar that time.'

'Yes,' said Miss Northcott, 'I think that Jack ought to be very proud of his strength of mind; don't you, Mr Armitage?'

'It took me all my time, though,' my friend said, seriously. 'You can't conceive what a strange feeling I had once or twice. All the strength seemed to have gone out of me – especially just before he collapsed himself.'

I walked round with Cowles, in order to see the ladies home. He walked in front with Mrs Merton, and I found myself behind with the young lady. For a minute or so I walked beside her without making any remark, and then I suddenly blurted out, in a manner which must have seemed somewhat brusque to her—

'You did that, Miss Northcott.'

'Did what?' she asked, sharply.

'Why, mesmerized the mesmerizer – I suppose that is the best way of describing the transaction.'

'What a strange idea!' she said, laughing. 'You give me credit for a strong will then?'

'Yes,' I said. 'For a dangerously strong one.'

'Why dangerous?' she asked, in a tone of surprise.

'I think,' I answered, 'that any will which can exercise such power is dangerous – for there is always a chance of its being turned to bad uses.'

'You would make me out a very dreadful individual, Mr Armitage,' she said, and then, looking up suddenly in my face – 'You have never liked me. You are suspicious of me and distrust me, though I have never given you cause.'

The accusation was so sudden and so true that I was unable to find any reply to it. She paused for a moment, and then said, in a voice which was hard and cold—

'Don't let your prejudice lead you to interfere with me, however, or say anything to your friend, Mr Cowles, which might lead to a difference between us. You would find that to be very bad policy.'

There was something in the way she spoke which gave an indescribable air of a threat to these few words.

'I have no power,' I said, 'to interfere with your plans for the future. I cannot help, however, from what I have seen and heard, having fears for my friend.'

'Fears!' she repeated, scornfully. 'Pray what have you seen and heard? Something from Mr Reeves, perhaps – I believe he is another of your friends?'

'He never mentioned your name to me,' I answered, truthfully enough. 'You will be sorry to hear that he is dying.' As I said it, we passed by a lighted window, and I glanced down to see what effect my words had upon her. She was laughing – there was no doubt of it; she was laughing quietly to herself. I could see merriment in every feature of her face. I feared and mistrusted the woman from that moment more than ever.

We said little more that night. When we parted she gave me a quick, warning glance, as if to remind me of what she had said about the danger of interference. Her cautions would have made little difference to me could I have seen my way to benefiting Barrington Cowles by anything which I might say. But what could I say? I might say that her former suitors had been unfortunate. I might say that I believed her to be a cruel-hearted woman. I might say that I considered her to possess wonderful, and almost preternatural, powers. What impression would any of these accusations make upon an ardent lover – a man with my friend's enthusiastic temperament? I felt that it would be useless to advance them, so I was silent.

And now I come to the beginning of the end. Hitherto much has been surmise and inference and hearsay. It is my painful task to relate now, as dispassionately and as accurately as I can, what actually occurred under my own notice, and to reduce to writing the events which preceded the death of my friend.

Towards the end of the winter, Cowles remarked to me that he intended to marry Miss Northcott as soon as possible – probably some time in the spring. He was, as I have already remarked, fairly well off, and the young lady had some money of her own, so that there was no pecuniary reason for a long engagement. 'We are going to take a little house out at Corstorphine,' he said, 'and we hope to see your face at our table, Bob, as often as you can possibly come.' I thanked him, and tried to shake off my apprehensions and persuade myself that all would yet be well.

It was about three weeks before the time fixed for the marriage, that Cowles remarked to me one evening that he feared he would be late that night. 'I have had a note from Kate,' he said, 'asking me to call about eleven o'clock tonight, which seems rather a late hour, but perhaps she wants to talk over something quietly after old Mrs Merton retires.'

It was not until after my friend's departure that I suddenly recollected the mysterious interview which I had been told of as preceding the suicide of young Prescott. Then I thought of the ravings of poor Reeves, rendered more tragic by the fact that I had heard that very day of his death. What was the meaning of it all? Had this woman some baleful secret to disclose which must be known before her marriage? Was it some reason which forbade her to marry? Or was it some reason which forbade others to marry her? I felt so uneasy that I would have followed Cowles, even at the risk of offending him, and endeavoured to dissuade him from keeping his appointment, but a glance at the clock showed me that I was too late.

I was determined to wait up for his return, so I piled some coals upon the fire and took down a novel from the shelf. My thoughts proved more interesting than the book, however, and I threw it on one side. An indefinable feeling of anxiety and depression weighed upon me. Twelve o'clock came, and then half-past, without any sign of my friend. It was nearly one when I heard a step in the street outside, and then a knocking at the door. I was surprised as I knew that my friend always carried a key – however, I hurried down, and undid the latch. As the door flew open I knew in a moment that my worst apprehensions had been fulfilled. Barrington Cowles was leaning against the railings outside with his face sunk upon his breast, and his whole attitude expressive of the most intense despondency. As he passed in he gave a stagger, and would have fallen had I not thrown my left arm around him. Supporting him with this, and holding the lamp in my other hand, I led him slowly upstairs into our sitting-room. He sank down upon the sofa without a word. Now that I could get a good view of him, I was horrified to see the change which had come over him. His face was deadly pale, and his very lips were bloodless. His cheeks and forehead were clammy, his eyes glazed, and his whole expression altered. He looked like a man who had gone through some terrible ordeal, and was thoroughly unnerved.

'My dear fellow, what is the matter?' I asked, breaking the silence. 'Nothing amiss, I trust? Are you unwell?'

'Brandy!' he gasped. 'Give me some brandy!'

I took out the decanter, and was about to help him, when he snatched it from me with a trembling hand, and poured out nearly half a tumbler of the spirit. He was usually a most abstemious man, but he took this off at a gulp without adding any water to it. It seemed to do him good, for the colour began to come back to his face, and he leaned upon his elbow.

'My engagement is off, Bob,' he said, trying to speak calmly, but with a tremor in his voice which he could not conceal. 'It is all over.'

'Cheer up!' I answered, trying to encourage him. 'Don't get down on your luck. How was it? What was it all about?'

'About?' he groaned, covering his face with his hands. 'If I did tell you, Bob, you would not believe it. It is too dreadful – too horrible – unutterably awful and incredible! Oh, Kate, Kate!' and he rocked himself to and fro in his grief; 'I pictured you an angel and I find you a—'

'A what?' I asked, for he had paused.

He looked at me with a vacant stare, and then suddenly burst out, waving his arms: 'A fiend!' he cried. 'A ghoul from the pit! A vampire soul behind a lovely face! Now, God forgive me!' he went on in a lower tone, turning his face to the wall; 'I have said more than I should. I have loved her too much to speak of her as she is. I love her too much now.'

He lay still for some time, and I had hoped that the brandy had had the effect of sending him to sleep, when he suddenly turned his face towards me.

'Did you ever read of wehr-wolves?' he asked.

I answered that I had.

'There is a story,' he said, thoughtfully, 'in one of Marryat's books, about a beautiful woman who took the form of a wolf at night and devoured her own children. I wonder what put that idea into Marryat's head?'

He pondered for some minutes, and then he cried out for some more brandy. There was a small bottle of laudanum upon the table, and I managed, by insisting upon helping him myself, to mix about half a drachm with the spirits. He drank it off, and sank his head once more upon the pillow. 'Anything better than that,' he groaned. 'Death is better than that. Crime and cruelty; cruelty and crime. Anything is better than that,' and so on, with the monotonous refrain, until at last the words became indistinct, his eyelids closed over his weary eyes, and he sank into a profound slumber. I carrried him into his bedroom without arousing him; and making a couch for myself out of the chairs, I remained by his side all night.

In the morning Barrington Cowles was in a high fever. For weeks he lingered between life and death. The highest medical skill of

Edinburgh was called in, and his vigorous constitution slowly got the better of his disease. I nursed him during this anxious time; but through all his wild delirium and ravings he never let a word escape him which explained the mystery connected with Miss Northcott. Sometimes he spoke of her in the tenderest words and most loving voice. At others he screamed out that she was a fiend, and stretched out his arms, as if to keep her off. Several times he cried that he would not sell his soul for a beautiful face, and then he would moan in a most piteous voice, 'But I love her – I love her for all that; I shall never cease to love her.'

When he came to himself he was an altered man. His severe illness had emaciated him greatly, but his dark eyes had lost none of their brightness. They shone out with startling brilliancy from under his dark, overhanging brows. His manner was eccentric and variable – sometimes irritable, sometimes recklessly mirthful, but never natural. He would glance about him in a strange, suspicious manner, like one who feared something, and yet hardly knew what it was he dreaded. He never mentioned Miss Northcott's name – never until that fatal evening of which I have now to speak.

In an endeavour to break the current of his thoughts by frequent change of scene, I travelled with him through the highlands of Scotland, and afterwards down the east coast. In one of these peregrinations of ours we visited the Isle of May, an island near the mouth of the Firth of Forth, which, except in the tourist season, is singularly barren and desolate. Beyond the keeper of the lighthouse there are only one or two families of poor fisher-folk, who sustain a precarious existence by their nets, and by the capture of cormorants and Solan geese. This grim spot seemed to have such a fascination for Cowles that we engaged a room in one of the fishermen's huts, with the intention of passing a week or two there. I found it very dull, but the loneliness appeared to be a relief to my friend's mind. He lost the look of apprehension which had become habitual to him, and became something like his old self. He would wander round the island all day, looking down from the summit of the great cliffs which gird it round, and watching the long green waves as they came booming in and burst in a shower of spray over the rocks beneath.

One night – I think it was our third or fourth on the island –

Barrington Cowles and I went outside the cottage before retiring to rest, to enjoy a little fresh air, for our room was small, and the rough lamp caused an unpleasant odour. How well I remember every little circumstance in connection with that night! It promised to be tempestuous, for the clouds were piling up in the north-west, and the dark wrack was drifting across the face of the moon, throwing alternate belts of light and shade upon the rugged surface of the island and the restless sea beyond.

We were standing talking close by the door of the cottage, and I was thinking to myself that my friend was more cheerful than he had been since his illness, when he gave a sudden, sharp cry, and looking round at him I saw, by the light of the moon, an expression of unutterable horror come over his features. His eyes became fixed and staring, as if riveted upon some approaching object, and he extended his long thin forefinger, which quivered as he pointed.

'Look there!' he cried. 'It is she! It is she! You see her there coming down the side of the brae.' He gripped me convulsively by the wrist as he spoke. 'There she is, coming towards us!'

'Who?' I cried, straining my eyes into the darkness.

'She – Kate – Kate Northcott!' he screamed. 'She has come for me. Hold me fast, old friend. Don't let me go!'

'Hold up, old man,' I said, clapping him on the shoulder. 'Pull yourself together; you are dreaming; there is nothing to fear.'

'She is gone!' he cried, with a gasp of relief. 'No, by heaven! there she is again, and nearer – coming nearer. She told me she would come for me, and she keeps her word.'

'Come into the house,' I said. His hand, as I grasped it, was as cold as ice.

'Ah, I knew it!' he shouted. 'There she is, waving her arms. She is beckoning to me. It is the signal. I must go. I am coming, Kate; I am coming!'

I threw my arms around him, but he burst from me with super-human strength, and dashed into the darkness of the night. I followed him, calling to him to stop, but he ran the more swiftly. When the moon shone out between the clouds I could catch a glimpse of his dark figure, running rapidly in a straight line, as if to reach some definite goal. It may have been imagination, but it seemed to me that in the flickering light I could distinguish a vague something in front of him – a shimmering form which eluded his grasp and led him onwards. I saw his outlines stand out hard against the sky behind him as he surmounted the brow of a little hill, then he disappeared, and that was the last ever seen by mortal eye of Barrington Cowles.

The fishermen and I walked round the island all that night with lanterns, and examined every nook and corner without seeing a trace of my poor lost friend. The direction in which he had been running terminated in a rugged line of jagged cliffs overhanging the sea. At one place here the edge was somewhat crumbled, and there appeared marks upon the turf which might have been left by human feet. We lay upon our faces at this spot, and peered with our lanterns over the edge, looking down on the boiling surge two hundred feet below. As we lay there, suddenly, above the beating of the waves and the howling of the wind, there rose a strange, wild screech from the abyss below. The fishermen – a naturally superstitious race – averred that it was the sound of a woman's laughter, and I could hardly persuade them to continue the search. For my own part I think it may have been the cry of some seafowl startled from its nest by the flash of the lantern. However that may be, I never wish to hear such a sound again.

And now I have come to the end of the painful duty which I have undertaken. I have told as plainly and as accurately as I could the story of the death of John Barrington Cowles, and the train of events which preceded it. I am aware that to others the sad episode seemed commonplace enough. Here is the prosaic account which appeared in the *Scotsman* a couple of days afterwards:—

'Sad Occurrence on the Isle of May. – The Isle of May has been the scene of a sad disaster. Mr John Barrington Cowles, a gentleman well known in university circles as a most distinguished student, and the present holder of the Neil Arnott prize for physics, has been recruiting his health in this quiet retreat. The night before last he suddenly left his friend, Mr Robert Armitage, and he has not since been heard of. It is almost certain that he has met his death by falling over the cliffs which surround the island. Mr Cowles' health has been failing for some time, partly from over-study and partly from worry connected with family affairs. By his death the University loses one of her most promising alumni.'

I have nothing more to add to my statement. I have unburdened my mind of all that I know. I can well conceive that many, after weighing all that I have said, will see no ground for an accusation against Miss Northcott. They will say that, because a man of a naturally excitable disposition says and does wild things, and even eventually commits self-murder after a sudden and heavy disappointment, there is no reason why vague charges should be advanced against a young lady. To this, I answer that they are welcome to their opinion. For my own part, I ascribe the death of William Prescott, of Archibald Reeves, and of John Barrington Cowles to this woman with as much confidence as if I had seen her drive a dagger into their hearts.

You ask me no doubt, what my own theory is which will explain all these strange facts. I have none, or, at best, a dim and vague one. That Miss Northcott possessed extraordinary powers over the minds, and through the minds over the bodies, of others, I am convinced, as well as that her instincts were to use this power for base and cruel purposes. That some even more fiendish and terrible phase of character lay behind this – some horrible trait which it was necessary for her to reveal before marriage – is to be inferred from the experience of her three lovers, while the dreadful nature of the mystery thus revealed can only be surmised from the fact that the very mention of it drove from her those who had loved her so passionately. Their subsequent fate was, in my opinion, the result of her vindictive remembrance of their desertion of her, and that they were forewarned of it at the time was shown by the words of both Reeves and Cowles. Above this, I can say nothing. I lay the facts soberly before the public as they came under my notice. I have never seen Miss Northcott since, nor do I wish to do so. If by the words I have written I can save any one human being from the snare of those bright eyes and that beautiful face, then I can lay down my pen with the assurance that my poor friend has not died altogether in vain.

MANOR

Karl Heinrich Ulrichs

Karl Heinrich Ulrichs (1825–1895) was born in Aurich, then part of the Kingdom of Hanover, in present-day North-Western Germany. He graduated in law and theology from Göttingen University in 1846, and from 1846 to 1848 studied history at Berlin University, later working as a legal advisor. An advocate of rights for homosexuals at a time when homosexuality was illegal in many European countries, Ulrichs is now regarded as a pioneer of the modern gay rights movement, and there are streets named after him in several German cities. 'Manor' received its first book publication in 1885 in an anthology titled *Matrosengeschichten*, which translates into English as *Sailors' Tales*. While there had been vampire stories before 'Manor' that hinted at a same-sex relationship between the main protagonists, Ulrichs' story was the first to explicitly depict one between two men, making it an important milestone in the history of the vampire story.

I

FAR north in the Atlantic Ocean lies a solitary and forsaken group of thirty-five islands, equally distant from Scotland, Iceland, and Norway, called the Faroe Islands. Desolate, rocky, veiled by clouds, filled with the melancholy cries of fluttering gulls, and noisy with crashing breakers, they are almost always enveloped by fog. In summer the mountain tops, 1,800 and 2,000 feet above the sea, show rough crags, gloomy ravines, primitive fir forests, and thousands of springs, which often tumble down from great heights, foaming from boulder to boulder. The coastline is deeply cut by bays and fjords; ringed by high rocks, it is almost unapproachable everywhere. The sea, which is full of reefs all around, so as here and there to form a complete barricade, is ruffled by whirlpools formed by wild currents. Only seventeen of the islands are populated. Strömö and Vaagö are separated only by a narrow channel, which can be swum, although it takes a daring swimmer to do it. Many place names recall the time when there were no churches on the Faroe Islands and the old belief was not yet driven out, e.g., Thorshavn on the coast of Strömö, whose name itself means 'island of currents.'

In those days a fisherman rowed from Strömö with his fifteen-year-old son into the open sea. A storm came up, overturning the boat and throwing the son onto the reefs of Vaagö. A young boatman on Vaagö saw this. He leaped into the waves, swam between the reefs, seized the floating body, and drew it onto land. He sat with him on a rock, holding the half-stiff body on his knees and nursing him in his arms. The boy opened his eyes.

Boatman: 'Who are you?'

Boy: 'Har. I'm from Strömö.'

He rowed him across the channel back to Strömö, taking him to Laera, his mother. Gratefully the boy embraced his rescuer around the neck as they parted. (The corpse of his father was later thrown up onto land by the waves.) The boatman, who was named Manor, was an orphan, four years older than Har.

Manor grew fond of Har and longed to see him again. In the evening, when his day's work was finished, he sometimes rowed over to Strömö or swam the lukewarm waves, now that summer had come. Har went to the coast, climbed a cliff, and waved his kerchief when he saw Manor's boat coming in the distance. Then they stayed together an hour or two. If the sea was calm they rowed out and sang sailor songs. Or, stripping themselves of their clothing, they dove into the waves and swam to the nearby sandbar, which lay opposite; the seals, sunning themselves on the sand, fled. Or they walked in the dark green forest of tall fir trees, whose rustling tops proclaimed the speech of Thor. Or they sat down under the branches of an old birch on a rock. They chatted and made plans. If a ship were to come, which was sailing in search of whales, they both wanted to go along. As they sat there on the rock, Manor would lay his arm around Har's shoulder and call him 'my boy'; and the boy never felt more content than when Manor held him in that way. If it was already late when he came, then he quietly went up to the lilac bush which shaded Har's window and knocked on the pane. Har would wake up and slip out to him. He felt so happy, if he could be with Manor!

II

A Danish three-master arrived and anchored in Vaagö safe bay, looking for sailors for a two-month voyage to catch whales. Manor went aboard and the captain immediately took on the slender-grown lad, who was in the bloom of youth. Har wanted to go along as cabin boy, but Laera complained: 'You are my only child! The sea swallowed up your father. Will you abandon me?' Thus Har remained, but Manor left when the ship heaved anchor.

Two months passed; it was already wintry again. Har would climb a cliff and gaze into the distance. One morning he saw the ship coming and joyously waved his kerchief. But it was stormy and the surf was up. The ship steered toward the bay of Vaagö, but could not reach it and was thrown onto the dangerous reefs of Strömö, running aground before Har's eyes. He saw how the shipwrecked men fought the waves, and he caught a glimpse of one of them gripping a plank with his powerful arm. In the next moment he was sucked under, along with the plank, into the whirlpool of the surf. Har recognized him – it was Manor!

The flood tide brought many bodies onto land. Straw was prepared on the beach and corpses were laid on it, one next to the other. Manor's body was also brought there and laid on the straw. There he lay before Har, driven up by the sea water, with wet hair, eyes closed and cold, with pale lips and colourless cheeks from which the blood had drained. His slender form was good-looking even in death. 'This is the way I have to see you again, Manor!' Har cried, and threw himself sobbing across the beloved body, for a moment tasting again the bliss of an embrace.

The bodies were brought across the channel and buried the same day in the sand dunes of Vaagö.

III

In the evening Har sat in his hut, sad and silent. Laera wanted to comfort him, but he would not be comforted; he cursed the gods. He went to bed, but could not sleep. Toward midnight he fell into a half-slumber.

Then a noise awakened him. He looked up. Something was outside at the window. The branches of the lilac bush were rubbing against themselves and their dry leaves rustled. The window opened and a figure climbed inside. Aha! He knew that figure! In spite of the darkness he recognized it immediately! With slow steps it came up to him and laid itself on him in the bed, Har shivered, but he offered no resistance. It caressed his cheeks, though with a cold hand, oh! so cold, so cold! A feverish chill made him shudder. It kissed the warm, quivering boy-mouth with ice-cold lips. He felt the wet garment of the kissing figure, whose wet hair hung down onto his forehead. A feeling of dread passed through him, but it was mixed with bliss. The figure sighed. It sounded to him as if it wished to say: 'Longing drives me to you! I find no rest in the grave!'

He dared not speak; he scarcely dared to breathe. The figure had already raised itself and sighed as if it wished to say: 'Now I must go back.' It climbed onto the windowsill and left the way it had come.

'Manor was here,' said Har softly to himself.

That same night a fisherman from Strömö was out in the channel with his boat. The sea was lighted, so that gleaming drops fell from his oar. Then, shortly before midnight, he heard a strange sound. He saw something dart through the lighted waves in the direction of Strömö, something whose form he could not make out, but which had the speed of a large fish. But it was not a fish; that much he could recognize in the darkness.

The next night Manor came again, ice-cold as before, yet he stayed longer. He embraced the boy with cold arms, kissed his cheeks and mouth, and laid his head on the soft breast. Har trembled. His heart began to pound at this intimate embrace, and Manor laid his head directly over the pounding heart. His lips sought the gently heaving knob over his heart, which had been set into motion by its pounding. Then he began to suck, demandingly and thirstily, like a nursing infant at its mother's breast. After only a few moments, however, he left off, raised himself, and departed. It seemed to Har as if a sucking animal had filled itself on him.

That night, too, the fisherman was at work in the channel. At exactly the same hour as the night before the noise came again. This time it passed close by him. In the pale moonlight he was able to recognize it; it was a swimming man. He swam lying on the right side, as sailors sometimes swim, but was dressed in a shroud. The swimmer seemed not to notice him, even though he kept his face turned toward him. He swam with eyes closed. The sight was so disturbing that the fisherman pulled up his nets and rowed away.

Manor returned the following nights also. Sometimes he embraced the boy in his sleep, for now and then sleep overcame Har before Manor arrived. He awoke then in his embrace. Each time his lips sought the soft elevation over his heart. When it became day, Har saw now and again how yet another weak little drop of blood dripped from his left nipple. He wiped it away with his shirt. A drop had doubtless already flowed by itself onto his shirt. Only on a night of the full moon did Manor not come.

A dead person is often so strongly filled with longing for one or another of his loved ones left behind that he leaves his grave in the night and comes to him. For this is the old belief, that at midnight Urda gives back a brief half-life to many and then lends them strange powers from beyond the grave. It especially happens to young people, whom a bitter death has snatched away in the blossom of their years. He who returns is filled with a great need for blood and warmth at the same time. He yearns for the fresh blood of the living and, like a lover, for embraces. He also imparts great longing, however, and often produces a violent torment.

So it was here. Har tormented himself the whole day and was afflicted. With impatience, however, he waited for night and longed for the blissful thrill of the midnight embrace.

IV

Twelve days passed thus.

Laera: 'You are so pale and colourless. What is the matter, Har?'

He: 'Nothing, Mother.'

She: 'You are so quiet.'

He only sighed.

In the last cabin of the village there lived a wise woman, who knew all kinds of mysteries, and the worried mother went to her. The wise woman cast runic sticks.

Wise woman: 'The dead are visiting him.'

Laera: 'The dead?'

Wise woman: 'Yes, at night; and he must die of this, if an early halt is not put to the visits before it is too late.'

Laera returned home in dismay.

She: 'Is it true, Har, that you are receiving visits from the dead?'

He looked at the floor. 'Manor was here,' he said softly and sank onto her breast crying.

She: 'May the gods be merciful to you!'

He: 'The gods? Bah! What are the gods to do for me now? As he clung to the plank, alas! That was the time to be merciful, if they wished. But they let him sink under without mercy. Oh, how dear he was to me!'

Then she noticed the blood stains on his shirt, so she went to the village elders. They rowed across to Vaagö with the mother and son, and they took the wise woman along. To the people of Vaagö she said:

'Your graves are not closed. One body leaves his grave each night, comes across to us, and sucks himself full of the blood of this boy.'

The Vaagöers: 'Well, we'll fasten him.'

They took a fir stake, as long as a man and thick as his arm, and hewed it on four sides with a hatchet, making a foot-long point at the end. They walked to the dunes, one carrying the stake, another a heavy axe. They opened Manor's grave. He lay there before them, peaceful and quiet in his burial shroud.

First Vaagöer: 'Look! He is lying just as we laid him down.'

Wise woman: 'Because each time he again lays himself in the old position.'

Second Vaagöer: 'His face is indeed almost fresher than usual.'

Wise woman: 'No wonder. For that, Har's face is now all the more colourless.'

Har climbed down and threw himself once more on the beloved body.

'Manor! Manor!' he cried in a voice full of anguish. 'They want to impale you. Manor, wake up! Open your eyes! Your Har is calling you!'

But he did not open his eyes. He lay there motionless under Har's embrace, just as twelve days before on the straw on the beach.

Har did not want to let him loose. They tore him away and set the point of the stake on Manor's breast. Moaning, Har turned and fell on his mother's neck, hiding his face on her shoulder.

'Mother!' he cried out. 'Why have you done this to me?'

He heard the flat head of the axe fall into the stake, making the stake groan. A stronger blow, again a blow, and a half dozen more.

First Vaagöer: 'Now he's fastened.'

Second: 'Now he'll have to give up his returning.'

They carried Har away, half fainting.

'Now he'll leave you in peace, my dear child!' said Laera when they were again in their hut.

He went to bed grieving. 'Now he will come no more!' he said to himself sorrowfully. He was tired and faint. Disturbed and restless, however, he tossed on his bed. Slowly the minutes crept by; the hours lazily crawled past. Midnight came and still no sleep sank over his eyelids.

Listen! What is that? In the lilac bush . . . But no, of course that was impossible. And yet! Again, as before, the branches of the bush rustled and the window was opened. Manor was there again. He sighed deeply. In his breast he had a huge wound, which was square and went all the way through to his back. He lay again on Har, embraced him, and sucked. He sucked more demandingly and thirstily than before.

But Laera next door woke up that night, listened, and shivered. Early in the morning she came in and went up to Har's bed.

She: 'My poor child! He was here again after all.'

He: 'Yes, Mother. He was with me again.'

The bed was indeed spotted with the corpse's blood, which had trickled from the great wound.

V

Some hours later a boat was again rowed over the channel, but without Har. They again walked to the dunes, again opened the grave. The square stake was still stuck in the tomb, but no longer in Manor's breast. He lay bent around the stake. The stake hindered his lying stretched out.

Wise woman: 'He was able to get loose. The stake is the same thickness above and below.'

First Vaagöer: 'He was able to twist himself from below to the top of the stake.'

Second: 'But it must have cost him a monstrous effort.'

On the advice of the wise woman they hewed that day a stronger stake, which they left twice as thick above as below, so that it looked like a nail with a head. They pulled away the old stake and drove in the new one.

'There! Now he's nailed in,' said the axeman, as he gave the stake's head the last blow.

Second Vaagöer: 'Let him twist and turn; he'll never twist himself loose from this.'

Laera returned to Har and told him what had happened. 'Now it's over,' she said to herself, as she went to bed. She lay there sleepless. Midnight came and still all was quiet. Nothing rustled outside at the window in the branches of the lilac bush. No swimmer frightened the fisherman anymore, such as had cut through the billows at night with closed eyes.

Laera: 'Now you are at peace from him. He tormented you so!'

He: 'Oh, Mother! Mother! He did not torment me!'

He pined away in vain longing. 'Mother!' he said. 'It's all over with me now.' He wasted away, so that he was no longer able to raise himself from his bed.

She: 'You are so tired and weak, my dear son!'

He: 'He is drawing me down to him.'

One morning she sat by his bed while he still slept. A month had gone by since the shipwreck. It was still early. She was crying. Then he opened his eyes.

'Mother,' he said in a weak voice, 'I must die.'

She: 'Oh no, my child! You should not die so young!'

He: 'But yes! He was with me again. We talked with one another. We sat on the rock under the old birch in the forest as usual. He wrapped his arm again around my neck and called me "my boy." Tonight he will come again and fetch me. He promised it to me. I can bear it no longer without him.'

She bent over him and her tears flowed copiously onto his bed. 'My poor child!' she said and laid her hand on his forehead.

When night came she lit a lamp and watched at his bedside. He lay there quietly. He did not sleep, but stared silently before him.

He: 'Mother!'

She: 'What do you want, my good son?'

He: 'Lay me with him in his grave! Yes? And pull the horrible stake out of his breast!'

She promised it to him with a clasp of her hand and a kiss.

He: 'Oh, it must be so sweet to lie by him in the grave!'

Then midnight arrived. All at once his features were transfigured. He raised his head a bit, as if he were listening. With shining eyes he looked toward the window and the branches of the lilac bush.

'See, Mother, there he comes.'

Those were his last words. Then his eyes closed. He sank back onto the pillow and died.

And she did as he had requested.

First book publication in Karl Heinrich Ulrichs's *Matrosengeschichten* (*Sailors' Tales*, Leipzig: F. E. Fischer, 1885); later printed separately and anthologised.
Translated from the German by Hubert Kennedy.

OLD AESON

Arthur Quiller-Couch

Sir Arthur Thomas Quiller-Couch (1863–1944) was a highly respected
Cornish writer who often used the informal pen-name 'Q.' Early on
in his career he worked as a journalist and a book reviewer, and
published his first novel, *Dead Man's Rock* (1887), at the age of twenty-
four. Over the next fifty years, many other novels and some notable
short stories flowed from his pen, all written in a clear and seemingly
effortless style. His best-known supernatural stories are 'The Roll-Call
of the Reef' (1895) and 'A Pair of Hands' (1898), both of which have
been anthologised many times. 'Old Aeson,' which follows, is a wryly
humorous take on the psychic vampire theme, which originally
appeared in *The Speaker* (25 October, 1890) and received its first book
publication in *Noughts and Crosses: Stories, Studies and Sketches* (1891).

JUDGE between me and my guest, the stranger within my gates, the
man whom in his extremity I clothed and fed.

I remember well the time of his coming, for it happened at the end
of five days and nights during which the year passed from strength
to age; in the interval between the swallow's departure and the
redwing's coming; when the tortoise in my garden crept into his
winter quarters, and the equinox was on us, with an east wind that
parched the blood in the trees, so that their leaves for once knew
no gradations of red and yellow, but turned at a stroke to brown,
and crackled like tinfoil.

At five o'clock in the morning of the sixth day I looked out. The wind still whistled across the sky, but now without the obstruction of any cloud. Full in front of my window Sirius flashed with a whiteness that pierced the eye. A little to the right, the whole constellation of Orion was suspended clear over a wedge-like gap in the coast, wherein the sea could be guessed rather than seen. And, travelling yet further, the eye fell on two brilliant lights, the one set high above the other – the one steady and a fiery red, the other yellow and blazing intermittently – the one Aldebaran, the other revolving on the lighthouse top, fifteen miles away.

Half-way up the east, the moon, now in her last quarter and decrepit, climbed with the dawn close at her heels. And at this hour they brought in the Stranger, asking if my pleasure were to give him clothing and hospitality.

Nobody knew whence he came – except that it was from the wind and the night – seeing that he spoke in a strange tongue, moaning and making a sound like the twittering of birds in a chimney. But his journey must have been long and painful; for his legs bent under him, and he could not stand when they lifted him. So, finding it useless to question him for the time, I learnt from the servants all they had to tell – namely, that they had come upon him, but a few minutes before, lying on his face within my grounds, without staff or scrip, bareheaded, spent, and crying feebly for succour in his foreign tongue; and that in pity they had carried him in and brought him to me.

Now for the look of this man, he seemed a century old, being bald, extremely wrinkled, with wide hollows where the teeth should be, and the flesh hanging loose and flaccid on his cheekbones; and what colour he had could have come only from exposure to that bitter night. But his eyes chiefly spoke of his extreme age. They were blue and deep, and filled with the wisdom of years; and when he turned them in my direction they appeared to look through me, beyond me, and back upon centuries of sorrow and the slow endurance of man, as if his immediate misfortune were but an inconsiderable item in a long list. They frightened me. Perhaps they conveyed a warning of that which I was to endure at their owner's hands. From compassion, I ordered the servants to take him to my wife, with word that I wished her to set food before him, and see that it passed his lips.

So much I did for this Stranger. Now learn how he rewarded me.

He has taken my youth from me, and the most of my substance, and the love of my wife.

From the hour when he tasted food in my house, he sat there without hint of going. Whether from design, or because age and his sufferings had really palsied him, he came back tediously to life and warmth, nor for many days professed himself able to stand erect. Meanwhile he lived on the best of our hospitality. My wife tended him, and my servants ran at his bidding; for he managed early to make them understand scraps of his language, though slow in acquiring ours – I believe out of calculation, lest someone should inquire his business (which was a mystery) or hint at his departure. I myself often visited the room he had appropriated, and would sit for an hour watching those fathomless eyes while I tried to make head or tail of his discourse. When we were alone, my wife and I used to speculate at times on his probable profession. Was he a merchant? – an aged mariner? – a tinker, tailor, beggarman, thief? We could never decide, and he never disclosed.

Then the awakening came. I sat one day in the chair beside his, wondering as usual. I had felt heavy of late, with a soreness and languor in my bones, as if a dead weight hung continually on my shoulders, and another rested on my heart. A warmer colour in the Stranger's cheek caught my attention; and I bent forward, peering under the pendulous lids. His eyes were livelier and less profound. The melancholy was passing from them as breath fades off a pane of glass. *He was growing younger.* Starting up, I ran across the room, to the mirror.

There were two white hairs in my forelock; and, at the corner of either eye, half a dozen radiating lines. I was an old man.

Turning, I regarded the Stranger. He sat phlegmatic as an Indian idol; and in my fancy I felt the young blood draining from my own heart, and saw it mantling in his cheeks. Minute by minute I watched the slow miracle – the old man beautified. As buds unfold, he put on a lovely youthfulness; and, drop by drop, left me winter.

I hurried from the room, and seeking my wife, laid the case

before her. 'This is a ghoul,' I said, 'that we harbour: he is sucking my best blood, and the household is clean bewitched.' She laid aside the book in which she read, and laughed at me. Now my wife was well-looking, and her eyes were the light of my soul. Consider, then, how I felt as she laughed, taking the Stranger's part against me. When I left her, it was with a new suspicion in my heart. 'How shall it be,' I thought, 'if after stealing my youth, he go on to take the one thing that is better?'

In my room, day by day, I brooded upon this – hating my own alteration, and fearing worse. With the Stranger there was no longer any disguise. His head blossomed in curls; white teeth filled the hollows of his mouth: the pits in his cheeks were heaped full with roses, glowing under a transparent skin. It was Aeson renewed and thankless; and he sat on, devouring my substance.

Now, having probed my weakness, and being satisfied that I no longer dared to turn him out, he, who had half-imposed his native tongue upon us, constraining the household to a hideous jargon, the bastard growth of two languages, condescended to jerk us back rudely into our own speech once more, mastering it with a readiness that proved his former dissimulation, and using it henceforward as the sole vehicle of his wishes. On his past life he remained silent; but took occasion to confide in me that he proposed embracing a military career, as soon as he should tire of the shelter of my roof.

And I groaned in my chamber; for that which I feared had come to pass. He was making open love to my wife. And the eyes with which he looked at her, and the lips with which he coaxed her, had been mine; and I was an old man. Judge now between me and this guest.

One morning I went to my wife; for the burden was past bearing, and I must satisfy myself. I found her tending the plants on her window ledge; and when she turned, I saw that years had not taken from her comeliness one jot. And I was old.

So I taxed her on the matter of this Stranger, saying this and that, and how I had cause to believe he loved her.

'That is beyond doubt,' she answered, and smiled.

'By my head, I believe his fancy is returned!' I blurted out.

And her smile grew radiant, as, looking me in the face, she answered, 'By my soul, husband, it is.'

Then I went from her, down into my garden, where the day grew hot and the flowers were beginning to droop. I stared upon them and could find no solution to the problem that worked in my heart. And then I glanced up, eastward, to the sun above the privet-hedge, and saw him coming across the flower beds, treading them down in wantonness. He came with a light step and a smile, and I waited for him, leaning heavily on my stick.

'Give me your watch!' he called out, as he drew near.

'Why should I give you my watch?' I asked, while something worked in my throat.

'Because I wish it; because it is gold; because you are too old, and won't want it much longer.'

'Take it,' I cried, pulling the watch out and thrusting it into his hand. 'Take it – you who have taken all that is better! Strip me, spoil me—'

A soft laugh sounded above, and I turned. My wife was looking down on us from the window, and her eyes were both moist and glad.

'Pardon me,' she said, 'it is you who are spoiling the child.'

THE MASK

Richard Marsh

Richard Marsh was the pseudonym of the English novelist and short story writer Richard Bernard Heldmann (1857–1915). He began his literary career in his early twenties writing for boys' magazines, eventually becoming the associate editor of *The Union Jack*. There would, however, be an ignominious end to his association with the magazine when, in 1884, he was sentenced to eighteen months hard labour for forging cheques. On his release from prison, Heldmann took up writing again, using the aforementioned pseudonym 'Richard Marsh,' which is a combination of his first name and his mother's maiden name. Now writing mainly weird and sensational fiction, he had his biggest success with the supernatural thriller *The Beetle* (1897), the novel initially outselling Bram Stoker's *Dracula*, which had also come out that year. Equally sensational is the following story, which had its first publication in the December 1892 issue of *Gentleman's Magazine*. It features a deranged vampiress with a genius for disguise, who is undoubtedly one of the most fascinating femmes fatales in the whole of horror fiction.

I

What Happened in the Train

'Wigmakers have brought their art to such perfection that it is difficult to detect false hair from real. Why should not the same skill be shown in the manufacture of a mask? Our faces, in one sense, are nothing but masks. Why should not the imitation be as good as the reality? Why, for instance, should not this face of mine, as you see it, be nothing but a mask – a something which I can take off and on?'

She laid her two hands softly against her cheeks. There was a ring of laughter in her voice.

'Such a mask would not only be, in the highest sense, a work of art, but it would also be a thing of beauty – a joy for ever.'

'You think that I am beautiful?'

I could not doubt it – with her velvet skin just tinted with the bloom of health, her little dimpled chin, her ripe red lips, her flashing teeth, her great, inscrutable dark eyes, her wealth of hair which gleamed in the sunlight. I told her so.

'So you think that I am beautiful? How odd – how very odd!'

I could not tell if she was in jest or earnest. Her lips were parted by a smile. But it did not seem to me that it was laughter which was in her eyes.

'And you have only seen me, for the first time, a few hours ago?'

'Such has been my ill-fortune.'

She rose. She stood for a moment looking down at me. 'And you think there is nothing in my theory about – a mask?'

'On the contrary, I think there is a great deal in any theory you may advance.'

A waiter brought me a card on a salver. 'Gentleman wishes to see you, sir.' I glanced at the card. On it was printed, 'George Davis, Scotland Yard'. As I was looking at the piece of pasteboard she passed behind me.

'Perhaps I shall see you again, when we will continue our discussion about – a mask.'

I rose and bowed. She went from the verandah down the steps into the garden. I turned to the waiter. 'Who is that lady?'

'I don't know her name, sir. She came in last night. She has a private sitting-room at No. 22.' He hesitated. Then he added, 'I'm not sure, sir, but I think the lady's name is Jaynes – Mrs Jaynes.'

'Where is Mr Davis? Show him into my room.'

I went to my room and awaited him. Mr Davis proved to be a short, spare man, with iron-grey whiskers and a quiet, unassuming manner.

'You had my telegram, Mr Davis?'

'We had, sir.'

'I believe you are not unacquainted with my name?'

'Know it very well, sir.'

'The circumstances of my case are so peculiar, Mr Davis, that, instead of going to the local police, I thought it better to at once place myself in communication with headquarters.' Mr Davis bowed. 'I came down yesterday afternoon by the express from Paddington. I was alone in a first-class carriage. At Swindon a young gentleman got in. He seemed to me to be about twenty-three or four years of age, and unmistakably a gentleman. We had some conversation together. At Bath he offered me a drink out of his flask. It was getting evening then. I have been hard at it for the last few weeks. I was tired. I suppose I fell asleep. In my sleep I dreamed.'

'You dreamed?'

'I dreamed that I was being robbed.' The detective smiled. 'As you surmise, I woke up to find that my dream was real. But the curious part of the matter is that I am unable to tell you where my dream ended, and where my wakefulness began. I dreamed that something was leaning over me, rifling my person – some hideous, gasping thing which, in its eagerness, kept emitting short cries which were of the nature of barks. Although I say I dreamed this, I am not at all sure I did not actually see it taking place. The purse was drawn from my trousers pocket; something was taken out of it. I distinctly heard the chink of money, and then the purse was returned to where it was before. My watch and chain were taken, the studs out of my shirt, the links out of my wristbands. My pocketbook was treated as my purse had been – something was taken out of it and the book returned. My keys were taken. My dressing bag was taken from the rack, opened, and articles were taken out of it, though I could not see what articles they were. The bag was replaced on the rack, the keys in my pocket.'

'Didn't you see the face of the person who did all this?'

'That was the curious part of it. I tried to, but I failed. It seemed to me that the face was hidden by a veil.'

'The thing was simple enough. We shall have to look for your young gentleman friend.'

'Wait till I have finished. The thing – I say the thing because, in my dream, I was strongly, nay, horribly under the impression that I was at the mercy of some sort of animal, some creature of the ape or monkey tribe.'

'There, certainly, you dreamed.'

'You think so? Still, wait a moment. The thing, whatever it was, when it had robbed me, opened my shirt at the breast, and, deliberately tearing my skin with what seemed to me to be talons, put its mouth to the wound, and, gathering my flesh between its teeth, bit me to the bone. Here is sufficient evidence to prove that then, at least, I did not dream.'

Unbuttoning my shirt I showed Mr Davis the open cicatrice.

'The pain was so intense that it awoke me. I sprang to my feet. I saw the thing.'

'You saw it?'

'I saw it. It was crouching at the other end of the carriage. The door was open. I saw it for an instant as it leaped into the night.'

'At what rate do you suppose the train was travelling?'

'The carriage blinds were drawn. The train had just left Newton Abbot. The creature must have been biting me when the train was actually drawn up at the platform. It leaped out of the carriage as the train was restarting.'

'And did you see the face?'

'I did. It was the face of a devil.'

'Excuse me, Mr Fountain, but you're not trying on me the plot of your next novel – just to see how it goes?'

'I wish I were, my lad, but I am not. It was the face of a devil – so hideous a face that the only detail I was able to grasp was that it had a pair of eyes which gleamed at me like burning coals.'

'Where was the young gentleman?'

'He had disappeared.'

'Precisely. And I suppose you did not only dream you had been robbed?'

'I had been robbed of everything which was of the slightest value, except eighteen shillings. Exactly that sum had been left in my purse.'

'Now perhaps you will give me a description of the young gentleman and his flask.'

'I swear it was not he who robbed me.'

'The possibility is that he was disguised. To my eye it seems unreasonable to suppose that he should have removed his disguise while engaged in the very act of robbing you. Anyhow, you give me his description, and I shouldn't be surprised if I was able to lay my finger on him on the spot.'

I described him – the well-knit young man, with his merry eyes, his slight moustache, his graceful manners.

'If he was a thief, then I am no judge of character. There was something about him which, to my eyes, marked him as emphatically a gentleman.'

The detective only smiled. 'The first thing I shall have to do will be to telegraph all over the country a list of the stolen property. Then I may possibly treat myself to a little private think. Your story is rather a curious one, Mr Fountain. And then later in the day I may want to say a word or two with you again. I shall find you here?'

I said that he would. When he had gone I sat down and wrote a letter. When I had finished the letter I went along the corridor towards the front door of the hotel. As I was going I saw in front of me a figure – the figure of a man. He was standing still, and his back was turned my way. But something about him struck me with such a sudden force of recognition that, stopping short, I stared. I suppose I must, unconsciously, have uttered some sort of exclamation, because the instant I stopped short, with a quick movement, he wheeled right round. We faced each other.

'You!' I exclaimed. I hurried forward with a cry of recognition. He advanced, as I thought, to greet me. But he had only taken a step or two in my direction when he turned into a room upon his right, and, shutting the door behind him, disappeared.

'The man in the train!' I told myself. If I had had any doubt upon the subject his sudden disappearance would have cleared my doubt away. If he was anxious to avoid a meeting with me, all the more reason why I should seek an interview with him. I went to the door of the room which he had entered and, without the slightest hesitation, I turned the handle. The room was empty – there could be no doubt of that. It was an ordinary hotel sitting-room, own brother to the one which I occupied myself, and, as I saw at a glance, contained no article of furniture behind which a person could be concealed. But at the other side of the room was another door.

'My gentleman,' I said, 'has gone through that.' Crossing the room again I turned the handle. This time without result – the door was locked. I rapped against the panels. Instantly someone addressed me from within.

'Who's that?'

The voice, to my surprise, and also somewhat to my discomfiture, was a woman's:

'Excuse me, but might I say one word to the gentleman who has just entered the room?'

'What's that? Who are you?'

'I'm the gentleman who came down with him in the train.'

'What?'

The door opened. A woman appeared – the lady whom the waiter had said he believed was a Mrs Jaynes, and who had advanced that curious story about a mask being made to imitate the human face. She had a dressing jacket on, and her glorious hair was flowing loose over her shoulders. I was so surprised to see her that for a moment I was tongue-tied. The surprise seemed to be mutual, for, with a pretty air of bewilderment, stepping back into the room she partially closed the door.

'I thought it was the waiter. May I ask, sir, what it is you want?'

'I beg ten thousand pardons; but might I just have one word with your husband?'

'With whom, sir?'

'Your husband.'

'My husband?'

Again throwing the door wide open she stood and stared at me.

'I refer, madam, to the gentleman whom I just saw enter the room.'

'I don't know if you intend an impertinence, sir, or merely a jest.' Her lip curled, her eyes flashed – it was plain she was offended.

'I just saw, madam, in the corridor a gentleman with whom I travelled yesterday from London. I advanced to meet him. As I did so he turned into your sitting-room. When I followed him I found it empty, so I took it for granted he had come in here.'

'You are mistaken, sir. I know no gentleman in the hotel. As for my husband, my husband has been dead three years.'

I could not contradict her, yet it was certain I had seen the stranger turn into the outer room. I told her so.

'If any man entered my sitting-room – which was an unwarrantable liberty to take – he must be in it now. Except yourself, no one
has come near my bedroom. I have had the door locked, and, as you
see, I have been dressing. Are you sure you have not been dreaming?'

If I had been dreaming I had been dreaming with my eyes open;
and yet, if I had seen the man enter the room – and I could have
sworn I had – where was he now? She offered, with scathing irony,
to let me examine her own apartment. Indeed, she opened the door
so wide that I could see all over it from where I stood. It was plain
enough that, with the exception of herself, it had no occupant.

And yet, I asked myself, as I retreated with my tail a little between
my legs, how could I have been mistaken? The only hypothesis I
could hit upon was, that my thoughts had been so deeply engaged
upon the matter that they had made me the victim of hallucination.
Perhaps my nervous system had temporarily been disorganised by
my misadventures of the day before. And yet – and this was the
final conclusion to which I came upon the matter – if I had not seen
my fellow-passenger standing in front of me, a creature of flesh and
blood, I would never trust the evidence of my eyes again. The most
ardent ghost-seer never saw a ghost in the middle of the day.

I went for a walk towards Babbacombe. My nerves might be a
little out of order – though not to the extent of seeing things which
were non-existent, and it was quite possible that fresh air and exercise might do them good. I lunched at Babbacombe, spending the
afternoon, as the weather was so fine, upon the seashore, in company
with my thoughts, my pipe, and a book. But as the day wore on a
sea mist stole over the land, and as I returned Torquay-wards, it was
already growing dusk. I went back by way of the seafront. As I was
passing Hesketh Crescent I stood for a moment looking out into the
gloom which was gathering over the sea. As I looked I heard, or I
thought that I heard, a sound just behind me. As I heard it the blood
seemed to run cold in my veins, and I had to clutch at the coping
of the seawall to prevent my knees from giving way under me. It
was the sound which I had heard in my dream in the train, and
which had seemed to come from the creature which was robbing
me: the cry or bark of some wild beast. It came once, one short,
quick, gasping bark, then all was still. I looked round, fearing to see
I know not what. Nothing was in sight. Yet, although nothing could

be seen, I felt that there was something there. But, as the silence continued, I began to laugh at myself beneath my breath. I had not supposed that I was such a coward as to be frightened at less than a shadow! Moving away from the wall, I was about to resume my walk, when it came again – the choking, breathless bark – so close to me that I seemed to feel the warm breath upon my cheek. Looking swiftly round, I saw, almost touching mine, the face of the creature which I had seen, but only for an instant, in the train.

II

Mary Brooker

'Are you ill?'

'I am a little tired.'

'You look as though you had seen a ghost. I am sure you are not well.'

I did not feel well. I felt as though I had seen a ghost, and something worse than a ghost! I had found my way back to the hotel – how, I scarcely knew. The first person I met was Mrs Jaynes. She was in the garden, which ran all round the building. My appearance seemed to occasion her anxiety.

'I am sure you are not well! Do sit down! Let me get you something to drink.'

'Thanks; I will go to my own room. I have not been very well lately. A little upsets me.'

She seemed reluctant to let me go. Her solicitude was flattering; though if there had been a little less of it I should have been equally content. She even offered me her arm. That I laughingly declined. I was not quite in such a piteous plight as to be in need of that. At last I escaped her. As I entered my sitting-room someone rose to greet me. It was Mr Davis.

'Mr Fountain, are you not well?'

My appearance seemed to strike him as it had struck the lady.

'I have had a shock. Will you ring the bell and order me some brandy?'

'A shock?' He looked at me curiously. 'What sort of a shock?'

'I will tell you when you have ordered the brandy. I really am in need of something to revive me. I fancy my nervous system must be altogether out of order.'

He rang the bell. I sank into an easy-chair, really grateful for the support which it afforded me. Although he sat still I was conscious that his eyes were on me all the time. When the waiter had brought the brandy Mr Davis gave rein to his curiosity. 'I hope that nothing serious has happened.'

'It depends upon what you call serious.' I paused to allow the spirit to take effect. It did me good. 'You remember what I told you about the strange sound which was uttered by the creature which robbed me in the train? I have heard that sound again.'

'Indeed!' He observed me attentively. I had thought he would be sceptical; he was not. 'Can you describe the sound?'

'It is difficult to describe, though when it is once heard it is impossible not to recognise it when it is heard again.' I shuddered as I thought of it. 'It is like the cry of some wild beast when in a state of frenzy – just a short, jerky, half-strangled yelp.'

'May I ask what were the circumstances under which you heard it?'

'I was looking at the sea in front of Hesketh Crescent. I heard it close behind me, not once, but twice; and the second time I – I saw the face which I saw in the train.'

I took another drink of brandy. I fancy that Mr Davis saw how even the mere recollection affected me.

'Do you think that your assailant could by any possibility have been a woman?'

'A woman!'

'Was the face you saw anything like that?'

He produced from his pocket a pocketbook, and from the pocketbook a photograph. He handed it to me. I regarded it intently. It was not a good photograph, but it was a strange one. The more I looked at it the more it grew upon me that there was a likeness – a dim and fugitive likeness, but still a likeness, to the face which had glared at me only half an hour before.

'But surely this is not a woman?'

'Tell me, first of all, if you trace in it any resemblance.'

'I do, and I don't. In the portrait the face, as I know it, is grossly flattered; and yet in the portrait it is sufficiently hideous.'

Mr Davis stood up. He seemed a little excited. 'I believe I have hit it!'

'You have hit it?'

'The portrait which you hold in your hand is the portrait of a criminal lunatic who escaped last week from Broadmoor.'

'A criminal lunatic!' As I looked at the portrait I perceived that it was the face of a lunatic.

'The woman – for it is a woman – is a perfect devil – as artful as she is wicked. She was there during Her Majesty's pleasure for a murder which was attended with details of horrible cruelty. She was more than suspected of having had a hand in other crimes. Since that portrait was taken she has deliberately burnt her face with a red-hot poker, disfiguring herself almost beyond recognition.'

'There is another circumstance which I should mention, Mr Davis. Do you know that this morning I saw the young gentleman too?'

The detective stared. 'What young gentleman?'

'The young fellow who got into the train at Swindon, and who offered me his flask.'

'You saw him! Where?'

'Here, in the hotel.'

'The devil you did! And you spoke to him?'

'I tried to.'

'And he hooked it?'

'That is the odd part of the thing. You will say there is something odd about everything I tell you; and I must confess there is. When you left me this morning I wrote a letter; when I had written it I left the room. As I was going along the corridor I saw, in front of me, the young man who was with me in the train.'

'You are sure it was he?'

'Certain. When first I saw him he had his back to me. I suppose he heard me coming. Anyhow, he turned, and we were face to face. The recognition, I believe, was mutual, because as I advanced—'

'He cut his lucky?'

'He turned into a room upon his right.'

'Of course you followed him?'

'I did. I made no bones about it. I was not three seconds after him, but when I entered, the room was empty.'

'Empty!'

'It was an ordinary sitting-room like this, but on the other side of it there was a door. I tried that door. It was locked. I rapped with my knuckles. A woman answered.'

'A woman?'

'A woman. She not only answered, she came out.'

'Was she anything like that portrait?'

I laughed. The idea of instituting any comparison between the horror in the portrait and that vision of health and loveliness was too ludicrous. 'She was a lady who is stopping in the hotel, with whom I already had had some conversation, and who is about as unlike that portrait as anything could possibly be – a Mrs Jaynes.'

'Jaynes? A Mrs Jaynes?' The detective bit his fingernails. He seemed to be turning something over in his mind. 'And did you see the man?'

'That is where the oddness of the thing comes in. She declared that there was no man.'

'What do you mean?'

'She declared that no one had been near her bedroom while she had been in it. That there was no one in it at that particular moment is beyond a doubt, because she opened the door to let me see. I am inclined to think, upon reflection, that, after all, the man may have been concealed in the outer room, that I overlooked him in my haste, and that he made good his escape while I was knocking at the lady's door.'

'But if he had a finger in the pie, that knocks the other theory upon the head.' He nodded towards the portrait which I still was holding in my hand. 'A man like that would scarcely have such a pal as Mary Brooker.'

'I confess, Mr Davis, that the whole affair is a mystery to me. I suppose that your theory is that the flask out of which I drank was drugged?'

'I should say upon the face of it that there can't be two doubts about that.' The detective stood reflecting. 'I should like to have a look at this Mrs Jaynes. I will have a look at her. I'll go down to the office here, and I think it's just possible that I may be treated to a peep at her room.'

When he had gone I was haunted by the thought of that criminal lunatic, who was at least so far sane that she had been able to make good her escape from Broadmoor. It was only when Mr Davis had left me that I discovered that he had left the portrait behind him. I looked at it. What a face it was! 'Think,' I said to myself, 'of being left at the mercy of such a woman as that!'

The words had scarcely left my lips when, without any warning, the door of my room opened, and, just as I was taking it for granted that it was Mr Davis come back for the portrait, in walked the young man with whom I had travelled in the train! He was dressed exactly as he had been yesterday, and wore the same indefinable but unmistakable something which denotes good breeding.

'Excuse me,' he observed, as he stood with the handle of the door in one hand and his hat in the other, 'but I believe you are the gentleman with whom I travelled yesterday from Swindon?' In my surprise I was for a moment tongue-tied. 'I do not think I have made a mistake.'

'No,' I said, or rather stammered, 'you have not made a mistake.'

'It is only by a fortunate accident that I have just learnt that you are staying in the hotel. Pardon my intrusion, but when I changed carriages at Exeter I left behind me a cigar-case.'

'A cigar-case?'

'Did you notice it? I thought it might have caught your eye. It was a present to me, and one I greatly valued. It matched this flask.' Coming a step or two towards me he held out a flask – the identical flask from which I had drunk! I stared alternately at him and at his flask.

'I was not aware that you changed carriages at Exeter.'

'I wondered if you noticed it. I fancy you were asleep.'

'A singular thing happened to me before I reached my journey's end – a singular and a disagreeable thing.'

'How do you mean?'

'I was robbed.'

'Robbed?'

'Did you notice anybody get into the carriage when you, as you say, got out?'

'Not that I am aware of. You know it was pretty dark. Why, good gracious! is it possible that after all it wasn't my imagination?'

'What wasn't your imagination?'

He came closer to me – so close that he touched my sleeve with his gloved hand. 'Do you know why I left the carriage when I did? I left it because I was bothered by the thought that there was someone in it besides us two.'

'Someone in it besides us two?'

'Someone underneath the seat. I was dozing off as you were doing. More than once I woke up under the impression that someone was twitching my legs beneath the seat; pinching them – even pricking them.'

'Did you not look to see if anyone was there?'

'You will laugh at me, but – I suppose I was silly – something restrained me. I preferred to make a bolt of it, and become the victim of my own imagination.'

'You left me to become the victim of something besides your imagination, if what you say is correct.'

All at once the stranger made a dart at the table. I suppose he had seen the portrait lying there, because, without any sort of cere-mony, he picked it up and stared at it. As I observed him, commenting inwardly about the fellow's coolness, I distinctly saw a shudder pass all over him. Possibly it was a shudder of aversion, because, when he had stared his fill, he turned to me and asked, 'Who, may I ask, is this hideous-looking creature?'

'That is a criminal lunatic who has escaped from Broadmoor – one Mary Brooker.'

'Mary Brooker! Mary Brooker! Mary Brooker's face will haunt me for many a day.' He laid the portrait down hesitatingly, as if it had for him some dreadful fascination which made him reluctant to let it go. Wholly at a loss what to say or do, whether to detain the man or to permit him to depart, I turned away and moved across the room. The instant I did so I heard behind me the sharp, frenzied yelp which I had heard in the train, and which I had heard again when I had been looking at the sea in front of Hesketh Crescent. I turned as on a pivot. The young man was staring at me. 'Did you hear that?' he said.

'Hear it! Of course I heard it.'

'Good God!' He was shuddering so that it seemed to me that he could scarcely stand. 'Do you know that it was that sound, coming from underneath the seat in the carriage, which made me make a bolt of it? I – I'm afraid you must excuse me. There – there's my card. I'm staying at the Royal. I will perhaps look you up again tomorrow.'

Before I had recovered my presence of mind sufficiently to inter-fere he had moved to the door and was out of the room. As he went out Mr Davis entered; they must have brushed each other as they passed.

'I forgot the portrait of that Brooker woman,' Mr Davis began.

'Why didn't you stop him?' I exclaimed.

'Stop whom?'

'Didn't you see him – the man who just went out?'

'Why should I stop him? Isn't he a friend of yours?'

'He's the man who travelled in the carriage with me from Swindon.'

Davis was out of the room like a flash of lightning. When he returned he returned alone.

'Where is he?' I demanded.

'That's what I should like to know.' Mr Davis wiped his brow. 'He must have travelled at the rate of about sixty miles an hour – he's nowhere to be seen. Whatever made you let him go?'

'He has left his card.' I took it up. It was inscribed 'George Etherege, Coliseum Club'. 'He says he is staying at the Royal Hotel. I don't believe he had anything to do with the robbery. He came to me in the most natural manner possible to inquire for a cigar-case which he left behind him in the carriage. He says that while I was sleeping he changed carriages at Exeter because he suspected that someone was underneath the seat.'

'Did he, indeed?'

'He says that he did not look to see if anybody was actually there because – well, something restrained him.'

'I should like to have a little conversation with that young gentleman.'

'I believe he speaks the truth, for this reason. While he was talking there came the sound which I have described to you before.'

'The sort of bark?'

'The sort of bark. There was nothing to show from whence it came. I declare to you that it seemed to me that it came out of space. I never saw a man so frightened as he was. As he stood trembling, just where you are standing now, he stammered out that it was because he had heard that sound come from underneath the seat in the carriage that he had decided that discretion was the better part of valour, and, instead of gratifying his curiosity, had chosen to retreat.'

III

The Secret of the Mask

Table d'hôte had commenced when I sat down. My right-hand neighbour was Mrs Jaynes. She asked me if I still suffered any ill effects from my fatigue.

'I suppose,' she said, when I assured her that all ill effects had passed away, 'that you have not thought anything of what I said to you this morning – about my theory of the mask?' I confessed that I had not. 'You should. It is a subject which is a crotchet of mine, and to which I have devoted many years – many curious years of my life.'

'I own that, personally, I do not see exactly where the interest comes in.'

'No? Do me a favour. Come to my sitting-room after dinner, and I will show you where the interest comes in.'

'How do you mean?'

'Come and see.'

She amused me. I went and saw. Dinner being finished, her proceedings, when together we entered her apartment – that apartment which in the morning I thought I had seen entered by my fellow-passenger – took me a little by surprise.

'Now I am going to make you my confidant – you, an entire stranger – you, whom I never saw in my life before this morning. I am a judge of character, and in you I feel that I may place implicit confidence. I am going to show you all my secrets; I am going to induct you into the hidden mysteries; I am going to lay bare before you the mind of an inventor. But it doesn't follow because I have confidence in you that I have confidence in all the world besides, so, before we begin, if you please, I will lock the door.'

As she was suiting the action to the word I ventured to remonstrate. 'But, my dear madam, don't you think—'

'I think nothing. I know that I don't wish to be taken unawares, and to have published what I have devoted the better portion of my life to keeping secret.'

'But if these matters are of such a confidential nature I assure you—'

'My good sir, I *will* lock the door.'

She did. I was sorry that I had accepted so hastily her invitation, but I yielded. The door was locked. Going to the fireplace she leaned her arm upon the mantelshelf.

'Did it ever occur to you,' she asked, 'what possibilities might be open to us if, for instance, Smith could temporarily become Jones?'

'I don't quite follow you,' I said. I did not.

'Suppose that you could at will become another person, and in the character of that other person could move about unrecognised among your friends, what lessons you might learn!'

'I suspect,' I murmured, 'that they would for the most part be lessons of a decidedly unpleasant kind.'

'Carry the idea a step further. Think of the possibilities of a dual existence. Think of living two distinct and separate lives. Think of doing as Robinson what you condemn as Brown. Think of doubling the parts and hiding within your own breast the secret of the double; think of leading a triple life; think of leading many lives in one – of being the old man and the young, the husband and the wife, the father and the son.'

'Think, in other words, of the unattainable.'

'Not unattainable!' Moving away from the mantelshelf she raised her hand above her head with a gesture which was all at once dramatic. 'I have attained!'

'You have attained? To what?'

'To the multiple existence. It is the secret of the mask. I told myself some years ago that it ought to be possible to make a mask which should in every respect so closely resemble the human countenance that it would be difficult, if not impossible, even under the most trying conditions, to tell the false face from the real. I made experiments. I succeeded. I learnt the secret of the mask. Look at that.'

She took a leather case from her pocket. Abstracting its contents, she handed them to me. I was holding in my hand what seemed to me to be a preparation of some sort of skin – gold-beater's skin, it might have been. On one side it was curiously, and even delicately, painted. On the other side there were fastened to the skin some oddly-shaped bosses or pads. The whole affair, I suppose, did not weigh half an ounce. While I was examining it Mrs Jaynes stood looking down at me.

'You hold in your hand,' she said, 'the secret of the mask. Give it to me.'

I gave it to her. With it in her hand she disappeared into the room beyond. Hardly had she vanished than the bedroom door reopened, and an old lady came out.

'My daughter begs you will excuse her.' She was a quaint old lady, about sixty years of age, with silver hair, and the corkscrew ringlets of a bygone day. 'My daughter is not very ceremonious, and is so wrapt up in what she calls her experiments that I sometimes tell her she is wanting in consideration. While she is making her preparations, perhaps you will allow me to offer you a cup of tea.'

The old lady carried a canister in her hand, which, apparently, contained tea. A tea service was standing on a little side table; a kettle was singing on the hob. The old lady began to measure out the tea into the teapot.

'We always carry our tea with us. Neither my daughter nor I care for the tea which they give you in hotels.'

I meekly acquiesced. To tell the truth, I was a trifle bewildered. I had had no idea that Mrs Jaynes was accompanied by her mother. Had not the old lady come out of the room immediately after the young one had gone into it I should have suspected a trick – that I was being made the subject of experiment with the mysterious 'mask'. As it was, I was more than half inclined to ask her if she was really what she seemed to be. But I decided – as it turned out most unfortunately – to keep my own counsel and to watch the sequence of events. Pouring me out a cup of tea, the old lady seated herself on a low chair in front of the fire.

'My daughter thinks a great deal of her experiments. I hope you will not encourage her. She quite frightens me at times; she says such dreadful things.'

I sipped my tea and smiled. 'I don't think there is much cause for fear.'

'No cause for fear when she tells one that she might commit a murder; that a hundred thousand people might see her do it, and that not by any possibility could the crime be brought home to her!'

'Perhaps she exaggerates a little.'

'Do you think that she can hear?' The old lady glanced round in the direction of the bedroom door.

'You should know better than I. Perhaps it would be as well to say nothing which you would not like her to hear.'

'But I must tell someone. It frightens me. She says it is a dream she had.'

'I don't think, if I were you, I would pay much attention to a dream.'

The old lady rose from her seat. I did not altogether like her manner. She came and stood in front of me, rubbing her hands, nervously, one over the other. She certainly seemed considerably disturbed. 'She came down yesterday from London, and she says she dreamed that she tried one of her experiments – in the train.'

'In the train!'

'And in order that her experiment might be thorough she robbed a man.'

'She robbed a man!'

'And in her pocket I found this.'

The old lady held out my watch and chain! It was unmistakable. The watch was a hunter. I could see that my crest and monogram were engraved upon the case. I stood up. The strangest part of the affair was that when I gained my feet it seemed as though something had happened to my legs – I could not move them. Probably something in my demeanour struck the old lady as strange. She smiled at me. 'What is the matter with you? Why do you look so funny?' she exclaimed.

'That is my watch and chain.'

'Your watch and chain – yours! Then why don't you take them?' She held them out to me in her extended palm. She was not six feet from where I stood, yet I could not reach them. My feet seemed glued to the floor.

'I – I cannot move. Something has happened to my legs.'

'Perhaps it is the tea. I will go and tell my daughter.' Before I could say a word to stop her she was gone. I was fastened like a post to the ground. What had happened to me was more than I could say. It had all come in an instant. I felt as I had felt in the railway carriage the day before – as though I were in a dream. I looked around me. I saw the teacup on the little table at my side, I saw the flickering fire, I saw the shaded lamps; I was conscious of the presence of all these things, but I saw them as if I saw them in a dream. A sense of nausea was stealing over me – a sense of horror. I was afraid of I knew not what. I was unable to ward off or to control my fear.

I cannot say how long I stood there – certainly some minutes – helpless, struggling against the pressure which seemed to weigh upon my brain. Suddenly, without any sort of warning, the bedroom door opened, and there walked into the room the young man who, before dinner, had visited me in my own apartment, and who yesterday had travelled with me in the train. He came straight across the room, and, with the most perfect coolness, stood right in front of me. I could see that in his shirt-front were my studs. When he raised his hands I could see that in his wristbands were my links. I could see that he was wearing my watch and chain. He was actually holding my watch in his hand when he addressed me.

'I have only half a minute to spare, but I wanted to speak to you about – Mary Brooker. I saw her portrait in your room – you remember? She's what is called a criminal lunatic, and she's escaped from Broadmoor. Let me see, I think it was a week today, and just about this time – no, it's now a quarter to nine; it was just after nine.' He slipped my watch into his waistcoat-pocket. 'She's still at large, you know. They're on the lookout for her all over England, but she's still at large. They say she's a lunatic. There are lunatics at Broadmoor, but she's not one. She's no more a lunatic than you or I.'

He touched me lightly on the chest; such was my extreme disgust at being brought into physical contact with him that even before the slight pressure of his fingers my legs gave way under me, and I sank back into my chair.

'You're not asleep?'

'No,' I said, 'I'm not asleep.' Even in my stupefied condition I was conscious of a desire to leap up and take him by the throat. Nothing of this, however, was portrayed upon my face, or, at any rate, he showed no sign of being struck by it.

'She's a misunderstood genius, that's what Mary Brooker is. She has her tastes and people do not understand them; she likes to kill – to kill! One of these days she means to kill herself, but in the meantime she takes pleasure in killing others.'

Seating himself on a corner of the table at my side, allowing one foot to rest upon the ground, he swung the other in the air. 'She's a bit of an actress too. She wanted to go upon the stage, but they said that she was mad. They were jealous, that's what it was. She's the finest actress in the world. Her acting would deceive the devil himself – they allowed that even at Broadmoor – but she only uses her powers for acting to gratify her taste – for killing. It was only the other day she bought this knife.'

He took, apparently out of the bosom of his vest, a long, glittering, cruel-looking knife. 'It's sharp. Feel the point – and the edge.'

He held it out towards me. I did not attempt to touch it; it is probable that I should not have succeeded even if I had attempted.

'You won't? Well, perhaps you're right. It's not much fun killing people with a knife. A knife's all very well for cutting them up afterwards, but she likes to do the actual killing with her own hands and nails. I shouldn't be surprised if, one of these days, she were to kill you – perhaps tonight. It is a long time since she killed anyone, and she is hungry. Sorry I can't stay; but this day week she escaped from Broadmoor as the clock had finished striking nine, and it only wants ten minutes, you see.' He looked at my watch, even holding it out for me to see.

'Goodnight.' With a careless nod he moved across the room, holding the glittering knife in his hand. When he reached the bedroom door he turned and smiled. Raising the knife he waved it towards me in the air; then he disappeared into the inner room.

I was again alone – possibly for a minute or more; but this time it seemed to me that my solitude continued only for a few fleeting seconds. Perhaps the time went faster because I felt, or thought I felt, that the pressure on my brain was giving way, that I only had to make an effort of sufficient force to be myself again and free. The power of making such an effort was temporarily absent, but something within seemed to tell me that at any moment it might return. The bedroom door – that door which, even as I look back, seems to have been really and truly a door in some unpleasant dream – reopened. Mrs Jaynes came in; with rapid strides she swept across the room; she had something in her right hand, which she threw upon the table.

'Well,' she cried, 'what do you think of the secret of the mask?'

'The secret of the mask?' Although my limbs were powerless throughout it all I retained, to a certain extent, the control of my own voice.

'See here, it is such a little thing.' She picked up the two objects which she had thrown upon the table. One of them was the preparation of some sort of skin which she had shown to me before. 'These are the masks. You would not think that they were perfect representations of the human face – that masterpiece of creative art – and yet they are. All the world would be deceived by them as you have been. This is an old woman's face, this is the face of a young man.' As she held them up I could see, though still a little dimly, that the objects which she dangled before my eyes were, as she said, veritable masks. 'So perfect are they, they might have been skinned from the fronts of living creatures. They are such little things, yet I have made them with what toil! They have been the work of years, these two, and just one other. You see nothing satisfied me but perfection; I have made hundreds to make these two. People could not make out what I was doing; they thought that I was making toys; I told them that I was. They smiled at me; they thought that it was a new phase of madness. If that be so, then in madness there is more cool, enduring, unconquerable resolution than in all your sanity. I meant to conquer, and I did. Failure did not dishearten me; I went straight on. I had a purpose to fulfil; I would have fulfilled it even though I should have had first to die. Well, it is fulfilled.'

Turning, she flung the masks into the fire; they were immediately in flames. She pointed to them as they burned.

'The labour of years is soon consumed. But I should not have triumphed had I not been endowed with genius – the genius of the actor's art. I told myself that I would play certain parts – parts which would fit the masks – and that I would be the parts I played. Not only across the footlights, not only with a certain amount of space between my audience and me, not only for the passing hour, but, if I chose, for ever and for aye. So all through the years I rehearsed these parts when I was not engaged upon the masks. That, they thought, was madness in another phase. One of the parts' – she came closer to me; her voice became shriller – 'one of the parts was that of an old woman. Have you seen her? She is in the fire.' She jerked her thumb in the direction of the fireplace. 'Her part is played – she had to see that the tea was drunk. Another of the parts was that of a young gentleman. Think of my playing the man! Absurd. For there is that about a woman which is not to be disguised. She always reveals her sex when she puts on men's clothes. You noticed it, did you not – when, before dinner, he came to you; when you saw him in the corridor this morning; when yesterday he spent an hour with you in the train? I know you noticed it because of these.'

She drew out of her pocket a handful of things. There were my links, my studs, my watch and chain, and other properties of mine. Although the influence of the drug which had been administered to me in the tea was passing off, I felt, even more than ever, as though I were an actor in a dream.

'The third part which I chose to play was the part of – Mrs Jaynes!' Clasping her hands behind her back, she posed in front of me in an attitude which was essentially dramatic.

'Look at me well. Scan all my points. Appraise me. You say that I am beautiful. I saw that you admired my hair, which flows loose upon my shoulders' – she unloosed the fastenings of her hair so that it did flow loose upon her shoulders – 'the bloom upon my cheeks, the dimple in my chin, my face in its entirety. It is the secret of the mask, my friend, the secret of the mask! You ask me why I have watched, and toiled, and schemed to make the secret mine.' She stretched out her hand with an uncanny gesture. 'Because I wished to gratify my taste for killing. Yesterday I might have killed you; tonight I will.'

She did something to her head and dress. There was a rustle of drapery. It was like a conjurer's change. Mrs Jaynes had gone, and instead there stood before me the creature with, as I had described it to Davis, the face of a devil – the face I had seen in the train. The transformation in its entirety was wonderful. Mrs Jaynes was a fine, stately woman with a swelling bust and in the prime of life. This was a lank, scraggy creature, with short, grey hair – fifty if a day. The change extended even to the voice. Mrs Jaynes had the soft, cultivated accents of a lady. This creature shrieked rather than spoke.

'I,' she screamed, 'am Mary Brooker. It is a week today since I won freedom. The bloodhounds are everywhere upon my track. They are drawing near. But they shall not have me till I have first of all had you.'

She came closer, crouching forward, glaring at me with a maniac's eyes. From her lips there came that hideous cry, half gasp, half yelp, which had haunted me since the day before, when I heard it in my stupor in the train.

'I scratched you yesterday. I bit you. I sucked your blood. Now I will suck it dry, for you are mine.'

She reckoned without her host. I had only sipped the tea. I had not, as I had doubtless been intended to do, emptied the cup. I was again master of myself; I was only awaiting a favourable opportunity to close. I meant to fight for life.

She came nearer to me and nearer, uttering all the time that bloodcurdling sound which was so like the frenzied cry of some maddened animal. When her extended hands were all but touching me I rose up and took her by the throat. She had evidently supposed that I was still under the influence of the drug, because when I seized her she gave a shriek of astonished rage. I had taken her unawares. I had her over on her back. But I soon found that I had undertaken more than I could carry through. She had not only the face of a devil, she had the strength of one. She flung me off as easily as though I were a child. In her turn she had me down upon my back. Her fingers closed about my neck. I could not shake her off. She was strangling me.

She would have strangled me – she nearly did. When, attracted by the creature's hideous cries, which were heard from without, they forced their way into the room, they found me lying unconscious, and, as they thought, dead, upon the floor. For days I hung between life and death. When life did come back again Mary Brooker was once more an inmate of Her Majesty's house of detention at Broadmoor.

THE LAST OF THE VAMPIRES

Phil Robinson

Born in Chunar, India, the son of an army chaplain, Philip Stewart Robinson (1847-1902) was educated in England at Marlborough College, after which he was employed as a war correspondent by the *Daily Telegraph*. He wrote a number of books reflecting his interest in natural history and humorous Anglo-Indian literature, but among connoisseurs of weird fiction he is chiefly known for his trio of vampire tales, 'The Man-Eating Tree,' 'Medusa,' and 'The Last of the Vampires,' which were collected in *Tales by Three Brothers* in 1902, the year of his death. 'The Man-Eating Tree' was subsequently reprinted in *Dracula's Brood* (1987), and 'Medusa' recently appeared in *Vintage Vampire Stories* (2011). The third story, 'The Last of the Vampires,' which is our next offering, was originally published in the March 1893 issue of *The Contemporary Review*, and features a most unusual vampire.

Do you remember the discovery of the 'man-lizard' bones in a cave on the Amazon some time in the sixties? Perhaps not; but it created a great stir at the time in the scientific world; and in a lazy sort of way, interested men and women of fashion. For a day or two it was quite the correct thing for Belgravia to talk of 'connecting links,' of 'the evolution of man from the reptile,' and 'the reasonableness of ancient myths' that spoke of Centaurs and Mermaids as actual existences.

The fact was that a German Jew, an india-rubber merchant, working his way with the usual mob of natives through a cahucho

forest along the Maranyon, came upon some bones on the riverbank where he had pitched his camp. Idle curiosity made him try
to put them together, when he found, to his surprise, that he had
before him the skeleton of a creature with human hands and feet,
a dog-like head and immense batlike wings. Being a shrewd man,
he saw the possibility of money being made out of such a curiosity;
so he put all the bones he could find into a sack and, on the back
of a llama, they were in due course conveyed to Chachapoyas, and
thence to Germany.

Unfortunately, his name happened to be the same as that of another
German Jew who had just then been trying to hoax the scientific
world with some papyrus rolls of a date anterior to the Flood, and
who had been found out and put to shame. So when his namesake
appeared with the bones of a winged man, he was treated with scant
ceremony.

However, he sold his india-rubber very satisfactorily, and as for
the bones, he left them with a young medical student of the ancient
University of Bierundwurst, and went back to his cahucho trees and
his natives and the banks of the Amazon. And there was an end of
him.

The young student one day put his fragments together, and, do
what he would, he could only make one thing of them – a winged
man with a dog's head.

There were a few ribs too many, and some odds and ends of
backbone, which were superfluous; but what else could be expected
of the anatomy of so extraordinary a creature? From one student
to another the facts got about, and at last the professors came to
hear of it; and, to cut a long story short, the student's skeleton was
taken to pieces by the learned heads of the college, and put together
again by their own learned hands.

But do what they would, they could only make one thing of it
– a winged man with a dog's head.

The matter now became serious: the professors were at first
puzzled, and then got quarrelsome; and the result of their squabbling
was that pamphlets and counterblasts were published; and so all
the world got to hear of the bitter controversy about the 'man-lizard
of the Amazon.'

One side declared, of course, that such a creature was an impossibility, and that the bones were a remarkably clever hoax. The other side retorted by challenging the sceptics to manufacture a duplicate, and publishing the promise of such large rewards to any one who could succeed in doing so, that the museum was beset for months by competitors. But no one could manufacture another man-lizard. The man part was simple enough, provided they could get a human skeleton. But at the angles of the wings were set huge claws, black, polished, and curved, and nothing that ingenuity could suggest would imitate them. And then the 'Genuinists,' as those who believed in the monster called themselves, set the 'Imposturists' another poser; for they publicly challenged them to say what animal either the head or the wings had belonged to, if not to the man-lizard? And the answer was never given.

So victory remained with them, but not, alas! the bones of contention. For the Imposturists, by bribery and burglary, got access to the precious skeleton, and lo! one morning the glory of the museum had disappeared. The man half of it was left, but the head and wings were gone, and from that day to this no one has ever seen them again.

And which of the two parties was right? As a matter of fact, neither; as the following fragments of narrative will go to prove.

Once upon a time, so say the Zaporo Indians, who inhabit the district between the Amazon and the Maranyon, there came across the Pampas de Sacramendo a company of gold-seekers, white men, who drove the natives from their workings and took possession of them. They were the first white men who had ever been seen there, and the Indians were afraid of their guns; but eventually treachery did the work of courage, for, pretending to be friendly, the natives sent their women among the strangers, and they taught them how to make tucupi out of the bread-fruit, but did not tell them how to distinguish between the ripe and the unripe. So the wretched white men made tucupi out of the unripe fruit, which brings on fits like epilepsy, and when they were lying about the camp, helpless, the Indians attacked them and killed them all.

All except three. These three they gave to the Vampire.

But what was the Vampire? The Zaporos did not know. 'Very long ago,' said they, 'there were many vampires in Peru, but they were all swallowed up in the year of the Great Earthquake when the Andes were lifted up, and there was left behind only one Arinchi, who lived where the Amazon joins the Maranyon, and he would not eat dead bodies – only live ones, from which the blood would flow.'

So far the legend; and that it had some foundation in fact is proved by the records of the district, which tell of more than one massacre of white gold-seekers on the Maranyon by Indians whom they had attempted to oust from the washings; but of the Arinchi, the Vampire, there is no official mention. Here, however, other local superstitions help us to the reading of the riddle of the man-lizard of the University of Bierundwurst.

When sacrifice was made to 'the Vampire,' the victim was bound in a canoe, and taken down the river to a point where there was a kind of winding backwater, which had shelving banks of slimy mud, and at the end there was a rock with a cave in it. And here the canoe was left. A very slow current flowed through the tortuous creek, and anything thrown into the water ultimately reached the cave. Some of the Indians had watched the canoes drifting along, a few yards only in an hour, and turning round and round as they drifted, and had seen them reach the cave and disappear within. And it had been a wonder to them, generation after generation, that the cave was never filled up, for all day long the sluggish current was flowing into it, carrying with it the flotsam of the river. So they said that the cave was the entrance to Hell, and bottomless.

And one day a white man, a professor of that same University of Bierundwurst, and a mighty hunter of beetles before the Lord, who lived with the Indians in friendship, went up the backwater right into the entrance, and set afloat inside the cave a little raft, heaped up with touch-wood and knots of the oil-tree, which he set fire to, and he saw the raft go creeping along all ablaze, for an hour and more lighting up the wet walls of the cave as it went on either side; and then *it was put out*.

It did not 'go' out suddenly, as if it had upset, or had floated over the edge of a waterfall, but it was as if it had been beaten out.

For the burning fragments were flung to one side and the other, and the pieces, still alight, glowed for a long time on the ledges and points of rock, where they fell, and the cave was filled with the sound of a sudden wind and the echoes of a noise as of great wings flapping.

And at last, one day, this professor went into the cave himself.

'I took,' he wrote, 'a large canoe, and from the bows I built out a brazier of stout cask-hoops, and behind it set a gold-washing tin dish for a reflector, and loaded the canoe with roots of the resin-tree, and oil-wood, and yams, and dried meat; and I took spears with me, some tipped with the woorali poison, that numbs but does not kill. And so I drifted inside the cave; and I lit my fire, and with my pole I guided the canoe very cautiously through the tunnel, and before long it widened out, and creeping along one wall I suddenly became aware of a moving of something on the opposite side.

'So I turned the light fair upon it, and there, upon a kind of ledge, sat a beast with a head like a large grey dog. Its eyes were as large as a cow's.

'What its shape was I could not see. But as I looked I began gradually to make out two huge bat-like wings, and these were spread out to their utmost as if the beast were on tip-toe and ready to fly. And so it was. For just as I had realised that I beheld before me some great bat-reptile of a kind unknown to science, except as prediluvian, and the shock had thrilled through me at the thought that I was actually in the presence of a living specimen of the so-called "extinct" flying lizards of the Flood, the thing launched itself upon the air, and the next instant it was upon me.

'Clutching on to the canoe, it beat with its wings at the flame so furiously that it was all I could do to keep the canoe from capsizing, and, taken by surprise, I was nearly stunned by the strength and rapidity of its blows before I attempted to defend myself.

'By that time – seemingly half a minute had elapsed – the brazier had been nearly emptied by the powerful brute; and the Vampire, mistaking me no doubt for a victim of sacrifice, had already taken hold of me. The next instant I had driven a spear deep into its body, and with a prodigious tumult of wings, the thing loosed its claws from my clothes and dropped off into the stream.

'As quickly as possible I rekindled my light, and now saw the Arinchi, with wings outstretched upon the water, drifting along on the current. I followed it.

'Hour after hour, with my reflector turned full upon that grey dog's head with cow-like eyes, I passed along down the dark and silent waterway. I ate and drank as I went along, but did not dare to sleep. A day must have passed, and two nights; and then, as of course I had all along expected, I saw right ahead a grey eye-shaped light, and knew that I was coming out into daylight again.

'The opening came nearer and nearer, and it was with intense eagerness that I gazed upon my trophy, the floating Arinchi, the last of the "winged reptiles."

'Already in imagination I saw myself the foremost of travellers of European fame – the hero of my day. What were Banks' kangaroos or Du Chaillu's gorilla to my discovery of the last survivor of the pterodactyle creatures of the Flood – the flying Saurians of the pre-Noachian epoch of catastrophe and mud?

'Full of these thoughts, I had not noticed that the Vampire was no longer moving, and suddenly the bow of the canoe bumped against it. In an instant it had climbed up on to the boat. Its great batlike wings once more beat me and scattered the flaming brands, and the thing made a desperate effort to get past me back into the gloom. It had seen the daylight approaching and rather than face the sun preferred to fight.

'Its ferocity was that of a maddened dog, but I kept it off with my pole, and seeing my opportunity as it clung, flapping its wings, upon the bow, gave it such a thrust as made it drop off. It tried to swim (I then for the first time noticed its long neck), but with my pole I struck it on the head and stunned it, and once more saw it go drifting on the current with me into daylight.

'What a relief it was to be out in the open air! It was noon, and as we passed out from under the entrance of the cave the river blazed so in the sunlight that after the two days of almost total darkness I was blinded for a time. I turned my canoe to the shore, to the shade of trees, and throwing a noose over the floating body, let it tow behind.

'Once more on firm land – and in possession of the Vampire!

'I dragged it out of the water. What a hideous beast it looked, this winged kangaroo with a python's neck! It was not dead; so I made a muzzle with a strip of skin, and then I firmly bound its wings together round its body. I lay down and slept. When I awoke, the next day was breaking; so, having breakfasted, I dragged my captive into the canoe and went on down the river. Where I was I had no idea, but I knew that I was going to the sea: going to Germany: that was enough.

* * * * * *

'For two months I have been drifting with the current down this never-ending river. Of my adventures, of hostile natives, of rapids, of alligators, and jaguars, I need say nothing. They are the common property of all travellers. But my Vampire! It is still alive. And now I am devoured by only one ambition – to keep it alive, to let Europe actually gaze upon the living, breathing survivor of the great Reptiles known to the human race before the days of Noah – the missing link between the reptile and the bird. To this end I deny myself food; deny myself even precious medicine. In spite of itself I gave it all my quinine, and when the miasma crept up the river at night, I covered it with my rug and lay exposed myself. If the black fever should seize me!

* * * * * *

'Three months, and still upon this hateful river! Will it never end? I have been ill – so ill, that for two days I could not feed it. I had not the strength to go ashore to find food, and I fear that it will die – die before I can get it home.

* * * * * *

'Been ill again – the black fever! But *it* is alive. I caught a vicuna swimming in the river, and it sucked it dry – gallons of blood. It had been unfed three days. In its hungry haste it broke its muzzle. I was almost too feeble to put it on again. A horrible thought possesses me. Suppose it breaks its muzzle again when I am lying ill, delirious, and it is ravenous? Oh! the horror of it! To see it eating is terrible. It links the claws of its wings together, and cowers over the body; its head is under the wings, out of sight. But the victim never moves. As soon as the Vampire touches it there seems to be a paralysis. Once those wings are linked there is absolute quiet.

Only the sound of sucking and heavy breathing. Horrible! horrible! But in Germany I shall be famous. *In Germany with my Vampire!*

* * * * * *

'Am very feeble. It broke its muzzle again. But it was in the daylight – when it is blind. Its great eyes are blind in sunlight. It was a long struggle. This black fever! and the horror of this thing! I am too weak now to kill it, if I would. I *must* get it home alive. Soon – surely soon – the river will end. O God! does it never reach the sea, reach white men, reach home? But if it attacks me I will throttle it. If I am dying I will throttle it. If we cannot go back to Germany alive, we will go together dead. I will throttle it with my two hands, and fix my teeth in it, and our bones shall lie together on the bank of this accursed river.'

* * * * * *

This is nearly all that was recorded of the Professor's diary. But it is enough to tell us of the final tragedy.

The two skeletons *were* found together on the very edge of the riverbank. Half of each, in the lapse of years, had been washed away at successive floodtides. The rest, when put together, made up the man-reptile which, to use a Rabelaisian phrase, 'metagrobolised all to nothing' the University of Bierundwurst.

THE STORY OF JELLA AND THE MACIC

Professor P. Jones

Little is known about the author of this story. The only clue to his identity is a newspaper report from 1894 which gives details about a fire which destroyed the valuable library of a Professor P. Jones, the Orientalist, who lived in Trieste. Judging by his novel *The Pobratim* (1895) – from which 'The Story of Jella and the Macic' is extracted – the Professor seems to have been an expert on the local customs and beliefs of the inhabitants of the Montenegro-Hungary region of the Balkans; and, although written as a work of fiction, *The Pobratim* is a veritable storehouse of Slavic legends and superstitions.

MILOS Bellacic swallowed another glass of *slivovitz*, leaving, however, a few drops at the bottom of his glass, which he spilt on the floor as a compliment to the *Starescina*, showing thereby that in his house there was not only enough and to spare, but even to be wasted. He then took a long pull at the amber mouthpiece of his long Marasca cherry pipe, let the smoke rise quietly and curl about his nose, and, after clearing his throat, began as follows:

THE STORY OF JELLA AND THE MACIC

Once upon a time there lived in a village of Crivoscie an old man and his wife; they had one fair daughter Jella and no more. This girl was beyond all doubt the prettiest maiden of the place. She was as beautiful as the rising sun, or the new moon, or as a *Vila*; so nothing more need be said about her good looks. All the young men of the village and of the neighbouring country were madly in love with her, though she never gave them the slightest encouragement.

Being now of a marriageable age, she was, of course, asked to every festivity. Still, being very demure, she would not go anywhere, as neither her father nor her mother, who were a sullen couple of stingy, covetous old fogeys, would accompany her.

At last her parents, fearing lest she might remain an old maid, and be a thorn rather than a comfort to them, insisted upon her being a little more sociable, and go out of an evening like the other girls. 'Moreover, if some rich young man comes courting you, be civil to him,' said the mother. 'For there are still fools who will marry a girl for her pretty face,' quoth the father. It was, therefore, decided that the very next time some neighbours gathered together to make merry, Jella should take part in the festivity. 'For how was she ever to find the husband of her choice if she always remained shut up at home?' said the mother.

Soon afterwards, a feast in honour of some saint or other happened to be given at the house of one of their wealthy neighbours, so Jella decked herself out in her finest dress and went. She was really beautiful that evening, for she wore a gown of white wool, all embroidered in front with a wreath of gay flowers, then an over-dress of the same material, the sleeves of which were likewise richly stitched in silks of many colours. Her belt was of some costly Byzantine stuff, all purfled with gold threads. On her head she wore a red cap, the headgear of the young Crivosciane.

As she entered the room, all the young men flocked around her to invite her to dance the *Kolo* with them, and to whisper all kinds of pretty things to her. But she, blushing, refused them all, declaring that she would not dance, elbowed her way to a corner of the room, where she sat down quite alone. All the young men soon came buzzing around her, like moths round a candle, each one hoping to be fortunate enough to become her partner. Anyhow, when the music struck up, and the *Kolo* began, their toes were now itching, and one by one they slunk away, and she, to her great joy, and the still greater joy of the other girls, was left quite by herself.

While she was looking at the evolutions of the *Kolo*, she saw a
young stranger enter the room. Although he wore the dress of the
Kotor, he evidently was from some distant part of the country. His
clothes – made out of the finest stuffs, richly braided and embroidered in gold – were trimmed with filigree buttons and bugles. The
pas, or sash, he wore round his waist was of crimson silk, woven
with gold threads; the wide morocco girdle – the *pripasnjaca* – was
purfled with lovely arabesques; his princely weapons, studded with
precious stones and damaskened, were numerous and costly. His
pipe, stuck not in his girdle like his arms, but 'twixt his blue satin
waistcoat – *jacerma* – and his shirt, had the hugest amber mouthpiece
that man had ever seen; aye, the Czar himself could not possibly
have a finer pipe. What young man, seeing that pipe with its silver
mounting, adorned with coral and turquoises, could help breaking
the Tenth Commandment? He was, moreover, as handsome as a
Macic, aye, as winsome as Puck.

He came in the room, doffed his cap to greet the company like
a well-bred young man, then set it pertly on his head again. After
that, he went about chatting with the lads, flirting with the lassies,
as if he had long been acquainted with them, like a youth accustomed to good company. He did not notice, however, poor Jella in
her corner. He took no part in the dances, probably because, every
Jack having found his Jill, there was nobody with whom he could
dance.

The girls all looked slily at him, and many a one wished in her
heart that she had not been so hasty in choosing her partner, nay,
that she had remained a wallflower for that night.

At last the young stranger wended his steps towards that corner
where Jella was sitting alone, moping. He no sooner caught sight
of her than he went gracefully up, and, looking at her with a merry
twinkle in his eyes, and a most mischievous smile upon his lips:

'And you, my pretty one? Don't you dance this evening?' he
asked.

'I never dance, either this evening or any other.'

'And why not?'

'Because there is not a single young man I care to dance with.'

'Oh, Jella!' whispered the girls, 'dance with him if he asks you;
we should so much like to see how he dances.'

'Then it would be useless asking you to dance the *Kolo* with me,
I suppose?'

'Oh, Jella! dance with him,' whispered the young men; 'it would
be an unheard-of rudeness to refuse dancing with a stranger who
has no partner.'

'Even if I did not care about dancing, I should do so for the sake
of our village.'

'Then you only dance with me that it might not be said: "He was
welcomed with the sour lees of wine"?'

'I dance with you because I choose to do so.'

'Thank you, pretty one.'

The two thereupon began to go through the maze of the *Kolo*,
and, as he twisted her round, they both moved so gracefully, keeping
time to the music, that they looked like feathery boughs swayed by
the summer breeze.

About ten o'clock the dances came to an end, and every youth,
having gone to thank his host for the pleasant evening he had
passed, went off with his partner, laughing and chatting all the way.

'And you, my lovely one, where do you live?' asked the stranger
of Jella.

'In one of the very last houses of the village, quite at the end of
the lane.'

'Will you allow me to see you home?'

'If I am not taking you out of your way.'

'Even if it were, it would be a pleasure for me.'

Jella blushed, not knowing what to answer to so polite a youth.

They, therefore, went off together, and in no time they reached
her house. Jella then bid the stranger goodbye, and, standing on
the door-step, she saw him disappear in the darkness of the night.

Whither had he gone? Which turning had he taken? She did not
know.

A feeling of deep sadness came over her; for the first time in her
life she felt a sense of bereavement and loneliness.

Would this handsome young man come back again? She almost
felt like running after the stranger to ask him if they would meet
on the morrow, or, at least, after some days. Being a modest girl,
she, of course, could not do so; moreover, the youth had already
disappeared.

'Did you bring me any cakes?' was the mother's first question, peevish at being awakened in her first sleep.

'Oh, no! *mati*; I never ate a crumb of a cake myself.'

'And you enjoyed yourself?'

'Oh! very much so; far more than I ever thought.'

Thereupon she began to relate all that had happened, and would have made a long description of the young man who had danced with her, but her father woke in the midst of a tough snore and bade her hold her tongue.

On the morrow there was again a party in the village, for it was carnival, the time of the year when good folks make merry. When night came on, Jella went to the dance without needing to be much pressed by her parents. She was anxious to know if the young stranger would be there, and, also, if he would dance with her or with some other girl.

'Remember,' said her mother to her as she was going off, 'do not dance with him "like a fly without a head"; but measure him from top to toe, and think how lucky it would be if he, being well off, would marry a dowerless girl like you. The whole village speaks of him, of his weapons and his pipe; still, he might be "like a drop of water suspended on a leaf," without house or home. Therefore, remember to question him as to his land, his castle, and so forth; try and find out if he is an only son and from where he comes, for "Marry with your ears and not with your eyes," as the saying is.'

'Anyhow, take this tobacco pouch,' added the old man, 'and offer it to him before he leaves you.'

'Why?' asked Jella, guilelessly.

'Because it is made out of a muskrat, and so it will be easy to follow him whithersoever he goes, even in the darkness of the night.'

Jella, being a simple kind of a girl, did not like the idea of entrapping a young man; moreover, if she admired the stranger, it was for his good looks and his wit rather than for his rich clothes; but being frightened both of her father and her mother, who had never had a kind word for her, she promised to do as she was bidden. She then went to the party, and there everything happened as upon the preceding evening.

The girls all waited for the handsome young man to make his

appearance, and put off accepting partners till the last moment, each one hoping that she might be the chosen one. The hour upon which he had come the evening before was now past, and still they all waited in vain. The music had begun, and the young men, impatient to be up and doing, were heavily beating time with their feet. At last the *Kolo* began. They had just taken their places, and all except Jella had forgotten the stranger, when he all at once stepped into the room, bringing with him a number of bottles of maraschino, and cakes overflowing with honey and stuffed with pistachios.

He, as upon the evening before, went round the room, talking with the young men and teasing the prettiest girls. Then he stepped up to Jella, and asked her to dance with him.

The *Kolo* at last came to an end, the boys went off with the girls, the old folks hobbled after them, and the unknown youth, putting his arm round his partner's waist, as if he had been engaged to her, accompanied her home.

They soon reached her house; Jella then gave the stranger the tobacco-pouch, and, having bid him goodnight, she stood forlorn on the door-step, to see him go off. No sooner had he turned his back, than the father, who was holding the door ajar and listening to every word they said, slipped out, like a weasel, and followed him by the smell of his musk pouch.

The night was as still as it was dark, the moon had not yet risen, a hushed silence seemed to have fallen over nature, and not the slightest animal was heard stirring abroad.

The young fellow, after following the road for about a hundred paces, left the highway and took a short cut across the fields. The old man was astounded to see that, though a stranger, he was quite familiar with the country, for he knew not only what lane to take, but also what path to follow in the darkness of the night, almost better than he did himself. He climbed over walls, slipped through the gaps in the hedges, leapt over ditches, just as if it had been broad daylight.

Jella's father had a great ado to follow him; still, he managed to hobble along, like an ungainly, bow-legged setter, as fast as the other one capered. They crossed a wood, where the boles of the trees had weird and fantastic shapes, where thorny twigs clutched him by his clothes; then they came out on a plain covered with sharp flints, where huge scorpions lurked under every stone. Afterwards they reached a blasted heath, where nothing grew but gnarled, knotty, and twisted roots of trees, which, by the dusky light of the stars, looked like huge snakes and fantastical reptiles; there, in the clumps of rank grass, the horned vipers curled themselves. After this they crossed a morass, amidst the croaking of the toads and the hooting of owls, where unhallowed will-o'-the-wisps flitted around him.

The old man was now sorely frightened; the country they were crossing was quite unknown to him, and besides, it looked like a spot cursed by God, and leading to a worse place still. He began to lag. What was he to do? – go back? – he would only flounder in the mire. He crossed himself, shut his eyes tightly, and followed the smell of the musk. He thus walked on for some time, shivering with fear as he felt a flapping of wings near him, and ever and anon a draught of cold air made him lose the scent he was following.

At last he stopped, hearing a loud creaking sound, a grating stridulous noise, like that of the rusty hinges of some heavy iron gate which was being closed just behind him.

A gate in the midst of a morass! thought he; where the devil could he have come to? As he uttered the ominous word of *Kudic* he heard the earth groan under his feet.

It is a terrible thing to hear the earth groan; it does so just before an earthquake!

He did not dare to open his eyes; he listened, awed, and then the faint sound of a distant bell fell upon his ears.

It was midnight, and that bell seemed to be slowly tolling – aye, tolling for the dead, the dead that groan in the bosom of the earth.

A shiver came over him, big drops of cold sweat gathered on his forehead. He sniffed the cold night air; it smelt earthy and damp, the scent of musk had quite passed away.

At last he half-opened his eyes, to see if he could perceive anything of the young stranger. The moon, rising behind a hillock, looked like a weird eye peeping on a ghastly scene. What did he see – what were those uncouth shapes looming in the distance, amidst the surrounding mist?

Why was the earth newly dug at his feet, shedding a smell of clay and mildew?

He felt his head spinning, and everything about him seemed to whirl.

What was that dark object dangling down, as from a huge gallows?

Whither was he to go? – back across the wide morass, where the earth, soft and miry, sank under his feet, where the unhallowed lights lead the wanderers into bottomless quagmires?

He opened his eyes widely, and began to stare around. He saw strange shapes flit through the fog, figures darker than the fog itself rise, mist-like, from the earth. Were they night-birds or human beings? He could not tell.

All at once he bethought himself that they were witches and wizards, *carovnitsi* and *viestitche*, the *morine* or nightmares, and all the creatures of hell gathering together for their nightly frolic.

Fear prompted him to run off as fast as he possibly could, but huge pits were yawning all around him; moreover, curiosity held him back, for he would have liked to see where the damned store away their gold; so, between these two feelings, he stood there rooted to the earth.

At last, when fear prevailed over covetousness, he was about to flee; he felt the ground shiver under his feet, a grave slowly opened on the spot where he stood, for – as you surely must have understood – he was in the very midst of a burying-ground. At midnight in a burying-ground, when the tombs gape and give out their dead! His hair stood on end, his blood was curdling within his veins, his very heart stopped beating.

Can you fancy his terror in seeing a *voukoudlak,* a horrid vampire all bloated with the blood it nightly sucks? Slowly he saw them rise one after the other, each one looking like a drowsy man awaking from deep slumbers. Soon they began to shake off their sluggishness, and leap and jump and frolic around, and as the mist cleared he could see all the other uncouth figures whirl about in a mazy dance, like midges on a rainy day.

It was too late to run away now, for as soon as these bloodsuckers saw him, they surrounded him, capering and yelling, twisting their boneless and leech-like bodies, grinning at him with delight, at the thought of the good cheer awaiting them, telling him that it was by no means a painful kind of death, and that afterwards he himself would become a vampire and have a jolly time of it.

At the sight of these dead-and-alive kind of ghosts, the poor man wished he had either a pentacle, a bit of consecrated candle, or even a medal of the Virgin; but he had nothing, he was at the mercy of the fiends; therefore, overpowered by fear, he fell down in a fainting-fit.

That night, and the whole of the following day, Jella and her mother waited for the old man to come back; but they waited in vain. When the evening came on, her mother persuaded her to go to the dancing-party and see if the young stranger would come again.

'Perhaps,' said she, 'he might tell you something about your father; if not, ask no questions. Anyhow, take this ball of thread, which I have spun myself, and on bidding him goodbye, manage to cast this loop on one of his buttons, drop the ball on the ground, and leave everything to me. Very likely your father has lost the scent of the musk, and is still wandering about the country. This thread, which is as strong as wire, is a much surer guide to go by.'

Jella did as she was bid. She went to the house where the *Kolo* was being danced; she spent the whole evening with the young stranger, who never said a word about her father, and when the moment of parting on the threshold of the door arrived, she deftly fastened the end of the thread to one of his buttons, and then stood watching him go off.

The ball having slowly unwound itself, the old woman darted out and caught hold of the other end of the string. Then she followed the youth in the darkness, through thorns and thickets, through brambles and briars, as well as her tottering legs could carry her, much in the same way her husband had done the evening before.

That night and the day afterwards, Jella waited for her father and mother, but neither of them returned. When evening came on, afraid of remaining alone, she again went to dance the *Kolo*.

The evening passed very quickly, and the rustic ball came to an end. The youth accompanied her home as he had done the evening before, and on their way he whispered words of love in her ear, that made her heart beat faster, and her head grow quite giddy, words that made her forget her father and mother, and the dreaded night she was to pass quite alone. Still, as they got in sight of the house, Jella, who was very frightened, grew all at once quite thoughtful and gloomy. Seeing her so sorrowful, the young stranger put again his arm round her waist, and looking deep into her dark blue eyes, he asked her why she was so sad.

She thereupon told him the cause of all her troubles.

'Never mind, my darling,' said the youth, 'come along with me.'

'But,' faltered Jella, hesitatingly, 'do you go far?'

'No, not so very far either.'

'Still, where do you go?'

'Come and see, dear.'

Jella did not exactly know what to do. She fain would go with him, and yet she was afraid of what people might say about her, and again she shuddered at the thought of having to remain at home quite alone.

'You are not afraid to come with me,' he asked; 'are you?'

'Afraid? No, why should I be? you surely would take care of me?'

'Of course; why do you not come, then?'

'Because the old women might say that it is improper.'

'Oh,' quoth he, laughing, 'only old women who have daughters of their own to marry, say such things!'

Thereupon he offered her his arm, and off they went.

Soon leaving the village behind them, they were in the open fields, beyond the vineyards and the orchards, in the untilled land where the agaves shoot their gaunt stalks up towards the sky, where the air is redolent with the scent of thyme, sage and the flowering Agnus castus bushes; then again they went through leafy lanes of myrtle and pomegranate trees and meadows where orchids bloomed and sparkling brooks were babbling in their pebbly beds.

Though they had been walking for hours, Jella did not feel in the least tired; it seemed as if she had been borne on the wings of the wind. Moreover, all sense of gloom and sadness was over, and she was as blithe and as merry as she had ever been.

At last – towards dawn – they reached a dense wood, where stately oaks and fine beech trees formed fretted domes high up in the air. There nightingales warbled erotic songs, and the merle's throat burst with love; there the crickets chirped with such glee that you could hardly help feeling how pleasant life was. The moon on its wane cast a mellow, silvery light through the shivering leaves, whilst in the east the sky was of the pale saffron tint of early dawn.

'Stop!' said the young girl, laying her hand on the stranger's arm. 'Do you not see there some beautiful ladies dancing under the trees, swinging on the long pendant branches and combing the pearly drops of dew from their black locks?'

'I see them quite well.'

'They must be *Vile*?'

'I am sure they are.'

'Fairies should not be seen by mortal eyes against their wish. Then do not let us seek their wrath.'

'Do not be afraid, sweet child; we are no ordinary mortals, you and I.'

'You, perhaps, are not; but as for me, I am only a poor peasant girl.'

'No, my love, you are much better than you think. Look there! the fairies have seen you, and they are beckoning you to go to them.'

'But, then, tell me first what I am.'

'You are a foundling; the old man and woman with whom you lived were not your parents. They stole you when you were an infant for your beauty and the rich clothes you wore.'

'And you, who are you, *gospod*?'

'I?' said the young man, laughing. 'I am *Macic*, the merry, the mischievous sprite. I have known you since a long time. I loved you from the first moment I saw you, and I always hoped that, "as like matches with like," you yourself might perhaps some day get to like me and marry me. Tell me, was I right?' said he, looking at her mischievously.

Jella told him he was a saucy fellow to speak so lightly about such a grave subject, but then – woman-like – she added that he was not wrong.

They were forthwith welcomed by the *Vile* with much glee, and, soon afterwards, their wedding was celebrated with great pomp and merriment.

'But what became of the old man and his wife?' asked an interested listener.

'They met with the punishment their curiosity deserved. They

were found a long time afterwards locked up in an old disused
burying-ground. They were both of them quite dead, for when they
fainted at the terrible sights they saw, the vampires availed themselves of their helplessness to suck up the little blood there was in
them.'

'May St John preserve us all from such a fate,' said Milos Bellacic,
crossing himself devoutly.

THE RING OF KNOWLEDGE

William Beer

William Beer is a forgotten author about whom nothing appears to be known, other than that he had two stories – 'The Casa Principessa' and 'The Ring of Knowledge' – published in *Atalanta*, a British monthly magazine that flourished briefly in the late 19th century. Primarily intended for young middle class women readers, it, nevertheless, published a wide range of stories, of which the most outstanding was Clemence Housman's 'The Were-Wolf.' Surprisingly, Beer's story 'The Ring of Knowledge,' which appeared in the November 1896 issue, has never been reprinted until now, making it one of the rarest stories in this anthology.

'DEAR Mr Vere, – We much regret to learn that you have not succeeded in finding Madame Augarde: but it is, of course, some satisfaction to know that you are certain she is no longer in Paris; and if you are correct in your inference that she has taken refuge in Berlin, we are sure to be able to find her shortly, thanks to the admirable police arrangements of that city. We shall be glad for you to remain some time longer in France, as we shall require your ability in unravelling a case placed in our hands. You probably know the particulars of "L'affaire Viroflay" as well as we do. The widow of the deceased Count is looked upon with suspicion by his relatives as having had some connection with his death: and now her brother-in-law (who is an Englishman) has placed the matter unreservedly with us. We hope, with your help, to clear away the mystery that now surrounds the Count's demise.' So ran the letter from my chief. I had read this letter and the papers accompanying it through and through again. I had been to the chateau where the accident, crime, or tragedy – whichever it was – occurred, had questioned the servants, and prosecuted enquiries in every conceivable direction without the slightest result; and L'affaire Viroflay seemed in a fair way to remain as much a mystery to me as it had already proved to the French police.

I was again in Paris, in my old rooms in the Place St Antoine-des-Cochons – two rooms and an anteroom, on the fifth, it's true, but which had the advantage of opening on a wide balcony which gave me a view, not only of the Place below, with its beds of brilliant flowers and falling spray of the fountain, but also of the ceaseless ebb and flow of life, the bustle and noise in the Boulevard St Michel – the dear old Boule Miche of one's student days – how long ago they seemed, those salad days, and so far away were scattered those I used to know, that they might have been a handful of leaves in the wind that is called time, and I a ghost, come back to haunt my old habitat in the Quartier Latin.

I had finished my *déjeûner*, sent in from a neighbouring restaurant, seasoning my meal with some such melancholy thoughts as these; and while lingering over my coffee and cognac I took out my instructions and read them over for the hundredth time. What was the use of it, come to a deadlock as I was? I thrust them impatiently into my pocketbook, and made up my mind to sit *chez moi* no longer, debating uselessly: I would go out and see if there were any letters awaiting me at the post office, and chance should arrange the rest of the day for me: perhaps I would dine on the other side of the river: perhaps I would go as far as the Bois – *cela dépend*!

I descended the Boulevard and walked along the Quai Voltaire, spending some pleasant minutes at the secondhand bookstalls which line the river parapet, turning over the books and quaint prints displayed, and looking into all the curio shops I passed, as was my wont.

One window displayed a show of battered brooches, rings, and a hundred small and doubtful objects of 'bigotry and virtue.' There was only one thing worth looking at twice in the whole window, and at first I passed it over: my second glance, however, showed me a very uncommon ring.

It was undoubtedly a genuine antique; a large cameo cut in sard and curiously set in thick, dark gold: the cameo itself – a head, full face – delicately cut, and the setting uncommon. I could see that some characters were cut in the gold on the inner side, characters such as are written on the Incantation Bowls in the Louvre, that were dug up by M. Botta from the stone-heaps marking the site of long-forgotten Chaldean cities, cities of the Sun and Moon and the Fish. I was so impressed with the look of the ring that I entered the shop to enquire its price. A frowsy little old woman, wrapped apparently in a bedgown of some dark printed stuff, with a red and yellow handkerchief worn turban-wise on her head, shuffled forward, and, peering up at me through her spectacles, demanded, in no civil manner, what I wanted. 'How much do you ask for that ring? The third in that tray.' 'Ring?' helping herself copiously to snuff. 'All in that tray 65 francs 50, except the turquoise, that's 80; and the pearl ring in the next tray is 100, and worth 125.' 'This one is 65.50, then?' I said, taking up the one I coveted and slipping it on my finger.

'Yes; but the pearl one is the best: worth 125'; more graciously, 'Monsieur should have it for 100, for 95 even,' snuffing vigorously the while. 'Yes, no doubt the pearl ring is *bon marché*; but this one takes my fancy, so I will have it.' '*Eh bien, chacun à son goût; mais Monsieur se trompe – merci!*' sweeping up the 65.50, with a hand that, with the help of age, dirt and snuff, resembled more the claw of some bird of prey than the hand of a human being.

I went on my way rejoicing, crossed the Pont des Tuilleries, strolled through the Gardens, out by the Golden Gates, into the Place de la Concorde and up the Rue Royale, determining as I went that I would dine at Duval's, opposite the Madeleine.

Being early, I hoped to get a table by the window, at the corner of the boulevard, but I found the best place occupied. Still, there was room for two, and the second seat was not to be scorned; and before I had taken two more steps I knew that fortune was friends with me still, for the other diner was my old comrade, Adolphe. The recognition and the pleasure of it were mutual, and in another second Adolphe was on his feet, shaking both my hands in the hearty British fashion I had taught him years ago. We wondered at the happy chance that had reunited us, and congratulated ourselves upon it, and then fell to discussing our dinner together, what time we talked of old days in the Quartier. 'How long have you been in Paris? Where are you living? What are you doing? How has fate used you?' from Adolphe, as he ate.

'In the old Hotel; in the Place St Antoine des Cochons.'

'No? But how droll!'

'And you, Adolphe?'

'Oh, I am at Barbizon. You remember Emile: he and I and Pierre – you do not know him – rent a cottage there. Pierre is Pierre Esme Vouard, the poet, thou knowest,' tutoring me in the old fashion. 'And you remember Mère Charcot?'

'I should think so.'

'Aie! the life we led her. Well, she keeps house and looks after us, and we get on famously – but famously! And Emile has a picture in the salon, a fine thing – "Le Philosophe et le Cupidon"; and I,' with a shrug, 'Oh, I do well. I have sold several sketches to Maupas – he is an old thief, *bien entendu*, but what would you? He has sent me a rich American, who has commissioned a large landscape. It is as broad as it is long: that was one of your sayings.'

'And Marie?'

'Is married, pretty as ever, and keeps a restaurant out by the Porte Maillot,' Adolphe said, succinctly.

'And Jules has gone to Rome,' I said, passing him my cigarette-case. 'Poor Jules! I was sorry to hear that he had thrown up painting and gone in for being *dévot*. Were not you, Adolphe? He was good company, Jules, in the old times.'

'*Mais oui*,' Adolphe said, vaguely, with his eyes on my ring. He had always been a dabbler in all sorts of out-of-the-way lore and antiquities, I remembered, and, seeing that my new acquisition had attracted his interest, it struck me that he might be able to decipher the letters engraved on the gold.

'Oh, Adolphe!' I said; 'can you tell me the meaning of this—,' trying to take the ring off my finger, but to my great surprise I was unable to remove it, although it slipped on with the greatest ease. 'I can't get it off!' I continued, holding out my hand. 'I suppose my finger must have swollen, the result of our good dinner,' laughingly. 'But it is a quaint old ring, is it not?'

'Yes, very old,' Adolphe said, with emphasis. 'I suppose you know the sort of superstition attached to that ring?'

'Indeed I don't. What is it?'

'No! Is it possible that you don't know the history of your find? I believe there never existed but seven of them, and of these all but three were supposed to have been destroyed. They were called the Thirsty Rings.'

'What an extraordinary name!'

'The Thirsty Rings, or the Rings of Knowledge, which you will, had extraordinary histories,' Adolphe said, drily. 'Whoever owned one had only to let his blood drop on it and in some unexplained way it would tell him whatever of the past or future he desired to know.'

'Extraordinary!' I said again, looking at my ring with double interest and excitement. 'Go on.'

'Catherine de Medicis had one, and it foretold to her the death of all her sons and the accession of Henri Quatre, and in her rage at the unwelcome prophecy she threw it into the fire. To come to our own time, Josephine had one, and it showed her her divorce and Napoleon's downfall. Old Pio Nono had another, taken from the sarcophagus of Augustus, *on dit*, and it foretold him the loss of the Temporal Power. The third ring is in the Sultan's treasury.'

'Then this must be Josephine's, for I picked it up today at a curio shop in the Quai Voltaire,' I said, as we called for our account and settled it. 'I got it for a song, too.'

'Ah! it is better to be born lucky than rich. Take good care of that ring; the Thirsty Rings are famous for unaccountable disappearances,' Adolphe said, as we went down into the Place de la Madeleine, and arranging a day whereon to meet at Barbizon, we parted, Adolphe going towards the Gare St Lazare, and I turning down the Rue Royale, on my way homewards.

I don't know what I had done to tire me, but, soon after I reached my rooms I fell into a sound sleep, and never woke until some time past sunset. The room was already full of shadows, though there was a little afterglow in the sky, and I lighted my lamp and closed the windows, and settled myself at my desk, grudgingly enough, for I hated to report another failure to the chief. It had to be done, however, so I did it: and then I threw my pen down, and gave myself up to discontented thought. I fell to idly turning the ring round and round on my finger. It slipped off quite easily now, to my surprise, for I remembered that I had tried in vain to remove it from my finger at the restaurant; and in spite of myself, I began to recall the story Adolphe had told me, and I examined the ring more minutely, turning it this way and that, and finally holding it up to the lamp. The cameo was a very large one, seven-eighths of an inch long, at least, by five-eighths, and the carving of the head was masterly. The face was that of a youth, in the first flush of manhood, the lips parted, and the head set in a kind of cloud. 'Why should I not work the charm; at least, I could try, and if it failed—. It would fail, of course: it could do nothing but fail. It was all ridiculous rubbish, and the day had gone by for such superstitious notions. Still—' I took up the ring again, looked at the parted lips, and made up my mind to try. I opened my penknife and pricked my wrist, letting the drops of crimson blood fall exactly on the open mouth. 'One, two, three! No change. Of course, what else did I expect? Four, five, six. Merciful Heavens! were the old tales true, after all?' I threw the ring on the table as if it had burnt me, and stared at it aghast. The face was growing, growing, and the cloud which framed it was moving – swirling and circling slowly like the vapour in a retort, changing its colour like an opal: now white, now blue, now faintly rosy, while points of brilliant light seemed constantly to thread their way through the vapour.

The face was now a human face, and it seemed to grow no more. It was still pallid, the face of one dead, slowly life seemed to pass into it. Colour came into the cheeks, and presently the closed eyelids opened to show eyes almost insupportably bright, and the full red lips were parted in a smile.

For some minutes I sat stupefied, nervously grasping the carved arms of my chair; then I took my courage in both hands and spoke, but my voice sounded low and far away, and utterly unfamiliar in my own ears.

'Who are you? What are you?'

'I am the shadow of the shade of That which men call knowledge, and gods another name – that for which men venture all; and which gained is bitterness of spirit and vexation of heart.' I cannot say I heard, I rather seemed to understand than absolutely hear.

'You speak my language well,' I said, more taken aback than ever.

'All tongues are but fragments of that great speech which all once knew in that which men call the past, and which all must speak again in that which mortals call eternity. But why have you enquired of me, oh child of the later time?

'Ask, and I must answer thee. For now I am of thee, and thou of me, for evil or for good, blood of thy blood, and life of thy life.'

'Well,' I said, gathering courage, 'I am in a difficulty, my reputation is at stake, and perhaps my future career. I have come to Paris to trace out a mysterious crime, and I am further from the light than ever. The Comte de Viroflay perished from poison, and I must find by whom it was administered. Can you tell me? If so, name your price?' I added, rather bitterly, 'for I suppose knowledge is not given for nothing?'

'I ask no price,' It said. 'Said I not that, for a little season, thou art of me and I of thee? Blood of thy blood, and life of thy life? I can tell thee, or, better, show thee, all. Say, wilt thou see?'

'Yes; I will see,' I replied.

Slowly the face – I saw the ring no longer – raised itself till it was beside my face, and ever the opal-coloured cloud whirled and swirled and circled around it: and the ineffable sweetness of the immortal eyes looked into mine, but the smile that curved the full red lips was edged with bitter contempt. 'Look,' It said, and as It spoke a light mist gathered at the end of the room, towards which we were looking, It and I. As I looked the mist drew slowly right and left like parted curtains, and I saw a familiar scene. It was the garden of the Chateau de Viroflay. I knew it again in a moment: and where I sat motionless in my chair I saw the roses on the terrace nodding gently in the evening wind, and saw the green reaches of the garden sloping softly down to the lake below. Down the curving pathway a man and woman were walking. I had seen their painted presentments, and I knew them at once for the dead Comte and Madame la Comtesse. I rose from my chair to see them better, almost wondering that they did not see me: and still they came close and closer yet, until I could see the adoration in the Comte's dark eyes, and the bored expression of Madame's charming face. They turned when they were almost beside me, went slowly up the steps to the terrace, and so disappeared through an open window into the chateau. The mist dropped swiftly upon the garden, blotting out its light and colour, then rolled up again like a shrivelling leaf. 'Look again,' said the voice by my side. It was night this time, and though I could not see the moon there was a broad stream of light on the lake, darkened every now and again, I suppose, by a cloud passing over the moon. The window that was open on the terrace before was open still, and from its shadow a cloaked figure steals forth. The Comtesse! She descends the steps leading from the terrace to the garden. She seems to have some steady purpose in her mind, for she looks neither to right nor left of her as she goes. Had she done so she must have seen the figure that followed in her footsteps: closely and noiselessly as her shadow. I could not see the face, but the build and height helped me at once to guess that Madame's shadow was no other than her husband. She went swiftly along the path between the Diane and Minerve fountains, and in a second she stood on the bank of the lake, watching – watching for some one. Ah! she has not long to wait, for almost immediately a boat came out of the shadow of the balustrade and pulled up close under Madame's feet. I can see the rower; it is Madame's cousin, le Capitaine de Vionville. He was standing on the bank beside Madame, when I looked again, and the boat was abandoned to her own devices, while he stood, talking eagerly, with Madame's eyes fixed on his face.

'It is not love,' whispers the Thing beside me, in answer to my unspoken thoughts. 'It has been love, and might be love again, if she were free. This meeting is not of her seeking, and she would but say farewell. The man who has her hand, has her truth, too.' M. le Comte was too far away to hear what Madame said, or to see the unmistakable air of repulse with which she at last turned away from her cousin. 'Had he done so he would live now, but this was not to be.' Slowly the Comtesse turned and moved away, and softly her shadow followed her again: softly, too, the mist fell, blotting it all out. When it again clears it is a white and dusty road winding along between tall poplars which I see. There is a small town in the distance, and the gleam of water between the poplar trees, and along the dusty road some figures walking briskly, all dyed in the mellow light of sunset. The pictures passed before me like a pano-rama: the white and dusty road, the passing peasants, and presently, walking amid them, a spare and upright figure – the Comte again. Then the town: its narrow streets and little lighted shops: through the open doors sudden glimpses of crowded cabarets, or quiet rooms where white-capped women prepare the evening meal. We follow a narrow winding street: Rue St Louis le Grand, I notice it is named. Here there were many little shops of indifferent prosperity, among them a dingy-looking pharmacien's opposite a fountain. The door was closed, and remained inhospitably shut heedless of the Comte's summons; but he knocked again, this time with so peremptory a hand that the door opened grudgingly, and the shrivelled head of a little old man peeped out. Seeing M. le Comte, he opens wider the door and bids him enter, and we follow. I see the shop itself, with its outer door jealously barred and bolted, its dusty ill-furnished shelves and bottles, the old pharmacien standing behind the counter, and M. le Comte, pale and stern, whispering something, with his mouth on a level with the old man's ear.

The pharmacien grinned, rather than smiled, drew back, and shook his head, gesticulating vigorously the while. Again the Comte whispered, and perhaps this time it was rather a threat than a request, for the pharmacien trembles violently. He seems to attempt to expos-tulate, but M. le Comte, with a vehement gesture, turns towards the door, and, afraid, perhaps, that the *seigneur* was really going to carry out his whispered threat, the little old man threw up his hands and, reluctantly shuffling away, proceeded to search for something among the bottles in a cupboard at the back of the shop. After much fumbling in its dark recesses he returns with a tiny phial in his hand, which he gave to Monsieur de Viroflay, with a sinister smile. ''Tis not wide, nor deep, but 'twill serve,' and M. le Comte seemed contented enough with his purchase as he put louis after louis into the pharmacien's shaking hand. 'I should know that sinister old face again anywhere, if only by a villainous-looking scar which runs right across his brow, from temple to eye.' Then the mist engulfed all, the Comte, the evil-looking pharmacien, and the little dimly-lighted shop. When it again cleared, it was the ballroom at the chateau which I saw, brilliantly illuminated from end to end, its walls banked with flowers of the rarest kinds, its floor covered with guests dancing to the music of a band, stationed in the musicians' gallery, at the far end. Madame la Comtesse I could easily distinguish, radiant with health and beauty, waltzing with her cousin de Vionville, a gallant figure in his gay uniform, and M. le Comte, dark and sad, dancing with *his* cousin, Madame des Greux. I could not tell if she complained of fatigue, or faintness, but I saw the Comte lead her to a seat in one of the window-recesses, and there leave her, after bowing with the court-liness for which all the de Viroflays had been distinguished. The scene shifted now to the supper-room, where every detail was perfect and everything ready, but for the moment it was empty. There were three supper-tables, exquisitely arranged with damask roses and stephanotis – Madame's favourite flowers – the stephanotis massed in low glass troughs, the roses in tall silver vases, and trails of roses covering the delicate damask. The tables followed three sides of the room, the fourth end being the great folding-doors leading to the ballroom. Through these, as I looked, the Comte comes stealthily into the empty supper-room; and for a little while he stands still at the head of the first table, looking at the flowers with dreamy eyes. Here they were in even greater profusion: roses heaped up recklessly round the tall vases, and not an inch of cloth to be seen for the stephanotis showered upon it.

'Stephanotis – and Stephanie is Madame's name.' I said to myself. 'It is the anniversary of her wedding, I know, but is it anything else?'

'It is her fete-day,' It said in my ear. 'Have you forgotten? The Comte will call upon his guests to pledge his wife, and then—.' My eyes went from the Comte's gloomy face to the four places at the head of the first table, where, among the other glasses, stood four magnificent Venetian goblets, two trumpet-shaped and two globular.

'Those four places are for madame and her husband, and the two cousins, I suppose,' I said, my eyes straying back to the Comte, who was stooping over the table now, with one hand in his waist-coat pocket and one busy with a tall Venetian glass. There was the chink of glass against glass, the falling of two or three drops from a little vial into the tall goblet, and then the Comte turned quickly away, and left the room.

Turned quickly away – and in turning disarranged the trail of crimson roses which surrounded his glasses; a small thing to do, but it cost him his life – on such trifling causes do great events hinge.

Scarcely had he left the room when a grey-headed butler came quickly in, followed by a young footman. His accustomed eye saw that the flowers had been disarranged at once, and he began to replace them, grumbling the while. In so doing his hand caught M. le Comte's Venetian goblet and overturned it; hastily calling the footman Ambroise to remove the broken glass, he moved the next tall goblet – that intended for the Capitaine with which the Comte had been meddling – into the place of the broken one, the footman bringing a tall goblet for M. le Capitaine from the last place at the table.

Hardly had the change been effected when the double doors opened wide, and M. le Comte and Madame entered, followed by the guests. They were soon seated, and the supper begins. By-and-by the Comte rises, and turning slightly towards Madame, made (I suppose) some pretty speech, while the servants were busy filling the guests' goblets. The Comte's speech soon ended, and as he lifted his glass, his guests arose to their feet, following suit and turning their smiling faces towards Madame. The Comte gave the toast, turned to his wife with a bow, and drank off the contents of his glass. The next minute an extraordinary spasm passed over his face, and for a second he stood fighting for breath, his eyes fixed on his wife's horror-struck face. The guests are too startled and terrified to more than gaze in horror. Madame has sprung to her feet. With a cry of 'You— you—' (the first sound I had heard since the drama had re-enacted itself before me) he fell heavily across the table and lay there face downwards, crushing the roses to pieces. The cloud gathered quickly this time, and hid everything. I passed my hand across my face, and when I looked again the mist had vanished, the Face too; the ring lay, a harmless-looking thing, on the table in front of me. Surely I had been dreaming? But no; there was blood still on the ring, on the table, on the arm of the chair, where, no doubt, it had trickled from my wounded wrist.

I stepped out on the balcony. The moon had already risen, and the cool night air soon enabled me to regather my scattered senses.

I had the end of the clue in my hands now, and the sooner I cleared up the whole mystery the better; I should recognise the street, the pharmacien, and his shop again directly. I would start at once for Fesonsac, and by travelling all night I might reach the chateau tomorrow. I went back into my room, took some papers and loose money from my desk, and telling the concierge I might be away some days I hailed a passing fiacre and drove to the Gare d'Orleans.

I just managed to catch the train, and tired out by the strain of my weird experience I slept soundly till we arrived at Fesonsac.

I could see the white towers of the chateau through the woods, and, yes! surely this was the road I had seen – at any rate I would try it; so I bargained for the solitary conveyance that I found at the station. 'Whereto, Monsieur?' 'Ah! straight on. I will tell you when to turn.' We had been driving for nearly two hours along a straight road and I was beginning to doubt, when quite suddenly a bend in the highway brought town walls and a gate into view. 'Through the gate,' I called cheerily to the *cocher* 'up the Rue St-Louis-le-Grand and to the Bureau de Police.' It was no mere vision then, no phantasy of an overwrought imagination! Here was the dark medieval gateway with its obliterated shields, here the twisting streets I had seen, the fountain with its battered saint; here, the ill-paved street of Louis-le-Grand and the pharmacien's shop – and the very man himself peering from the open door. I sat well back in the carriage, and a few minutes more brought me to the Bureau de Police, with the familiar tricolour flapping lazily in the morning wind over the *porte-cochère*. 'You may remain; I may want you for some time.' '*Bien*, Monsieur.' I was soon closeted with the Chief of Police, and explained my errand as briefly as possible.

'But yes! he knew the man well; he was of doubtful reputation. If monsieur's information was correct it would clear up the mystery, and, yes! lift an undeserved stigma from a noble lady. How had monsieur acquired his knowledge? It was wonderful! *Tiens*, he would go with me himself, if I would permit.' It was the very thing I wanted, so I 'permitted' it cheerfully. Confronted with the agent of the law the pharmacien confessed that, under a threat to reveal some discreditable secret of his past, the Comte had forced him to part with a certain minute portion of a deadly Eastern drug. This drug dissolved in a certain medium would immediately evaporate, leaving the poison invisibly attached to the vessel into which it had been poured, to be redissolved by any liquid poured into this same vessel. Supplied with this important link in our chain we drove thence to the chateau de Viroflay, and sought the last link – the old butler, Josef.

'Did he remember the night of his late master's death? Everything that occurred?'

'But yes, perfectly.'

'The incident of the broken and replaced glass, for instance?'

'Ah, yes! but how does monsieur know that?'

'Monsieur had extraneous information. Well?'

'M. le Comte told me to use the Venetian service of glass – it was presented to one of his ancestors by the King – or something – of Venice, at whose court he had been the ambassador of Le Grand Monarque.'

'Presented by one of the Doges. Yes! Well?'

'M. le Comte gave me instructions that these Venice glasses were not to be filled till he rose to propose Madame's health; and I obeyed his orders, of course. I thought it very strange, but Monsieur le Comte would brook no questions. Yes, I had a misfortune, and broke the glass laid for the Comte himself, the flowers had become disarranged—'

'*Bon jour, mon ami*, that is all we want of you.' And as we went out the chief turned to me with a look of relief, 'Your information was correct in every detail, and I felicitate monsieur on solving a riddle that baffled us. So the Comte fell a victim to his own villainy? but, *Mon Dieu!* what a narrow escape for *le pauvre Capitaine* – what a narrow escape! Will monsieur honour me by taking *déjeûner* with me?'

'A thousand thanks and a thousand apologies, but, no; I must return at once to Paris. Business calls me.'

It was not until I was once more in the train that I noticed the ring was not on my finger – nor could I remember having noticed it on my hand since I left Paris. In my haste I must have left it on the table in my rooms; but I had locked the door on leaving, so, of course, it would be safe enough. It was night when I got back to Paris, and after a hasty inquiry 'Any letters – any visitors,' answered in the negative by the sleepy concierge, I took my key and hurried upstairs, taking the steps two at a time in my haste.

I unlocked the door, lighted my lamp, and gave a hurried glance round my room. All was just as I had left it, even my desk, which I had omitted to lock in my haste; the spots of blood still on table cloth and chair, but look as I might, search as I would, the Ring of Knowledge was nowhere to be found.

A BEAUTIFUL VAMPIRE

Arabella Kenealy

Arabella Kenealy (1859–1938) was born at Portslade, Sussex, and was one of the eleven legitimate children of the Irish barrister Edward V. H. Kenealy. She was educated at the London School of Medicine for Women, and subsequently practised medicine in London. 'A Beautiful Vampire' – her only story to utilise the vampire theme – clearly draws its inspiration from the Countess Bathory legend, and is one of a series of stories chronicling the cases of an occult detective named Lord Syfret. The twelve stories in which he appears – collectively known as *Some Experiences of Lord Syfret* – were originally published in the *Ludgate Magazine*. "A Beautiful Vampire" was in November 1896 issue, and achieved book publication the following year in *Belinda's Beaux and Other Stories*.

———————————————

I

THERE was a flutter indeed in the little town of Argles, when it became known that Dr Andrew had made an attempt upon the life of Lady Deverish. Andrew was a youngish, good-looking fellow, junior partner in the firm of Byrne & Andrew, the principal doctors in the place. Everybody liked him. He was as clever as he was kind. He would take equal pains to pull the ninth child of a navvy through a croup seizure as he would have done had it been heir to an earldom. Some people thought this mistaken kindness on the doctor's part – the navvy's ninth could well have been spared, especially as the navvy drank, and in any case was unable to provide properly for eight. Some went so far even as to assert that Andrew was flying in the face of Providence – to say nothing of the ratepayers – when he brought this superfluous ninth triumphantly through its fifth attack of croup. Otherwise, he was as popular as a man may be in a world wherein flaws and scandal lend to tea and bread-and-butter a stimulating quality denied to blamelessness and good repute.

'The butler says he heard raised voices,' it was whispered over dainty cups, 'and then Lady Deverish shrieked for help, and he ran in and found the doctor clutching her round the throat.'

'And only just in time. Her face was perfectly black!'

'Isn't it awful? Such a kind man as he has always seemed. Is there any madness in the family?'

'It is not certain. They say his mother was peculiar. Wrote books, and did other extraordinary things. Always wore very large hats with black feathers. Quite out of fashion, Mrs Byass tells me. She knew her.'

'What have they done with him?'

'That is the strangest part of it. She wouldn't charge him – said it was all a mistake. So he just got into his carriage, and continued his rounds.'

'Gracious! Strangling everybody?'

'Oh, I believe not.'

'Her throat was bruised black and blue. Old Dr Byrne went at once and saw to her. He got a new nurse down from London. They say it was a nurse they quarrelled about, you know.'

'Well, they won't get anyone to believe that, my dear.'

'No, because she was as plain as could be. And Lady Deverish's groom told cook that Dr Andrew scarcely looked at her.'

'And I never heard that he admired Lady Deverish.'

'Ah! well, most men do.'

'I don't see what she wants a nurse at all for. She's the picture of health.'

'She says she suffers from nerves.'

'If all of us who suffer from "nerves" were to have trained nurses looking after us, there wouldn't be enough trained nurses to go round.'

'No, but all of us are not widows with the incomes of two rich dear departeds at our bankers, my dear.'

Now, knowing both her charming ladyship and Andrew, I was naturally interested as to why he had put hands about her beautiful throat in anything other than loving kindness. Therefore, I made a point of drinking tea with a number of amiable and gracious persons of my acquaintance during the week following this most notable attempt. All the information I got for my pains has been condensed into the foregoing gossip, and since it was insufficient for my purposes I set about seeking more. I called early at the Manor. I did not entirely credit rumour's whisper concerning the victim's mangled throat, but I knew Andrew's muscular lean hands, if he had been in earnest, would, to say the least of it, have rendered prudent her retirement for the space of some days, so that I did not expect to see anybody but her companion, Mrs Lyall.

'Gracious, how ill you look!' I could not help exclaiming, as she entered.

I had known her some months earlier as a buxom matron. Now she was a haggard old woman. Her features worked and twisted. She slid into a chair, her hands and members shaking like those of one with palsy. For several minutes she could not speak.

'You must have been sadly troubled,' I said.

She was a mild and somewhat flaccid person, one of those plump anaemic women who give one the impression that in their veins run milk. But as I spoke her face became contorted. She struggled up and brandished a trembling, clenched hand.

'If he had only done it!' she cried passionately, 'if by some mercy of Providence he had only done it!'

She was transformed – distorted. It was as though some mild and milky Alderney had suddenly developed claws. She slid trembling again into her chair.

'My dear Mrs Lyall,' I remonstrated, 'if he had only done it, the world would have lost a beautiful and accomplished member of your sex – and poor Andrew's career would have come to a summary and lamentable end.'

'No jury would have convicted him,' she protested, '*not when they knew*.' She dropped her voice and searched the room with apprehensive eyes. Then she whispered, 'She is a devil.'

Now I was aware that some plain and very good women are in the habit of regarding every comely member of their sex as allied in one or another way with the Father of Evil, but it was clear that some sentiment stronger than general principles was moving Mrs Lyall.

My interest was roused. But she had come to the end of her remarks. She glanced round timorously.

'For Heaven's sake, Lord Syfret, do not mention a word of this,' she stammered. 'I am sadly unnerved. I scarcely know what I say. Poor Lady Deverish has been rather trying.' She shut her weak lips obstinately. I assured her of my discretion. I expressed sympathy, and went my way.

Byrne had nothing to tell. 'Andrew will not say a word,' he said. 'He was over-taxed. Been up several nights. She must have exasperated him somehow. Shouldn't have thought he had it in him. He has always been the kindest of fellows.'

'What does she say?'

'Laughs it off, though she don't seem amiable. Looks as if she don't want things to come out.'

'You don't mean—?'

'My dear fellow, whatsoever I mean, I do not say.'

It has always been my habit in life to take the bull by the horns whensoever circumstances have rendered this feat at the same time possible and prudent. I determined to attempt it now. Andrew, after all, was a very mild and tractable bull, despite his recent outbreak.

'I will not disguise the object of my visit,' I informed him. 'You know my weakness. Anything you tell me will go no further. The ball of Argles' scandal will get no push from me. But I like to probe human motive; and you must admit the situation is suggestive.'

He smiled – a nervous smile. I had never seen him so careworn. He shook his head. 'She has tied my hands,' he said. 'If they had let me I would have strangled her.'

'I do not wonder you are hard hit,' I adventured, watching him. 'She is certainly a siren of the first water.'

He burst out laughing. 'Great Scott!' he said. 'Is that what they say? Do they think I am aspiring to the Deverish's hand and acres? No, no; I am not altogether a fool.'

At this moment somebody ran up the stairs and after a preliminary knock, burst into the room.

'Please, doctor, come quick,' a pageboy blurted. 'There's Lady Deverish's nurse has fallen down in the road, and they says she's dying.'

The same change came over Andrew that had come over Mrs Lyall. His face became contorted. He held a clenched fist in the air. 'Damn her!' he cried, and rushed out.

Now this ejaculation had every appearance of applying to her ladyship's nurse, and would point to an amount of callousness on Andrew's part – considering the moribund condition of that unfortunate young person – whereof I am sure he was incapable. I hasten, therefore, to inform the reader that it was intended solely and absolutely for her ladyship's bewitching self. It was as fervid and whole-souled a fulmination as I remember to have heard. It left no doubt in my mind whatsoever as to the fact of her ladyship owing her life to that timely advent of her butler. My interest was not abated. I followed Andrew out. In the next street a knot of curious persons were assembled.

'Stand back,' the doctor called as we went up. 'Give her air.'

The circle widened, disclosing the figure of a young woman in nursing dress, lying senseless on the pavement. Her upturned face was curiously pinched, though the conformation was young, and her hair fallen loose about her cheek hung in girlish rings.

'She does not look strong enough for nursing,' I remarked to Byrne, who came up at the moment.

'Strong enough,' he echoed testily. 'A week ago she was sturdy and robust. The Deverish takes care of that. Can't stand sickliness about her.' He added half to himself, 'Must be something wrong with the house. Ventilation bad or something. One after another they've gone off like this.' The girl now began to show signs of consciousness. She opened her eyes, and seeing Andrew, smiled faintly. Presently she sat up.

'When you feel equal to it, my dear,' Dr Byrne said, 'we will help you to my carriage, and you can drive straight back.'

'Back,' she repeated wildly, 'where?'

'Why, to the Manor. You must—'

She interrupted him; she caught his hand. 'No, no,' she gasped, 'not there, never there. I cannot stand another hour of it.'

'The beautiful Deverish must be something of a vixen,' I reflected, seeing the expression on the girl's face.

Andrew was helping her to her feet. 'Don't be afraid,' he said quietly, 'I will see that you do not go back.'

She looked into his face. 'What is it?' she whispered, with white lips. 'Do you know?'

'Yes, I know,' he answered, meeting her look.

I had an inspiration. Among my clientele I numbered several trained nurses. I called at the post office on my way home and wired for one. In less than two hours she was with me. I despatched her to the Manor. 'Say you have been sent from Heaven or Buckingham Palace, or any other probable and impressive source, and keep your eyes and ears open,' I enjoined her, with that utter disregard for truth and scrupulousness which I have found the greatest of all aids to me in my researches.

She returned in an hour. There was anger in her eyes. The gauze veil streaming from her bonnet fluttered manelike to the offended toss of her head.

'You did not stay long,' I said.

'My lord,' she returned, 'I did not have the opportunity. Lady Devilish – I believe you called her Devilish – just came into the room and gave a little cry, and turned her back on me as if I'd been an ogre. "Oh, you would never suit," she said, "I must have someone young" – my lord, I am twenty-six – "and plump" – I weigh ten stone – "and healthy" – I have never had a day's illness. "Send someone young, and plump, and healthy," and she marched out.'

'I suppose that would not be difficult?' I commented.

'Not at all,' she said resolutely, 'a little padding, a touch of rouge, and some minor details are all that are needed.'

'You mean to go yourself, then?'

'Yes, I mean to go,' she returned. 'If there is anything to find out she may be sorry she wasn't more civil,' she added meditatively.

'Would she not recognize you?'

I admire grit. I admired the uncompromising and superior disdain with which she met my question. She turned and left without condescending a word. In fifteen minutes she came back, or, rather, somebody did whose voice was all I recognized. Her disguise was perfect. Before, she had certainly looked neither youthful (despite her assurance as to twenty-six), nor plump (despite her boasted avoirdupois), nor healthy. Now she was plump, and young, and rosy.

She had been dark; now a profusion of rich red hair rippled from her brows. I wondered why she did not always go about disguised. She explained.

'In most houses, my lord,' she said, 'there are sons, and brothers, and husbands. A woman who has her living to get by nursing can only afford to sport cherry cheeks under exceptional circumstances.'

When she had gone I dipped my pen in coloured ink and entered her name in my diary. Whether or not she succeeded with Lady 'Devilish', she was a capable person. And capable persons are red-letter persons in a world where incompetency rules seven days out of most weeks.

II

Nurse Marian's Story

She received me with open arms. 'You are just what I want,' she said effusively. 'I loathe sickliness. There was a gaunt, haggard creature here an hour ago. Ugh!' she shuddered, 'I would not have employed her for worlds.'

I may be prejudiced, but after her remark I confess, to feeling somewhat antipathetic to her ladyship. She has a curious way of staring. I suspect her of being short-sighted and shirking glasses for the sake of her looks. Certainly I have never seen anybody so brilliantly beautiful.

Upstairs I was introduced to her companion, Mrs Lyall. She did not strike me as being altogether sane. She has rather a grim smile.

'You'll soon lose those fine cheeks,' she said the moment she saw me.

'I trust not,' I returned, with some amount of confidence. (I had only just opened a new packet.) 'Is Lady Devilish rather a trying patient, then?' I asked.

She broke into a laugh. 'What did you call her?'

'I understood her name to be Devilish,' I said.

'No, it's her nature,' she retorted, looking furtively about. 'Her name has an "r" instead of an "l".'

Her ladyship was plainly no favourite of Mrs Lyall's. Indeed, everybody in the house seemed to be in mortal terror of her. The servants would not, if they could help it, enter a room where she was.

From the unhealthy faces of the household I came to the conclusion that the house was thoroughly unsanitary. I determined to investigate the drains. Whatsoever there might be that was unwholesome it did not affect the mistress. Her energy was marvellous. She never tired. When after a long day picnicking or a late ball, everybody looked as white as paper, she was as fresh and blooming and gay-spirited as possible. It seemed a mere farce for her to employ a nurse. But she had a fad about massage, and insisted on being 'massed' morning and night.

'You don't look tired,' she remarked in a puzzled way, at the end of my first night's operations. She was staring curiously at my rouged cheeks. Strangely enough I was feeling actually faint. Strong-nerved as I am, I fairly reeled.

'Whatsoever I look,' I answered her, a little irritably, 'I certainly feel more tired than I ever remember feeling.'

I thought she seemed pleased. Certainly I had said nothing to please her. No doubt she was thinking her own thoughts.

Her engagement to be married again was announced the day after my arrival. She had been already married twice. The young man – the Earl of Arlington – was, with a number of other persons, stopping in the house. He was handsome and pleasant-looking. I was told he had thrown over a girl he had cared for and who had cared for him for years in order to propose to Lady Deverish. He did not look capable of it. But, to all appearance, he was head over heels in love. He could not keep his eyes from her. He sat like a man bewitched, and neither ate nor rested.

'Poor young gentleman! He'll go the way of the others,' Mrs Plimmer, the housekeeper, confided to me.

'You don't suspect Lady Deverish of poisoning her husbands?' I returned.

'It isn't my place to suspect my betters, Nurse,' she said with dignity, 'All I say is there's something terrible mysterious. Why does everybody who comes to the Manor fail in health?'

'Drains,' I suggested.

She tossed her ample chin. 'Why did her two young husbands,

as likely men as might be, sicken from the day she married them, and die consumptive? Was that drains, can you tell me?'

I thought it might have been, but having no evidence, did not commit myself.

Mrs Plimmer tossed her ample chin again, this time triumphantly. 'And why,' she proceeded, 'did Dr Andrew, as kind a gentleman as walks, try to strangle her?'

I braved her scorn and ventured 'jealousy.'

She eyed me witheringly. 'The doctor's no lady's man,' she said, 'and besides if he was, it's no reason for strangling them.'

I was unable to find any fault with the drains. I began to grow interested. I myself felt strangely out of sorts – a new experience for me.

Lord Arlington's infatuation amounted to possession. He sat staring at her in a kind of ecstasy of fascination. He was pale and moody and obviously unhappy. I was told he had lost health and spirits markedly since his engagement. Probably his conscience troubled him about the other woman. At breakfast one morning he unwrapped a little packet which had come by post for him, without, it is to be supposed, observing the handwriting. As he undid it mechanically there dropped from the wrappings a ring, a knot of ribbon, and a bundle of letters. He seemed stunned. Without a word he gathered them together and quitted the room. I met him later pacing the garden like a madman.

Poor man! His love affair was short-lived.

A week later I was involuntary witness to a curious scene. I was sitting late one evening in the garden. Lady Deverish would not need me until bedtime, when her massage was due. Suddenly he and she, talking excitedly, came round the shrubbery.

'I have been mad,' he exclaimed, in a hoarse, passionate voice. 'For God's sake let me go free. They say her heart is broken.'

She put her two hands on his shoulders, and lifted her face to his.

'I will never let you go,' she said, with a curious ring as of metal in her voice. She wound her arms about his neck and kissed his throat. 'And you love me too much,' she added.

'Heaven only knows if it is love,' he answered, 'it seems to me like madness. I had loved her faithfully for years.'

'And now you love me, and there is no way out of it,' she whispered. She leaned up again and kissed him. Then with a little cooing laugh she left him.

He remained looking after her. 'Yes, there is one way out of it,' I heard him say slowly.

That night he shot himself.

Now, although I had known her but a fortnight, I had known her long enough to believe her superior to the weakness of being very deeply in love. Yet the night he died I was inclined to alter my opinion. He had bidden her a hasty goodbye, saying he was summoned to town. He took the last train up.

During the night I was called to her. I found her sitting up in bed, her face ashen pale, her eyes distended, her hands clasped to her head. She was gasping for breath. She seemed like one stricken; her features were picked out by deep grey lines. She did not speak, but pointed with an insistent finger to her right temple. I put my hand upon it. Then I called quickly for a light; for my fingers slipped along that which seemed to be a moist and clammy aperture, moist with a horrible, unmistakable clamminess. But when the light was brought there was neither blood nor aperture, only a curious, blanched spot, chill to the touch.

I gave her brandy, and put hot bottles in her bed. She was shaking as with ague. She clutched my hands, holding them against that ice-spot in her temple till I was sick and faint. Soon she seemed better. Some colour returned to her.

'My God, he is dead!' she said, through chattering teeth. Then she crouched down in the bed, a shuddering heap.

Next morning the news came. In that same hour he had put a bullet through his right temple. She was ill all that day, nerveless and almost pulseless. She looked ten years older. I never saw so singular a change. I sent for Dr Byrne, who attributed it to the shock of bad news. Why it developed some hours before the news arrived he did not explain. He only said: 'Tut, tut, Nurse, life is full of coincidences'; and prescribed ammonia.

Next day she was better, and suggested getting up, but changed her mind after having seen a mirror. 'Gracious!' she said, with a shudder, 'I look like an old woman.' She broke into feeble weeping. 'He ought to have thought of me,' she cried angrily.

She demanded wine and meat-juices, taking them with a curious solicitude, and carefully looking into her mirror for their effect. But she saw little there to comfort her.

'Do you think it might be my death-blow?' she questioned once through quivering lips. I shook my head. 'Ah, you don't know all,' she muttered.

In the afternoon she asked that the gardener's child should be brought to her. He was a chubby, rosy little fellow, whom everybody petted. 'I must have something to liven me,' she said. I had never supposed her fond of children. But she held her arms hungrily for him, and strained him to her breast. Her spirits rose. Her eyes brightened: she got colour. Soon she was laughing and chatting in her accustomed manner. The child had fallen asleep, but she would not part with him. When at last she let him go, I was horrified to find him cold and pallid. He was breathing heavily, and quite unconscious. I concluded the poor little chap was sickening for something. Later, I was surprised to receive a note from Dr Andrew, whom I did not know. I dismissed him as I had done Mrs Lyall, and probably Mrs Plimmer, as not altogether sane. 'I have been called in to attend Willy Daniels,' the note ran. 'For Heaven's sake, do not let her get hold of any more children.'

Next day she was better. She seemed to have forgotten Arlington and talked only of her health. She asked again for the boy. I told her he was ill. She broke into a curious laugh which seemed uncalled for. 'Thank goodness, I haven't lost my power,' she said a minute later. But she did not explain the saying.

She was in high spirits all the morning, talking and singing and trying on new laces and bonnets. She still complained of pain in the right temple. After her massage she turned peevish, protesting that it did her no good. 'If you hadn't such a colour I should not believe you healthy,' she said crossly.

She had the parson's children to tea. It would amuse her, she said, to see them eat their strawberries. They seemed afraid of her, and eyed her from a distance. When she attempted to take the little one, it clung to me and shrieked. But she persisted, and it soon fell asleep in her arms. On presently taking it from her, I found it chilled and breathing stertorously and quite unconscious. I thought of Dr Andrew's injunction. Heavens! what had she done? Was she a secret poisoner? I dismissed the notion forthwith. I had not left the room a moment during the time the child was with her, nor had it taken anything to eat or drink.

'What is the matter?' I demanded.

Her eye avoided mine. She answered nonchalantly: 'What does one expect? Children are everlastingly teething or over-feeding or having measles.'

Next morning I was called up at daybreak. Dr Andrew was waiting to see me. I threw on my things and went down. He was stalking up and down the drawing-room. He stared.

'You seem to have resisted her,' he muttered, looking at my cheeks. I have a long memory, and had not forgotten my rouge. He told me a wild and incredible story. He wound up by handing me a small bottle.

'Give her that dose so soon as she wakes,' he said. The man was probably a better doctor than he was an actor. His manner paraded the nature of the dose. I took out the cork and smelt it. It was as I suspected. I walked across the room and emptied its contents out of the window. 'Pardon me,' I said, 'but you are exceeding your duty.'

'Is she to be allowed to go on murdering people?' he protested. 'Do you know I have been up all night with that unfortunate baby? Do you know Willy Daniels is not yet out of danger? Good Heavens! if I am willing to take the consequences, how can one who knows the circumstances hesitate?'

'I have a safer and more justifiable plan,' I said. 'If what you say is true the remedy is simple, and poison is uncalled for. After all, Dr Andrew, your story would sound lame enough in a lawcourt. By my plan you run no risks.'

I laid it before him. He seemed interested. But he would not, after the manner of men in their dealings with women, permit me to take too much credit to myself.

'It might work,' he said lukewarmly, 'and as you say it would certainly be safer.'

I went to my room and opened a further packet of rouge. I applied it lavishly. I began to see that the health tint on my cheeks had an important bearing on the situation. I put vermilion on my lips. Then I carried my patient her breakfast.

She seemed restored and lay in her rose-pink bed, a smiling Venus. She fairly glowed with beautiful health. I thought of that poor little sick boy. 'Goodness!' I said with a start, 'how ill you look!' She ceased from smiling. She leapt across the floor, her draperies clinging round her pink flushed toes. She fled to the glass. She turned on me peevishly. 'Why did you tell me?' she protested. 'I should have thought I looked well.'

I went and stood beside her. 'Compare yourself with me.'

She was pale enough indeed by the time she had done so. 'Am I losing my power after all?' she muttered. 'Heavens! shall I grow old like other people?'

Suddenly she flung herself upon me. She pressed her lips and cheeks against my throat and face.

'Give *me* some of it,' she cried ravenously. 'You have so much vitality. Let me drain some of that rich health and colour.'

I nearly fell. It seemed as if she were actually sucking out my life. I reeled and sickened. Then with a tremendous effort I pushed her away and stumbled from the room. Was Andrew's story indeed true? Was she a monster or merely a monomaniac?

Years ago he had said she was dying of consumption. So far as physical signs could be trusted, she had not a week to live. Suddenly she began to recover. She made flesh rapidly, gained health, and came back to life from the very jaws of death. Meanwhile, her sister, a schoolgirl, whom she insisted on having always with her, sickened and died.

Then a brother died, then her mother. By this time she had grown quite strong. Since then she had lived on the vital forces of those surrounding her. 'The law of life,' he said, 'makes creatures inter-dependent. Physical vitality is subject to physical laws of diffusion and equalisation. One person below par absorbs the nerve and life sources of healthier persons with them. Many old, debilitated subjects live on the animal forces of the cat they keep persistently in their chair, and die when it dies. Wives and husbands, sisters and brothers, friends and acquaintances: there is a constant interchange of vital force. Lady Deverish has to my knowledge been the actual cause of death of a dozen persons. Besides these she has drained the health of everybody associated with her. And in her case – a rare and extreme one – the faculty is conscious and voluntary. She was living on Arlington. The man was powerless. She paralysed his will, his mind, his energies. She robbed him of strength to resist her. The sequel is interesting, psychologically. She being for the time charged with his vitality, his sudden death, by some curious sympathy, affected her in the way you have described. She was all at once and violently bereft of the source whence she was drawing energy. But she will soon, if she be allowed, find some other to prey on. For some years I have studied her closely. She is the archetype of a class of persons I have long had under observation. I find such power depends largely on force of will and concentration. If she can maintain these there is no reason why she should not live to be a hundred. There will always be persons of less assertive selfishness to serve as reservoirs of vital strength to her. At present her confidence is shaken, her power – therefore her life trembles in the balance. In the interests of humanity and justice she must not be allowed to regain her confidence. She lives by wholesale murder.'

III

I drank a glass of port and went back to my patient. She lay panting on her bed.

'Fie!' I said; 'that was a bit of hysteria. Come now, take your breakfast.'

She looked me in the face. A terror of death stood in beads on her skin. 'I have heard of transfusion,' she said faintly; 'if you will let me have some of the rich red blood run out of your veins into mine I will settle £500 a year on you.'

I shook my head.

'A thousand,' she said. 'Fifteen hundred.'

'I should be cheating you,' I insisted, 'even were I willing. The operation has never been really successful.'

She broke into raving and tears.

'I cannot die,' she said; 'I love life. I love being beautiful and rich; I love admiration. I must have admiration! I love my beautiful, beautiful body and the joy of life! I cannot, cannot die!'

'What nonsense!' I said. 'You are not going to die.'

'If I could only get it,' she raved, 'I would drink blood out of living bodies rather than I would die.'

An hour later she summoned the housekeeper. She had been cogitating with a fold between her brows; her teeth set like pearls in the red of her lower lip.

'Plimmer,' she said, 'give all the servants a month's wages and an hour's notice to quit. I cannot endure their sickly faces. Get in a staff of decently healthy people. These cadaverous wretches are killing me.'

Plimmer left the room without a word. At the door she cast one look toward me and threw her hands up, as one who says: 'The Lord have mercy on us!'

I followed, and bade her stay her hand. Whether Andrew's theories were true, or whether my lady were but a person with a mania, there was no doubt but that her convictions played an important part in the case.

I threw on my things and expended a half-sovereign at the chemist's. I came back the possessor of sundry packets. These I distributed among the household with explicit directions. Her ladyship was not well; her whim must be humoured.

It is surprising what a little rouge will do. In a few minutes the servants' hall was a scene Arcadian. Even the elderly butler reverted to blooming youth. Then I said to her cheerfully:

'You are making a mistake about the servants. For my part I am struck with their healthy looks.'

'Since I have been ill?' she faltered.

She lay quiet, breathing hard through her dilated nostrils. 'Send some of them in,' she said presently.

By the time they had gone she was as white as paper. 'Good Heavens!' I heard her mutter, 'I have lost my power. I am a dead woman.'

Then she flung out her arms and wept. 'Get me healthy children,' she cried; 'I must have health about me.'

Dr Byrne, who was attending her, assented in all innocence. 'Why, of course,' he said; 'it will be cheerful for you. Get in some cherry-cheeked children to amuse her ladyship, Nurse.'

I nodded – in token that I was not deaf – not at all in acquiescence. Food and wine I supplied in plenty, but neither children nor adults. I isolated her in toto. I allowed her maids only to come near her long enough to dust and arrange the room. I have seen her fix

them with a basilisk stare, straining her will. She had undoubtedly
some baleful hypnotic power which set them trembling and stumbling about in curious, aimless fashion. They would seem drawn,
as by some spell, to stand motionless and dazed beside her bed.
Then I would turn them face about and parading their roseate tints,
scold them for idleness and dismiss them. She would stare after
them in a despair which, under other circumstances, would have
been pitiful. The sense that her power was gone robbed her actually
of power. She raved and cursed her self-murdered lover for involving
her in his death.

Whether Dr Andrew and I were justified in that we did I sometimes wonder now. Then I had no room for doubt. In face of the
horrible facts it did not occur to me to question it. If that she believed
were true, we were assuredly justified; if not, that we did could not
affect results.

Andrew's theory of those results is that she had lived so long on
human energy that food in the crude state stood her in little stead.
Certainly, though she was fed unremittingly on the choicest and
most nourishing of diets, she was an aged and haggard woman in
a week. Nobody would have recognized her. She shrivelled and
shrank like one cholera-stricken. One day her dog stole into the
room. She put out her hand and clutched it voraciously. I took it
an hour later from her. It was dead and stiff.

How I myself, and a nurse I had called in to help me, kept life
in us I cannot say. I had been an abstainer. Now I drank wine like
water. All round her bed was an atmosphere as of a vault, though
outside it was sunny June.

She raged like one possessed. 'You are murdering, murdering
me,' she cried incessantly.

Dr Byrne thought her mind wandering. I knew it centred with
a monstrous, selfish sanity. He sent for one of the first London
consultants. After a lengthy investigation the great man pronounced
her suffering from some obscure nervous disease. 'Nothing to be
done,' he said. 'I give her three days: most interesting case. Hope
you will succeed in getting a post-mortem.'

Once she fixed me with her baleful eyes, how baleful was seen
now that their fine lustre and the bloom beneath them were gone.

'I have had ten years more of life and pleasure than my due,' she chuckled in her shrivelled throat – the throat now of an old, old woman.

Then she broke into dry-eyed crying. 'I thought I could have lived another ten.' She begged once for a mirror. I thank Heaven that with all my heat of indignation against her, I was not guilty of that cruelty.

Dr Andrew called daily for my bulletin. Everything science afforded in the way of food and stimulant, he scrupulously got down from London.

'We must give her every chance,' he said, 'every justifiable chance, that is.'

After a few days I was again single-handed. My nurse-colleague succumbed. I felt my powers failing. I could scarcely drag about. I prayed Providence for strength to last so long as she should. Even in the moment of dissolution, such was her frenzied greed of life, that I believed should some non-resistant person take my place, she would struggle back to health.

Once when I arranged her pillows, she seized my hand, and before I could withdraw it she had carried it to her mouth and bitten into it. I felt her suck the blood voraciously. She cried out and struck at me as I wrenched it away.

She died in the third week of her isolation. I saw the death change come into her shrivelled face. Then in the moment wherein life left her she made one supremest effort.

It seemed as though my heart stopped. My head took on my chest, my hands dropped at my side. Then I swayed and fell headlong across her bed. They found me later lying on her corpse. I am convinced that had she been a moment earlier, had she nerved her powers the instant before, rather than on the instant life was leaving her, she would be alive to this day, and I – As it was, I did not leave my bed for a month.

'If I were to write that story in the *Lancet*,' Dr Andrew said, 'I should be the laughing-stock of the profession. Yet it is the very keynote of human health and human disease, this interchange of vital force which goes on continually between individuals. Such rapacity and greed as the Deverish's are, fortunately, rare; but there are a score such vampires in this very town, vampires in lesser degree. When

A. talks with me ten minutes I feel ten years older. It takes me an hour to bring my nerve-power up to par again. People call him a bore. In reality he is a rapacious egotist hungrily absorbing the life-force of anyone with whom he comes into relation – in other words, a human vampire.'

THE STORY OF BAELBROW

E. & H. Heron

E. & H. Heron was the joint pseudonym of the mother-and-son
writing team, Kate O'Brien Ryall Prichard (1851–1935) and Hesketh
Vernon Prichard (1876–1922). Hesketh, who did most of the writing,
was born in Jhansi, India, the son of an officer in the King's Own
Scottish Borderers. One of the most accomplished Englishmen of his
generation, he led an extremely active life and was, among other things,
an international reporter and war correspondent, an explorer, a
big-game hunter, a prominent conservationist, a first-class cricketer,
and an expert marksman, who was placed in charge of the training
of the British Army's sniper squads during the First World War. Prichard
also found time to write novels and short stories – most of them in
collaboration with his mother. His circle of literary friends included
Arthur Conan Doyle and J. M. Barrie; and it was the latter who
introduced him to press baron Cyril Arthur Pearson, who suggested
that Prichard and his mother write a series of ghost stories for *Pearson's
Magazine*. The invitation was accepted and the duo penned a total of
twelve stories, each featuring Flaxman Low, a psychic detective special-
ising in investigating supernatural mysteries. This popular series included
the following story, which appeared in the April 1898 issue of the
magazine.

It is a matter for regret that so many of Mr Flaxman Low's remi-
niscences should deal with the darker episodes of his career. Yet
this is almost unavoidable, as the more purely scientific and less

strongly marked cases would not, perhaps, contain the same elements of interest for the general public, however valuable and instructive they might be to the expert student. It has also been considered better to choose the completer cases, those that ended in something like satisfactory proof, rather than the many instances where the thread broke off abruptly amongst surmisings, which it was never possible to subject to convincing tests.

North of a low-lying strip of country on the East Anglian coast, the promontory of Bael Ness thrusts out a blunt nose into the sea. On the Ness, backed by pinewoods, stands a square, comfortable stone mansion, known to the countryside as Baelbrow. It has faced the east winds for close upon three hundred years, and during the whole period has been the home of the Swaffam family, who were never in any wise put out of conceit of their ancestral dwelling by the fact that it had always been haunted. Indeed, the Swaffams were proud of the Baelbrow Ghost, which enjoyed a wide notoriety, and no one dreamt of complaining of its behaviour until Professor Jungvort, of Nuremburg, laid information against it, and sent an urgent appeal for help to Mr Flaxman Low.

The Professor, who was well acquainted with Mr Low, detailed the circumstances of his tenancy of Baelbrow, and the unpleasant events that had followed thereupon.

It appeared that Mr Swaffam, senior, who spent a large portion of his time abroad, had offered to lend his house to the Professor for the summer season. When the Jungvorts arrived at Baelbrow, they were charmed with the place. The prospect, though not very varied, was at least extensive, and the air exhilarating. Also the Professor's daughter enjoyed frequent visits from her betrothed – Harold Swaffam – and the Professor was delightfully employed in overhauling the Swaffam library.

The Jungvorts had been duly told of the ghost, which lent distinction to the old house, but never in any way interfered with the comfort of the inmates. For some time they found this description to be strictly true, but with the beginning of October came a change. Up to this time and as far back as the Swaffam annals reached, the ghost had been a shadow, a rustle, a passing sigh – nothing definite or troublesome. But early in October strange things began to occur, and the terror culminated when a housemaid was found dead in a corridor three weeks later. Upon this the Professor felt that it was time to send for Flaxman Low.

Mr Low arrived upon a chilly evening when the house was already beginning to blur in the purple twilight, and the resinous scent of the pines came sweetly on the land breeze. Jungvort welcomed him in the spacious, firelit hall. He was a stout German with a quantity of white hair, round eyes emphasised by spectacles, and a kindly, dreamy face. His life-study was philology, and his two relaxations chess and the smoking of a big Bismarck-bowled meerschaum.

'Now, Professor,' said Mr Low when they had settled themselves in the smoking-room, 'how did it all begin?'

'I will tell you,' replied Jungvort, thrusting out his chin, and tapping his broad chest, and speaking as if an unwarrantable liberty had been taken with him. 'First of all, it has shown itself to me!'

Mr Flaxman Low smiled and assured him that nothing could be more satisfactory.

'But not at all satisfactory!' exclaimed the Professor. 'I was sitting here alone, it might have been midnight – when I hear something come creeping like a little dog with its nails, tick-tick, upon the oak flooring of the hall. I whistle, for I think it is the little "Rags" of my daughter, and afterwards opened the door, and I saw' – he hesitated and looked hard at Low through his spectacles, 'something that was just disappearing into the passage which connects the two wings of the house. It was a figure, not unlike the human figure, but narrow and straight. I fancied I saw a bunch of black hair, and a flutter of something detached, which may have been a handkerchief. I was overcome by a feeling of repulsion. I heard a few, clicking steps, then it stopped, as I thought, at the museum door. Come, I will show you the spot.'

The Professor conducted Mr Low into the hall. The main staircase, dark and massive, yawned above them, and directly behind it ran the passage referred to by the Professor. It was over twenty feet long, and about midway led past a deep arch containing a door reached by two steps. Jungvort explained that this door formed the entrance to a large room called the Museum, in which Mr Swaffam, senior, who was something of a dilettante, stored the various curios he picked up during his excursions abroad. The Professor went on to say that he immediately followed the figure, which he believed had gone into the museum, but he found nothing there except the cases containing Swaffam's treasures.

'I mentioned my experience to no one. I concluded that I had seen the ghost. But two days after, one of the female servants coming through the passage in the dark, declared that a man leapt out at her from the embrasure of the Museum door, but she released herself and ran screaming into the servants' hall. We at once made a search but found nothing to substantiate her story.

'I took no notice of this, though it coincided pretty well with my own experience. The week after, my daughter Lena came down late one night for a book. As she was about to cross the hall, something leapt upon her from behind. Women are of little use in serious investigations – she fainted! Since then she has been ill and the doctor says "Run down."' Here the Professor spread out his hands. 'So she leaves for a change tomorrow. Since then other members of the household have been attacked in much the same manner, with always the same result, they faint and are weak and useless when they recover.

'But, last Wednesday, the affair became a tragedy. By that time the servants had refused to come through the passage except in a crowd of three or four – most of them preferring to go round by the terrace to reach this part of the house. But one maid, named Eliza Freeman, said she was not afraid of the Baelbrow Ghost, and undertook to put out the lights in the hall one night. When she had done so, and was returning through the passage past the Museum door, she appears to have been attacked, or at any rate frightened. In the grey of the morning they found her lying beside the steps dead. There was a little blood upon her sleeve but no mark upon her body except a small raised pustule under the ear. The doctor said the girl was extraordinarily anæmic, and that she probably died from fright, her heart being weak. I was surprised at this, for she had always seemed to be a particularly strong and active young woman.'

'Can I see Miss Jungvort tomorrow before she goes?' asked Low, as the Professor signified he had nothing more to tell.

The Professor was rather unwilling that his daughter should be questioned, but he at last gave his permission, and next morning

Low had a short talk with the girl before she left the house. He found her a very pretty girl, though listless and startlingly pale, and with a frightened stare in her light brown eyes. Mr Low asked if she could describe her assailant.

'No,' she answered, 'I could not see him, for he was behind me. I only saw a dark, bony hand, with shining nails, and a bandaged arm pass just under my eyes before I fainted.'

'Bandaged arm? I have heard nothing of this.'

'Tut – tut, mere fancy!' put in the Professor impatiently.

'I saw the bandages on the arm,' repeated the girl, turning her head wearily away, 'and I smelt the antiseptics it was dressed with.'

'You have hurt your neck,' remarked Mr Low, who noticed a small circular patch of pink under her ear.

She flushed and paled, raising her hand to her neck with a nervous jerk, as she said in a low voice:

'It has almost killed me. Before he touched me, I knew he was there! I felt it!'

When they left her the Professor apologised for the unreliability of her evidence, and pointed out the discrepancy between her statement and his own.

'She says she sees nothing but an arm, yet I tell you it had no arms! Preposterous! Conceive a wounded man entering this house to frighten the young women! I do not know what to make of it! Is it a man, or is it the Baelbrow Ghost?'

During the afternoon when Mr Low and the Professor returned from a stroll on the shore, they found a dark-browed young man with a bull neck, and strongly marked features, standing sullenly before the hall fire. The Professor presented him to Mr Low as Harold Swaffam.

Swaffam seemed to be about thirty, but was already known as a far-seeing and successful member of the Stock Exchange.

'I am pleased to meet you, Mr Low,' he began, with a keen glance, 'though you don't look sufficiently high-strung for one of your profession.'

Mr Low merely bowed.

'Come, you don't defend your craft against my insinuations?' went on Swaffam. 'And so you have come to rout out our poor old ghost from Baelbrow? You forget that he is an heirloom, a family

possession! What's this about his having turned rabid, eh, Professor?'
he ended, wheeling round upon Jungvort in his brusque way.

The Professor told the story over again. It was plain that he stood
rather in awe of his prospective son-in-law.

'I heard much the same from Lena, whom I met at the station,'
said Swaffam. 'It is my opinion that the women in this house are
suffering from an epidemic of hysteria. You agree with me, Mr Low?'

'Possibly. Though hysteria could hardly account for Freeman's
death.'

'I can't say as to that until I have looked further into the particulars. I have not been idle since I arrived. I have examined the
Museum. No one has entered it from the outside, and there is no
other way of entrance except through the passage. The flooring is
laid, I happen to know, on a thick layer of concrete. And there the
case for the ghost stands at present.' After a few moments of dogged
reflection, he swung round on Mr Low, in a manner that seemed
peculiar to him when about to address any person. 'What do you
say to this plan, Mr Low? I propose to drive the Professor over to
Ferryvale, to stop there for a day or two at the hotel, and I will also
dispose of the servants who still remain in the house for, say, forty-
eight hours. Meanwhile you and I can try to go further into the
secret of the ghost's new pranks?'

Flaxman Low replied that this scheme exactly met his views, but
the Professor protested against being sent away. Harold Swaffam
however was a man who liked to arrange things in his own fashion,
and within forty-five minutes he and Jungvort departed in the
dogcart.

The evening was lowering, and Baelbrow, like all houses built in
exposed situations, was extremely susceptible to the changes of the
weather. Therefore, before many hours were over, the place was
full of creaking noises as the screaming gale battered at the shuttered
windows, and the tree branches tapped and groaned against the
walls.

Harold Swaffam, on his way back, was caught in the storm and
drenched to the skin. It was therefore, settled that after he had
changed his clothes he should have a couple of hours' rest on the
smoking-room sofa, while Mr Low kept watch in the hall.

The early part of the night passed over uneventfully. A light burned faintly in the great wainscotted hall, but the passage was dark. There was nothing to be heard but the wild moan and whistle of the wind coming in from the sea, and the squalls of rain dashing against the windows. As the hours advanced, Mr Low lit a lantern that lay at hand, and, carrying it along the passage, tried the Museum door. It yielded, and the wind came muttering through to meet him. He looked round at the shutters and behind the big cases which held Mr Swaffam's treasures, to make sure that the room contained no living occupant but himself.

Suddenly he fancied he heard a scraping noise behind him, and turned round, but discovered nothing to account for it. Finally, he laid the lantern on a bench so that its light should fall through the door into the passage, and returned again to the hall, where he put out the lamp, and then once more took up his station by the closed door of the smoking-room.

A long hour passed, during which the wind continued to roar down the wide hall chimney, and the old boards creaked as if furtive footsteps were gathering from every corner of the house. But Flaxman Low heeded none of these; he was waiting for a certain sound.

After a while, he heard it – the cautious scraping of wood on wood. He leant forward to watch the Museum door. Click, click, came the curious dog-like tread upon the tiled floor of the Museum, till the thing, whatever it was, paused and listened behind the open door. The wind lulled at the moment, and Low listened also, but no further sound was to be heard, only slowly across the broad ray of light falling through the door grew a stealthy shadow.

Again the wind rose, and blew in heavy gusts about the house, till even the flame in the lantern flickered: but when it steadied once more, Flaxman Low saw that the silent form had passed through the door, and was now on the steps outside. He could just make out a dim shadow in the dark angle of the embrasure.

Presently, from the shapeless shadow came a sound Mr Low was not prepared to hear. The thing sniffed the air with the strong, audible inspiration of a bear, or some large animal. At the same moment, carried on the draughts of the hall, a faint, unfamiliar odour reached his nostrils. Lena Jungvort's words flashed back upon him – this, then, was the creature with the bandaged arm!

Again, as the storm shrieked and shook the windows, a darkness passed across the light. The thing had sprung out from the angle of the door, and Flaxman Low knew that it was making its way towards him through the illusive blackness of the hall. He hesitated for a second; then he opened the smoking-room door.

Harold Swaffam sat up on the sofa, dazed with sleep.

'What has happened? Has it come?'

Low told him what he had just seen. Swaffam listened half-smilingly.

'What do you make of it now?' he said.

'I must ask you to defer that question for a little,' replied Low.

'Then you mean me to suppose that you have a theory to fit all these incongruous items?'

'I have a theory, which may be modified by further knowledge,' said Low. 'Meantime, am I right in concluding from the name of this house that it was built on a barrow or burying-place?'

'You are right, though that has nothing to do with the latest freaks of our ghost,' returned Swaffam decidedly.

'I also gather that Mr Swaffam has lately sent home one of the many cases now lying in the Museum?' went on Mr Low.

'He sent one, certainly, last September.'

'And you have opened it,' asserted Low.

'Yes; though I flattered myself I had left no trace of my handi-work.'

'I have not examined the cases,' said Low. 'I inferred that you had done so from other facts.'

'Now, one thing more,' went on Swaffam, still smiling. 'Do you imagine there is any danger – I mean to men like ourselves? Hysterical women cannot be taken into serious account.'

'Certainly; the gravest danger to any person who moves about this part of the house alone after dark,' replied Low.

Harold Swaffam leant back and crossed his legs.

'To go back to the beginning of our conversation, Mr Low, may I remind you of the various conflicting particulars you will have to reconcile before you can present any decent theory to the world?'

'I am quite aware of that.'

'First of all, our original ghost was a mere misty presence, rather guessed at from vague sounds and shadows – now we have a something that is tangible, and that can, as we have proof, kill with fright. Next Jungvort declares the thing was a narrow, long and distinctly armless object, while Miss Jungvort has not only seen the arm and hand of a human being, but saw them clearly enough to tell us that the nails were gleaming and the arm bandaged. She also felt its strength. Jungvort, on the other hand, maintained that it clicked along like a dog – you bear out this description with the additional information that it sniffs like a wild beast. Now what can this thing be? It is capable of being seen, smelt, and felt, yet it hides itself successfully in a room where there is no cavity or space suffi-cient to afford covert to a cat! You still tell me that you believe that you can explain?'

'Most certainly,' replied Flaxman Low with conviction.

'I have not the slightest intention or desire to be rude, but as a mere matter of common sense, I must express my opinion plainly. I believe the whole thing to be the result of excited imaginations, and I am about to prove it. Do you think there is any further danger tonight?'

'Very great danger tonight,' replied Low.

'Very well; as I said, I am going to prove it. I will ask you to allow me to lock you up in one of the distant rooms, where I can get no help from you, and I will pass the remainder of the night walking about the passage and hall in the dark. That should give proof one way or the other.'

'You can do so if you wish, but I must at least beg to be allowed to look on. I will leave the house and watch what goes on from the window in the passage, which I saw opposite the Museum door. You cannot, in any fairness, refuse to let me be a witness.'

'I cannot, of course,' returned Swaffam. 'Still, the night is too bad to turn a dog out into, and I warn you that I shall lock you out.'

'That will not matter. Lend me a macintosh, and leave the lantern lit in the Museum, where I placed it.'

Swaffam agreed to this. Mr Low gives a graphic account of what followed. He left the house and was duly locked out, and, after groping his way round the house, found himself at length outside the window of the passage, which was almost opposite to the door of the Museum. The door was still ajar and a thin band of light cut

out into the gloom. Further down the hall gaped black and void.
Low, sheltering himself as well as he could from the rain, waited
for Swaffam's appearance. Was the terrible yellow watcher balancing
itself upon its lean legs in the dim corner opposite, ready to spring
out with its deadly strength upon the passer-by?

Presently Low heard a door bang inside the house, and the next
moment Swaffam appeared with a candle in his hand, an isolated
spread of weak rays against the vast darkness behind. He advanced
steadily down the passage, his dark face grim and set, and as he
came Mr Low experienced that tingling sensation, which is so often
the forerunner of some strange experience. Swaffam passed on
towards the other end of the passage. There was a quick vibration
of the Museum door as a lean shape with a shrunken head leapt
out into the passage after him. Then all together came a hoarse
shout, the noise of a fall and utter darkness.

In an instant, Mr Low had broken the glass, opened the window,
and swung himself into the passage. There he lit a match and as it
flared he saw by its dim light a picture painted for a second upon
the obscurity beyond.

Swaffam's big figure lay with outstretched arms, face downwards,
and as Low looked a crouching shape extricated itself from the fallen
man, raising a narrow vicious head from his shoulder.

The match spluttered feebly and went out, and Low heard a
flying step click on the boards, before he could find the candle
Swaffam had dropped. Lighting it, he stooped over Swaffam and
turned him on his back. The man's strong colour had gone, and the
wax-white face looked whiter still against the blackness of hair and
brows, and upon his neck under the ear, was a little raised pustule,
from which a thin line of blood was streaked up to the angle of his
cheekbone.

Some instinctive feeling prompted Low to glance up at this
moment. Half extended from the Museum doorway were a face and
bony neck – a high-nosed, dull-eyed, malignant face, the eye sockets
hollow, and the darkened teeth showing. Low plunged his hand into
his pocket, and a shot rang out in the echoing passageway and hall.
The wind sighed through the broken panes, a ribbon of stuff fluttered
along the polished flooring, and that was all, as Flaxman Low half
dragged, half carried Swaffam into the smoking-room.

It was some time before Swaffam recovered consciousness. He listened to Low's story of how he had found him with a red angry gleam in his sombre eyes.

'The ghost has scored off me,' he said with an odd, sullen laugh, 'but now I fancy it's my turn! But before we adjourn to the Museum to examine the place, I will ask you to let me hear your notion of things. You have been right in saying there was real danger. For myself I can only tell you that I felt something spring upon me, and I knew no more. Had this not happened I am afraid I should never have asked you a second time what your idea of the matter might be,' he ended with a sort of sulky frankness.

'There are two main indications,' replied Low. 'This strip of yellow bandage, which I have just now picked up from the passage floor, and the mark on your neck.'

'What's that you say?' Swaffam rose quickly and examined his neck in a small glass beside the mantelshelf.

'Connect those two, and I think I can leave you to work it out for yourself,' said Low.

'Pray let us have your theory in full,' requested Swaffam shortly.

'Very well,' answered Low good-humouredly – he thought Swaffam's annoyance natural under the circumstances – 'The long, narrow figure which seemed to the Professor to be armless is developed on the next occasion. For Miss Jungvort sees a bandaged arm and a dark hand with gleaming – which means, of course, gilded – nails. The clicking sound of the footstep coincides with these particulars, for we know that sandals made of strips of leather are not uncommon in company with gilt nails and bandages. Old and dry leather would naturally click upon your polished floors.'

'Bravo, Mr Low! So you mean to say that this house is haunted by a mummy!'

'That is my idea, and all I have seen confirms me in my opinion.'

'To do you justice, you held this theory before tonight – before, in fact, you had seen anything for yourself. You gathered that my father had sent home a mummy, and you went on to conclude that I had opened the case?'

'Yes. I imagine you took off most of, or rather all, the outer bandages, thus leaving the limbs free, wrapped only in the inner bandages which were swathed round each separate limb. I fancy this mummy was preserved on the Theban method with aromatic spices, which left the skin olive-coloured, dry and flexible, like tanned leather, the features remaining distinct, and the hair, teeth, and eyebrows perfect.'

'So far, good,' said Swaffam. 'But now, how about the intermittent vitality? The pustule on the neck of those whom it attacks? And where is our old Baelbrow ghost to come in?'

Swaffam tried to speak in a rallying tone, but his excitement and lowering temper were visible enough, in spite of the attempts he made to suppress them.

'To begin at the beginning,' said Flaxman Low, 'everybody who, in a rational and honest manner, investigates the phenomena of spiritism will, sooner or later, meet in them some perplexing element, which is not to be explained by any of the ordinary theories. For reasons into which I need not now enter, this present case appears to me to be one of these. I am led to believe that the ghost which has for so many years given dim and vague manifestations of its existence in this house is a vampire.'

Swaffam threw back his head with an incredulous gesture.

'We no longer live in the middle ages, Mr Low! And besides, how could a vampire come here?' he said scoffingly.

'It is held by some authorities on these subjects that under certain conditions a vampire may be self-created. You tell me that this house is built upon an ancient barrow, in fact, on a spot where we might naturally expect to find such an elemental psychic germ. In those dead human systems were contained all the seeds for good and evil. The power which causes these psychic seeds or germs to grow is thought, and from being long dwelt on and indulged, a thought might finally gain a mysterious vitality, which could go on increasing more and more by attracting to itself suitable and appropriate elements from its environment. For a long period this germ remained a helpless intelligence, awaiting the opportunity to assume some material form, by means of which to carry out its desires. The invisible is the real; the material only subserves its manifestation. The impalpable reality already existed, when you provided for it a physical medium for action by unwrapping the mummy's form. Now, we can only judge of the nature of the germ by its manifestation through matter. Here we have every indication of a vampire intelligence touching into life and energy the dead human frame. Hence the mark on the neck of its victims, and their bloodless and anæmic condition. For a vampire, as you know, sucks blood.'

Swaffham rose, and took up the lamp.

'Now, for proof,' he said bluntly. 'Wait a second, Mr Low. You say you fired at this appearance?' And he took up the pistol which Low had laid down on the table.

'Yes, I aimed at a small portion of its foot which I saw on the step.'

Without more words, and with the pistol still in his hand, Swaffam led the way to the Museum.

The wind howled round the house, and the darkness, which precedes the dawn, lay upon the world, when the two men looked upon one of the strangest sights it has ever been given to men to shudder at.

Half in and half out of an oblong wooden box in a corner of the great room, lay a lean shape in its rotten yellow bandages, the scraggy neck surmounted by a mop of frizzled hair. The toe strap of a sandal and a portion of the right foot had been shot away.

Swaffam, with a working face, gazed down at it, then seizing it by its tearing bandages, he flung it into the box, where it fell into a lifelike posture, its wide, moist-lipped mouth gaping up at them.

For a moment Swaffam stood over the thing; then with a curse he raised the revolver and shot into the grinning face again and again with a deliberate vindictiveness. Finally he rammed the thing down into the box, and, clubbing the weapon, smashed the head into fragments with a vicious energy that coloured the whole horrible scene with a suggestion of murder done.

Then, turning to Low, he said:

'Help me to fasten the cover on it.'

'Are you going to bury it?'

'No, we must rid the earth of it,' he answered savagely. 'I'll put it into the old canoe and burn it.'

The rain had ceased when in the daybreak they carried the old canoe down to the shore. In it they placed the mummy case with its ghastly occupant, and piled faggots about it. The sail was raised and the pile lighted, and Low and Swaffam watched it creep out on the ebb tide, at first a twinkling spark, then a flare of waving fire, until far out to sea the history of that dead thing ended 3000 years after the priests of Armen had laid it to rest in its appointed pyramid.

THE PURPLE TERROR

Fred M. White

Fred Merrick White (1859–1935) was born in West Bromwich, in the West Midlands, and was a prolific author of novels and short stories. Like Conan Doyle, he was renowned for his immaculate handwritten manuscripts. An article in *The New York Tribune*, 24 May 1908, states that: 'Probably the most minute as well as the neatest handwriting is that of Fred M. White. Mr White writes with his own hand every word of his stories and novels. His manuscript, though so microscopic, is wonderfully clear and well formed, and easy to read when one gets accustomed to his many peculiarities.' Today, this author is chiefly remembered for his 'Doom of London' science fiction stories. Six in total, they were published in *Pearson's Magazine* between January 1903 and June 1904. The following story, a contribution to *The Strand Magazine* in September 1899, is White's only known excursion into vampire territory.

LIEUTENANT Will Scarlett's instructions were devoid of problems, physical or otherwise. To convey a letter from Captain Driver of the Yankee Doodle, in Porto Rico Bay, to Admiral Lake on the other side of the isthmus, was an apparently simple matter.

'All you have to do,' the captain remarked, 'is to take three or four men with you in case of accidents, cross the isthmus on foot, and simply give this letter into the hands of Admiral Lake. By so doing we shall save at least four days, and the aborigines are presumedly friendly.'

The aborigines aforesaid were Cuban insurgents. Little or no strife had taken place along the neck lying between Porto Rico and the north bay where Lake's flagship lay, though the belt was known to be given over to the disaffected Cubans.

'It is a matter of fifty miles through practically unexplored country,' Scarlett replied; 'and there's a good deal of the family quarrel in this business, sir. If the Spaniards hate us, the Cubans are not exactly enamoured of our flag.'

Captain Driver roundly denounced the whole pack of them.

'Treacherous thieves to a man,' he said. 'I don't suppose your progress will have any brass bands and floral arches to it. And they tell me the forest is pretty thick. But you'll get there all the same. There is the letter, and you can start as soon as you like.'

'I may pick my own men, sir?'

'My dear fellow, take whom you please. Take the mastiff, if you like.'

'I'd like the mastiff,' Scarlett replied; 'as he is practically my own, I thought you would not object.'

Will Scarlett began to glow as the prospect of adventure stimulated his imagination. He was rather a good specimen of West Point naval dandyism. He had brains at the back of his smartness, and his geological and botanical knowledge were going to prove of considerable service to a grateful country when said grateful country should have passed beyond the rudimentary stages of colonization. And there was some disposition to envy Scarlett on the part of others floating for the past month on the liquid prison of the sapphire sea.

A warrant officer, Tarrer by name, plus two A.B.'s of thews and sinews, to say nothing of the dog, completed the exploring party. By the time that the sun kissed the tip of the feathery hills they had covered some six miles of their journey. From the first Scarlett had been struck by the absolute absence of the desolation and horror of civil strife. Evidently the fiery cross had not been carried here; huts and houses were intact; the villagers stood under sloping eaves, and regarded the Americans with a certain sullen curiosity.

'We'd better stop for the night here,' said Scarlett.

They had come at length to a village that boasted some pretensions. An adobe chapel at one end of the straggling street was faced by a wine house at the other. A padre, with hands folded over a bulbous, greasy gabardine, bowed gravely to Scarlett's salutation. The latter had what Tarrer called 'considerable Spanish.'

'We seek quarters for the night,' said Scarlett. 'Of course, we are prepared to pay for them.'

The sleepy padre nodded towards the wine house.

'You will find fair accommodation there,' he said. 'We are friends of the Americanos.'

Scarlett doubted the fact, and passed on with florid thanks. So far, little signs of friendliness had been encountered on the march. Coldness, suspicion, a suggestion of fear, but no friendliness to be embarrassing.

The keeper of the wine shop had his doubts. He feared his poor accommodation for guests so distinguished. A score or more of picturesque, cut-throat-looking rascals with cigarettes in their mouths lounged sullenly in the bar. The display of a brace of gold dollars enlarged mine host's opinion of his household capacity.

'I will do my best, senors,' he said. 'Come this way.'

So it came to pass that an hour after twilight Tarrer and Scarlett were seated in the open amongst the oleanders and the trailing gleam of the fireflies, discussing cigars of average merit and a native wine that was not without virtues. The long bar of the wine house was brilliantly illuminated; from within came shouts of laughter mingled with the ting, tang of the guitar and the rollicking clack of the castanets.

'They seem to be happy in there,' Tarrer remarked. 'It isn't all daggers and ball in this distressful country.'

A certain curiosity came over Scarlett.

'It is the duty of a good officer,' he said, 'to lose no opportunity of acquiring useful information. Let us join the giddy throng, Tarrer.'

Tarrer expressed himself with enthusiasm in favour of any amusement that might be going. A month's idleness on shipboard increases the appetite for that kind of thing wonderfully. The long bar was comfortable, and filled with Cubans who took absolutely no notice of the intruders. Their eyes were turned towards a rude stage at the far end of the bar, whereon a girl was gyrating in a dance with a celerity and grace that caused the wreath of flowers around her shoulders to resemble a trembling zone of purple flame.

'A wonderfully pretty girl and a wonderfully pretty dance,' Scarlett murmured, when the motions ceased and the girl leapt gracefully to the ground. 'Largesse, I expect. I thought so. Well, I'm good for a quarter.'

The girl came forward, extending a shell prettily. She curtsied before Scarlett and fixed her dark, liquid eyes on his. As he smiled and dropped his quarter-dollar into the shell a coquettish gleam came into the velvety eyes. An ominous growl came from the lips of a bearded ruffian close by.

'Othello's jealous,' said Tarrer. 'Look at his face.'

'I am better employed,' Scarlett laughed. 'That was a graceful dance, pretty one. I hope you are going to give us another one presently—'

Scarlett paused suddenly. His eyes had fallen on the purple band of flowers the girl had twined round her shoulder. Scarlett was an enthusiastic botanist; he knew most of the gems in Flora's crown, but he had never looked upon such a vivid wealth of blossom before.

The flowers were orchids, and orchids of a kind unknown to collectors anywhere. On this point Scarlett felt certain. And yet this part of the world was by no means a difficult one to explore in comparison with New Guinea and Sumatra, where the rarer varieties had their homes.

The blooms were immensely large, far larger than any flower of the kind known to Europe or America, of a deep pure purple, with a blood-red centre. As Scarlett gazed upon them he noticed a certain cruel expression on the flower. Most orchids have a kind of face of their own; the purple blooms had a positive expression of ferocity and cunning. They exhumed, too, a queer, sickly fragrance. Scarlett had smelt something like it before, after the Battle of Manila. The perfume was the perfume of a corpse.

'And yet they are magnificent flowers,' said Scarlett. 'Won't you tell me where you got them from, pretty one?'

The girl was evidently flattered by the attention bestowed upon her by the smart young American. The bearded Othello alluded to edged up to her side.

'The senor had best leave the girl alone,' he said, insolently.

Scarlett's fist clenched as he measured the Cuban with his eyes. The Admiral's letter crackled in his breast pocket, and discretion got the best of valour.

'You are paying yourself a poor compliment, my good fellow,' he said, 'though I certainly admire your good taste. Those flowers interested me.'

The man appeared to be mollified. His features corrugated in a smile.

'The senor would like some of those blooms?' he asked. 'It was I who procured them for little Zara here. I can show you where they grow.'

Every eye in the room was turned in Scarlett's direction. It seemed to him that a kind of diabolical malice glistened on every dark face there, save that of the girl, whose features paled under her healthy tan.

'If the senor is wise,' she began, 'he will not—'

'Listen to the tales of a silly girl,' Othello put in, menacingly. He grasped the girl by the arm, and she winced in positive pain. 'Pshaw, there is no harm where the flowers grow, if one is only careful. I will take you there, and I will be your guide to Port Anna, where you are going, for a gold dollar.'

All Scarlett's scientific enthusiasm was aroused. It is not given to every man to present a new orchid to the horticultural world. And this one would dwarf the finest plant hitherto discovered.

'Done with you,' he said; 'we start at daybreak. I shall look to you to be ready. Your name is Tito? Well, goodnight, Tito.'

As Scarlett and Tarrer withdrew the girl suddenly darted forward. A wild word or two fluttered from her lips. Then there was a sound as of a blow, followed by a little stifled cry of pain.

'No, no,' Tarrer urged, as Scarlett half turned. 'Better not. They are ten to one, and they are no friends of ours. It never pays to interfere in these family quarrels. I daresay, if you interfered, the girl would be just as ready to knife you as her jealous lover.'

'But a blow like that, Tarrer!'

'It's a pity, but I don't see how we can help it. Your business is the quick dispatch of the Admiral's letter, not the squiring of dames.'

Scarlett owned with a sigh that Tarrer was right.

* * * * * *

It was quite a different Tito who presented himself at daybreak the following morning. His insolent manner had disappeared. He was cheerful, alert, and he had a manner full of the most winning politeness.

'You quite understand what we want,' Scarlett said. 'My desire is to reach Port Anna as soon as possible. You know the way?'

'Every inch of it, senor. I have made the journey scores of times. And I shall have the felicity of getting you there early on the third day from now.'

'Is it so far as that?'

'The distance is not great, senor. It is the passage through the woods. There are parts where no white man has been before.'

'And you will not forget the purple orchids?'

A queer gleam trembled like summer lightning in Tito's eyes. The next instant it had gone. A time was to come when Scarlett was to recall that look, but for the moment it was allowed to pass.

'The senor shall see the purple orchid,' he said; 'thousands of them. They have a bad name amongst our people, but that is nonsense. They grow in the high trees, and their blossoms cling to long, green tendrils. These tendrils are poisonous to the flesh, and great care should be taken in handling them. And the flowers are quite harmless, though we call them the devil's poppies.'

To all of this Scarlett listened eagerly. He was all-impatient to see and handle the mysterious flower for himself. The whole excursion was going to prove a wonderful piece of luck. At the same time he had to curb his impatience. There would be no chance of seeing the purple orchid today.

For hours they fought their way along through the dense tangle. A heat seemed to lie over all the land like a curse – a blistering sweltering, moist heat with no puff of wind to temper its breathlessness. By the time that the sun was sliding down, most of the party had had enough of it.

They passed out of the underwood at length, and, striking upwards, approached a clump of huge forest trees on the brow of a ridge. All kinds of parasites hung from the branches; there were ropes and bands of green, and high up a fringe of purple glory that caused Scarlett's pulses to leap a little faster.

'Surely that is the purple orchid?' he cried.

Tito shrugged his shoulders contemptuously.

'A mere straggler or two,' he said, 'and out of reach in any case. The senor will have all he wants and more tomorrow.'

'But it seems to me,' said Scarlett, 'that I could—'

Then he paused. The sun like a great glowing shield was shining full behind the tree with its crown of purple, and showing up every green rope and thread clinging to the branches with the clearness of liquid crystal. Scarlett saw a network of green cords like a huge spider's web, and in the centre of it was not a fly, but a human skeleton!

The arms and legs were stretched apart as if the victim had been crucified. The wrists and ankles were bound in the cruel web. Fragments of tattered clothing fluttered in the faint breath of the evening breeze.

'Horrible,' Scarlett cried, 'absolutely horrible!'

'You may well say that,' Tarrer exclaimed, with a shudder. 'Like the fly in the amber or the apple in the dumpling, the mystery is how he got there.'

'Perhaps Tito can explain the mystery,' Scarlett suggested.

Tito appeared to be uneasy and disturbed. He looked furtively from one to the other of his employers as a culprit might who feels he has been found out. But his courage returned as he noted the absence of suspicion in the faces turned upon him.

'I can explain,' he exclaimed, with teeth that chattered from some unknown terror or guilt. 'It is not the first time that I have seen the skeleton. Some plant-hunter doubtless who came here alone. He climbed into the tree without a knife, and those green ropes got twisted round his limbs, as a swimmer gets entangled in the weeds. The more he struggled, the more the cords bound him. He would call in vain for anyone to assist him here. And so he must have died.'

The explanation was a plausible one, but by no means detracted from the horror of the discovery. For some time the party pushed their way on in the twilight, till the darkness descended suddenly like a curtain.

'We will camp here,' Tito said; 'it is high, dry ground, and we have this belt of trees above us. There is no better place than this for miles around. In the valley the miasma is dangerous.'

As Tito spoke he struck a match, and soon a torch flamed up. The little party were on a small plateau, fringed by trees. The ground

was dry and hard, and, as Scarlett and his party saw to their astonishment, littered with bones. There were skulls of animals and skulls
of human beings, the skeletons of birds, the frames of beasts both
great and small. It was a weird, shuddering sight.

'We can't possibly stay here,' Scarlett exclaimed.

Tito shrugged his shoulders.

'There is nowhere else,' he replied. 'Down in the valley there
are many dangers. Further in the woods are the snakes and jaguars.
Bones are nothing. Peuf, they can be easily cleared away.'

They had to be cleared away, and there was an end of the matter.
For the most part the skeletons were white and dry as air and sun
could make them. Over the dry, calcined mass the huge fringe of
trees nodded mournfully. With the rest, Scarlett was busy scattering
the mocking frames aside. A perfect human skeleton lay at his feet.
On one finger something glittered – a signet ring. As Scarlett took
it in his hand he started.

'I know this ring!' he exclaimed; 'it belonged to Pierre Anton,
perhaps the most skilled and intrepid plant-hunter the Jardin des
Plantes ever employed. The poor fellow was by way of being a friend
of mine. He met the fate that he always anticipated.'

'There must have been a rare holocaust here,' said Tarrer.

'It beats me,' Scarlett responded. By this time a large circle had
been shifted clear of human and other remains. By the light of the
fire loathsome insects could be seen scudding and straddling away.
'It beats me entirely. Tito, can you offer any explanation? If the
bones were all human I could get some grip of the problem. But
when one comes to birds and animals as well! Do you see that the
skeletons lie in a perfect circle, starting from the centre of the clump
of trees above us? What does it mean?'

Tito professed utter ignorance of the subject. Some years before
a small tribe of natives invaded the peninsula for religious rites.
They came from a long way off in canoes, and wild stories were
told concerning them. They burnt sacrifices, no doubt.

Scarlett turned his back contemptuously on this transparent tale.
His curiosity was aroused. There must be some explanation, for
Pierre Anton had been seen of men within the last ten years.

'There's something uncanny about this,' he said, to Tarrer. 'I mean
to get to the bottom of it, or know why.'

'As for me,' said Tarrer, with a cavernous yawn, 'I have but one ambition, and that is my supper, followed by my bed.'

* * * * * *

Scarlett lay in the light of the fire looking about him. He felt restless and uneasy, though he would have found it difficult to explain the reason. For one thing, the air trembled to strange noises. There seemed to be something moving, writhing in the forest trees above his head. More than once it seemed to his distorted fancy that he could see a squirming knot of green snakes in motion.

Outside the circle, in a grotto of bones, Tito lay sleeping. A few moments before his dark, sleek head had been furtively raised, and his eyes seemed to gleam in the flickering firelight with malignant cunning. As he met Scarlett's glance he gave a deprecatory gesture and subsided.

'What the deuce does it all mean?' Scarlett muttered. 'I feel certain yonder rascal is up to some mischief. Jealous still because I paid his girl a little attention. But he can't do us any real harm. Quiet, there!'

The big mastiff growled and then whined uneasily. Even the dog seemed to be conscious of some unseen danger. He lay down again, cowed by the stern command, but he still whimpered in his dreams.

'I fancy I'll keep awake for a spell,' Scarlett told himself.

For a time he did so. Presently he began to slide away into the land of poppies. He was walking amongst a garden of bones which bore masses of purple blossoms. Then Pierre Anton came on the scene, pale and resolute as Scarlett had always known him; then the big mastiff seemed in some way to be mixed up with the phantasm of the dream, barking as if in pain, and Scarlett came to his senses.

He was breathing short, a beady perspiration stood on his forehead, his heart hammered in quick thuds – all the horrors of nightmare were still upon him. In a vague way as yet he heard the mastiff, howl, a real howl of real terror, and Scarlett knew that he was awake.

Then a strange thing happened. In the none too certain light of the fire, Scarlett saw the mastiff snatched up by some invisible hand, carried far on high towards the trees, and finally flung to the earth with a crash. The big dog lay still as a log.

A sense of fear born of the knowledge of impotence came over Scarlett; what in the name of evil did it all mean? The smart scientist had no faith in the occult, and yet what did it all mean?

Nobody stirred. Scarlett's companions were soaked and soddened with fatigue; the rolling thunder of artillery would have scarce disturbed them. With teeth set and limbs that trembled, Scarlett crawled over to the dog.

The great, black-muzzled creature was quite dead. The full chest was stained and soaked in blood; the throat had been cut apparently with some jagged, saw-like instrument, away to the bone. And, strangest thing of all, scattered all about the body was a score or more of the great purple orchid flowers broken off close to the head. A hot, pricking sensation travelled slowly up Scarlett's spine and seemed to pass out at the tip of his skull. He felt his hair rising.

He was frightened. As a matter of honest fact, he had never been so horribly scared in his life before. The whole thing was so mysterious, so cruel, so bloodthirsty.

Still, there must be some rational explanation. In some way the matter had to do with the purple orchid. The flower had an evil reputation. Was it not known to these Cubans as the devil's poppy?

Scarlett recollected vividly now Zara's white, scared face when Tito had volunteered to show the way to the resplendent bloom; he remembered the cry of the girl and the blow that followed. He could see it all now. The girl had meant to warn him against some nameless horror to which Tito was leading the small party. This was the jealous Cuban's revenge.

A wild desire to pay this debt to the uttermost fraction filled Scarlett, and shook him with a trembling passion. He crept along in the drenching dew to where Tito lay, and touched his forehead with the chill blue rim of a revolver barrel. Tito stirred slightly.

'You dog!' Scarlett cried. 'I am going to shoot you.'

Tito did not move again. His breathing was soft and regular. Beyond a doubt the man was sleeping peacefully. After all he might be innocent; and yet, on the other hand, he might be so sure of his quarry that he could afford to slumber without anxiety as to his vengeance.

In favour of the latter theory was the fact that the Cuban lay beyond the limit of what had previously been the circle of dry bones. It was just possible that there was no danger outside that pale. In that case it would be easy to arouse the rest, and so save them from the horrible death which had befallen the mastiff. No doubt these were a form of upas tree, but that would not account for the ghastly spectacle in mid-air.

'I'll let this chap sleep for the present,' Scarlett muttered.

He crawled back, not without misgivings, into the ring of death. He meant to wake the others and then wait for further developments. By now his senses were more alert and vigorous than they had ever been before. A preternatural clearness of brain and vision possessed him. As he advanced he saw suddenly falling a green bunch of cord that straightened into a long, emerald line. It was triangular in shape, fine at the apex, and furnished with hooked spines. The rope appeared to dangle from the tree overhead; the broad, sucker-like termination was evidently soaking up moisture.

A natural phenomenon evidently, Scarlett thought. This was some plant new to him, a parasite living amongst the treetops and drawing life and vigour by means of these green, rope-like antennae designed by Nature to soak and absorb the heavy dews of night.

For a moment the logic of this theory was soothing to Scarlett's distracted nerves, but only for a moment, for then he saw at regular intervals along the green rope the big purple blossoms of the devil's poppy.

He stood gasping there, utterly taken aback for the moment. There must be some infernal juggling behind all this business. He saw the rope slacken and quiver, he saw it swing forward like a pendulum, and the next minute it had passed across the shoulders of a sleeping seaman.

Then the green root became as the arm of an octopus. The line shook from end to end like the web of an angry spider when invaded by a wasp. It seemed to grip the sailor and tighten, and then, before Scarlett's, afrighted eyes, the sleeping man was raised gently from the ground.

Scarlett jumped forward with a desire to scream hysterically. Now that a comrade was in danger he was no longer afraid. He whipped a jackknife from his pocket and slashed at the cruel cord. He half expected to meet with the stoutness of a steel strand, but to his surprise the feeler snapped like a carrot, bumping the sailor heavily on the ground.

He sat up, rubbing his eyes vigorously.

'That you, sir?' he asked. 'What is the matter?'

'For the love of God, get up at once and help me to arouse the others,' Scarlett said, hoarsely. 'We have come across the devil's workshop. All the horrors of the inferno are invented here.'

The bluejacket struggled to his feet. As he did so, the clothing from his waist downwards slipped about his feet, clean cut through by the teeth of the green parasite. All around the body of the sailor blood oozed from a zone of teeth marks.

Two-o'clock-in-the-morning courage is a virtue vouchsafed to few. The tar, who would have faced an ironclad cheerfully, fairly shivered with fright and dismay.

'What does it mean, sir?' he cried. 'I've been—'

'Wake the others,' Scarlett screamed; 'wake the others.'

Two or three more green tangles of rope came tumbling to the ground, straightening and quivering instantly. The purple blossoms stood out like a frill upon them. Like a madman, Scarlett shouted, kicking his companions without mercy.

They were all awake at last, grumbling and moaning for their lost slumbers. All this time Tito had never stirred.

'I don't understand it at all,' said Tarrer.

'Come from under those trees,' said Scarlett, 'and I will endeavour to explain. Not that you will believe me for a moment. No man can be expected to believe the awful nightmare I am going to tell you.'

Scarlett proceeded to explain. As he expected, his story was followed with marked incredulity, save by the wounded sailor, who had strong evidence to stimulate his otherwise defective imagination.

'I can't believe it,' Tarrer said, at length. They were whispering together beyond earshot of Tito, whom they had no desire to arouse for obvious reasons. 'This is some diabolical juggling of yonder rascally Cuban. It seems impossible that those slender green cords could—'

Scarlett pointed to the centre of the circle.

'Call the dog,' he said grimly, 'and see if he will come.'

'I admit the point as far as the poor old mastiff is concerned. But at the same time I don't – however, I'll see for myself.'

By this time a dozen or more of the slender cords were hanging pendent from the trees. They moved from spot to spot as if jerked up by some unseen hand and deposited a foot or two farther. With the great purple bloom fringing the stem, the effect was not unlovely save to Scarlett, who could see only the dark side of it. As Tarrer spoke he advanced in the direction of the trees.

'What are you going to do?' Scarlett asked.

'Exactly what I told you. I am going to investigate this business for myself.'

Without wasting further words Scarlett sprang forward. It was no time for the niceties of an effete civilization. Force was the only logical argument to be used in a case like this, and Scarlett was the more powerful man of the two.

Tarrer saw and appreciated the situation.

'No, no,' he cried; 'none of that. Anyway, you're too late.'

He darted forward and threaded his way between the slender emerald columns. As they moved slowly and with a certain stately deliberation there was no great danger to an alert and vigorous individual. As Scarlett entered the avenue he could hear the soak and suck as the dew was absorbed.

'For Heaven's sake, come out of it,' he cried.

The warning came too late. A whip-like trail of green touched Tarrer from behind, and in a lightning flash he was in the toils. The tendency to draw up anything and everything gave the cords a terrible power. Tarrer evidently felt it, for his breath came in great gasps.

'Cut me free,' he said, hoarsely; 'cut me free. I am being carried off my feet.'

He seemed to be doomed for a moment, for all the cords there were apparently converging in his direction. This, as a matter of fact, was a solution of the whole sickening, horrible sensation. Pulled here and there, thrust in one direction and another, Tarrer contrived to keep his feet.

Heedless of possible danger to himself Scarlett darted forward, calling to his companions to come to the rescue. In less time than it takes to tell, four knives were at work ripping and slashing in all directions.

'Not all of you,' Scarlett whispered. So tense was the situation that no voice was raised above a murmur. 'You two keep your eyes open for fresh cords, and cut them as they fall, instantly. Now then.'

The horrible green spines were round Tarrer's body like snakes. His face was white, his breath came painfully, for the pressure was terrible. It seemed to Scarlett to be one horrible dissolving view of green, slimy cords and great weltering, purple blossoms. The whole of the circle was strewn with them. They were wet and slimy underfoot.

Tarrer had fallen forward half unconscious. He was supported now by but two cords above his head. The cruel pressure had been relieved. With one savage sweep of his knife Scarlett cut the last of the lines, and Tarrer fell like a log unconscious to the ground. A feeling of nausea, a yellow dizziness, came over Scarlett as he staggered beyond the dread circle. He saw Tarrer carried to a place of safety, and then the world seemed to wither and leave him in the dark.

'I feel a bit groggy and weak,' said Tarrer an hour or so later: 'but beyond that this idiot of a Richard is himself again. So far as I am concerned, I should like to get even with our friend Tito for this.'

'Something with boiling oil in it,' Scarlett suggested, grimly. 'The callous scoundrel has slept soundly through the whole of this business. I suppose he felt absolutely certain that he had finished with us.'

'Upon my word, we ought to shoot the beggar!' Tarrer exclaimed.

'I have a little plan of my own,' said Scarlett, 'which I am going to put in force later on. Meanwhile we had better get on with breakfast. When Tito wakes a pleasant little surprise will await him.'

Tito roused from his slumbers in due course and looked around him. His glance was curious, disappointed, then full of a white and yellow fear. A thousand conflicting emotions streamed across his dark face. Scarlett read them at a glance as he called the Cuban over to him.

'I am not going into any unnecessary details with you,' he said. 'It has come to my knowledge that you are playing traitor to us.

Therefore we prefer to complete our journey alone. We can easily find the way now.'

'The senor may do as he pleases,' he replied. 'Give me my dollar and let me go.'

Scarlett replied grimly that he had no intention of doing anything of the kind. He did not propose to place the lives of himself and his comrades in the power of a rascally Cuban who had played false.

'We are going to leave you here till we return,' he said. 'You will have plenty of food, you will be perfectly safe under the shelter of these trees, and there is no chance of anybody disturbing you. We are going to tie you up to one of these trees for the next four-and-twenty hours.'

All the insolence died out of Tito's face. His knees bowed, a cold dew came out over the ghastly green of. his features. From the shaking of his limbs he might have fared disastrously with ague.

'The trees,' he stammered, 'the trees, senor! There is danger from snakes, and – and from many things. There are other places—'

'If this place was safe last night it is safe today,' Scarlett said, grimly. 'I have quite made up my mind.'

Tito fought no longer. He fell forward on his knees, he howled for mercy, till Scarlett fairly kicked him up again.

'Make a clean breast of it,' he said, 'or take the consequences. You know perfectly well that we have found you out, scoundrel.'

Tito's story came in gasps. He wanted to get rid of the Americans. He was jealous. Besides, under the Americanos would Cuba be any better off? By no means and assuredly not. Therefore it was the duty of every good Cuban to destroy the Americanos where possible.

'A nice lot to fight for,' Scarlett muttered. 'Get to the point.'

Hastened to the point by a liberal application of stout shoe leather, Tito made plenary confession. The senor himself had suggested death by medium of the devil's poppies. More than one predatory plant-hunter had been lured to his destruction in the same way. The skeleton hung on the tree was a Dutchman who had walked into the clutch of the purple terror innocently. And Pierre Anton had done the same. The suckers of the devil's poppy only came down at night to gather moisture; in the day they were coiled up like a spring. And anything that they touched they killed. Tito had watched more than one bird or small beast crushed and mauled by these cruel spines with their fringe of purple blossoms.

'How do you get the blooms?' Scarlett asked.

'That is easy,' Tito replied. 'In the daytime I moisten the ground under the trees. Then the suckers unfold, drawn by the water. Once the suckers unfold one cuts several of them off with long knives. There is danger, of course, but not if one is careful.'

'I'll not trouble the devil's poppy any further at present,' said Scarlett, 'but I shall trouble you to accompany me to my destination as a prisoner.'

Tito's eyes dilated.

'They will not shoot me?' he asked, hoarsely.

'I don't know,' Scarlett replied. 'They may hang you instead. At any rate, I shall be bitterly disappointed if they don't end you one way or the other. Whichever operation it is, I can look forward to it with perfect equanimity.'

GLÁMR

Sabine Baring-Gould

This story is based on a famous episode in Iceland's *Grettir's Saga*, which
was first written down in the early 14th century. It tells of a fight to
the death between Grettir, a mighty warrior, and a vampire named Glámr.
The latter is a *draugr*, which is the name the Icelanders of that period
gave to an animated corpse. In appearance these restless dead are hideous
to look at and carry the unmistakable stench of the grave, from which
they periodically emerge to prey on the living. Unlike ghosts, they have
a corporeal body and possess superhuman strength; and they can also
increase their size at will, making them formidable adversaries.

Baring-Gould (1834–1924) first told the story of Glámr in chapter
seven of *Iceland: Its Scenes and Sagas* (1863), under the heading 'The
Vampire's Grave,' and later included the same tale in his collection of
short stories *A Book of Ghosts* (1904), retitling it 'Glámr.' An English
clergyman, hagiographer, and prolific storyteller, Baring-Gould is also
remembered as the composer of hymns, the best-known being 'Onward,
Christian Soldiers.'

———————————

The following story is found in the Gretla,[3] an Icelandic Saga,
composed in the thirteenth century, or that comes to us in the form
then given to it; but it is a redaction of a Saga of much earlier date.
Most of it is thoroughly historical, and its statements are corrobo-
rated by other Sagas. The following incident was introduced to

3 Also known as *Grettir's Saga*.

account for the fact that the outlaw Grettir would run any risk rather than spend the long winter nights alone in the dark.

At the beginning of the eleventh century there stood, a little way up the Valley of Shadows in the north of Iceland, a small farm, occupied by a worthy bonder, named Thorhall, and his wife. The farmer was not exactly a chieftain, but he was well enough connected to be considered respectable; to back up his gentility he possessed numerous flocks of sheep and a goodly drove of oxen. Thorhall would have been a happy man but for one circumstance – his sheepwalks were haunted.

Not a herdsman would remain with him; he bribed, he threatened, entreated, all to no purpose; one shepherd after another left his service, and things came to such a pass that he determined on asking advice at the next annual council. Thorhall saddled his horses, adjusted his packs, provided himself with hobbles, cracked his long Icelandic whip, and cantered along the road, and in due time reached Thingvellir.

Skapti Thorodd's son was lawgiver at that time, and as everyone considered him a man of the utmost prudence and able to give the best advice, our friend from the Vale of Shadows made straight for his booth.

'An awkward predicament, certainly – to have large droves of sheep and no one to look after them,' said Skapti, nibbling the nail of his thumb, and shaking his wise head – a head as stuffed with law as a ptarmigan's crop is stuffed with blaeberries. 'Now I'll tell you what – as you have asked my advice, I will help you to a shepherd; a character in his way, a man of dull intellect, to be sure, but strong as a bull.'

'I do not care about his wits so long as he can look after sheep,' answered Thorhall.

'You may rely on his being able to do that,' said Skapti. 'He is a stout, plucky fellow; a Swede from Sylgsdale, if you know where that is.'

Towards the break-up of the council – 'Thing' they call it in Iceland – two greyish-white horses belonging to Thorhall slipped their hobbles and strayed; so the good man had to hunt after them himself, which shows how short of servants he was. He crossed

Sletha-asi, thence he bent his way to Armann's-fell, and just by the Priest's Wood he met a strange-looking man driving before him a horse laden with faggots. The fellow was tall and stalwart; his face involuntarily attracted Thorhall's attention, for the eyes, of an ashen grey, were large and staring, the powerful jaw was furnished with very white protruding teeth, and around the low forehead hung bunches of coarse wolf-grey hair.

'Pray, what is your name, my man?' asked the farmer, pulling up.

'Glámr, an please you,' replied the wood-cutter.

Thorhall stared; then, with a preliminary cough, he asked how Glámr liked faggot-picking.

'Not much,' was the answer; 'I prefer shepherd life.'

'Will you come with me?' asked Thorhall; 'Skapti has handed you over to me, and I want a shepherd this winter uncommonly.'

'If I serve you, it is on the understanding that I come or go as it pleases me. I tell you I am a bit truculent if things do not go just to my thinking.'

'I shall not object to this,' answered the bonder. 'So I may count on your services?'

'Wait a moment! You have not told me whether there be any drawback.'

'I must acknowledge that there is one,' said Thorhall; 'in fact, the sheepwalks have got a bad name for bogies.'

'Pshaw! I'm not the man to be scared at shadows,' laughed Glámr; 'so here's my hand to it; I'll be with you at the beginning of the winter night.'

Well, after this they parted, and presently the farmer found his ponies. Having thanked Skapti for his advice and assistance, he got his horses together and trotted home.

Summer, and then autumn passed, but not a word about the new shepherd reached the Valley of Shadows. The winter storms began to bluster up the glen, driving the flying snowflakes and massing the white drifts at every winding of the vale. Ice formed in the shallows of the river; and the streams, which in summer trickled down the ribbed scarps, were now transmuted into icicles.

One gusty night a violent blow at the door startled all in the farm. In another moment Glámr, tall as a troll, stood in the hall glowering out of his wild eyes, his grey hair matted with frost, his teeth rattling and snapping with cold, his face blood-red in the glare of the fire which smouldered in the centre of the hall. Thorhall jumped up and greeted him warmly, but the housewife was too frightened to be very cordial.

Weeks passed, and the new shepherd was daily on the moors with his flock; his loud and deep-toned voice was often borne down on the blast as he shouted to the sheep driving them into fold. His presence in the house always produced gloom, and if he spoke it sent a thrill through the women, who openly proclaimed their aversion for him.

There was a church near the byre, but Glámr never crossed the threshold; he hated psalmody; apparently he was an indifferent Christian. On the vigil of the Nativity Glámr rose early and shouted for meat.

'Meat!' exclaimed the housewife; 'no man calling himself a Christian touches flesh today. Tomorrow is the holy Christmas Day, and this is a fast.'

'All superstition!' roared Glámr. 'As far as I can see, men are no better now than they were in the bonny heathen time. Bring me meat, and make no more ado about it.'

'You may be quite certain,' protested the good wife, 'if Church rule be not kept, ill-luck will follow.'

Glámr ground his teeth and clenched his hands. 'Meat! I will have meat, or—' In fear and trembling the poor woman obeyed.

The day was raw and windy; masses of grey vapour rolled up from the Arctic Ocean, and hung in piles about the mountaintops. Now and then a scud of frozen fog, composed of minute particles of ice, swept along the glen, covering bar and beam with feathery hoar-frost. As the day declined, snow began to fall in large flakes like the down of the eider-duck. One moment there was a lull in the wind, and then the deep-toned shout of Glámr, high up the moor slopes, was heard distinctly by the congregation assembling for the first vespers of Christmas Day. Darkness came on, deep as that in the rayless abysses of the caverns under the lava, and still the snow fell thicker. The lights from the church windows sent a yellow haze far out into the night, and every flake burned golden as it swept within the ray. The bell in the lychgate clanged for evensong, and the wind puffed the sound far up the glen; perhaps it reached the herdsman's ear. Hark! Someone caught a distant sound or shriek, which it was he could not tell, for the wind muttered and mumbled about the church eaves, and then with a fierce whistle scudded over the graveyard fence. Glámr had not returned when the service was over. Thorhall suggested a search, but no man would accompany him; and no wonder! it was not a night for a dog to be out in; besides, the tracks were a foot deep in snow. The family sat up all night, waiting, listening, trembling; but no Glámr came home. Dawn broke at last, wan and blear in the south. The clouds hung down like great sheets, full of snow, almost to bursting.

A party was soon formed to search for the missing man. A sharp scramble brought them to high land, and the ridge between the two rivers which join in Vatnsdalr was thoroughly examined. Here and there were found the scattered sheep, shuddering under an icicled rock, or half buried in a snowdrift. No trace yet of the keeper. A dead ewe lay at the bottom of a crag; it had staggered over in the gloom, and had been dashed to pieces.

Presently the whole party were called together about a trampled spot in the heath, where evidently a death-struggle had taken place, for earth and stone were tossed about, and the snow was blotched with large splashes of blood. A gory track led up the mountain, and the farm servants were following it, when a cry, almost of agony, from one of the lads, made them turn. In looking behind a rock, the boy had come upon the corpse of the shepherd; it was livid and swollen to the size of a bullock. It lay on its back with the arms extended. The snow had been scrabbled up by the puffed hands in the death-agony, and the staring glassy eyes gazed out of the ashen-grey, upturned face into the vaporous canopy overhead. From the purple lips lolled the tongue, which in the last throes had been bitten through by the white fangs, and a discoloured stream which had flowed from it was now an icicle.

With trouble the dead man was raised on a litter, and carried to a gill-edge, but beyond this he could not be borne; his weight waxed more and more, the bearers toiled beneath their burden, their foreheads became beaded with sweat; though strong men they were crushed to the ground. Consequently, the corpse was left at the ravine-head, and the men returned to the farm. Next day their efforts to lift Glámr's bloated carcass, and remove it to consecrated ground, were unavailing. On the third day a priest accompanied them, but the body was nowhere to be found. Another expedition without the priest was made, and on this occasion the corpse was discovered; so a cairn was raised over the spot.

Two nights after this one of the thralls who had gone after the cows burst into the hall with a face blank and scared; he staggered to a seat and fainted. On recovering his senses, in a broken voice he assured all who crowded about him that he had seen Glámr walking past him as he left the door of the stable. On the following evening a houseboy was found in a fit under the farmyard wall, and he remained an idiot to his dying day. Some of the women next saw a face which, though blown out and discoloured, they recognised as that of Glámr, looking in upon them through a window of the dairy. In the twilight, Thorhall himself met the dead man, who stood and glowered at him, but made no attempt to injure his master. The haunting did not end there. Nightly a heavy tread was heard around the house, and a hand feeling along the walls, sometimes thrust in at the windows, at others clutching the woodwork, and breaking it to splinters. However, when the spring came round the disturbances lessened, and as the sun obtained full power, ceased altogether.

That summer a vessel from Norway dropped anchor in the nearest bay. Thorhall visited it, and found on board a man named Thorgaut, who was in search of work.

'What do you say to being my shepherd?' asked the bonder.

'I should very much like the office,' answered Thorgaut. 'I am as strong as two ordinary men, and a handy fellow to boot.'

'I will not engage you without forewarning you of the terrible things you may have to encounter during the winter night.'

'Pray, what may they be?'

'Ghosts and hobgoblins,' answered the farmer; 'a fine dance they lead me, I can promise you.'

'I fear them not,' answered Thorgaut; 'I shall be with you at cattle-slaughtering time.'

At the appointed season the man came, and soon established himself as a favourite in the house; he romped with the children, chucked the maidens under the chin, helped his fellow-servants, gratified the housewife by admiring her curd, and was just as much liked as his predecessor had been detested. He was a devil-may-care fellow, too, and made no bones of his contempt for the ghost, expressing hopes of meeting him face to face, which made his master look grave, and his mistress shudderingly cross herself. As the winter came on, strange sights and sounds began to alarm the folk, but these never frightened Thorgaut; he slept too soundly at night to hear the tread of feet about the door, and was too short-sighted to catch glimpses of a grisly monster striding up and down, in the twilight, before its cairn.

At last Christmas Eve came round, and Thorgaut went out as usual with his sheep.

'Have a care, man,' urged the bonder; 'go not near to the gill-head, where Glámr lies.'

'Tut, tut! fear not for me. I shall be back by vespers.'

'God grant it,' sighed the housewife; 'but 'tis not a day for risks, to be sure.'

Twilight came on: a feeble light hung over the south, one white streak above the heath land to the south. Far off in southern lands it was still day, but here the darkness gathered in apace, and men came from Vatnsdalr for evensong, to herald in the night when Christ was born. Christmas Eve! How different in Saxon England! There the great ashen faggot is rolled along the hall with torch and taper; the mummers dance with their merry jingling bells; the boar's head, with gilded tusks, 'bedecked with holly and rosemary,' is brought in by the steward to a flourish of trumpets.

How different, too, where the Varanger cluster round the imperial throne in the mighty church of the Eternal Wisdom at this very hour. Outside, the air is soft from breathing over the Bosphorus, which flashes tremulously beneath the stars. The orange and laurel leaves in the palace gardens are still exhaling fragrance in the hush of the Christmas night.

But it is different here. The wind is piercing as a two-edged sword; blocks of ice crash and grind along the coast, and the lake waters are congealed to stone. Aloft, the Aurora flames crimson, flinging long streamers to the zenith, and then suddenly dissolving into a sea of pale green light. The natives are waiting round the church-door, but no Thorgaut has returned.

They find him next morning, lying across Glámr's cairn, with his spine, his leg, and arm-bones shattered. He is conveyed to the churchyard, and a cross is set up at his head. He sleeps peacefully. Not so Glámr; he becomes more furious than ever. No one will remain with Thorhall now, except an old cowherd who has always served the family, and who had long ago dandled his present master on his knee.

'All the cattle will be lost if I leave,' said the carle; 'it shall never be told of me that I deserted Thorhall from fear of a spectre.'

Matters grew rapidly worse. Outbuildings were broken into of a night, and their woodwork was rent and shattered; the house door was violently shaken, and great pieces of it were torn away; the gables of the house were also pulled furiously to and fro.

One morning before dawn, the old man went to the stable. An hour later, his mistress arose, and taking her milking pails, followed him. As she reached the door of the stable, a terrible sound from within – the bellowing of the cattle, mingled with the deep notes of an unearthly voice – sent her back shrieking to the house. Thorhall leaped out of bed, caught up a weapon, and hastened to the cowhouse. On opening the door, he found the cattle goring each other. Slung across the stone that separated the stalls was something. Thorhall stepped up to it, felt it, looked close; it was the cowherd, perfectly dead, his feet on one side of the slab, his head on the other, and his spine snapped in twain. The bonder now moved with his family to Tunga, another farm owned by him lower down the valley; it was too venturesome living during the midwinter night at the haunted farm; and it was not till the sun had returned as a bridegroom out of his chamber, and had dispelled night with its phantoms, that he went back to the Vale of Shadows. In the meantime, his little girl's health had given way under the repeated alarms of the winter; she became paler every day; with the autumn flowers she faded, and was laid beneath the mould of the churchyard in time for the first snows to spread a virgin pall over her small grave.

At this time Grettir – a hero of great fame, and a native of the north of the island – was in Iceland, and as the hauntings of this vale were matters of gossip throughout the district, he inquired about them, and resolved on visiting the scene. So Grettir busked himself for a cold ride, mounted his horse, and in due course of

time drew rein at the door of Thorhall's farm with the request that
he might be accommodated there for the night.

'Ahem!' coughed the bonder; 'perhaps you are not aware—'

'I am perfectly aware of all. I want to catch sight of the troll.'

'But your horse is sure to be killed.'

'I will risk it. Glámr I must meet, so there's an end of it.'

'I am delighted to see you,' spoke the bonder; 'at the same time,
should mischief befall you, don't lay the blame at my door.'

'Never fear, man.'

So they shook hands; the horse was put into the strongest stable,
Thorhall made Grettir as good cheer as he was able, and then, as
the visitor was sleepy, all retired to rest.

The night passed quietly, and no sounds indicated the presence
of a restless spirit. The horse, moreover, was found next morning
in good condition, enjoying his hay.

'This is unexpected!' exclaimed the bonder, gleefully. 'Now,
where's the saddle? We'll clap it on, and then goodbye, and a merry
journey to you.'

'Goodbye!' echoed Grettir; 'I am going to stay here another
night.'

'You had best be advised,' urged Thorhall; 'if misfortune should
overtake you, I know that all your kinsmen would visit it on my
head.'

'I have made up my mind to stay,' said Grettir, and he looked
so dogged that Thorhall opposed him no more.

All was quiet next night; not a sound roused Grettir from his
slumber. Next morning he went with the farmer to the stable. The
strong wooden door was shivered and driven in. They stepped across
it; Grettir called to his horse, but there was no responsive whinny.

'I am afraid—' began Thorhall. Grettir leaped in, and found the
poor brute dead, and with its neck broken.

'Now,' said Thorhall quickly, 'I've got a capital horse – a skewbald
– down by Tunga, I shall not be many hours in fetching it; your
saddle is here, I think, and then you will just have time to reach—'

'I stay here another night,' interrupted Grettir.

'I implore you to depart,' said Thorhall.

'My horse is slain!'

'But I will provide you with another.'

'Friend,' answered Grettir, turning so sharply round that the
farmer jumped back, half frightened, 'no man ever did me an injury
without rueing it. Now, your demon herdsman has been the death
of my horse. He must be taught a lesson.'

'Would that he were!' groaned Thorhall; 'but mortal must not
face him. Go in peace and receive compensation from me for what
has happened.'

'I must revenge my horse.'

'An obstinate man will have his own way! But if you run your
head against a stone wall, don't be angry because you get a broken
pate.'

Night came on; Grettir ate a hearty supper and was right jovial;
not so Thorhall, who had his misgivings. At bedtime the latter crept
into his crib, which, in the manner of old Icelandic beds, opened
out of the hall, as berths do out of a cabin. Grettir, however, determined on remaining up; so he flung himself on a bench with his
feet against the posts of the high seat, and his back against Thorhall's
crib; then he wrapped one lappet of his fur coat round his feet, the
other about his head, keeping the neck-opening in front of his face,
so that he could look through into the hall.

There was a fire burning on the hearth, a smouldering heap of
red embers; every now and then a twig flared up and crackled,
giving Grettir glimpses of the rafters, as he lay with his eyes
wandering among the mysteries of the smoke-blackened roof. The
wind whistled softly overhead. The clerestory windows, covered
with the amnion of sheep, admitted now and then a sickly yellow
glare from the full moon, which, however, shot a beam of pure
silver through the smoke-hole in the roof. A dog without began to
howl; the cat, which had long been sitting demurely watching the
fire, stood up with raised back and bristling tail, then darted behind
some chests in a corner. The hall door was in a sad plight. It had
been so riven by the spectre that it was made firm by wattles only,
and the moon glinted athwart the crevices. Soothingly the river,
not yet frozen over, prattled over its shingly bed as it swept round
the knoll on which stood the farm. Grettir heard the breathing of
the sleeping women in the adjoining chamber, and the sigh of the
housewife as she turned in her bed.

Click! click! – It is only the frozen turf on the roof cracking with

the cold. The wind lulls completely. The night is very still without.
Hark! a heavy tread, beneath which the snow yields. Every footfall
goes straight to Grettir's heart. A crash on the turf overhead! By
all the saints in paradise! The monster is treading on the roof. For
one moment the chimney-gap is completely darkened: Glámr is
looking down it; the flash of the red ash is reflected in the two
lustreless eyes. Then the moon glances sweetly in once more, and
the heavy tramp of Glámr is audibly moving towards the farther
end of the hall. A thud – he has leaped down. Grettir feels the
board at his back quivering, for Thorhall is awake and is trembling
in his bed. The steps pass round to the back of the house, and then
the snapping of the wood shows that the creature is destroying
some of the outhouse doors. He tires of this apparently, for his
footfall comes clear towards the main entrance to the hall. The
moon is veiled behind a watery cloud, and by the uncertain glimmer
Grettir fancies that he sees two dark hands thrust in above the
door. His apprehensions are verified, for, with a loud snap, a long
strip of panel breaks, and light is admitted. Snap – snap! another
portion gives way, and the gap becomes larger. Then the wattles
slip from their places, and a dark arm rips them out in bunches,
and flings them away. There is a crossbeam to the door, holding a
bolt which slides into a stone groove. Against the grey light, Grettir
sees a huge black figure heaving itself over the bar. Crack! that has
given way, and the rest of the door falls in shivers to the earth.

'Oh, heavens above!' exclaims the bonder.

Stealthily the dead man creeps on, feeling at the beams as he
comes; then he stands in the hall, with the firelight on him. A
fearful sight; the tall figure distended with the corruption of the
grave, the nose fallen off, the wandering, vacant eyes, with the glaze
of death on them, the sallow flesh patched with green masses of
decay; the wolf-grey hair and beard have grown in the tomb, and
hang matted about the shoulders and breast; the nails, too, they
have grown. It is a sickening sight – a thing to shudder at, not to
see.

Motionless, with no nerve quivering now, Thorhall and Grettir
held their breath.

Glámr's lifeless glance strayed round the chamber; it rested on
the shaggy bundle by the high seat. Cautiously he stepped towards

it. Grettir felt him groping about the lower lappet and pulling at it. The cloak did not give way. Another jerk; Grettir kept his feet firmly pressed against the posts, so that the rug was not pulled off. The vampire seemed puzzled, he plucked at the upper flap and tugged. Grettir held to the bench and bed board, so that he was not moved, but the cloak was rent in twain, and the corpse staggered back, holding half in its hands, and gazing wonderingly at it. Before it had done examining the shred, Grettir started to his feet, bowed his body, flung his arms about the carcass, and, driving his head into the chest, strove to bend it backward and snap the spine. A vain attempt! The cold hands came down on Grettir's arms with diabolical force, riving them from their hold. Grettir clasped them about the body again; then the arms closed round him, and began dragging him along. The brave man clung by his feet to benches and posts, but the strength of the vampire was the greater; posts gave way, benches were heaved from their places, and the wrestlers at each moment neared the door. Sharply writhing loose, Grettir flung his hands round a roof beam. He was dragged from his feet; the numbing arms clenched him round the waist, and tore at him; every tendon in his breast was strained; the strain under his shoulders became excruciating, the muscles stood out in knots. Still he held on; his fingers were bloodless; the pulses of his temples throbbed in jerks; the breath came in a whistle through his rigid nostrils. All the while, too, the long nails of the dead man cut into his side, and Grettir could feel them piercing like knives between his ribs. Then at once his hands gave way, and the monster bore him reeling towards the porch, crashing over the broken fragments of the door. Hard as the battle had gone with him indoors, Grettir knew that it would go worse outside, so he gathered up all his remaining strength for one final desperate struggle. The door had been shut with a swivel into a groove; this groove was in a stone, which formed the jamb on one side, and there was a similar block on the other, into which the hinges had been driven. As the wrestlers neared the opening, Grettir planted both his feet against the stone posts, holding Glámr by the middle. He had the advantage now. The dead man writhed in his arms, drove his talons into Grettir's back, and tore up great ribbons of flesh, but the stone jambs held firm.

'Now,' thought Grettir, 'I can break his back,' and thrusting his head under the chin, so that the grisly beard covered his eyes, he forced the face from him, and the back was bent as a hazel rod.

'If I can but hold on,' thought Grettir, and he tried to shout for Thorhall, but his voice was muffled in the hair of the corpse.

Suddenly one or both of the doorposts gave way. Down crashed the gable trees, ripping beams and rafters from their beds; frozen clods of earth rattled from the roof and thumped into the snow. Glámr fell on his back, and Grettir staggered down on top of him. The moon was at her full; large white clouds chased each other across the sky, and as they swept before her disk she looked through them with a brown halo round her. The snowcap of Jorundarfell, however, glowed like a planet, then the white mountain ridge was kindled, the light ran down the hillside, the bright disk stared out of the veil and flashed at this moment full on the vampire's face. Grettir's strength was failing him, his hands quivered in the snow, and he knew that he could not support himself from dropping flat on the dead man's face, eye to eye, lip to lip. The eyes of the corpse were fixed on him, lit with the cold glare of the moon. His head swam as his heart sent a hot stream to his brain. Then a voice from the grey lips said—

'Thou hast acted madly in seeking to match thyself with me. Now learn that henceforth ill luck shall constantly attend thee; that thy strength shall never exceed what it now is, and that by night these eyes of mine shall stare at thee through the darkness till thy dying day, so that for very horror thou shalt not endure to be alone.'

Grettir at this moment noticed that his dirk had slipped from its sheath during the fall, and that it now lay conveniently near his hand. The giddiness which had oppressed him passed away, he clutched at the sword haft, and with a blow severed the vampire's throat. Then, kneeling on the breast, he hacked till the head came off.

Thorhall appeared now, his face blanched with terror, but when he saw how the fray had terminated he assisted Grettir gleefully to roll the corpse on the top of a pile of faggots, which had been collected for winter fuel. Fire was applied, and soon far down the valley the flames of the pyre startled people, and made them wonder what new horror was being enacted in the upper portion of the Vale of Shadows.

Next day the charred bones were conveyed to a spot remote from the habitations of men, and were there buried.

What Glámr had predicted came to pass. Never after did Grettir dare to be alone in the dark.

THE VAMPIRE NEMESIS

'Dolly'

During the late nineteenth and early twentieth centuries, several British expatriates living and working in China and Hong Kong wrote works of fiction set in East Asia, which often explored the cultural conflicts between British residents and their Chinese subordinates, of which the following story is an interesting example. Although sometimes falsely credited to Mrs Vernon F. Creighton, the author of this story was actually Leonard D'Oliver, who at the time it was written was the Chief Officer on the steamer S.S. *Kut Sang*, the newest, most up-to-date ship in the fleet of the Indo-China Steam Navigation Company of Hong Kong. In his spare time he wrote short stories, the best of which were collected in *The Vampire Nemesis and Other Weird Stories of the China Coast* (1905).

IN setting down the train of events that occurred at Ningpo on that horror-filled night of August, 18—, I shall make no attempt to justify or excuse my own conduct, nor that of my friend, the end of whose troubled career I shall here endeavour to portray.

Nor would I wish that any who should scan this page should believe that there was aught supernatural about the occurrence. I make no doubt but that all could be readily explained away on grounds purely natural by one who had been a calm observer of the facts, if facts they were, and not some horrible nightmare on which I look back shuddering – one not possessed of the overwrought mind, in a state of nervous tension, such as at the time was mine.

I set them forth here for what they may be worth, and leave the reader to draw his own conclusions.

My reason for reverting at all to so painful a subject, the bare recollection of which, even now, causes the cold beads of terror to gather, must be that the spirit of my friend and college chum cries to me from the grave that justice be done him; that his memory be cleared of the foul stain of murder, leaving nevertheless that of base treachery and fiendish cruelty.

After years of wavering irresolution, I take up my pen to reopen that chapter of horror.

One word more ere I commence. Those who were at Ningpo at that period, now so many years ago, will doubtless remember some of the incidents which at that time made such a sensation, and should they here, under the assumed names, recognise the actors in the terrible tragedy, let them know that hereby one of them sends greetings.

Fergusson and I had been close friends since those early days at Cambridge when all the world looked rosy and life lay before us. Study had never been our forte, and it was perhaps in a mutual avoidance of lectures that we were thrown so much together.

In all the sports we had stood premier. Fergusson had had the proud distinction of pulling in the college eight, while I had competed, unsuccessfully it is true, for the Diamond Sculls at Henley. At cricket and football we were both adepts, and with the gloves neither of us were to be lightly handled; it was only within the bounds of the lecture room that we allowed our inferiority to any, and these, as I said before, we avoided as religiously as our remaining at college would admit. The very natural result of which was that on our leaving and stepping on to the platform of the world we found, to our chagrin, that it was heads that were required there in the scrimmage, and that arms, be they never so well seasoned, were almost a superfluity, unless one had a fancy for bricklaying or some kindred occupation.

It was about this time that glowing reports commenced to reach England of the gold that lay beneath the fertile soil of British Guiana, the old El Dorado of Sir Walter Raleigh, and Fergusson and I resolved upon going out to see for ourselves if somewhere at least sinews were not in requisition. As a result we did dig some gold, or rather washed it, for it was all alluvial deposits, but we buried much more silver, and after a year we came away in disgust.

Our next billet was at the other end of the world, where, still together, we each got a berth on the two papers that the tiny town in the Malay States could boast. There, being better hands at satire than the respective editors, we used to write the slashing editorials about each other that was nearly all the papers contained. To an outsider, with a sense of humour, it must have been intensely amusing to see the two who in the columns of their journals had been vilifying each other, seeking among their extensive vocabulary for a name black enough, drinking an amicable glass together later in the day.

However, there being not enough inhabitants able to read to keep one paper going, the two journals, with a praiseworthy pertinacity, choked each other to death, and with their demise Fergusson and I were once more thrown on our own resources. Yet there exists a certain gentleman of much-maligned character who is reported to look after his own, and he now led us to join the Chinese Imperial Custom Service; thus we drifted from port to port until we were finally stationed at Ningpo, with every prospect of it being a permanency; and it is here that my story may be said to commence.

There being then no Customs quarters there, we each rented a small flat by the riverside, on opposite sides of the stone-flagged street, and about fifty yards apart, and, with a Chinese girl as housekeeper, proceeded to make our lives as comfortable as might be.

I have no desire to pose as a model of virtue. We were neither of us married, but those girls were as faithful to us as any European woman firmly tied in the bonds of Western wedlock could have been.

And here, in relating how Fergusson came by his housekeeper, I must paint in the first dark stain that marred his character. Under him was a half-caste watcher who had a lovely young wife, a girl of little more than eighteen, also with an obvious strain of Western blood in her veins, though she affected the Chinese costume and spoke but little better pidgin-English than her pure-blooded sisters.

This man Fergusson pursued with the most implacable hatred I have ever seen him exhibit towards any human being, until the poor fellow, who went by the name of Mathews (God knows where he got it from!) was never out of hot water. Fine after fine was imposed upon him – sometimes with justice, however unmerciful; more often without – until one day I angrily remonstrated with Fergusson on his gross injustice.

His only reply was a curtly-expressed desire that I would mind my own business, and as I did not care to come to an open rupture with him for the sake of a half-caste, nothing more was said.

At last poor Mathews fell into a trap which I firmly believe had been deliberately laid for him at the instigation of Fergusson, and was dismissed from the service.

This misfortune reduced the unhappy pair to the verge of starvation, and it was then that I saw the ghastly malignity of Fergusson's relentless persecution. He had been paying surreptitious attentions, when chance offered, to the young girl-wife, and now, having so successfully ruined the husband, he offered her a home beneath his own roof, which she accepted with alacrity.

I suppose I must confess that, after the first burst of anger at Fergusson's treachery to the watcher, I condoned the hideous offence. After all, Fergusson was my old college chum, and perhaps at heart I was as bad myself, lacking but opportunity.

And so for five months everything ran smoothly. 'May,' as Fergusson called his partner in guilt, took readily to her altered fortunes and changed manner of living, nor seemed in the least to regret the loss of her legitimate lord. Ibe, we heard, had taken to opium-smoking, and during his few hours of wakefulness sought employment as a coolie in the rice-fields on the opposite side of the river. Ibe had never been more than a barely perceptible step above the surrounding Chinamen, but now, in his degradation, he had sunk to the level of the lowest. Yet Fergusson felt no remorse for what was so obviously his handiwork.

One dark night early in February Fergusson and I returned late from the newly-erected Customs Club, and stopped opposite my door. He had taken to drinking rather deeply, and I had stayed on beyond my usual hour to keep an eye on him and prevent him, if possible, from imbibing to excess.

The flat I occupied was over a Chinese shop, and to reach the staircase one had to go through the small go-down to the side to a little courtyard at the back, and so through the door leading to the stairs.

Now, as we stood talking, Fergusson was pressing me to step round to his place and sample a bottle of particularly good whisky he had obtained from a ship on which he had been stationed. But I firmly declined. It was late, I said, past midnight. Fergusson would take no denial.

'Come along,' he said, 'it isn't twelve yet. May will have something hot in readiness for us. You need not stay long.'

'Not twelve?' I echoed. 'I wouldn't mind betting it is past one!'

'Done for five dollars,' said Fergusson, smiling.

'Right; come upstairs and look at the clock.'

We turned and walked through the go-down into the courtyard beyond. But we had no need to ascend the stairs. As we stood there the little clock I kept in my room ('Bow Bells' Fergusson called it) chimed out musically, and we both stood still to listen. I thought as we stood there that I heard a faint stir as of someone entering in the go-down beyond, but paid no heed. The little clock ran through its preliminary chime, then struck one.

'There!' I cried triumphantly.

But scarcely had the sound died away on the stairs when there came the thunderous report of a revolver, fired point-blank in a confined space, and as the reverberations echoed through the go-down Fergusson staggered, with a stifled cry, to the wall. Another shot followed closely on the other, and locating the marksman by the flash of the weapon in the darkness of the go-down, I made a rush at him, and went sprawling over something soft and yielding lying full across the doorway. I struck a match and bent over it. It was Mathews, or rather the wreck of Mathews, lying there with a tiny stream of blood bubbling out from his temple and trickling across the floor, a smoking pistol – an antiquated 'bulldog' – gripped in his hand.

Without waiting to see more, I threw the match away and ran back to see how Fergusson had fared. I found him leaning against the wall, pale but smiling, trying to staunch the flow of blood from a flesh wound in the shoulder.

'Near thing that, Ward,' he said coolly, as I inquired anxiously where he was hit. 'A little lower, and it would have finished me.'

'Where are you hit?' I asked again.

'Left shoulder – mere scratch!'

He sat down on an empty box while I helped him off with his coat.

'Wonder who was the potter?' he said presently.

'Mathews,' I answered.

'Damn him!' cried Fergusson furiously, springing to his feet. 'The cursed swine! He shall pay for this!'

'He has paid already,' I said quietly.

'How?'

'He is outside with a bullet in his brain,' I answered briefly. This night's work was not to my liking.

'That's right,' Fergusson said brutally. 'I'm glad he did the job neatly on himself, just as glad as that he bungled it on me.'

'Fergusson,' I said sternly, 'this is your doing.'

'Pshaw! Nonsense! The girl did not want to stay with him, and one must oblige a lady when it lies in one's power so to do.'

A crowd was already gathering, attracted by the report; and as Fergusson did not want to be mixed up in the matter, he hastily slipped up to my room and washed and bandaged his arm. Then we sauntered down to where they were gathered round the dead man, leaving it to be inferred that he had simply committed suicide in the street and tumbled into the open doorway.

'Jolly glad,' said Fergusson when all was quiet again, 'that it did not happen at my place – people would have twigged. I suppose he was lying in wait for me at my door, and when he saw us come in here followed with the intention of potting me when I came out.'

Things fell back into their old groove, and months slid by. The only change was that, despite my efforts to keep him straight, Fergusson took to drinking deeper and deeper, and poor May had a hard time of it when he came home drunk, for he ill-used her shamefully. Remonstrance was in vain; when he was in his cups it was utterly useless to attempt to argue with him, and next morning when he was sobered no one was more contrite, as he viewed the bruises on the girl's tender flesh, than Fergusson himself. Still she stuck to him, doing her best to keep him from the drink, nor ever complaining to him or anyone else of his brutality.

So matters went on until that eventful August night, when began the most frightful series of events it has ever been the lot of mortal man to witness or chronicle.

It was a close, sultry night, with that ominous stillness which, to my mind, always presages some form of disaster. My housekeeper had long ago retired for the night, and I was sitting near the open window smoking and wondering idly what had become of Fergusson, whom I had not seen for three days. On one of his bursts again, was my conclusion. I would have to look him up in the morning and give him a talking to, though I smiled bitterly to myself as I thought of how little use that would be. Things could not go on like this, however, if Fergusson did not want to be dismissed from the service. While I yet pondered on his folly, footsteps creaked on the stairs without, and I looked round to see the man of whom I was thinking standing in the doorway. His eyes were bloodshot and protruding, and his hair – he had come in without a hat – fairly standing on end. His clothes were in disorder, and there was a look of wild terror in his face, as he staggered into the room, that for the moment alarmed me.

The next I muttered to myself, 'Drunk again!' as I crossed to the table beside which he had collapsed into a chair.

He raised his head as I sat down opposite him and looked wildly round the room, as though searching for a presence he could feel but could not see.

'Ward,' he said suddenly, turning his terror-stricken eyes on me, 'do you believe in ghosts?'

'Spirits?' I asked, contempt in my tones as I pointed to the whisky-bottle on the sideboard. 'Yes! So do you, or you would not be here now in that disgusting state.'

He flung up his head impatiently.

'Do you believe in transmigration?' he asked again. Fergusson, the cool, the resolute, was trembling like a scared kitten.

'I thought we settled all that to our entire satisfaction years ago at coll.,' I told him.

But he went on wildly, unheeding my jesting treatment of the matter.

'Ward, do you think it possible that a man, we will say a Chinaman, could come back to earth in the form of a vampire, to haunt one who has wronged him?'

'Why?' I queried amusedly. 'Have you seen him?'

His face was ashen with terror and his lips livid as he muttered—
'I have!'

'My dear man,' I laughed, 'you've got 'em again, got 'em badly,
for this time your rats have wings!'

He answered nothing, only looked apprehensively round the
room. I went on:

'Best rat poison for vampires and such, Fergusson, is a course of
strict teetotalism, and a few doses of bromide, administered not to
them but to yourself.'

But my irony was lost on him.

'Listen, Ward!' said he, gripping my arm as in a vice, and there
was something of deadly earnestness in his voice that forced my
attention. 'Last night I came home from the club as usual' – I had no
need to ask him in what state 'as usual' was, I knew, alas! too well
– 'and went to the little cupboard where I had stowed three bottles
of whisky that I had obtained from the chief officer of one of
Butterfield's boats discharging sugar in the river, in order to continue
the orgy, and found them gone.'

He stopped and glanced round the room again.

'Good job for you!' said I unsympathetically.

He continued—

'I went in and shook May out of her sleep, and asked her what
she had done with them; but she professed entire ignorance of them
until I gripped her arm till she writhed in pain' – he groaned, and
from that I concluded that he must be sober now, but suffering from
delirium tremens – 'then she cried out in her agony that she had
smashed them so that I should not drink myself to death.

'But I told her roughly she lied, and that I would not release her
until she showed me where she had hidden them. She only sobbed,
"Have makee break! Have makee break!" Then, Ward, in a frenzy
of drunken passion I got a length of cord and bound her slender
wrists and ankles to the head and foot rails of the bed. Bound them'
– he shuddered violently – 'until I could see the cords cutting into
the tender flesh, and her delicate limbs swelling under the torture,
and I stood beside her and laughed in glee while she moaned, "Have
makee break! True, have makee break!"'

His head sank on his arms and he groaned again in anguish of remorse. I rose to my feet in sudden heat and strode to his side, shaking him roughly by the collar.

'Fergusson!' I cried fiercely, 'is this true? Answer me, man! Is this true?'

'As true,' he replied miserably, 'as that I look forward to burning in hell for it!'

'You cur!' I cried, flinging him from me, for I knew the depth of the girl's devotion to him.

He did not resent it nor attempt to excuse himself, only looked up at me with a bitter laugh – a laugh that reminded me of the savage snarl of a wounded hyena – and I shuddered involuntarily.

'Listen, Ward, for there is more to come!'

I took two or three hasty turns to and fro, then sat down opposite to him again. He went on with feverish haste, eager to get it over.

'I left her there, Ward! Left her in torture!' His voice rose almost to a wail. 'Left her, and went back into the other room. A gust of wind from the open window had blown the lamp out and the room was in darkness, and as I stood there gloating like a fiend over the moans that came from the bed in the other room something swept up against the closed window; a moment later it had returned and fluttered in through the open one.'

He stopped suddenly, and a violent trembling shook his frame.

'Ward, it was the "Thing"!'

'What the—'

'Yes!' he cried eagerly, 'the vampire!'

I felt in no mood to laugh at his absurd fancy now. I felt too shocked at the cruel treatment he had meted out to May.

'It came into the room, Ward, and flapped in ever lessening circles round my head. I struck out wildly at It, for I was intoxicated and did not fear It at the time. But It took no notice of my vicious lunges; It sailed three times round my head, then as I thought flapped its way out again through the open window. I looked at my watch; it was exactly one o'clock.

'Firm set on getting more drink, I left the house again, leaving May to her agony, and made my way back to the club. It was closed, but I made the boy give me a full bottle of whisky, saying I wanted a peg, and brought it away with me.

'I must have drunk half of it before I got back to the house, and when I went in I found the groans had ceased. I went to May's bedside—'

The curtains at the window stirred slightly, and he broke off suddenly with a great start, terror writ large in his face.

'Ward!' he cried, with livid lips, 'It is coming! The "Thing"!'

'Nonsense!' I said. 'That was a puff of wind.'

The man was utterly unnerved. I had to pacify him as one soothes a little child.

'Go on with your vile story!' I told him at last.

'I went to May's side, and there, Ward, was the "Thing" on her face. It had Its head just under her ear, with its great wings slowly fanning. Ward!' he almost shrieked, 'It was sucking her life's blood! Do you hear me? Sucking her blood! She had swooned with the pain of the cords and the horror of this "Thing", and I – I stood there, made fearless with drink, laughing in devilish joy at the sight I saw. How long I stayed I do not know, but at last I sank down in stupor beside the bed. I knew nothing more until this morning.'

'And then?' I asked. I was getting interested in this curious mental aberration of Fergusson's.

'Then, when I arose,' he broke out in sudden fury, 'she was dead! Dead, Ward! Dead! dead! dead!'

Suddenly he grew deadly calm, going on with the quietness of a surgeon diagnosing a case.

'There was a tiny puncture under her ear, just on the jugular vein, with a little globule of blood no bigger than a bead exuding from it; but the pillow was bathed in blood, soaked through and through.'

Matters were looking black indeed, for I had no doubt at the time that Fergusson had killed her in the frenzy of his drunken passion. Afterward I had no cause to change my mind.

'I think it must have dazed me, for I threw myself across her cold body and lay there until the moment before you saw me,' he continued vacantly. 'I got up then, leaving her poor stiffened limbs still bound to the bed-rails, and came on here.'

'Fergusson,' I said gravely, 'do you realise what this means, lad? It means murder, and murder is an ugly word – even in China, Fergusson!'

Tomorrow at dawn he was to escape to safety in the outgoing Jardine steamer, and as yet we fancied ourselves secure in the certainty of no one having entered the house of death.

But Fergusson seemed to have abandoned all hope of flight, or, rather, a gloomy despondency that whispered to him of its futility, had settled like a black pall over his being.

All through the early part of that dreadful night I sat talking to him, trying one moment to soothe his craven fears, and the next to rouse him from the apathy of his despair. He was completely unnerved, and had a shuddering premonition that the Thing was hovering near, in spite of my repeated assurances that, except for ourselves, the room was empty.

Suddenly, far into the night – how far I knew not then, for I had tried not to count the chimes of the little clock – his terror-sharpened perceptions caught the sharp tramp of distant feet on the flags of the little street below. He rose with shaking knees to his feet and tottered to the window. I had heard the sound too, and followed him, peering over his shoulder. What we saw was the chief of police, with four men in the uniform of the Imperial Constabulary, standing outside Fergusson's door.

As we watched, Major Barnes gave an order in a low undertone, and he and two constables advanced into the house.

We stood watching, frozen into inaction, until they emerged again, and with a low whistle, answered from somewhere behind us, strode straight towards my door.

Then, as the blood rushed back to my palpitating heart, I saw what this meant for Fergusson. By some means the crime had already been discovered, and the hounds of the law were on his trail.

I ran round the room, looking frantically for some means of escape. The front door was impossible; the wall that bounded one side of the little court was far too high for a man to scale without due preparation; and on either side impassable go-downs, with blank walls, having nor door nor window by which to gain access.

He was fairly trapped like a rat in its hole!

But as I gazed in despair at the wall which formed the boundary of the lane that separated us from the British Consul's grounds, my heart went bounding into my throat with joy and hope, for I beheld,

'I realise what it means,' he answered gloomily, 'and I almost rejoice at it. It will prove one thing – it will prove that Justice, though in the abstract drawing a wrong conclusion from her premises, will yet be right in the fundamental fact.'

'What fact?' For, having come to the same conclusion myself, I did not follow the drift of his reasoning.

'The fact,' he replied with a harsh laugh, 'that I murdered her; though I swear to you, Ward, that no drop of her blood was shed by hand of mine.'

I smiled pityingly, and as I still smiled the little clock in the next room chimed out, then paused for a second and struck one. The smile and the words I was about to utter froze on my lips, for I felt the hair gradually rising on my head with vague, undefined apprehension. At the same moment something struck with a muffled thud against the side of the open window, and I heard a soft, insistent flapping of wings. A sudden puff of wind from somewhere fanned my cheek, as on the floor I saw the dark shadow of some huge 'Thing' that was fluttering slowly round the room.

For a space I was too terrified to look up, and when I raised my eyes it was to see a black, shapeless mass flapping through the open window into the blackness of the night beyond. Fergusson had covered his eyes with his hand as he cowered in his chair, shrunk into himself. Now he raised his head and put out a palsied hand, seizing my arm, as he whispered hoarsely—

'Ward, did you see It?'

'See what?' I asked uneasily, more to give myself time to recover my equanimity.

'It! The "Thing"!'

By this I had regained my composure, and was ready to laugh at my foolish fancy.

'What thing?' I asked him again.

'The vampire!' said Fergusson in the same sepulchral whisper.

'Bosh!' I answered lightly. 'There was something came into the room, but it was merely a large bat attracted hither by the light.'

'It was a vampire,' insisted he, '*the* vampire!'

'We are not in South America now,' I replied testily, thoroughly ashamed of my sudden fears, 'and there are no vampires in China.'

'Nevertheless,' Fergusson repeated doggedly, 'it was a vampire.'

'A flying-fox, perhaps,' I told him, 'and they are harmless, herbivorous like the bats.'

I was puzzled what to do with Fergusson. I could not leave my old chum to be taken in my own house, much as he might deserve it. At last an idea came to me that would at least give us more time.

'Fergusson,' I asked, breaking in on the dream into which he had fallen, 'did you lock your door before you came away?'

'Lock it? No! Why?'

'Give me your keys,' was all I said.

He handed them to me, and leaving him sitting there I sped across the road and gained his house.

Everything was in darkness, but prompted by an impulse of curiosity I could not control, I crept softly into the bedroom and struck a match. Perhaps, after all, the whole thing was but a fancy of his distorted brain, and all might yet be well.

As the match flared up, I held it above my head and looked around. Ah, no! There was the poor girl lashed, as he had described, to the bed, the cords sunk deep in the tender flesh. The pillow, too, was drenched in blood, as he had said, and as I bent over her I saw a small incision in her neck, just below the ear.

It was true enough, then! But in spite of that curious little puncture in the fair skin, I still believed this ghastly thing was the terrible handiwork of my friend, and turned away with a shudder, locking the door ere I left.

I returned to Fergusson, trying by my relation of plans for his escape, to rouse him from the apathy into which he had sunk.

To have attempted to get away by one of the regular Shanghai boats would have been suicidal folly; but there was a Jardine steamer sailing for Hong Kong in two or three days' time, and if he could stow away in her I hoped he might be able to conceal himself in some remote corner of the world before the hounds of justice were set on his track. I explained to him that I would report him ill to the comptroller, so allaying suspicion for his non-appearance; and when the boat was ready to sail he was to slip out and sneak on board, trusting to chance to explain away his presence when she was once at sea. No one would be likely to go to his rooms, and provided he lay low in mine he would have a very fair chance of success.

Fergusson, for his part, looked on the whole matter indifferently and took very little interest in the maturing of the plans for his own safety.

Very surprised was my little housekeeper to find when she awoke next morning that my friend had spent the night on the couch in the other room. Of course we told her nothing of what had occurred. Nor did we think it wise to tell her that he would spend two or three days with us, deeming it better to let her find out for herself as the time passed and he still made no move to go to his own home.

Now that I come to the last part of this terrible history I hesitate to set it down, lest it should be looked upon as a mere freak of my imagination. And yet I have not said enough to clear my old friend's name of the black stain of murder and establish his innocence, wherefore I must proceed, though discredit be cast upon the close of the tragedy.

Yet I myself, as I look back from the vantage-coign of these after years, feel a dread steal over me lest, after all, it should be nothing but the coincidence of a large bat having flown into my room at the precise hour of one, and on another night having hovered near Fergusson's head at the same eerie hour. The rest may have been but the delusions of his drink-maddened brain and my own overwrought fancy. I dread the thought that it may be so, for if such a series of extraordinary coincidences be possible, then it means that Fergusson was a foul murderer.

But speculation is idle; let me finish the gruesome narrative.

That night of pain and horror wore slowly away, and never before or since have I watched the grey dawn creep slowly up from the East with such feelings of gratitude and relief.

The ensuing day, too, passed away without event; so also another night and a day crept by.

I had to leave Fergusson during each day in order to attend to my duties; but I reported him at headquarters unwell, telling the Customs doctor that it was his intention to call shortly and let him prescribe.

The fourth night since the poor girl, lying now so stark and swollen in that silent house, had met her death closed in, and a strange change fell upon Fergusson.

what before had escaped my attention, a stout wire stay that, leading from the roof of the go-down beside my window, was made fast to the flagstaff within the grounds, from which in the daytime floated the British Jack. It was nearly horizontal, inclining if anything slightly downwards for about thirty yards until it reached the staff. It passed well clear of the high wall, and should present no obstacle to a desperate man to traverse.

I swung hurriedly towards Fergusson, who was standing at the window, his hands thrust deep in his pockets, gazing moodily down at the advancing constables.

'Fergusson' – I was almost jocular in the intensity of my relief – 'are your muscles as fit as in the old coll. days?'

'Pretty well,' he answered absently, without taking his eyes from the street below.

I seized his arm and dragged him forcibly to the rear window.

'See that wire stay?' I cried exultantly, 'you can easily traverse that hand over hand to the flag-staff; slide down and slip through the consul's grounds to the river side; then take – steal if necessary – a sampan, and try to get down to Chin Hai. There get aboard one of the outward-bound junks, bound anywhere, so you can get another chance of freedom. The night is dark, and not expecting to find you overhead, they are safe not to see you cross.'

While I spoke I had been hastily cramming what loose money I had in the house into his pocket. He roused himself with an effort, and extended his hand.

'Goodbye, Ward, old friend!' he said huskily.

There was a desolate sadness – a hopelessness – in his face and voice that appalled me. He was as a man to whom an impending doom had shown itself clear and strong.

I grasped his hand, gulping down a lump that had risen in my throat.

'Goodbye!' I said. 'Now go, there is not a moment to lose! We shall meet again.'

But he turned to me once more.

'Never! Ward, you do believe that I did not murder her, do you not? I have been a brute, but say you believe me innocent of *that*.'

'Yes, yes!' I cried eagerly, pushing him toward the open window. 'Quick! Get out on the sill!'

He stood on the windowsill and climbed up on to the wire, swinging himself out with an agility that showed me he had lost little of his old form.

I stood at the window watching him with a feeling of thankfulness swing lightly along, when – I saw the 'Thing' sail swiftly out from under the overhanging eaves and flap toward him.

He did not see it at first as it circled round his head, while I stood there rooted to the spot, unable to stir a finger. Suddenly it swooped down, down, until I could see the blackness of it dimly outlined against his shoulders.

I could not see clearly what happened during those ten awful seconds, but his face was hidden from view – covered by the 'Thing.' I heard him give a stifled scream of horror that sounded far away, as though a blanket was being pressed firmly over mouth and nose, and he had stopped clambering. Then he let go one hand to try to tear the bat from his face and draw a breath; but he swung half round on the other arm, and had to clutch the wire again with both hands to save himself from falling.

He turned in frantic terror, trying to regain the window ledge, and as he came on I, with the cold sweat standing thick on my brow, could see the frightful form pressed close to his face. Three steps he took like that; then he stopped, and his body swayed helplessly, as, with another muffled scream, his hold of the wire relaxed, and he went crashing down to the courtyard beneath.

I heard his skull crush in like an eggshell as his head struck the stone flags thirty feet below, and while I yet gazed, sick at heart, with the blood frozen in my veins, the horrible 'Thing' rose from where he had fallen and fluttered up toward me.

Still, I could not stir, only gaze horrified at the monster as it flapped to the wire, and, hooking on its hinder claws about six feet from the window, hung suspended head down.

A ray of light from the lamp at my back fell upon It, as It turned Its hideous head toward me, and I could see the malignant, beady eyes looking piercingly into mine; *I saw, too, the triangular piece of erect cartilage on the end of the nose that distinguishes the vampire.*

And as I sank to the floor in merciful oblivion the handle of the door rattled, as it swung open, disclosing Major Barnes with four constables at his back.

For an instant I saw him standing there, peering anxiously about the room. Then, as the darkness swept down and engulfed my failing spirit, the little clock within chimed out merrily, paused for a moment, and tolled – One!

THE ELECTRIC VAMPIRE

F. H. Power

Nothing is known about the author of 'The Electric Vampire,' but there has been speculation that 'F. H. Power' could be a pseudonym. When this story made its first appearance in the October 1910 issue of *The London Magazine*, a note preceding the story claimed that, although it was but a figment of the author's imagination, it was based on fact, explaining that it drew its inspiration from experiments conducted by the eccentric British scientist Andrew Crosse (1784–1855), who was an early pioneer and experimenter in the use of electricity. It is thought that a lecture he gave on the subject in the early 1800s may have influenced Mary Shelley's choice of electricity as the agent for animating the man-made monster in her 1818 novel, *Frankenstein*, but the main link to Crosse that this story has is that in 1836 he achieved unwanted notoriety by claiming he had unintentionally created microscopic insects from a lifeless chemical compound by means of a process known as electrocrystallisation.

I WAS at breakfast when the note reached me. 'My dear Charles,' it ran – 'I shall be glad if you can come round to my place tonight, as I have something to show you, which I think will interest you. I have also asked Vane.'

It did not take a moment for me to make up my mind to go. Dr Vane and I often spent an evening at George Vickers's house. We were bachelors, and as we were all fond of things scientific, the time passed very pleasantly – so pleasantly that very often it was two or three o'clock in the morning before he saw us off his premises.

During the day I found myself speculating as to what our friend intended to show us. I recalled some of the weird and fascinating electrical experiments he had performed in his laboratory. 'I bet it's another experiment with electricity,' I said to myself, but I was only partly correct.

I arrived at the house about six o'clock, and found Vane had already arrived, and, as usual, had taken the easiest armchair in which to rest his lean body. Our host, with his ruddy, smiling face, stood with his back to the fireplace.

'I'm glad you have come, Charlie,' he said. 'You will be able to relieve me from that living mark of interrogation.' And he nodded towards the doctor, who sat twirling an imaginary moustache.

'Well, why can't he indicate what he has dragged us round here for?' the doctor asked plaintively. 'And fancy having as an excuse that he doesn't want to spoil my appetite for dinner!'

'Eh, what?' I ejaculated.

'Oh, now you are going to start. For goodness' sake find something else to talk about until we have had something to eat,' said Vickers, and he suggested aeroplanes.

We let him have his own way, and very soon after sat down to dinner. Our conversation during the meal would have been dry to many, but it was after our own hearts, and never flagged for a moment. The doctor's speciality was biology. My hobby is chemistry, and it was through an explosion which nearly blinded me that I first made his acquaintance, and subsequently introduced him to George Vickers.

At last George leaned back in his chair, and, lighting a cigar, said:

'You fellows, of course, want to know what on earth I am keeping up my sleeve. Before I show you, I want you to listen to this short extract from a series of lectures given by a man named Noad, and published in 1844.'

He fetched the book, and read:

'"It was in the course of his experiments in electrocrystallisation that that extraordinary insect about which so much public curiosity has been expended, was first noticed by Mr Crosse."'

Here Vickers looked up from the volume, and remarked:

'Mr Crosse I might say, was a gentleman who stood foremost as one of the individuals in this country who have distinguished themselves by their researches in atmospheric electricity.'

He turned to the book again:

'"In justice to this talented individual, who was most shamefully and absurdly assailed by some ignorant people on account of this insect, and who underwent much calumny and misrepresentation in consequence of experiments 'which in this nineteenth century it seems a crime to have made,' I shall give a detailed account of that experiment in which the Acarus first made its appearance."'

'Here follows,' said George, 'a minute description of the apparatus Crosse used. Briefly a basin containing practically a saturated solution of soluble silica is placed in a funnel, and a piece of flannel hangs over the side of the basin and acts as a syphon. The liquid falls in drops on a piece of porous red oxide of iron from Vesuvius, kept constantly electrified by a voltaic battery.'

Again he turned to the book and read:

'"On the fourteenth day from the commencement of the experiment, Mr Crosse observed through a lens a few small whitish excrescences or nipples projecting from about the middle of the electrified iron, and nearly under the dropping of the fluid above. On the eighteenth day these projections enlarged, and seven or eight filaments, each of them longer than the excrescence from which it grew, made their appearance on each of the nipples. On the twenty-second day, these appearances were more elevated and distinct; and on the twenty-sixth day each figure assumed the form of a *perfect insect* standing erect on a few bristles which formed its tail. Till this period Mr Crosse had no notion that these appearances were any other than an incipient mineral formation, but it was not until the twenty-eighth day, when he plainly perceived these little creatures move their legs, that he felt any surprise. In a few days they separated themselves from the stone, and moved about at pleasure. They appeared to feed by suction." . . . Mr Crosse adds: "*I have never ventured an opinion as to the cause of their birth;* and for a very good reason – I was unable to form one."'

Vickers shut the book up.

'There's a lot more about it, but I think I have read all that is necessary. If either of you would like some more information on those early experiments, you will find it in the "Transactions of the Electrical Society".'

There was silence whilst we puffed at our cigars. At length, Dr Vane said:

'I was under the impression that subsequent experimentalists were not so successful as Mr Crosse?'

Vickers smiled enigmatically.

'If you will just come this way, I fancy I shall be able to prove to you that at least one other experimentalist has been fairly successful.' And beckoned us to follow him.

I had often been in his laboratory, but to my surprise he led us to a room at the top of the house, and, as he inserted the key, drew our attention to the Yale lock.

'I rely on you chaps to keep to yourselves what I am going to show you, because I am preparing a paper on this experiment, and I want to surprise 'em,' he said, and pushed the door open.

Dr Vane, with an eager look on his face, entered boldly. I followed close behind, and I remembered wondering why George, usually so unemotional, appeared to be in a state of suppressed excitement.

And then I saw what it was. May I, a man, be forgiven if I trembled from head to foot!

On a low plain wood table was a sheet of some metal about four feet square. From a cistern fixed above, and pierced by many minute holes, some liquid dropped on the slab incessantly. But these things I barely noticed, for my attention was riveted to the centre of that slab, on which sprawled a creature which I can only liken to an immense spider, its length being about two feet.

Two legs appeared from behind each side of the head, and four longer ones – they must have been nearly as long as the body – at the back. Projecting from its head, where you would expect to find the mouth, was a trunk-like object which went in and out like the trunk of a fly. All over the body about an inch apart long filaments stood out. Its colour was drab, and it was apparently covered with slime. Its eyes were like the eyes of an owl, and never blinked.

We stared at the fearsome object in dead silence.

Vickers was the first to speak.

'Pretty, isn't it?' he said, with a laugh, but the laugh seemed strangely out of place.

I glanced at the doctor. His hands were clenched, and his eyes so wide open that the whites could be seen all round.

'My God, George, what is that thing?' he whispered.

'That, my dear doctor, is the result of years of experimenting. It first became visible to the naked eye five years ago today, but it does not appear to have grown during the last six months. It vindicates Crosse absolutely. Don't you think it is superb?'

'Superb? Oh, yes, it's superb!' said the doctor. He kept muttering to himself as he walked round the table, glaring at the thing on it, but from the few words I caught he was not calling it superb or anything like it.

At last his love of biology overcame his repugnance.

'I should like to feel one of those filaments,' he said, and stretched out his hand.

Like a flash of lightning Vickers seized his wrist, and his face was the colour of chalk. Dr Vane looked astonished and hurt.

'I am sorry, doctor, but I forgot to tell you it can give a terrific electric shock,' he said apologetically.

Vane looked somewhat scared, but his interest was plainly increased.

'Then it is some sort of relation to the Gymnotus, or electric eel of Venezuela?' he asked.

'Or the Torpedo of the Mediterranean,' I suggested.

Vickers shrugged his shoulders.

'I only know that poor old Tippoo' – a splendid collie and great favourite of us all – 'happened to accompany me to this room yesterday, and poked his nose a bit too near, when he suddenly toppled over dead as a doornail. He was horribly burnt down one side.'

Our friend spoke quietly, but it was easy to see he was deeply affected as he related the tragedy.

'That must have startled you,' I said.

'Well, no, I cannot say it was a surprise. I received a very nasty shock when it was quite small – perhaps I was not handling it as carefully as I might have. But' – here he turned to that monstrous creature, and actually passed his hand down one of its hairy legs – 'but you know who feeds you, don't you, my beauty?'

The thing evidently did know, for that trunk-like object went in and out rapidly. And I might say here that was the only movement we noticed in it that evening.

The startled look on our faces seemed to amuse Vickers.

'It's all right; it knows me. I have watched it grow day by day, and—'

Here the doctor cut in with a question.

'What do you feed the brute on?' he asked.

Vickers hesitated a moment, and looked at us. Then he walked to the other side of the room, and opened a box which had airholes pierced in it.

'The trunk,' he explained, 'is fitted with two small pointed teeth at the end, and the blood of the victim is gradually sucked out.' He anticipated our next question. 'No. It does not kill it first,' he said, and shut the lid.

The box contained live mice.

It was exactly ten days later that I was sitting with Vane in his study over a game of chess. At least, we were supposed to be playing chess. As a matter of fact, the doctor was again telling me what he thought of our friend's experiment, and the game had languished.

'I tell you it's the greatest discovery ever made – the greatest!' And his fist thumped the table, making the pieces on the board dance again. His eyes shone with excitement, but this died away as his thoughts travelled in a different channel. 'But of all the ugly things God ever created—'

He stopped abruptly.

'Do you know,' he continued presently, 'that Vickers's interesting pet belongs to the family of mites – ticks, as they are popularly called – notwithstanding its extraordinary size? All these creatures are furnished with suckers through which they can draw the juices of the animals on which they are parasitic, and in tropical countries – well, I will just say they are considerably more than annoying, and leave the rest to your imagination. They are small and flat when they first settle themselves on their victim, but they gradually swell and redden, until at last, when they are fully gorged, they are as large as broad-beans, and as easily crushed as ripe gooseberries.

'It seems to me from its mode of formation that George has discovered the link between the inorganic world and the world of life – the link which is indispensable to a complete scheme of evolution; but the great objection to this idea is the creature's obvious complexity—'

My further remarks were interrupted by a knock at the door, and the doctor's maid Emily entered.

'Mr Vickers's housekeeper would like to speak to you, sir.'

I heard Vane's 'Ah!' although it was said very softly. I remember my heart was beating at a ridiculous rate, and I tried hard to calm myself as I reflected that probably the old lady had come about her 'screws,' as she called her rheumatism, and which I knew had been troubling her more than usual.

But Dr Vane went down the two flights of stairs to his surgery two steps at a time. At the door he turned round and simply nodded to me, and we entered together.

Mrs Jones, Vickers's housekeeper, was waiting, with her veil pushed up until it looked like a black bandage across her forehead.

'Is it Mr Vickers?' Vane asked abruptly.

Mrs Jones never spoke quickly, and she did not intend to be hurried that day. Her reply came slowly, so deliberately that I thought my supply of patience would ebb away long before that simple question was answered.

'Well, sir, I don't know as there is anything the matter with Mr Vickers, but he ain't had a bite since one o'clock yesterday, and yet I feel certain as he is in the house. He went upstairs—'

I think Mrs Jones had reason to look astonished, for Dr Vane, noted for his precise ways and highly professional manner, dashed to the house-telephone and shouted into the mouthpiece: 'Tell John to bring the car round at once! You understand? He is not to delay one moment!' Then he turned to the housekeeper, who stood with her mouth half open, and said rapidly: 'You will come with us, and give us further particulars on the road.'

What had happened? I dreaded to think of what that upstairs room would reveal to us. The doctor and I looked at each other. Then he placed his hand on my arm.

'Charlie,' he whispered, 'you can depend on it George has got foul of that monster. I have felt something would happen, ever since he showed it to us, and it looks very much as if that something has happened.'

'I pray God we shall not be too late!' I said fervently, but I thought of that Thing, with the never-winking eyes, and shuddered.

'Have you a revolver?' I asked.

He nodded, and left the surgery.

A few moments later the motor arrived. We bundled Mrs Jones in; and as Vane gave the chauffeur the address, he added: 'Drive like hell!' I shall not forget that ride in a hurry, and I am quite sure Mrs Jones won't. We plied her with questions, but her replies were so incoherent we soon gave it up. She sat with bulging eyes, one hand clutching the side of the car, the other my coat, and every time it bumped over an obstacle she shrieked. More than once I bawled into her ear: 'It's all right!' but I might have saved my breath, for she made no sort of variation on her terror-stricken cry: 'Stop it! Stop it!'

A scared-looking maid let us in. We brushed past her, and went straight upstairs. Arriving at the door of that room, we stopped and listened, but could detect not the slightest sound. We tried the door – it was locked. So, after all that tearing hurry we were met by a well-built door, and Vickers had the key. We looked at each other in despair, but with Dr Vane it lasted but a moment, and was succeeded by a look of grim determination.

'He is in there, and we have got to get to him,' he said decisively.

'I'll fetch a locksmith: I think that will turn out to be the quickest way out of the difficulty,' I said, and was on the point of moving off when the doctor whispered excitedly: 'Wait! Listen! He is speaking!'

I tiptoed back to the door, and listened with loudly beating heart, but hardly breathing: there was silence, a long silence, then I heard a voice, but what it said I could not distinguish. It seemed to come from afar off, like a voice on a telephone that had been badly connected up. Vane shook his head.

'Speak up, old man! We can't hear you!' he shouted.

Again we listened, and this time we could just make out the words '. . . key . . . false . . . bottom . . . desk,' then all was quiet again.

'Which drawer, and how do you open it?' the doctor asked loudly. But not another sound came from the room, although he repeated the question twice.

Vane turned to me. 'That's a piece of luck. I wonder why he had two keys made? Well, we have got to find that duplicate, quick,' he said.

We rapidly made our way to Vickers's study, where we knew

there was a roller-top desk. We thanked Heaven when we found the door open, and also the desk. It was a beautiful piece of furniture, and the top was rolled back, showing the row of pigeon-holes and small drawers. Tucked in one of the pigeon-holes was a bunch of keys.

'Now, where the dickens is the drawer with the false bottom?' said Vane, and he hurriedly tried to find the keys which fitted the drawers.

Now, investigations of this sort cannot be hurried, and, swearing softly, he demonstrated this fact completely. The swearing grew louder and louder, till, for a moment, I lost sight of the object of the search in amazement at the extent of his vocabulary.

I relieved him of the bunch when he had opened half the drawers. Eventually we unlocked the lot, but although we quickly took a large number of measurements, we could not find the slightest indication of a false bottom to any of them.

Our nerves were in a high state of tension before we entered the study; by this time, mine were in a deplorable condition. The doctor's face was lined with anxiety.

Silently he handed me a poker, and from the wall took down an old Malay kriss, which did duty for an ornament.

'You take the right side of the desk; I'll take the other,' I said.

We found the precious key, but the desk—

Again we were at the door upstairs, and, although I turned the lock, I dreaded pushing it open. The whole business was so uncanny. Was that horrible creature prowling about the room ready to rush at us the moment we entered? How should we find Vickers?

I glanced at Vane. His jaw was set, and he had taken the revolver out of his pocket. The only sounds we could hear were some carts rumbling along the roadway, and the whistling from a train a long way off.

But the business in hand was very real and desperately urgent, and I do not think anyone would have noticed any hesitancy in pushing that door open; yet the next moment we were suddenly struck motionless as a low whisper reached us: 'For God's sake, move as quietly as you can!' We entered on tiptoe.

There are some scenes which are stamped on the memory in such a way that they are never forgotten. Years after they can be called to the eye of the mind with wonderful fidelity to detail. The scene which met us was such a one.

A broad beam from the setting sun came through the bottom of one of the windows, where the blind had not been completely drawn, and we saw. Very plainly, too, for the beam fell straight on it.

Vickers lay stretched on his back in the middle of the room, with that grisly Thing straddled across his chest, its sucker buried in his throat. His face and lips were quite bloodless. His eyes were closed, and I could detect no sort of movement.

I looked at Vane. His brows were contracted till they almost met, and his breath came and went through his teeth with a little hissing noise. I reminded him of the revolver ready cocked in his hand.

'Don't be a fool!' he said irritably. 'Get some brandy, and, for Heaven's sake, look slippy!'

When I returned he had his fingers on the poor fellow's wrist, and the frown was still on his face, but the revolver was on the box which was pierced with airholes.

I suppose I must have looked puzzled. Vane spoke impatiently, yet his voice was hardly above a whisper.

'Look here: what guarantee is there I should kill this vampire before it had time to discharge its deadly current through George's body? You know as well as I do that creatures low down in the scale of creation take a lot of killing. We can't risk it, and I am sure we can't risk hauling it off.'

The brandy was doing its work, and Vickers must have heard some of our conversation, because his eyes opened, and he said, with a ghost of a smile: 'Have you ever seen a leech applied, Charlie?'

I started violently.

'Good heavens! you don't mean to say Vane and I have to hang about with our hands in our pockets doing nothing except speculating whether – whether—'

'Whether I shall be able to stand the drain till it shifts?'

Vickers smiled again as he took the words out of my mouth.

The thought was intolerable; surely there must be some way!

For hours Vane sat waiting. I also was waiting, but on a couch in another room, getting over the effects of a little blood transfusion. 'It is very necessary,' Vane had said, as he skilfully made the arrangements, so skilfully that the creature was not disturbed. The improved appearance of poor George was my reward.

Wearied in mind and body I fell asleep, and dreamed dreams of men and women I knew, but I gazed at them with horror, for they all had drawn, blanched faces, with great staring eyes, and something with its body across their chests and with its head buried at their throats, and they beseeched me by all I held sacred to take it from them, but I was bound by invisible bands. How shall I tell of my agony of mind? I woke with a start, and in a terrible perspiration, and found the doctor looking at me, hollow-eyed and unshaved.

'Nightmare?' he asked. 'Where did you want to go, and who wouldn't let you? Steady, steady,' he added, as I jumped up and swayed, owing to the floor apparently moving about. As he pointed out, transfusion has no great tendency to make things appear as steady as rocks.

'Has the thing moved?' I asked.

'No,' he answered laconically.

We looked at each other in silence. I was hoping he would guess my next question, but I had to ask it.

'How is George?'

'Alive.' And I knew from the way he said it that he had told me simply the bare truth and that was all. There was another long silence.

'Oh! can't we do something?' I cried despairingly.

'Yes,' replied Vane. 'I am going to do something if that vampire does not move in ten minutes. The point has been reached when the risk is negligible, inasmuch as if it does not move now there will be no necessity of doing anything. I am going to shoot it.'

We returned to that chamber of horrors. Poor Vickers looked ghastly, and it did not require a trained eye to see that the end was not far off.

I took my watch out. 'Give it five minutes,' muttered Vane; and I sat on the box with the airholes, glancing first at the deathlike face of Vickers, then at Vane's set features as he stood stroking his unshaven chin, gazing at our friend.

'Time's up,' I said.

The doctor walked gently till he was opposite the creature's head, and droped on one knee, then lowered the revolver till it was within six inches of its head. His finger was on the trigger when a strange thing occurred: the bloated monster suddenly withdrew its sucker and glared at him as if it knew that its hour of death had arrived. I thought Vane was fascinated by those baleful eyes, for he did not stir as the creature commenced to move towards him.

'Look out!' I shouted, and he sprang back. None too soon, for the thing rushed at him with incredible swiftness.

Then I had an opportunity of witnessing Vane's beautiful nerve, for not until the last trailing filament had left Vickers did he fire. I saw his finger press the trigger. The next instant a terrific report shook the building, and my hands flew up to my eyes to shut out that terrible blinding flash. Women's screams, mingled with noises as if giant hands were tearing the house to pieces, floated up from below.

The sound of someone groaning made me rouse myself.

Vane lay face downwards in an immense pool of blood, his head hanging over a ragged hole in the floor. I thanked Heaven fervently when I found that he had only been stunned by the vast charge of static electricity the creature had suddenly let loose. Like a flash of lightning the charge had struck the floor, bursting it open, then torn its way through the house.

We turned to Vickers. Vane felt his pulse.

'I will save him,' he said. And he did.

BIBLIOGRAPHY

Alcott, Louisa May. 'Lost in a Pyramid; or, The Mummy's Curse.' *The New World*, 16 January, 1869 (as by 'L.M.A.'). Reprinted in *Into the Mummy's Tomb*, edited by John Richard Stephens. New York: Berkley Books, 2001.

Alden, W. L. 'A Modern Vampire.' *Cassell's Family Magazine*, March 1894.

Anon. (falsely attributed to Lord Byron). 'The Bride of the Isles: A Tale Founded on the Popular Legend of the Vampire.' Dublin: J. Charles, 1820. Reprinted in *The Shilling Shockers: Stories of Terror from the Gothic Bluebooks*. London: Victor Gollancz, 1978; New York: St. Martin's, 1979.

Anon. 'The Tomb Among the Pines.' *Household Words*, 21 November, 1894. Reprinted in the *Sacramento Daily Union*, 17 January, 1897.

Baldwin, E. E. *The Strange Story of Dr. Senex*. New York: Minerva, 1891.

Baring-Gould, Sabine. 'A Dead Finger.' *Woman*, 21 April–5 May 1897. First book publication in *A Book of Ghosts*. London: Methuen, 1904. Reprinted in *Dracula's Brood*, edited by Richard Dalby. Wellingborough, U.K.: Crucible, 1987; New York: Dorset Press, 1991; London: Harper, 2016.

——. 'Glámr.' In *A Book of Ghosts*. London: Methuen, 1904. Extracted from *Iceland: Its Scenes and Sagas*. London: Smith, Elder, 1863.

——. 'Margery of Quether.' *Cornhill Magazine*, April–May 1884. First book publication in *Margery of Quether and Other Stories*. London: Methuen, 1891; New York: J. W. Lovell, 1892. Reprinted in *Margery of Quether and Other Weird Tales*, edited by Richard Dalby. Mountain Ash, Wales: Sarob Press, 1999. Also included in *Vintage Vampire Stories*, edited by Robert Eighteen-Bisang and Richard Dalby. New York: Skyhorse Publishing, 2011.

Beer, William. 'The Ring of Knowledge.' *Atalanta*, November 1896.

Bérard, Cyprien. *Lord Ruthwen ou les Vampires*. Paris: Ladvocat, 1820. Translated into English by Brian Stableford as *The Vampire Lord Ruthwen*. Encino, Calif., U.S.: Black Coat Press, 2011.

Bertram, Sidney. 'With the Vampires.' *Phil May's Annual*, Winter 1899. Reprinted in *Vampires: Classic Tales*, edited by Mike Ashley. Mineola, N.Y.: Dover, 2011.

Bierce, Ambrose. 'The Death of Halpin Frayser.' *The Wave*, 19 December, 1891. First book publication in *Can Such Things Be?* New York: Cassell, 1893. Reprinted in *The Undead*, edited by James Dickie. London: Neville Spearman, 1971.

Blackwood, Algernon. 'The Singular Death of Morton.' *The Tramp*, December 1910. First book publication in *Dracula's Brood*, edited by Richard Dalby. Wellingborough, U.K.: Crucible, 1987; New York: Dorset Press, 1991; London: Harper, 2016.

Braddon, Mary E. 'Good Lady Ducayne.' *The Strand*, February 1896. Reprinted in *Dracula's Brood*, edited by Richard Dalby. Wellingborough, U.K.: Crucible, 1987; New York: Dorset Press, 1991; London: Harper, 2016.

——. 'Herself.' *Sheffield Weekly Telegraph*, 17 November, 1894. Reprinted in *Vintage Vampire Stories*, edited by Robert Eighteen-Bisang and Richard Dalby. New York: Skyhorse Publishing, 2011.

Capuana, Luigi. 'A Vampire' (1907). Translated into English, by Gillian Riley, for *The Vampire*, edited by Ornella Volta and Valeria Riva. London: Neville Spearman, 1963. Also included, under the title 'A Case of Alleged Vampirism,' in *The Vampire Archives*, edited by Otto Penzler. New York: Vintage, 2009; U.K. edition retitled *The Vampire Archive*. London: Quercus, 2009.

Chaytor, H. J. *The Light of the Eye*. London: Digby, Long, 1897. [s.l.]: British Library, Historical Print Editions, 2011.

Cholmondeley, Mary. 'Let Loose.' *Temple Bar*, April 1890. First book publication in *Moth and Rust, and Other Stories*. New York: Dodd, Mead, 1902. Reprinted in *Dracula's Brood*, edited by Richard Dalby. Wellingborough, U.K.: Crucible, 1987; New York: Dorset Press, 1991; London: Harper, 2016.

Clarke, C. Langton. 'The Elixir of Life.' *Argosy*, December 1903. Reprinted in *People of the Pit*, edited by Gene Christie. New York: Black Dog, 2010.

Cobban, James Maclaren. *Master of His Fate*. Edinburgh: Blackwood & Sons, 1890; New York: Frank F. Lovell, 1890. [s.l.]: British Library, Historical Print Editions, 2011.

Crawford, Anne. 'A Mystery of the Campagna.' Originally published under the pseudonym 'Von Degen' in *Unwin's Annual for 1887*. London: T. Fisher Unwin, 1886. Reprinted in *Dracula's Brood*, edited by Richard Dalby. Wellingborough, U.K.: Crucible, 1987; New York: Dorset Press, 1991; London: Harper, 2016.

Crawford, F. Marion. 'For the Blood is the Life.' *Collier's*, 16 December, 1905. First book publication in *Wandering Ghosts*. New York: Macmillan, 1911; U.K. edition retitled *Uncanny Tales*. London: T. Fisher Unwin, 1911. Reprinted in *Children of the Night: Classic Vampire Stories*, edited by David Stuart Davies. Ware, U.K.: Wordsworth Editions, 2007.

Daniels, Cora Linn. *Sardia: A Story of Love*. Boston: Lee and Shepard, 1891. Charleston, S.C., U.S.: BiblioLife, 2009. London: Forgotten Books, 2012.

'Dolly.' (pseudonym of Leonard D'Oliver). 'The Vampire Nemesis.' In *The Vampire Nemesis and Other Weird Stories of the China Coast*. Bristol: Arrowsmith, 1905. Reprinted in *The Dark Shadows Book of Vampires and Werewolves*, selected by Barnabas and Quentin Collins. New York: Paperback Library, 1970.

Donovan, Dick (pseudonym of James Edward Muddock). 'The Woman with the "Oily Eyes".' In *Tales of Terror*. London: Chatto & Windus, 1899. Reprinted in *Vintage Vampire Stories*, edited by Robert Eighteen-Bisang and Richard Dalby. New York: Skyhorse Publishing, 2011.

——. 'The Story of Annette (from Official Records): Being the Sequel to 'The Woman with the "Oily Eyes".' In *Tales of Terror*. London: Chatto & Windus, 1899. Reprinted in *Vintage Vampire Stories*, edited by Robert Eighteen-Bisang and Richard Dalby. New York: Skyhorse Publishing, 2011. Actually a prequel rather than a sequel.

Doyle, Arthur Conan. 'John Barrington Cowles.' *Cassell's Saturday Journal*, 12–19 April, 1884. First book publication in *Dreamland and Ghostland, Vol. III*, edited Anon. London: George Redway, 1887. Reprinted in *Vampire Stories of Sir Arthur Conan Doyle*, edited by Robert Eighteen-Bisang and Martin H. Greenberg. New York: Skyhorse Publishing, 2009.

——. 'The Parasite.' *Harper's Weekly*, 10 November–1 December 1894. First book publication in *The Parasite*. Westminster, U.K.: Constable, 1894. Reprinted in *Dracula's Brood*, edited by Richard Dalby. Wellingborough, U.K.: Crucible, 1987; New York: Dorset Press, 1991; London: Harper, 2016.

Dumas, Alexandre. 'The Pale Lady.' Originally an episode in *The Thousand and One Phantoms* (1848). Translated into English for

Tales of the Supernatural. London: Methuen, 1910. Reprinted in *Vampires: Classic Tales*, edited by Mike Ashley. Mineola, N.Y.: Dover, 2011.

Erckmann-Chatrian (joint pen name of Émile Erckmann and Alexandre Chatrian). 'The Burgomaster in Bottle.' Originally appeared, as 'Le Bourgmestre en Bouteille,' in *Le Démocrate du Rhin*, 12 June, 1849. First book publication in *Histoires et Contes Fantastiques*. Strasbourg: Ph.-Alb. Dannbach, 1849. Translated into English for *The Polish Jew (and Other Stories)*. London: Ward, Lock, 1873. Reprinted in *The Invisible Eye*, edited by Hugh Lamb. Ashcroft, B.C., Canada: Ash-Tree Press, 2002.

——. 'The Crab Spider.' Originally published, as 'L'Araignée Crabe,' in *Les Contes Fantastiques*. Paris: Hachette, 1860. Translated into English, under the title 'The Crab Spider,' for the October 1893 issue of *Romance Magazine*, and was reprinted, with this title, in *The Invisible Eye*, edited by Hugh Lamb. Ashcroft, B.C., Canada: Ash-Tree Press, 2002. Also appeared in *The Strand Magazine* for October 1899 under the title 'The Spider of Guyana,' and was reprinted, with this title, in *Ghostly by Gaslight*, edited by Sam Moskowitz and Alden H. Norton. New York: Pyramid, 1971.

Falkner, J. Meade. *The Lost Stradivarius*. Edinburgh: Blackwood & Sons, 1895. New York: Appleton, 1896. Leyburn, U.K.: Tartarus Press, 2000.

Féval, Paul. *Le Chevalier Ténèbre* (1860). Translated into English by Brian Stableford as *Knightshade*. Mountain Ash, Wales: Sarob Press, 2001. Encino, Calif., U.S.: Black Coat Press, 2003.

——. *La Vampire* (1865). Translated into English by Brian Stableford as *The Vampire Countess*. Encino, Calif., U.S.: Black Coat Press, 2003.

——. *La Ville Vampire* (1874). Translated into English by Brian Stableford as *Vampire City*. Mountain Ash, Wales: Sarob Press, 2001. Encino, Calif., U.S.: Black Coat Press, 2003.

Fortune, Mary. 'The White Maniac: A Doctor's Tale.' *The Australian Journal*, 13 July, 1867 (as by 'Waif Wander'). Reprinted in *Vintage Vampire Stories*, edited by Robert Eighteen-Bisang and Richard Dalby. New York: Skyhorse Publishing, 2011.

Freeman, Mary E. Wilkins. 'Luella Miller.' *Everybody's Magazine*, December 1902. First book publication in *The Wind in the Rose-Bush, and Other Stories of the Supernatural*. New York: Doubleday, Page, 1903; London: John Murray, 1903. Reprinted in *Vampires: Encounters with the Undead*, edited by David Skal. New York: Black Dog, 2001.

Gautier, Théophile. 'La Morte Amoureuse.' *La Chronique de Paris*, 23 and 26 June, 1836. The first English translation by Lafcadio Hearn, titled 'Clarimonde,' appeared in *One of Cleopatra's Nights and Other Fantastic Romances*. New York: B. Worthington, 1882. Reprinted, with this title, in *Clarimonde and Other Stories*. Leyburn, U.K.: Tartarus Press, 2011. Other titles given to English translations of this story include: 'The Amorous Corpse,' 'The Beautiful Dead,' 'The Dead in Love,' 'The Dead Leman,' 'The Deathly Lover,' 'The Dreamland Bride,' and 'Loving Lady Death.'

Gilbert, William. 'The Last Lords of Gardonal.' *Argosy*, July–September 1867. First book publication in *The Wizard of the Mountain*. London: A. Strahan, 1867. Reprinted in *Dracula's Brood*, edited by Richard Dalby. Wellingborough, U.K.: Crucible, 1987; New York: Dorset Press, 1991; London: Harper, 2016.

Gilchrist, R. Murray. 'The Crimson Weaver.' *The Yellow Book*, July 1895. Reprinted in *Vampires: Classic Tales*, edited by Mike Ashley. Mineola, N.Y.: Dover, 2011.

——. 'The Lover's Ordeal.' *The London Magazine*, June 1905. Reprinted in *Vintage Vampire Stories*, edited by Robert Eighteen-Bisang and Richard Dalby. New York: Skyhorse Publishing, 2011.

Gogol, Nikolai. 'Viy.' In *Mirgorod* (1835). Reprinted in *The Vampire*, edited by Ornella Volta and Valeria Riva. London: Neville Spearman, 1963.

Gordon, Julien (pseudonym of Julie Grinnell Cruger). *Vampires*. Published in tandem with another novel in *Vampires; Mademoiselle Reseda*. Philadelphia: Lippincott, 1891.

Halidom, M. Y. (pseudonym of Alexander Huth). *The Woman in Black*. London: Greening & Co., 1906. Ashcroft, B.C., Canada: Ash-Tree Press, 2007.

Hawthorne, Julian. 'Ken's Mystery.' *Harper's New Monthly Magazine*, November 1883. First book publication in *David Poindexter's Disappearance, and Other Stories*. New York: Appleton, 1888. Reprinted in *Dracula's Brood*, edited by Richard Dalby. Wellingborough, U.K.: Crucible, 1987; New York: Dorset Press, 1991; London: Harper, 2016.

Heron, E. & H. (joint pseudonym of Kate and Hesketh Prichard). 'The Story of Baelbrow.' *Pearson's Magazine*, April 1898. First book publication in *Ghosts: Being the Experiences of Flaxman Low*. London: C. A. Pearson, 1899. Reprinted in *Flaxman Low, Psychic Detective*, edited by Richard Dalby. London: Ghost Story Press, 1993.

——. 'The Story of the Grey House.' *Pearson's Magazine*, May 1898. First book publication in *Ghosts: Being the Experiences of Flaxman Low*. London: C. A. Pearson, 1899. Reprinted in *Flaxman Low, Psychic Detective*, edited by Richard Dalby. London: Ghost Story Press, 1993.

——. 'The Story of the Moor Road.' *Pearson's Magazine*, March 1898. First book publication in *Ghosts: Being the Experiences of Flaxman Low*. London: C. A. Pearson, 1899. Reprinted in *Flaxman Low, Psychic Detective*, edited by Richard Dalby. London: Ghost Story Press, 1993.

Heyse, Paul. *The Fair Abigail*. New York: Dodd, Mead, 1894.

Hume, Fergus. 'Professor Brankel's Secret.' Originally appeared in Dunedin's *Saturday Advertiser*, November–December 1882. Subsequently published as a paperback in Melbourne, Australia by W. N. Baird, Railway Bookstalls, 1886.

James, M. R. 'Count Magnus.' In *Ghost Stories of an Antiquary*. London: Edward Arnold, 1904. Reprinted in *Vampires: Encounters with the Undead*, edited by David Skal. New York: Black Dog, 2001.

Jones, Professor P. 'The Priest and His Cook.' In *Vintage Vampire Stories*, edited by Robert Eighteen-Bisang and Richard Dalby. New York: Skyhorse Publishing, 2011. Extracted from *The Pobratim: A Slav Novel*. London: H. S. Nichols, 1895. [s.l.]: British Library, Historical Print Editions, 2011.

———. 'The Story of Jella and the Macic.' Extracted from *The Pobratim: A Slav Novel*. London: H. S. Nichols, 1895. [s.l.]: British Library, Historical Print Editions, 2011.

Kenealy, Arabella. 'A Beautiful Vampire.' *The Ludgate*, November 1896. First book publication in *Belinda's Beaux, and Other Stories*. London: Bliss, Sands, and Foster, 1897. Reprinted in *The Vampire Hunters' Casebook*, edited by Peter Haining. New York: Barnes & Noble, 1995. London: Warner UK, 1996.

Kingston, William H. G. 'The Vampire; or, Pedro Pacheco and the Bruxa.' In *Tales for All Ages*. London: Bickers & Bush, 1863. Reprinted in *Vintage Vampire Stories*, edited by Robert Eighteen-Bisang and Richard Dalby. New York: Skyhorse Publishing, 2011.

Le Fanu, Joseph Sheridan. 'Carmilla.' *The Dark Blue*, December 1871–March 1872. First book publication in *In a Glass Darkly*. London: Bentley, 1872. Reprinted in *The Blood Delirium: The Vampire in 19th Century European Literature*, edited by Candice Black. London: Sun Vision Press, 2013.

Linton, Eliza Lynn. 'The Fate of Madame Cabanel.' *All the Year Round*, 16 December, 1872. First book publication in *With a Silken Thread, and Other Stories*. London: Chatto & Windus, 1880. Reprinted in *Dracula's Brood*, edited by Richard Dalby. Wellingborough, U.K.: Crucible, 1987; New York: Dorset Press, 1991; London: Harper, 2016.

Loring, F. G. 'The Tomb of Sarah.' *Pall Mall Magazine*, December 1900. First book publication in *Victorian Ghost Stories*, edited by Montague Summers. London: Fortune Press, 1933. Reprinted in *The Book of the Living Dead*, edited by John Richard Stephens. New York: Berkley Books, 2010.

MacDonald, George. *Lilith*. London: Chatto & Windus, 1895. Whitefish, Mont., U.S.: Kessinger, 2011. [s.l.]: British Library, Historical Print Editions, 2011.

Marryat, Florence. *The Blood of the Vampire*. London: Hutchinson, 1897. Kansas City, Mont., U.S.: Valancourt Books, 2009. [s.l.]: British Library, Historical Print Editions, 2011.

Marsh, Richard (pseudonym of Richard B. Heldmann). 'The Mask.' *Gentleman's Magazine*, December 1892. First book publication in *Marvels and Mysteries*. London: Methuen, 1900. Reprinted in *The Haunted Chair and Other Stories*, edited by Richard Dalby. Ashcroft, B.C., Canada: Ash-Tree Press, 1997.

Maupassant, Guy de. 'The Horla.' *Gil Blas*, 26 October, 1886. A revised version was published in 1887, and the first English translation appeared in *Modern Ghosts, Selected and Translated from the Works of Guy de Maupassant (etc.)*. New York: Harper, 1890. Reprinted in *The Blood Delirium: The Vampire in 19th Century European Literature*, edited by Candice Black. London: Sun Vision Press, 2013.

McCrae, Hugh. 'The Vampire.' *The Bulletin*, November 1901 (as by 'W. W. Lamble'). Reprinted in *Vintage Vampire Stories*, edited by Robert Eighteen-Bisang and Richard Dalby. New York: Skyhorse Publishing, 2011.

Meade, L. T. (working name of Elizabeth Thomasina Meade Smith). *The Desire of Men: An Impossibility*. London: Digby, Long, 1899.

Milne, Robert Duncan. 'A Man Who Grew Young Again.' *The Argonaut*, February 1887. Reprinted in *Into the Sun and Other Stories*, edited by Sam Moskowitz. West Kingston, R.I., U.S.: Donald M. Grant, 1980.

Nisbet, Hume. 'The Old Portrait.' In *Stories Weird and Wonderful*. London: F. V. White, 1900. Reprinted in *Dracula's Brood*, edited by Richard Dalby. Wellingborough, U.K.: Crucible, 1987; New York: Dorset Press, 1991; London: Harper, 2016.

——. 'The Vampire Maid.' In *Stories Weird and Wonderful*. London: F. V. White, 1900. Reprinted in *Dracula's Brood*, edited by Richard Dalby. Wellingborough, U.K.: Crucible, 1987; New York: Dorset Press, 1991; London: Harper, 2016.

Norris, Frank. 'Grettir at Thorhall-stead.' *Everybody's Magazine*, April 1903. First book publication in *Horrors Unknown*, edited by Sam Moskowitz. New York: Walker, 1971. Reprinted in *The Vampire Omnibus*, edited by Peter Haining. London: Orion, 1995; Edison, N.J., U.S.: Chartwell Books, 1995.

O'Sullivan, Vincent. 'Will.' In *The Green Window*. London: Leonard Smithers, 1899. Reprinted in *Dracula's Brood*, edited by Richard Dalby. Wellingborough, U.K.: Crucible, 1987; New York: Dorset Press, 1991; London: Harper, 2016.

Paulding, James Kirke. 'The Vroucolacas: A Tale.' *Graham's Magazine*, June 1846.

Pigault-Lebrun, Charles. 'The Unholy Compact Abjured.' According to Peter Haining, the first English translation of this story appeared, c. 1825, in a British periodical titled *The French Novelist*. Reprinted in *Gothic Tales of Terror, Volume II: Europe and America*, edited by Peter Haining. London: Gollancz, 1972.

Poe, Edgar Allan. 'Berenice.' *Southern Literary Messenger*, March 1835. First book publication in *Tales of the Grotesque and Arabesque*. Philadelphia: Lea and Blanchard, 1840. Reprinted in *Dead Brides: Vampire Tales*. London: Creation Books, 1999.

——. 'The Fall of the House of Usher.' *Burton's Gentleman's Magazine*, September 1839. First book publication in *Tales of the Grotesque and Arabesque*. Philadelphia: Lea and Blanchard, 1840. Reprinted in *Dead Brides: Vampire Tales*. London: Creation Books, 1999.

——. 'Ligeia.' *American Museum*, September 1838. First book publication in *Tales of the Grotesque and Arabesque*. Philadelphia: Lea and Blanchard, 1840. Reprinted in *Dead Brides: Vampire Tales*. London: Creation Books, 1999.

——. 'Morella.' *Southern Literary Messenger*, April 1835. First book publication in *Tales of the Grotesque and Arabesque*. Philadelphia: Lea and Blanchard, 1840. Reprinted in *Dead Brides: Vampire Tales*. London: Creation Books, 1999.

——. 'The Oval Portrait.' *Broadway Journal*, April 1845 (a revised version of 'Life in Death' in *Graham's Lady's and Gentleman's Magazine*, April 1842). First book publication in *The Works of the Late Edgar Allan Poe; Volume 1: Tales*, edited by Rufus Wilmot Griswold. New York: J. S. Redfield, 1850. Reprinted in *Dead Brides: Vampire Tales*. London: Creation Books, 1999.

Polidori, John William. 'The Vampyre.' *The New Monthly Magazine*, April 1819 (in which it was erroneously attributed to Lord Byron). The first book edition was titled *The Vampyre: A Tale Related by Lord Byron to Dr. Polidori*. London: Colburn & Co., 1819. Publication then swiftly passed to Sherwood, Neely, and Jones, these editions being the ones normally found at auction today. Reprinted in *The Best Vampire Stories 1800–1849*, edited by Andrew Barger. Memphis, Tenn., U.S.: Bottletree Classics, 2012.

Power, F. H. 'The Electric Vampire.' *The London Magazine*, October 1910. Reprinted in *The Man Who Was Frankenstein*, edited by Peter Haining. London: F. Muller, 1979.

Praed, Mrs. Campbell. *Affinities: A Romance of Today*. London: Richard Bentley, 1885 (2 vols.).

——. *The Soul of Countess Adrian*. London: Trischler, 1891; New York: United States Book Co., 1891.

Prest, Thomas Pecket. See under Rymer, James Malcolm.

Quiller-Couch, Arthur. 'The Legend of Sir Dinar.' *The Speaker*, 19 December, 1891 (as by 'Q'). First book publication in *Wandering Heath: Stories, Studies and Sketches*. London: Cassell, 1896. Reprinted in *The Horror on the Stair and Other Weird Tales*, edited by S. T. Joshi. Ashcroft, B.C., Canada: Ash-Tree Press, 2000.

——. 'Old Aeson.' *The Speaker*, 25 October, 1890 (as by 'Q'). First book publication in *Noughts and Crosses: Stories, Studies and Sketches*. London: Cassell, 1891. Reprinted in *The Horror on the Stair and Other Weird Tales*, edited by S. T. Joshi. Ashcroft, B.C., Canada: Ash-Tree Press, 2000.

Quiroga, Horacio. 'The Feather Pillow.' Originally published in 1907 in an Argentine magazine called *Caras y Caretas*. Reprinted in *Dracula's Brood*, edited by Richard Dalby. Wellingborough, U.K.: Crucible, 1987; New York: Dorset Press, 1991; London: Harper, 2016.

Raupach, Ernst. 'Wake Not the Dead.' In *Minerva*. Leipzig, 1822 (as 'Lasst die Toten Ruhen'). Translated into English for *Popular Tales and Romances of the Northern Nations*. London: Simpkin, Marshall, 1823. Although long-attributed to Johann Ludwig Tieck, recent research carried out by Rob Brautigam and Douglas A. Anderson has established that Raupach was the real author. The first anthology to correctly attribute this story to Raupach was *Vampires: Classic Tales*, edited by Mike Ashley. Mineola, N.Y.: Dover, 2011, in which it appears as 'Let the Dead Rest,' which is a literal translation of the original German title.

Roberts, Morley. 'The Blood Fetish.' In *Midsummer Madness*. London: Eveleigh Nash, 1909. Reprinted in *Vintage Vampire Stories*, edited by Robert Eighteen-Bisang and Richard Dalby. New York: Skyhorse Publishing, 2011.

Robinson, Phil. 'The Last of the Vampires.' *The Contemporary Review*, March 1893. First book publication in *Tales by Three Brothers*. London: Ibister & Co. Ltd., 1902. Reprinted in *Vampire: Chilling Tales of the Undead*, edited by Peter Haining. London: W. H. Allen/ Target, 1985.

——. 'The Man-Eating Tree.' In *Under the Punkah*. London: Sampson Low, 1881. Also included in *Tales by Three Brothers*. London: Ibister & Co. Ltd., 1902. *Dracula's Brood*, edited by Richard Dalby. Wellingborough, U.K.: Crucible, 1987; New York: Dorset Press, 1991; London: Harper, 2016.

——. 'Medusa.' In *Tales by Three Brothers*. London: Ibister & Co. Ltd., 1902. Reprinted in *Vintage Vampire Stories*, edited by Robert Eighteen-Bisang and Richard Dalby. New York: Skyhorse Publishing, 2011.

Rymer, James Malcolm; or Thomas Pecket Prest. *Varney the Vampyre; or, The Feast of Blood*. Originally appeared in 109 weekly instalments between 1845 and 1847. Subsequently published in book form in 1847 by London publisher Edward Lloyd, who attributed it to 'the author of Grace Rivers; or, The Merchant's Daughter.' Uncertainty about who this referred to has meant the authorship of this seminal work has long been in doubt, although stylistically it would appear to be the work of Rymer rather than Prest. After many years out of print, it was eventually rescued from obscurity in 1970 by the New York publisher Arno Press, who brought out a 3-volume facsimile edition attributed to Thomas Peckett Prest. Since then, further editions have appeared from the following publishers: New York: Dover, 1972. 2 vols. (attributed to Rymer). Whitefish, Mont., U.S.: Kessinger, 2004, 2010. 3 vols. (attributed to Prest). Ware, U.K.: Wordsworth Editions, 2010. Single vol. (attributed to Rymer).

Sands, Robert C. 'The Black Vampyre: A Legend of Saint Domingo' (as by 'Uriah Derick D'Arcy'). New York: Printed for the author, 1819. Reprinted in *The Best Vampire Stories 1800–1849*, edited by Andrew Barger. Memphis, Tenn., U.S.: Bottletree Classics, 2012.

Schwob, Marcel. 'Les Striges.' In *Coeur Double*. Paris: P. Ollendorff, 1891. Reprinted, under the title 'The Strigae,' in *The King in the Golden Mask and Other Stories*. Leyburn, U.K.: Tartarus Press, 2012.

Silberrad, U. L. *The Enchanter*. London: Macmillan, 1899.

Sparrow, Lionel. 'The Vengeance of the Dead.' *The Australian Journal*, July 1910. Reprinted in *Vintage Vampire Stories*, edited by Robert Eighteen-Bisang and Richard Dalby. New York: Skyhorse Publishing, 2011.

Stenbock, Count Stanislaus Eric. 'The True Story of a Vampire.' In *Studies of Death*. London: Nutt, 1894. Reprinted in *The Blood Delirium: The Vampire in 19th Century European Literature*, edited by Candice Black. London: Sun Vision Press, 2013. Also titled 'The Sad Story of a Vampire' in some anthologies.

Stockton, Frank R. 'A Borrowed Month.' *Century Magazine*, February–March 1886. First book publication in *The Christmas Wreck and Other Stories*. New York: Scribner's Sons, 1886. Reprinted in *A Borrowed Month, and Other Stories*. Edinburgh: David Douglas, 1887. Whitefish, Mont., U.S.: Kessinger, 2010.

Stoker, Bram. *Dracula*. Westminster, U.K.: Constable, 1897. London: Hutchinson, 1897 (Colonial edition). New York: Doubleday & McClure, 1899 (first U.S. edition). Westminster, U.K.: Constable, 1901 (first paperback edition; abridged by the author). White Rock, B.C., Canada: Transylvania Press, 1994 (hardback reprint of the 1901 edition). Many other editions have appeared over the years. Among the most recent are: London: Collins Classics/HarperCollins, 2011. London: Pan Macmillan, 2016. Charleston, S.C., U.S.: CreateSpace, 2016.

Strong, Louise J. 'An Unscientific Story.' *Cosmopolitan*, February 1903. Reprinted in *Dracula's Brood*, edited by Richard Dalby. Wellingborough, U.K.: Crucible, 1987; New York: Dorset Press, 1991; London: Harper, 2016.

Taylor, C. Bryson. *In the Dwellings of the Wilderness*. New York: Henry Holt, 1904. Whitefish, Mont., U.S.: Kessinger, 2007.

Tieck, Johann Ludwig. See under Raupach, Ernst.

Tolstoy, Aleksey Konstantinovich. 'The Family of the Vourdalak.' *The Russian Messenger*, January 1884. Translated into English for *Vampires: Stories of the Supernatural*. Harmondsworth, U.K.: Penguin, 1946; rpt. New York: Hawthorn Books, 1969. Reprinted in *Children of the Night: Classic Vampire Stories*, edited by David Stuart Davies. Ware, U.K.: Wordsworth Editions, 2007 (as 'The Curse of the Vourdalak').

——. 'Upyr' (aka 'The Vampire'). Originally published in St. Petersburg in 1841 under the pseudonym 'Krasnorogsky.' Reprinted in *Vampires: Stories of the Supernatural*. Harmondsworth, U.K.: Penguin, 1946; rpt. New York: Hawthorn Books, 1969.

Tozer, Basil. 'The Vampire.' In *Around the World with a Millionaire*. London: R. A. Everett, 1902.

Trent, John Jason. 'Phalaenopsis Gloriosa.' *The Monthly Story Magazine*, November 1905. Reprinted in *Pearson's Magazine*, July 1906. Alleged to have been written by Edgar Wallace.

Turgenev, Ivan. 'Phantoms' (1864). Translated into English for *Phantoms, and Other Stories*. New York: C. Scribner's Sons, 1904. Reprinted in *Vampire Stories*, edited by Richard Dalby. London: Michael O'Mara, 1992; Secaucus, N.J., U.S.: Castle Books, 1993.

Ulrichs, Karl Heinrich. 'Manor.' *L'Aquila*, 20–30 July, 1884. First book publication in *Matrosengeschichten*. Leipzig: F. E. Fischer, 1885. Translated into English for *Embracing the Dark*, edited by Eric Garber. Boston: Alyson, 1991.

Upton, Smyth. *The Last of the Vampires*. Weston-Super-Mare, U.K.: Columbian Press, 1845. Reprinted in *The Spectre Bridegroom and Other Horrors*, edited by R. Reginald and Douglas Melville. New York: Arno Press, 1976. Rockville, Md., U.S.: Wildside Press, 2008.

Urquhart, M. *The Island of Souls: Being a Sensational Fairy-tale*. London: Mills & Boon, 1910.

Viereck, George Sylvester. *The House of the Vampire*. New York: Moffatt, Yard, 1907. New York: Arno Press, 1976. North Stratford, N.H., U.S.: Ayer, 2001.

Wachsmann, Karl von. 'The Mysterious Stranger.' Originally published under the title 'Der Fremde' in *Erzahlungen und Novellen*, third series. Leipzig, 1844. Translated into English for its appearance in *Chambers's Repository*, February 1854. Reprinted in *Vampires: Classic Tales*, edited by Mike Ashley. Mineola, N.Y.: Dover, 2011. After being unattributed for many years, confirmation that Wachsmann was the author of this story was provided by Douglas A. Anderson in his article 'A Note on M. R. James and Dracula' (*Fastitocalon*, Vol. 1, No. 2, 2010).

Watson, H. B. Marriott. 'The Stone Chamber.' In *The Heart of Miranda, and Other Stories, Being Mostly Winter Tales*. London: John Lane, 1898. Reprinted in *Dracula's Brood*, edited by Richard Dalby. Wellingborough, U.K.: Crucible, 1987; New York: Dorset Press, 1991; London: Harper, 2016.

Webber, Charles Wilkins. *Spiritual Vampirism: The History of Etherial Softdown and Her Friends of the 'New Light.'* Philadelphia: Grambo, 1853. Charleston, S.C., U.S.: Nabu Press, 2010.

Wells, H. G. 'The Flowering of the Strange Orchid.' *Pall Mall Budget*, 2 August, 1894. First book publication in *The Stolen Bacillus, and Other Incidents*. London: Methuen, 1895. Reprinted in *Vampires, Wine and Roses*, edited by John Richard Stephens. New York: Berkley Books, 1997.

——. *The War of the Worlds*. Simultaneously serialised in *Pearson's Magazine* and *The Cosmopolitan Magazine*, April–December 1897. Book Versions include: London: Heinemann, 1898; New York: Harper & Bros., 1898. London and New York: Penguin, 2005. London: Gollancz, 2012. New York: Cosimo Classics, 2012. Minneapolis, Minn., U.S.: First Avenue Editions, 2014.

White, Fred M. 'The Purple Terror.' *The Strand*, September 1899. Reprinted in *Monsters Galore*, edited by Bernhardt J. Hurwood. New York: Fawcett, 1965.

Whyte-Melville, G. J. 'A Vampire.' An episode in *Bones and I; or, The Skeleton at Home*. London: Chapman and Hall, 1868. [s.l.]: HardPress Publishing, 2013. Published separately as 'Madame de St. Croix,' in *Vintage Vampire Stories*, edited by Robert Eighteen-Bisang and Richard Dalby. New York: Skyhorse Publishing, 2011.

Wilde, Oscar. *The Picture of Dorian Gray*. Originally published on 20th June, 1890 in the July 1890 edition of *Lippincott's Monthly Magazine*. Book versions include: London: Ward, Lock, 1891. New York: Vintage, 2011. London: Penguin, 2012. San Diego, Calif., U.S.: IDW Publishing, 2012. London: Arcturus, 2013.

Williams, Thaddeus W. *In Quest of Life*. London and New York: F. T. Neely, 1898.

X. L. (pseudonym of Julian Osgood Field). 'A Kiss of Judas.' *Pall Mall Magazine*, July 1893. First book publication in *Aut Diabolus aut Nihil, and Other Tales*. London: Methuen, 1894. Reprinted in *Vintage Vampire Stories*, edited by Robert Eighteen-Bisang and Richard Dalby. New York: Skyhorse Publishing, 2011.

Young, Arthur. 'Pepopukin in Corsica.' In *The Stanley Tales, Vol. 1*. London: Thomas Hurst & Co., 1827 (as by 'A. Y.'). Reprinted, as by 'Arthur Young,' in *The Best Vampire Stories 1800–1849*, edited by Andrew Barger. Memphis, Tenn., U.S.: Bottletree Classics, 2012. Barger's claim that Arthur Young is the author of this story is unsubstantiated, and must be regarded as an educated guess.

Compiled by Brian J. Frost

About the Editors

Richard Dalby is a professional author, bibliographer, researcher and bookdealer, specializing in supernatural fiction. His previous anthologies include *The Sorceress in Stained Glass* (1971), *Dracula's Brood* (1987; reprinted 2016), *The Virago Book of Ghost Stories* (1987–1991; three volumes), *The Mammoth Book of Ghost Stories* (1990–1995; three volumes), *Ghosts for Christmas* (1988) and five other Christmas volumes. He has also edited and collected numerous single-author collections by H. Russell Wakefield, E. F. Benson, S. Baring-Gould, John Metcalfe, W. F. Harvey, L. A. G. Strong, F. Marion Crawford, Eleanor Scott, Rosemary Timperley, and many others.

Brian J. Frost, a freelance writer and graphic artist, is widely regarded as one of the world's leading authorities on vintage weird fiction. He first became interested in vampires after reading Bram Stoker's *Dracula* while in his teens, and in 1989 published the first full-scale survey of vampire fiction, *The Monster with a Thousand Faces: Guises of the Vampire in Myth and Literature*. Brian has written two other books dealing with iconic supernatural monsters, *The Essential Guide to Werewolf Literature* (2003) and *The Essential Guide to Mummy Literature* (2008). *Dracula's Brethren* is the second anthology he has edited, the first being *Book of the Werewolf* (1973), which was a huge success. A talented artist, Brian specialises in fantasy and macabre illustrations, the best of which have appeared in books and magazines.

By the same editor

Dracula's Brood